PRAISE FO

THE ESCAPE ARTIST

"This novel is like a launched torpedo slashing through 400 pages of deep water before reaching impact. Enjoy one of the best thriller rides ever."
—David Baldacci

"THE ESCAPE ARTIST has a magic trick up its sleeve. Part Lisbeth Salander, part *Homeland*'s Carrie Mathison. One of the most memorable characters I've read in years. Look out—Nola's coming. This is Meltzer in peak form."
—Lisa Scottoline

"Highly entertaining...Meltzer keeps the action crackling... There's no escaping the solid storytelling of THE ESCAPE ARTIST."
—Oline Cogdill, *South Florida Sun-Sentinel*

"THE ESCAPE ARTIST is Brad Meltzer's best book in years...Meltzer weaves a stellar tale of history, government-insider knowledge, and thrills...the rare novel that one wants to read fast while also needing to go slow to savor every word."
—Jeff Ayers, Associated Press

"Brad Meltzer has done it again! THE ESCAPE ARTIST is an exciting, cutting-edge thriller you will not be able to put down. If you love twists, tension, and tons of amazing characters, treat yourself to this gripping tale by one of the absolute best in the business."
—Brad Thor

"Meltzer is a master and this is his best. Not since *The Girl with the Dragon Tattoo* have you seen a character like this. Get ready to meet Nola. If you've never tried Meltzer, this is the one."
—Harlan Coben

"THE ESCAPE ARTIST is a slingshot of a novel. Brad Meltzer expertly pulls it back and lets it go, propelling the unlikeliest of heroes forward in a high stakes, high tension thriller that never lets you catch your breath. My advice: Buckle up!"

—Michael Connelly

"A throat-clenching masterpiece of suspense—and damned ingenious to boot. My jaw dropped once more—and so will yours."

—James Rollins

"Stellar...With its remarkable plot and complex characters, this page-turner not only entertains but also provides a fascinating glimpse into American history."

—*Publishers Weekly* (starred review)

"Gripping...a true page-turner."

—*Library Journal* (starred review)

"Meltzer has based his literary career on conspiracy-themed stories, and he's very good at them. In Nola and Zig, too, he's created two of his most compellingly fresh characters. Nola, in particular, represents a high point in the author's career: a strong, resourceful, mysterious female lead who could go toe to toe with Jack Reacher, Bob Lee Swagger, and the other guys. First of a new series, according to the publisher, and that's just fine." —*Booklist*

THE
ESCAPE
ARTIST

ALSO BY BRAD MELTZER

THE
ESCAPE
ARTIST

BRAD MELTZER

GRAND CENTRAL
PUBLISHING

NEW YORK   BOSTON

This book is a work of fiction. Names, characters, places, and incidents are the product of the author's imagination or are used fictitiously. Any resemblance to actual events, locales, or persons, living or dead, is coincidental.

Copyright © 2018 Forty-four Steps, Inc.

Cover design by Jarrod Taylor
Cover photography by Getty Images
Cover copyright © 2018 by Hachette Book Group, Inc.

Hachette Book Group supports the right to free expression and the value of copyright. The purpose of copyright is to encourage writers and artists to produce the creative works that enrich our culture.

The scanning, uploading, and distribution of this book without permission is a theft of the author's intellectual property. If you would like permission to use material from the book (other than for review purposes), please contact permissions@hbgusa.com. Thank you for your support of the author's rights.

Grand Central Publishing
Hachette Book Group
1290 Avenue of the Americas, New York, NY 10104
grandcentralpublishing.com
twitter.com/grandcentralpub

Originally published in hardcover and ebook by Grand Central Publishing in March 2018
First Trade Paperback Edition: September 2018

Grand Central Publishing is a division of Hachette Book Group, Inc. The Grand Central Publishing name and logo is a trademark of Hachette Book Group, Inc.

The publisher is not responsible for websites (or their content) that are not owned by the publisher.

The Hachette Speakers Bureau provides a wide range of authors for speaking events. To find out more, go to www.hachettespeakersbureau.com or call (866) 376-6591.

That 2,000 Yard Stare. Oil on canvas, 36½ X 28½. Life Collection of Art WWII, U.S. Army Center of Military History, Fort Belvoir, Virginia. Image courtesy of the Tom Lea Institute.

Library of Congress Cataloging-in-Publication Data

Names: Meltzer, Brad, author.
Title: The escape artist / Brad Meltzer.
Description: First edition. | New York : Grand Central Publishing, 2018.
Identifiers: LCCN 2017041729| ISBN 9781455559527 (hardcover) | ISBN 9781455571222 (large print) | ISBN 9781478929871 (audio download)
Subjects: LCSH: Conspiracies—Fiction. | BISAC: FICTION / Mystery & Detective / Women Sleuths. | GSAFD: Mystery fiction.
Classification: LCC PS3563.E4496 E75 2018 | DDC 813/.54—dc23
LC record available at https://lccn.loc.gov/2017041729

ISBN: 978-1-4555-5952-7 (hardcover), 978-1-4555-5951-0 (ebook), 978-1-4555-7122-2 (large print), 978-1-5387-4678-3 (signed edition), 978-1-5387-4680-6 (B&N Exclusive Edition), 978-1-5387-4681-3 (B&N Exclusive Signed edition), 978-1-5387-4679-0 (Costco Exclusive Edition), 978-1-5387-4689-9 (Costco Exclusive Signed edition), 978-1-5387-4793-3 (trade paperback), 978-1-5387-1570-3 (Hudson Exclusive edition)

Printed in the United States of America

LSC-C

10 9 8 7 6 5 4 3 2 1

For Sally Katz,
my godmother,
the true reader in our family.
Your love is magic.

ACKNOWLEDGMENTS

Twenty years. This book marks *twenty years* (!) since my first novel was published. That means, dear reader, if you were there from the start, you're *old*. It also means I owe you big for giving me this writer's life.

This book is a mystery. It's also a mission. Six years ago, I went on a USO trip to entertain our troops in the Middle East. Soon after, I learned about the heroes at Dover Air Force Base. Looking back, it seems clear I was in the midst of my own crisis, examining my life and my place in this world. The point is, I believe every book is born from a need, and it was this book that helped me realize the difference between *being alive* and actually *living*. It's what gave birth to the two new characters in these pages.

With that said, I owe tremendous thank-yous to the following: My first lady, Cori, who opens my heart and brings me to life. She is in every single page of this novel. I love you for it, C. Jonas, Lila, and Theo are always my best blessings. With these kids, I know what I live for. Jill Kneerim, my friend and agent, is the great soul. I have been enriched by her soul for two decades. Friend and agent Jennifer Rudolph Walsh at WME goes to battle for us every day. Extra thanks to Hope Denekamp, Lucy Cleland, Ike Williams, and all our friends at the Kneerim & Williams Agency.

This book is about a fight for one's life. So I need to thank my sister, Bari, who was there as we fought for ours. Also to Bobby, Ami, Adam, Gilda, and Will, for always standing with us.

I pride myself on my loyalty. Noah Kuttler takes it one step further. I trust him like no one else. He is a vault and a well of kindness. My life is better with you in it, Noah. Ethan Kline dreams the big dreams with me. Then Dale Flam, Matt Kuttler, Chris Weiss, and Judd Winick pour through my various drafts, telling me all the parts that make no sense and all the jokes that aren't funny. They don't realize all my jokes are funny.

With every book, a few people become so vital to the process it's as if their souls get poured into these pages. So let me start with William "Zig" Zwicharowski. As the Port Mortuary Branch Chief at Dover, he spends every day taking care of our fallen troops, making sure they're treated with honor, dignity, and respect. I've spent twenty years doing research. I've never been more humbled by someone's work. I'm embarrassing him now, so let me just say this: To everyone on the Dover team, thank you for what you do for Gold Star families. In addition to Zig, a special thank-you to another of my heroes, former Dover man Matt Genereux, who kept me honest at every level. Matt and Zig are family to me—and were my moral compasses. (Heart!) Finally, my master of all things military and one of my oldest friends, Scott Deutsch. In junior high school, we went to Michael Jackson's Victory Tour together. Today, he works in the military. I asked him hundreds of inane questions and he gave me all the right answers. I'm the one who then screws it up. You inspire me every day, pal. Thanks for all your trust.

I also need to thank everyone at Dover, including Major Ray Geoffroy, Tracy E. Bailey, Edward Conway, Chris Schulze, Mary Ellen "Mel" Spera, and Master Gunnery Sergeant Frederick Upchurch. (And yes, I know what really happened to Building 1303.) Also, much appreciation to my friend Senator Chris Coons for the hospitality in his home state of Delaware.

Even more details came from First Sergeant Amy L. M. Brown, our real-life Army Artist-in-Residence; Chris Semancik and everyone at the US Army Center of Military History, Museum Support Center at Fort Belvoir; Mary Roach, whose mastery of the dead left me breathless (as you read this thriller, when I reference my "favorite professor," I'm referencing Mary—go buy her book *Stiff*; it's brilliant); Chuck Collins of Compassionate Friends (if you know someone who has lost a child, go to their site); Ben Becker, for the gun knowledge; Caleb Wilde (along with his dad, Bill, and grandfather Bud), who spent a day talking about the dead and Pennsylvania; Steve Whittlesey and Howland Blackiston, for the honeybee details; Joel Marlin for the best history of magic; Mark Dimunation and everyone in the Houdini Collection at the Library of Congress; The Amazing Mr. Ash at Ash's Magic Shop, and the ever elusive Master of the Book, who deserves to be acknowledged but will only do it with a code name.

Extra thanks to Eljay Bowron, Bob Mayer (the godfather to Zig), Jake Black, David Howard, and Mark Ginsberg; Dr. Lee Benjamin and Dr. Ronald K. Wright, for always helping me maim and kill with authority; and the rest of my own inner circle, who I bother for every book: Jim Day, Chris Eliopoulos, Jo Ayn Glanzer, Denise Jaeger, Katriela Knight, Jason Sherry, Marie Grunbeck, Nick Marell, Staci Schecter, Simon Sinek, Eling Tsai, and David Watkins. Finally, major thanks to everyone in the military and veterans community, especially family members of those who serve. Your sacrifice is never lost on me. To that end, if you are thinking about suicide, especially in the military, call 1-800-273-8255. You are not alone. And thanks to everyone else who anonymously enriched these pages. You know who you are.

The books *The Secret Life of Houdini* by William Kalush and Larry Sloman, *Art of the American Soldier* by Renée Klish, *Stories in Stone* by Douglas Keister, *Houdini!!!* by Kenneth Silverman, and articles including "The Things That Carried Him" by Chris Jones, "Making Toast" by Roger Rosenblatt, "What Suffering Does" by David Brooks, and the writings of Linton Weeks were all greatly informing to this process; "Last Inspection" by James Dao and "The Child Exchange" by Megan Twohey led me to both Zig and Nola; our family on *Decoded* and *Lost History*, and at HISTORY, including Nancy Dubuc, Paul Cabana, Mike Stiller, and Russ McCarroll, for bringing me Houdini; Rob Weisbach, for being the very first;

and of course, my family and friends, whose names forever inhabit these pages.

I also want to thank everyone at Grand Central Publishing: Michael Pietsch, Brian McLendon, Matthew Ballast, Caitlin Mulrooney-Lyski, Kyra Baldwin, Chris Murphy, Dave Epstein, Martha Bucci, Ali Cutrone, Karen Torres, Jean Griffin, Beth deGuzman, Andrew Duncan, Meriam Metoui, Bob Castillo, Mari Okuda, the kindest and hardest-working sales force in show business, and all my treasured friends there. I've said it before, and I'll never stop saying it: They are the true reason this book is in your hands. I need to add a special thank-you to Jamie Raab, who knows that no matter where she goes, she's always family. I also want to welcome superstar Wes Miller, who has edited and pushed me in the very best ways. I'm lucky to know him. Finally, I want to thank our new master of ceremonies, Ben Sevier. Let me say it as clearly as I can: He has been the champion of this book and the classiest of class acts. I am so thankful he's in my life. Thank you, Ben, for your faith.

In 1898, John Elbert Wilkie, a friend of Harry Houdini, was put in charge of the United States Secret Service. Wilkie was a fan of Houdini and did his own tricks himself.

It is the only time in history that a magician was in control of the Secret Service.

PROLOGUE

Copper Center, Alaska

These were the last thirty-two seconds of her life.

As the small plane—a twin-engine CASA used by the military—took off from the airfield, most of the seven passengers on board were staring out their windows, thinking themselves lucky. Few people got to see this side of the world, much less the private base that the Army had built out here. On maps, it didn't exist. On Google, it was permanently blurred.

In the last row of the plane, a woman with shoulder-length black hair was convinced she was blessed, marveling at the snow-dusted tops of Alaska's beautiful aspen trees. She loved that the roots of aspen trees often grew together, supporting each other and forming a giant organism. It was why she joined the Army all those years ago: to build something stronger, with others. She got just that when she came out here to the lush wilderness.

Definitely blessed, she told herself. Then, just like that, the plane began to vibrate.

Her initial reaction was, *Fix it—straighten us out*. She was annoyed that the vibrations were messing up her handwriting. On the open tray table, she was trying to write a letter—a dirty note—to her fiancé, Anthony, telling him what she was planning to do to him later that evening.

Her hope was to slip it into his back pocket, Anthony being

so surprised—and horny—from her traveling all the way to Fort Campbell on his birthday, he wouldn't notice her sliding some playful fun into his pocket. And even if he did, well...thanks to their Army schedules, she and Anthony hadn't been alone with each other in two months. He'd have no problem with a pretty girl's hand on his ass.

The intercom cracked to life. *"Prepare for—"*

The pilot never got the words out.

The plane tilted, nose down, like it was arcing over the peak of a roller coaster. The woman with the black hair felt her stomach twist. All that was left was the final drop. Suddenly, there were anvils on her shoulders, pressing her into her seat.

Diagonally across the aisle, an Army lieutenant with buzzed red hair and triangular eyes made a face and gripped his armrests, just beginning to realize how bad it was about to get.

The woman with the black hair was Army too—a twenty-seven-year-old supply sergeant—and on those first days of her Airborne training at Fort Benning, they taught her that when it comes to a plane crash, people don't panic. They become docile and silent. To save yourself, you need to take action.

The plane jolted, nearly knocking the pen from her hand. *The pen. Her letter.* She almost forgot she was writing it. She thought about Anthony, about writing a will... Then she replayed those last few minutes before she got on board. *Oh, God.* Now it made sense. Her stomach was up in her throat. The VIPs at the front of the plane were now screaming. She knew why this plane was going down. This wasn't an accident.

Frantically, she jotted a new note, her hand shaking, tears squeezing out from behind her eyes.

The plane jolted again. A fireball of jet fuel came in through the emergency door on her left, from outside. Her shirt was on fire. She patted it out. She could smell melting plastic, yet at the sight of the flames—

The door. She was seated at the emergency exit.

Still clutching tight to the scribbled note, she gripped the door's red handle with both hands and started to pull. It gave way, and she slid it sideways. There was a pop. The door was still closed, but the seal was broken.

Twenty seconds to go.

She tried to get out of her seat, but her seat belt— It was still buckled. In a frenzy, she clawed at it. *Click.* She was free.

Still holding the crumpled note, now damp in her sweaty fist, she put her palm to the exit door and gave it a shove. It was stuck from the fire. She gave it a kick. The door opened as a rodeo of wind whipped her black hair in every direction. Papers went flying through the cabin. A phone bounced against the ceiling. People were screaming, though she couldn't make out any of it.

Fourteen seconds to go.

Outside, the tall, snow-covered aspen trees that had looked so small were now racing at her, growing larger every second. She knew the odds. When you free-fall in a light aircraft, if fate's not on your side, you don't have a chance.

"*GO! GET OUT!*" a man's voice shouted.

She had barely turned as the lieutenant with the triangular eyes barreled into her, fighting to get to the emergency exit.

The plane was in free fall now, a reddish orange smoke filling the cabin. Eleven seconds to go. The man was pushing against her with all his weight. They both knew if they jumped too soon— above three hundred feet—they wouldn't survive the impact. Even if they were lucky enough to live, the compound fractures in their legs—if the bones came through their skin—it'd make them bleed out in no time.

No. This had to be timed just right.

Not until you're at the treetops, she told herself, remembering her training and eyeing the aspens, which were closer than ever. The wind blinded her. The smoke was in her lungs as she held the lieutenant at bay with one hand and held tight to the note with her other.

"*GO! NOW!*" the man screamed, and for a moment, it looked like his back was on fire.

Eight seconds to go.

The plane plummeted diagonally toward the ground. Without even thinking about it, she stuffed the note into the one place she thought it might survive.

"*WE DON'T HAVE—!*"

Six seconds.

She put her foot on the lip of the doorway, turned back to the lieutenant and grabbed him by his shirt, trying to pull him outside with her. This could work. She could save them both.

She was wrong.

The lieutenant pulled away. It was instinct. No one wants to be yanked from a plane. That was the end. The lieutenant with the triangular eyes would go down, literally, in flames.

With three seconds to go, the woman with black hair leapt from the plane. She would land on the balls of her feet, still trying to follow her training as she hit with a thud in the snow. A perfect landing. But also a deadly one. She'd break both legs and snap her neck on impact.

The emergency crews would find her name on the manifest. Nola Brown.

And the scribbled note—her final words—that she'd hidden so well? That would be found by the least likely person of all.

1

Dover Air Force Base, Delaware

Jim "Zig" Zigarowski knew the pain was coming. It didn't stop him. He was good with pain. Used to it. Still, he knew this one would sting. Since the day Zig arrived at this remote building at the back of Dover Air Force Base, every case was wrenching. Especially this one. Hence the pain.

"I thought Lou was on call today?" asked Dr. Womack, a short Hispanic man with a weak beard and baggy medical scrubs.

"We switched," Zig said, wheeling the gurney a bit faster up the hallway, hoping to leave Womack behind. "Lou had a dinner date."

"Really? I just saw Lou at dinner. All alone."

Zig stopped. This was the moment where it could all implode. Zig shouldn't be here. Shouldn't have taken this gurney, or what was hidden below the light blue sheet that covered it. Would Womack stop him? Only if he realized what was going on.

"Huh. Guess I heard it wrong," Zig said, flashing the same charming grin that made those first years after his divorce so eventful. With mossy green eyes, a hairline scar on his jaw, and silver-and-black hair cut like Cary Grant's, Zig didn't look fifty-two. But as he swiped his ID and the metal double doors popped open, leading to the heart of the military installation, he was feeling it.

A sign above the door read:

DANGER:

FORMALDEHYDE IRRITANT

AND POTENTIAL CANCER HAZARD

Womack paused, turning away. Zig grinned, picked up speed, and gave a hard push to the gurney that was draped with a light blue sheet, covering the corpse underneath. In between the corpse's legs, pinning the sheet down, was a one-pound silver bucket. *The gut bucket,* they called it, because after the autopsy, it held all the internal organs. As Zig would tell new cadets: No matter how fat, thin, tall, or short you are—for every single one of us—all our organs fit in a one-pound bucket. For Zig, it was usually reassuring to know we all have that in common. Though right now, it wasn't bringing the reassurance he needed.

Automatic lights blinked on, lighting the medical suite. With a pneumatic hiss, the double doors bit shut behind him. For well over a decade, Zig had spent his days working in this high-tech surgical room, which served as a mortuary for the US government's most top secret and high-profile cases. On 9/11, the victims of the Pentagon attack were brought here. So were the victims of the attack on the USS *Cole,* the astronauts from the space shuttle *Columbia,* and the remains of well over fifty thousand soldiers and CIA operatives who fought in Vietnam, Afghanistan, Iraq, and every secret location in between. Here, in Delaware of all places, at Dover Air Force Base, was America's most important funeral home.

Be quick, Zig told himself, though when it came to preparing our fallen heroes for burial, Zig was never quick. Not until the job was done.

Readjusting his own blue medical scrubs, Zig could feel the pain inching even closer. On the head of the gurney, he reread the name scrawled on a jagged strip of masking tape:

SGT. *1ST CLASS NOLA BROWN*

"Welcome home, Nola," he whispered.

The corpse swayed slightly as he locked the wheels on the gurney.

Sometimes at Dover, an incoming dead soldier would have your same birthday, or even your same name. Last year, a young Marine with the last name *Zigarowski* died of smoke inhalation at a base in Kosovo. Naturally, Zig grabbed that case.

Nola, named for New Orleans, Louisiana, was different.

"It's been a while, hasn't it?" Zig asked the shrouded body.

Lowering his head, he said a quick prayer—the same prayer he said in every case. *Please give me strength to take care of the fallen so their family can begin healing.* Zig knew too well how grieving families would need that strength.

On his left, on a medical rolling cart, were his tools in size order, from largest forceps to smallest scalpel. Zig reached for the blue plastic eye caps, which looked like contact lenses with small spikes on them. Zig generally was not a superstitious man, but he was superstitious about the eyes of the dead, which never close as easily as the movies would have you believe. When you look at a corpse, the corpse looks back. The eye caps were a mortician's trick for keeping a client's eyes shut.

How could he possibly have let another mortician work this case? Nola Brown wasn't a stranger. He knew this girl, even if she wasn't a girl anymore. She was twenty-six. Even from her outline under the sheet, he could see it: strong and built like a soldier. Zig knew her from Pennsylvania, back when she was twelve. She was friends—a fellow Girl Scout—with Zig's daughter, Maggie.

Magpie. His *Little Star,* Zig thought, reliving those easy days before everything went so bad. There it was, the pain that now made his bones feel like they were hollowed out, simple to snap.

Had Zig known Nola well? He remembered that night, back at the Girl Scout campout. Zig was a chaperone, Nola the new girl. Adopted. Naturally, the other girls seized on that. But it was more than that. Some girls are quiet. Nola was silent. Silent Nola. A few of the girls thought that made Nola tough. But Zig knew better. Sometimes silence is beaten into people.

When you looked Nola's way, her black eyes with flecks of gold would beg you not to engage. Zig had been warned: Silent Nola was already on her fourth school. *Expelled from the other three for fighting*, one girl said. *Knocked out someone's front teeth with the blunt end of a Yoo-hoo bottle.* Another of Magpie's friends said she was caught stealing too, but c'mon, ever since the Salem witch trials, groups of twelve-year-old girls couldn't be trusted.

"You really took a beating that night, didn't you?" Zig asked Nola's corpse as he grabbed the outdated iPod that sat in a SoundDock on a nearby shelf. With a few clicks, Meat Loaf's *Bat Out of Hell* was playing from the cheap speaker. Even morticians needed working music.

"I owe you forever for what you did that night," Zig sighed.

To this day, Zig still didn't know who threw the can of orange soda into the campfire, or how long it was there. He could still see the campfire's smoke blowing sideways. For a moment, there was a high-pitched whistle, like a shrieking teapot. Then, out of nowhere, a loud pop like a cherry bomb. Hunks of aluminum exploded in every direction. Most of the girls screamed, then laughed.

Maggie's instinct was to freeze. Silent Nola's instinct was to jump sideways. Nola slammed into Maggie, who was standing there, frozen in fear as shards of razor-sharp metal flew at Zig's daughter's face.

At the impact, Maggie crashed to the dirt, completely safe. Still in mid-fall, Silent Nola let out a yelp, a screech, like an injured dog, then held the side of her head, blood everywhere.

The metal can had sliced away a chunk of her ear. The smoke was still blowing sideways. To this day, Zig didn't know if Nola did it purposefully, tackling his daughter to protect her—or if it was just dumb luck, the fortunate result of Nola's flight reflex. All he knew for sure was, without Nola, his daughter would've taken that metal bomb in the face. Everyone agreed. On that night, Nola had saved Zig's daughter.

Before anyone could react, Zig had scooped Nola up and drove her to the nearest emergency room. Maggie sat next to Nola in the backseat, thanking her for what she did, and also looking at her dad in a whole new way. For those few moments, on the way to the hospital, Nola—and Zig for scooping her up—were heroes.

"Thank you!" his daughter kept saying to Nola. "Thank you for what y— You okay?"

Nola never answered. She sat there, knees to her chest, eyes down as she gripped her ear. No doubt, she was in pain. The top of her ear was gone. Tears ran down her cheeks. But she never made a sound. Silent Nola had learned to take it in quiet.

At the hospital, as the doctor got ready to stitch her up, a nurse told Nola to hold tight to Zig's hand. Nola shook her head.

Three hours and forty stitches later, Nola's adoptive father stormed into the emergency room, smelling of bourbon and the breath mints to cover it. The first words out of his mouth were, "The Girl Scouts better be paying for this!"

As Nola left the hospital that night, head down and shuffling her feet as she trailed meekly behind her dad, Zig wanted to say something. Wanted to thank this girl, but more than that— Wanted to help this girl. He never did.

Of course, Zig and Maggie brought a huge gift basket to Nola's house. Nola's adoptive dad opened the door, grabbed it from Maggie's hands, and grunted a thanks. Zig kept at it, making calls to see how Nola was doing. One night, he even stopped by to check in on her. He never got a response. Undeterred, Zig nominated her for one of the big Girl Scout honors. Nola missed the ceremony.

A year later, Zig had the very worst night of his life. It took his marriage, his life, and most important, it took his daughter, his Magpie. Nola had saved her on the night of the campfire, but all Maggie got was another eleven months. Zig would forever blame himself for all of it.

Though Zig didn't know it at the time, Nola had moved on to her fifth school. Zig never saw her again. Until tonight.

"Don't you worry, Nola, you're in good hands now," Zig promised as he gripped the surgical sheet in one hand and the eye caps in the other. "And thank you again for what you did."

In the Mortuary at Dover, some say they do the job because they see their own children in the lives of these dead soldiers. Zig shook his head at maudlin explanations like that. He did this job for one reason: He was good at it. This was the gift God gave him. He saw every dead body as a puzzle, and no matter how bad the wounds, he could put each body back together so the family could say a proper goodbye. He did it day after day, soldier after soldier— over two thousand of them by now—and none of them had made him see those darkest days with his own daughter. Until tonight, when he saw the woman who saved her.

As he rolled the sheet down to Nola's neck and slid the eye caps into place, shutting her eyes, his throat tightened like it was gripped by a fist. This was the pain he was dreading. Even when you're ready for it, nothing sneaks up on you like grief.

Nola's head was turned sideways, her left cheek flash-burned from the plane crash that killed her. Fallen #2,356.

"You have my word, Nola. We'll get you looking great in no time," Zig told her, fighting to keep his voice steady, even as he calculated how much makeup this one would take. He should've never grabbed this case. He should ask one of his fellow morticians to switch right now. But he wouldn't.

Since the moment he first saw Nola's name on Dover's official big board, Zig couldn't stop thinking about that night at the campfire...couldn't stop seeing Nola crashing into young Maggie, knocking her out of the way...couldn't stop seeing the smoke blowing sideways, or Nola's mangled left ear...and couldn't stop replaying that look in his daughter's eyes when she saw Zig as a hero. Today, Zig knew his daughter was wrong, even back then. He wasn't a hero. He wasn't even a good person. But damn, it felt good to be a dad again, or at least to play the role of Dad again, one last—

Mothertrucker.

Zig glanced down at Nola's left ear. It was charred but otherwise perfect. Not a piece missing. *How could that—?* He looked again. Her entire ear was there. There wasn't even the hint of a scar. He leaned closer to make sure. Could he have remembered it wrong? Maybe it was the other ear.

Gently, he turned Nola's head, faceup, her cold skin like a glass of ice water. On the right half of her face, her skin was perfect, not burned at all. According to the casualty report, her military plane crashed just after takeoff, outside of Copper Center, Alaska, on the edge of the national park. All seven people aboard, including the pilot, were killed. Nola was considered the lucky one, thrown clear of the plane—or maybe she jumped, considering the compound fractures in her legs. *Definitely a jump,* Zig thought, recalling Nola's instincts at the campfire. Since she landed in the snow, with the right side of her face in the slush, the ice protected her from the gruesome burns she would've suffered all over her body as the plane went up in flames.

"There you go, turn just like that," Zig whispered as he rotated Nola's head all the way and got his first good view of—

Look at that.

Nola's other ear was perfect too. Two pristine ears. No pieces missing, no scars. It made no sense.

Zig looked back down at Nola's face, at her closed eyes. He hadn't seen her since she was twelve. *Was her nose flat like that? Could she have had her ears repaired?* Absolutely. But as Zig knew firsthand, ears are difficult to rebuild, and however great the surgeon who did it, they always showed a hairline scar.

Zig stepped down to the foot of the table, rechecking the laminated bar code around Nola's ankle, matching it to the ones on the gurney itself. The Mortuary at Dover is considered one of the military's true no-fail missions. The most important part of all its jobs is to make sure that one body is never mixed up with another. When fallen soldiers come into Dover, they don't even get to morticians like Zig until their identity has been triple-checked: by DNA, then dental records, then fingerprints.

Fingerprints.

From under the surgical sheet, Zig reached for Nola's hands. Both were burned black. With charring this bad, they usually couldn't get fingerprints. But that didn't mean there weren't any.

Racing out into the hallway toward the kitchenette in the breakroom, Zig grabbed a metal pot from one of the cabinets, filled it with water, and put it on the stove. As he waited for the water to boil, he pulled out his phone and dialed one of the few numbers he knew by heart. Area code 202. Washington, DC.

"What do you want?" a female voice asked.

"Thanks, Waggs. So nice to hear your voi—"

"Don't sweet-talk. Spit it out. You want something."

"Just the same things I always want: true friendship...more two-in-one restaurants, like when they combine Dunkin' Donuts with Baskin-Robbins...oh, and an end to people who make you take off your shoes in their house. We need to band together and fight against those people."

He could practically hear Waggs rolling her eyes. "This better be something for work," she said.

Amy Waggs wasn't stupid. As head of the FBI unit that pulled terrorists' biometrics from explosive devices, she was a specialist in what people leave behind. She was even left behind herself when her husband of twelve years decided he was gay and wanted her permission to date his law partner Andrew. When it happened, Waggs couldn't tell anyone at work. But she told Zig.

"Let me know what you need," she said in exasperation.

"Oh jeez. You're one of those people who makes everyone take their shoes off, aren't you?"

"Zig, if this isn't important, you're now the only thing holding me back from my date night with a reality show about a little dwarf family. Tell me what's going on."

On the stove, wafts of steam rose from his pot of water. "I need you to run a fingerprint."

"You got the Fang?" she asked, referring to the FBI's best weapon.

"I will in a minute," Zig said, leaving the boiling water behind and heading back into the hallway. It was late—after 7 p.m.—in a military location. The building was a ghost town.

Zig's surgical shoe-covers whispered down the hallway as he headed toward the closed door of Waggs's former office: the FBI's Latent Print Unit, a section of the building for FBI employees only.

"Is this for something personal, or did Adrian okay it?" Waggs asked.

"Whattya think?"

"Zig, please don't tell me you're about to break into our office."

"I'm not. I'm just checking to see if you have the same old password. Yup. There it is. You really should update that code," he said as the door clicked open.

"Zig, don't do this. You know you're not allowed in there."

"And I'd never go in," Zig said, stepping inside. It was a small room, even by Dover standards: single desk, stand-alone computer terminal, and a cabinet to hold evidence. Plus one other tool.

From the top drawer of the desk, Zig pulled out a black device that looked like a cell phone made with mil-spec hardware, meaning you could drop it and it wouldn't break. Zig didn't plan on dropping it. The Fang cost more than his annual salary.

"Are you even listening?" Waggs shouted through the phone as Zig darted back to the breakroom. "If Adrian hears that you took that without his permission—"

"I have permission. I'm talking to you, aren't I?"

"Don't do that. It's not funny."

"I'm not trying to be funny. Funny is when I'm reminiscing about two-in-one restaurants."

"Zig, how long do I know you? If you're making jokes, especially weak ones like this—"

"Hold on, did you say *weak*?"

"Are you in trouble? Tell me what's going on."

Grabbing the pot of boiling water from the stove, Zig didn't answer. He raced back to Nola's body.

"Does the body at least have good prints to give?" Waggs added.

"Absolutely," Zig lied, swiping his ID, waiting for the lab doors to click, and once again approaching the gurney. From afar, even with the gut bucket between her legs, Nola almost looked like she was sleeping, but a dead body always lies differently. There's a permanence that's unmistakable.

At Nola's side, Zig grabbed her lifeless hand, scraped some of the black charring from her fingers, then held her hand over the pot of boiling water.

"Nola, I'm sorry for this," he whispered as he dunked her hand in the hot water. He had to do this part right. No more than a few seconds.

When hands get badly burned, the ridges of the epidermis become black and unreadable. But like a burnt steak, if you scrape the charring away, there's a pink layer underneath. The dermal layer. The only problem is, the dermal ridges are too flat to give a proper fingerprint. But as any medical examiner—or mortician—knows, if you dip that finger in boiling water for seven seconds, the ridges will plump up.

Sure enough, as Zig pulled Nola's hand from the steaming water, her pointer and middle fingers were thick and swollen.

"Turning on the Fang," Zig said as he hit a few buttons. The Fang got its name from the two green lasers that pointed out from the bottom of the device. Lining up the lasers with Nola's pointer finger, Zig hit another button, activating the scanner.

"Work email or home?" Zig asked.

"This official business or not?"

"Home it is," Zig said, hitting *Send*.

Through the phone, there was a musical ping. Fingerprint delivered. It'd take only a few minutes for Waggs to check the FBI database.

"What's the story with this soldier? Why the personal interest?" Waggs asked, already clicking on her keyboard.

"It's just a case," Zig said. "According to the ID here, she's Sergeant First Class Nola Brown, female, twenty-six years old."

"And that's all you know about her?"

"What else is there to know? It's just a case," Zig insisted, his voice unwavering.

"Ziggy, I love you, but do you have any idea why, when the corpses come in, you're the one who gets all the facial injuries?"

"What're you talking about?"

"Don't play modest. If a soldier gets shot in the chest, they get assigned to any mortician. But when someone takes three bullets to the face, why does that body always go to you?"

"Because I can sculpt. I'm good with the clay."

"It's more than talent. Last year, when that Marine was hit by ISIS rocket fire, every other mortician said it should be a closed casket—that you should wrap him in gauze. You were the only one stubborn enough to spend fourteen straight hours wiring together his shattered jaw, then smoothing it over with clay and makeup, just so you could give his parents far more ease than they ever should've expected at their son's funeral. But y'know what that makes you?"

"Someone who's proud to serve his country."

"I love my country too. I'm talking about your job, Zig. When you take these horrors—lost hands, lost faces, lost lips—and you make them more palatable, y'know what that makes you?" Before Zig could answer, Waggs blurted, "A master liar. That's what every mortician sells, Zig. Lies. You do it for the right reasons—you're trying to help people through their hardest times. But every day, to hide those horrors, you need to be a first-class liar. And you're getting far too good at it."

Zig went to say something, but nothing came out. Closing his eyes, he turned his back to the body.

There was a chime through the phone. Waggs had something. "Okay, I found Nola Brown. Twenty-six years old," Waggs said. "Same age as Maggie, isn't she?"

At just the mention of his daughter's name, Zig spun toward the body, moving so fast, and so off-balance, his elbow clipped the silver bucket that was filled with—

Nonono! The gut bucket...!

Zig lunged. The bucket, with its gruesome stew, began to tip.

Zig was still reaching for it, still holding tight to his phone, as he started to yell. The bucket continued to tip, its contents sliding toward the lip.

Pffftt.

There was a loud, wet splat. For two decades, Zig had become accustomed to the gore that accompanied death. But as he looked down at the mess across the shiny gray floor, something caught his eye.

"Ziggy, we have a problem," Waggs said in his ear.

Zig barely heard her, focusing on the gray mass that he recognized as the stomach. Something wasn't right. There was a round lump, like when a snake swallows a rat. He leaned closer, making sure he was seeing it right. He was. There was something inside.

"Ziggy, you there?" Waggs asked as Zig put the phone on speaker and set it down on the gurney.

He moved even closer. Whatever was inside, it wasn't round or smooth. It was jagged and poking at the inner wall like...like a crumpled piece of paper.

Zig's mouth went dry. He'd seen this before.

During 9/11, one of the victims on the Pentagon flight knew the end was coming...and was smart enough to know that if you're ever in a plane crash, the best way to leave a note to your loved ones is to write it down and swallow the paper. The liquids in your stomach and intestines can protect the paper, since those're the last parts of your body that burn. Back then, Zig found the note in the victim's intestine. He cut it open with a scalpel, then tweezed his fingers inside. It was perfectly preserved. For Fallen #227, a final private goodbye.

"—ou hearing me? I found the fingerprints!" Waggs shouted.

Zig still didn't answer. Grabbing a scalpel from his work station and readjusting his medical gloves, he got down on one knee and sliced, making the hole big enough to—

There.

Zig pulled out the crumpled piece of paper. It was squished and soggy—easy for a medical examiner to miss—but otherwise intact.

Slowly peeling it open and being careful not to rip it, he could see the thin gray pencil lines . . . with frantic, shaky letters. The ultimate message in the ultimate bottle.

"Zig, are you listening? I ran the prints. That body you're looking at—whoever she is—that's not Nola Brown."

Zig nodded to himself, his mouth sagging open as he read and reread the handwritten note—the dying words—of the female stranger lying on the table in front of him:

Nola, you were right.
Keep running.

2

For five hours, Daewon Yamaguchi had been staring at his laptop screen.

There were worse jobs, especially for a twenty-four-year-old who'd been arrested twice for forgery and computer trespass. He could be like his pal Z0rk, who used to hack credit card numbers from an auto parts chain until he was caught by the Feds and threatened with thirty years in prison.

Today, Z0rk was a $40,000/year employee for the US government. A few of Daewon's other friends took their talents (and a bit more money) to work for Syria and Iran. And still others honed their skills at local hacking conventions, though Daewon knew that most of those were government fronts designed to sniff out local prospects. This wasn't the go-go early 2000s anymore. These days, most hacking was state sponsored. But not all of it.

Sucking on a peanut M&M and letting the candy coating melt away, Daewon settled in for his sixth hour staring at the screen. It was the ultimate irony. Hackers get into hacking because they don't want desk jobs—but all hacking is is a desk job.

By hour seven, Daewon was still sitting there, staring. Same at hour eight. And hour nine. Then . . .

Ping.

There it was. On-screen.

Picking up his phone, Daewon dialed the number they made him learn by heart.

"Talk," a man with a woodchipper of a voice answered.

This was what they lied about. The worst part of the job wasn't staring at a screen. It was dealing with *him*.

He never gave a name. That didn't stop Daewon from looking for it. But what unnerved Daewon was that he couldn't find it. And Daewon could find anything.

"*Talk*," the man insisted.

"The site you asked me to watch... You said to call you when someone pinged it. I just... someone pinged it."

"Who?"

"A woman. Amy Waggs," Daewon replied, clicking through a few screens. "She's FBI, just like you said. Went straight for the Nola Brown file."

The man went silent. "Is Ms. Waggs looking for herself or someone else?"

"Checking," Daewon replied, tossing back another peanut M&M as a new screen loaded. "From what I can tell, she's on her phone right now. I'm trying to see who she's talking to."

"You're telling me you can hack into an FBI agent's phone?"

"Only when they're dumb enough to use their personal one instead of a secure line. Swear to Steve Jobs, whoever invented working from home should get a big wet kiss on the mouth."

The man with the woodchipper voice didn't say a word.

"Okay, here we go," Daewon eventually said, leaning closer to the screen. "302 phone number. Delaware. Truthfully, I didn't think they allowed anyone to live in Delaware anymore."

The man still didn't answer.

"Jim Zigarowski. That's who she's talking to," Daewon added. "Says he's employed at the Dover Port Mortuary, whatever that is."

There was a long silence on the other line. "Zig," the man finally whispered. "That's a name I haven't heard in a while."

3

Dover, Delaware

It was nearly midnight as Zig rang the doorbell of the split-level home. Of course there was no answer.

"C'mon, Guns, don't do this tonight!" Zig called out, hopping in place to stay warm.

The door still didn't open.

Zig rang the bell again out of spite, then followed the overgrown lawn to his left, toward the garage.

On cue, a *chuuk* and a loud *whirr* sent the garage door rolling upward.

"Slapshot!" a muscular black man called from inside, swiping a hockey stick as he faced the back wall of the garage. With a punishing swing that nearly knocked the glasses from his face, the man swatted an orange puck into a net. From there, on a flat-screen TV attached to the garage's back wall, a videogame hockey puck continued to fly, following the initial trajectory and going far wide of the computerized Russian goalie guarding the net.

"Why does Lake Placid hate me so much?" Marine Corps Master Gunnery Sergeant Francis Steranko asked.

"Weak players blame the field," Zig said.

"It's not a field; it's a rink."

"It's a *television*. Now you wanna hand me the twig?" Zig asked, reaching for the hockey stick. "I'm still three shots down from our last game. My manhood's on the line."

It wasn't Zig's best joke, but he'd known Master Guns for over a decade. They'd worked hundreds of cases, buried thousands of soldiers, and fought to stay sane in this very garage by drinking gallons of Master Guns's homemade gin while playing drunk videogame hockey (almost always against the Russians). The joke should've earned Zig a chuckle, or at the very least a cheap crack about his manhood. Instead, Master Guns held tight to the hockey stick, facing the TV screen on the wall. "Ziggy, I know you're not here to play hockey."

Master Guns never took long to reveal he was Dover's chief homicide investigator.

"You're wearing the scent," Master Guns said, his beefy military build practically bursting through his T-shirt and sweatpants. "I smell it from here."

Sometimes Zig forgot how sharp his friend was. Humans have a unique odor. For the dead, it was even more unmistakable, a mix of sweetness and rotting fish that dogs can smell for up to fourteen months after someone's killed. Zig had taken three showers before coming here, thinking the scent of death had been scrubbed away. Most people would be fooled. Master Guns had never been *most people*.

"This is about the woman in the plane crash, isn't it?" he asked. "Nola Brown."

Zig stayed silent as a burst of wind sliced through the garage. The place was decorated like a bachelor pad, complete with a cheap black leather sofa that sagged in the middle. The wind sent the hockey net swaying and lifted the pages of magazines on the glass coffee table. Zig eyed the door that led into Master Guns's house. This was a conversation that was better conducted inside. But Zig knew he'd never get there.

It was Master Guns's one rule: No one goes inside the house. Garage only. No exceptions. Master Guns might be Zig's closest work friend, but the emphasis had always been on the word *work*. They'd had BBQs in this garage, blown out birthday cakes, and even, on a winter night as cold as tonight, toasted Guns's dead brother-in-law, a fallen Marine whom Master Guns asked Zig to work on personally. With work like that, the only way to stay sane was to keep your work life separate from your home life. The door between the garage and the rest of the house was his dividing line.

"How'd you know this was about Nola?" Zig asked.

"Ziggy, it's midnight. On a weekday. Do I look like one of your girlfriends?"

"What's that mean?"

"C'mon now. Melinda in Legal has a crush on you. She's smart, good-looking, even age-appropriate, but you don't date her. Sherry in Case Management has been divorced for a year—same thing, same age as you—and you don't date her. And Esther in Veteran Affairs—"

"Esther in Veteran Affairs looks like Mrs. Howell from *Gilligan's Island*, if she were still alive today."

"All I'm saying, lovey, is that your last girlfriend—the sales rep for that energy drink company—how long did she stick around? Three weeks? A month? I know why you do it, Ziggy. Life is much easier if you surround yourself with people who will leave you. But don't tell me you're coming here to play hockey, then think you can slyly pump me for information without me knowing."

As he turned, Zig could finally read what was written on Master Guns's Marines T-shirt: *My Job Is To Save Your Ass, Not Kiss It*.

"The T-shirt's kinda heavy-handed, even for you," Zig said.

"Don't screw with me, Ziggy," Master Guns said as the big vein swelled in his neck. "Tell me why you're so interested in this Nola Brown case."

When Zig didn't answer, Master Guns used the heel of his palm to pound a button on the wall. The garage door whirred, slowly rolling downward. Time for some privacy.

"Ziggy..."

"I know her," Zig blurted. "Nola Brown. She's from Ekron. I knew her when she was little. She saved Maggie's life..."

"Ah, there's the reason."

"You're damn right that's the reason. What she did that night, for me and for Maggie—I need to pay that back—and I'm telling you, that body in the mortuary... That's not her." For the next few minutes, Zig laid out the rest, about what she did at the campfire, the piece that was missing from the real Nola's ear, the swallowed note, and how this made him think Nola was still alive and in danger.

With each new detail, Master Guns took a slow breath through his nose. It was an old investigator trick. The calmer he made you feel, the more he thought you'd talk. But Zig saw the way that Master Guns's caterpillar eyebrows were starting to knit together. Master Guns looked annoyed. He looked disturbed. But he didn't look the least bit surprised.

"You knew this already, didn't you?" Zig asked.

"That there was a secret note hidden in her body? How could I possibly know something like that?"

"That wasn't what I asked, Guns. Bodies don't get to me until DNA, dental, and fingerprints have been checked and verified. That means someone from the FBI did the match. But when I asked my friend in the Bureau, she pulled up their workboard. Guess what she found? The FBI still hasn't sent a fingerprint expert."

"Make your point."

"My point is, without that expert, the only way for this body to get to me in the mortuary was if someone high up—like our colonel...or, say, our chief investigator—signed off on it. Now c'mon. Tell me what you're not saying."

Master Guns was a decorated Marine. Zig was a civilian mortician with a knack for rebuilding dead bodies. To most, their difference in rank would be an issue. But for Master Guns, the only rank that mattered was this: *Heart* or *No heart*. They saw it every day: Do you believe in the mission of dealing with our fallen troops with honor, dignity, and respect? Or are you someone who, when you hear that a new body is coming in, looks at your watch to see if you can sneak out before the shift change? No question, Master Guns had heart. Zig? Master Guns knew the answer to that. Everyone knew the answer.

"Ziggy, in the autopsy report... Did you see how Nola died?"

"I told you, I don't think it's Nola."

"I heard you. Whoever she is. Did you read how she died?"

"Plane crash. In Alaska."

"That's right. And have you seen the coverage on the news?"

"I've been working on the body. Why? What're they saying?"

"That's the thing. They're saying nothing. And I mean *nothing*. Every other plane crash, no matter how far it is—the French Alps, Malaysia, wherever—the whole world knows the instant the plane goes down. But this seven-person flight Nola was on, it plummeted forty-eight hours ago, and the news is just now hitting the airwaves. You know what it takes to pull off two days of silence? Even *we* didn't hear about it until the body was on its way."

"Okay, so the same thing happened a couple years back when Senator Assa's plane went down with those CIA folks aboard. Whenever the secret squirrels get involved, we only get a few hours' notice."

"You're not listening. When Nola's body arrived, two men in crappy black suits were waiting in my office. With Colonel Hsu. They flashed IDs and politely told me that they had a special interest in this case. They also said they wanted the body the moment we were done with it. As in, immediately."

"So they're the ones who gave you Nola's fingerprints?"

"Forget the prints. The last time black suits showed up like that, two buildings had gone down in New York and we were scrambling to identify victims from the Pentagon crash."

When Zig closed his eyes, he still saw it so clearly. In the hours after 9/11, as the Pentagon victims started arriving, Zig was unpacking the burned body of a dark-skinned man with a missing arm. Out of nowhere, two FBI agents were standing over Zig's shoulder, watching a bit too intently. Zig quickly realized: He wasn't working on one of the victims. He had the pilot, one of the terrorists. Soon after, the FBI whisked the body away for their own private testing.

"You think Nola—or whoever she really is—is the one who crashed the plane?" Zig asked.

"I don't care if she did. What worries me more is who we're picking a fight with."

"*We?*" Zig asked hopefully.

"You," Master Guns clarified in deep baritone. "The black suits—Whatever they're looking at, this is far beyond the world where you and I live. Our job is to bring *closure*, not open up more problems."

"Closure doesn't exist. Not for anyone."

"No. Nuh-uh. Now you're getting emotional, and when you get emotional, you get stupid."

"Some things are worth being stupid over."

"Not *this*," Master Guns growled, pointing the hockey stick like a magician's wand.

On most nights, a threat from Master Guns might make Zig back off. But tonight, Zig wasn't intimidated or daunted in any way. No, since the moment he realized Nola was still out there, Zig was... he didn't have a word for it yet. But he could feel it. A need. He *needed* to know what happened to Nola, needed to find out if she was safe, but also... something else. Something that was tugging at him from his core—and lighting it up. Like a spark igniting a dormant fire. He needed to find the answer to this case. But he also needed the case itself.

"You think you're just searching for an old friend of your daughter—"

"She's more than a friend! She saved Maggie's life!"

"So now you have to save this girl's life? You're making a karmic trade?"

"You don't understand. We knew her. The whole community knew her. She gave me an extra year with my daughter."

"Which is absolutely commendable. I understand your need to do right by her—but you're sticking your head in a fire here, Ziggy. And not a little campfire that singes your ear. This'll burn you alive. Just like her."

"So I should just ignore that Nola's out there...that she might need help? Even forgetting that I know her...this body in our morgue—whoever she really is, that's someone's kid! Someone raised her, combed her hair, took pictures of her every year on her first day of school. And now we're supposed to do nothing even though we know she's misidentified?"

Guns didn't answer. He didn't have to. During their first weeks at Dover, Master Guns and Zig found out that one of their supervisors was sending unidentified remains—random bones, fingers, even someone's leg—to be dumped in a nearby landfill, just to clean house. The remains were old, impossible to ID, and taking up precious storage space. Master Guns and Zig were newbies, expected to go along and stay silent. *Why rock the boat and risk your job and your career in the military?* Because that's not how you honor our fallen brothers and sisters. The next day, they filed a report with the colonel. Their supervisor "voluntarily retired" soon after.

"I'm happy to do this alone," Zig said.

"You *are* doing this alone," Master Guns shot back, still pointing with the hockey stick.

"They really put the spook in you, didn't they?" Zig asked.

"Not they. *Him.*"

Zig cocked an eyebrow, lost.

"You don't even know who you're taking on, do you?" Master Guns asked, reaching for the TV remote.

With the flick of a button, the videogame was gone, replaced by CNN. The grisly image on-screen glowed on the wall, lighting the dark garage.

"It's all over the news. Nola's plane..." Master Guns explained as the camera pulled in on footage of a small plane mangled in the snow. Smoke twirled in the air, but the plane looked mostly intact. Behind them, the garage door was still closed, but to Zig, it was suddenly colder than ever. "Didn't you see who else was on that flight?"

4

Zig was home within the hour. His doormat sat askew on his front porch. Cursing the UPS guy, he kicked the mat back into place, opened the front door, and headed for the kitchen.

From his left pocket, he pulled out a lunch receipt and a loose Post-it, dumping them both in the trash. From his right, he took out his pocketknife, a small six-inch ruler, and his "wallet," a lean stack of cash, credit cards, and driver's license, all bound by a thick red rubber band. Zig didn't carry any photos or memorabilia. Working every day with death, he was keenly aware: You can't take anything with you.

Last year, he read that highly hyped book that said to find true happiness, you should pare down your life, throw away everything you don't regularly use, and save only the things that bring you joy. For Zig, that joy came from chisels and carving tools, along with the drill press and battered workbench in the extra bedroom upstairs that he'd converted into a shop. It also came from taking care of his "girls."

With a beer in his hand, he headed out to his small backyard, where, up on concrete blocks, there was a white wooden box that he'd built himself, with conspicuous dovetail joints that were hand cut with a backsaw and chisel. The box was the size of a two-drawer file cabinet with a small circular hole cut into it. A red-and-yellow sign on the side read, *Caution: Dangerous Bees.*

The bees weren't dangerous. Especially this hive, which had a wonderfully calm queen. But the sign kept the kids in the neighborhood away from the one thing that brought Zig more peace than anything else.

"Evening, ladies," he called out, approaching the wooden box and its forty thousand inhabitants. Zig got his first beehive back in college, for a hippie science class called Animals & Farming. Back then, he rolled his eyes when it was his week to take care of the professor's hive. His classmates hated it too.

Yet for Zig, from that very first day, there was one thing that fascinated him: Every creature in the hive, every single honeybee, had a purpose—a role it followed its entire life. Guard bees protected the hive, nurse bees took care of the babies, and architect bees built the hive's hexagon structure, making it mathematically perfect in every way.

There were even undertaker bees, who removed the dead from the hive and flew a hundred yards to dispose of the bodies. It was a job Zig knew well. Certainly, humans have purpose in their lives. But why were the bees so single-minded and committed to that purpose? It wasn't just for the good of the queen. It was for the good of each other, for their whole community. How could anyone not admire a beautiful world like that?

"Everyone okay?" Zig asked, knowing the answer. This late and this cold, the hive was quiet. But as Zig approached, he pulled out his phone and flicked on the flashlight. Something seemed...off.

He put his ear to the box. No buzzing. He put his face closer to the round hole he'd carved carefully in the wood. The guard bees, who sat right inside, should've already flown out.

Still nothing.

Zig stuffed his finger in his beer bottle, tapping the bottle lightly against the side of the wood. *Ping-pong-ping.* Sure enough, a few bees exited. And then, there it was—a low-pitched hum that

surrounded him, that embraced him, that soothed him when he
needed it most.

Mmmmmmmmmmmmmmm.

For the first ten years of his daughter's life, Zig looked in on her
every night, checking the rise and fall of Maggie's chest, checking
to make sure she was breathing. The hum of the bees, in its own
way, gave him that same feeling. Everything would be okay, even if,
deep down, he knew it wouldn't.

"Good night, girls," he said. Every fall, after the queen bee was
impregnated, all the male bees were murdered by the female bees.
Right now, every bee in the hive was a female.

"Also, thanks for stinging that freckly kid who threw a baseball
at the hive. He's not getting free honey this year," he added.

In every life, whatever you do, you either destroy or create. As a
mortician, Zig saw destruction every day. Beekeeping was his own
personal offset.

"*You have no messages,*" the ancient, robotic answering machine
voice announced as Zig returned to the kitchen.

Flipping open his laptop, he slid into the breakfast nook that
had taken him nearly half a year to make, also with hand-cut dovetail joints. On-screen, Facebook bloomed into view, to the only
page he went to. *Her* page.

Charmaine Clarke.

Every day, he'd tell himself not to look. But every day, he'd
be back. Charmaine's most recent status update was a photo—a
close-up of a T-shirt that read: *What If The Hokey-Pokey Really Is
What It's All About?*

Forty-two friends liked it, declaring it "So funny!" Someone
else added, "You're hysterical!!!" Like most things online, it was
an absurd overstatement. Still, there was one singular nugget even
Facebook tended to get right, on the left side of the screen:

Status: Single.

Outside, a lone honeybee bounced off the window, swirling in the moonlight. *Guard bee*, Zig thought, *though could be a forager.* Back when he set up his first hive, foragers were Zig's favorites. They were the only ones to actually leave the hive, the ones on the grand adventure. Lately, though, Zig realized there was a reason why foraging was saved for the eldest bees in the hive. It would be the last job they had. They'd literally work themselves to death, dying alone.

Suddenly, Zig's cell phone rang. Caller ID told him not to take it.

"What's wrong?" he answered.

"Nice to hear your voice too," Waggs pushed back, her work number showing she was still at the FBI. "Can't I just call to see how you're doing, and then you ask how I'm doing? That's how friendships work."

Zig pretended to laugh. "How are you doing, Waggs? How's Vincent?" he added, referring to Waggs's son.

"Too handsome for his own good. Thinks that just because he's twenty-four years old and starting a new job—selling timeshares, for Godsakes—that he's too busy to call his frightfully underappreciated mother who he owes everything to. Oh, and my brother asked to borrow money again. So, yeah, same crappiness as usual. How about you? That Nola Brown case...it shook you up, didn't it?"

"I appreciate you checking in, but I'm fine."

"You sound mopey."

"I'm great. Just got home," Zig said, turning back to his computer screen.

Status: Single.

"You're on Facebook, aren't you?" Waggs challenged.

Zig stared at the screen, trying not to see his own reflection. Nearly two decades ago, Waggs started at Dover two days before he did. But all these years later, their bond wasn't just from a mutual moment in time. She always understood him—and knew where his holes were. "I'm not on Facebook," he insisted.

"You do realize Facebook tells you when your friends are online? I'm on it right now. I can see you there, Ziggy."

He clicked to a new screen, hating himself for being such a cliché.

"If you want, Ziggy, I can go through Charmaine's profile and send you all the bad photos of her, or maybe just the good ones, depending on what kinda night you want."

Usually, he'd laugh at that joke. Not tonight, especially after everything with Nola and the churned-up memories of what she did for Maggie. Zig thought of his own daughter numerous times every day—in fact, he purposely said her name out loud each morning, just to make sure she wouldn't be forgotten—but today, after seeing that body, now he was picturing the worst of those days, back when he was standing at Magpie's closet, trying to decide what dress they should bury her in. "Waggs, it's late. I've got to be at work early tomorrow."

"You sure you're—"

"I'm fine. You're a good friend. Thanks for checking in."

"Truthfully, I just wanted to bitch about my brother. But we can take it up tomorrow. Oh and PS—no one's life is as good as it looks on Facebook."

As she hung up, Zig stared at the screen. Was he really that guy who spent his nights trolling online for the supposed love of his life? Zig didn't want to be that guy. He was done being that guy. Then again . . .

He clicked back to Charmaine's profile. Maybe the hokey-pokey really was what it's all about.

In the Facebook search box, he typed the name *Nola Brown*. A few faces came up. None of them was the adult version of hers. Same with Google. He was tempted to call Waggs back. But no, not yet.

"Nola, I know you're out there somewhere," Zig murmured. A few clicks of the keyboard took him over to CNN.com.

Rookstool, 6 Others Dead in Alaska Crash

Plane crashes were tragic enough, but it was worse when the press lasered in on the biggest bold name on board and turned the rest of the passengers into asterisks. In this case, the bold name was Nelson Rookstool, the head of the Library of Congress.

According to CNN, Rookstool was on a cross-country trip promoting literacy to rural Eskimo communities. Okay. That was his job. But as Master Guns had pointed out, the Librarian of Congress doesn't usually fly on military aircraft.

At the end of the CNN story, it said the other victims' names were being withheld until families could be notified. *Not true*, Zig thought. The plane crashed two days ago. That was plenty of time to notify, which meant if they were still withholding IDs, it was to cover up whatever was really going on in Alaska.

Clicking to a new screen, Zig logged into the mortuary's private intranet. The Board, they called it, named after the enormous board in HQ that showed the names of all the incoming fallen soldiers and citizens who were headed Zig's way.

According to the schedule, the remaining bodies from the Alaska crash would arrive first thing tomorrow. But as Zig scrolled down, he saw who else would be there to salute the flag-covered transfer cases that looked like caskets.

Under *Incoming Flights* was the one call sign that always meant a bad day:

M-1

He stared at it, listening to the hum of his laptop, the hum of the bees outside.

Marine One.

The big man himself was coming. The President of the United States.

According to CNN, the President had appointed Rookstool to the Librarian job. Apparently, they were old friends. But for the President to be coming for this...

Nola, what the hell'd you get yourself into?

5

Guidry, Texas
Nineteen years ago

This was Nola when she was seven.

She was a girl who noticed things. Even at that young age, she noticed the way her mom, Barb LaPointe, would check herself in the reflection of their shiny Home Depot kitchen faucet whenever she washed the dishes. She noticed how her dad, Walter, would move his lips—concentrating hard—when reading the newspaper.

Today, though, Nola didn't notice anything. She was too busy eating her favorite meal: *Space Jam* mac and cheese, chocolate milk, and Oreo cookies—Double Stuf, of course.

"Here you go, sweetie pie," Walter said. That should've been her first clue. She was never *sweetie pie*. Only his three biological kids were.

Knocking the Oreo plate aside, Walter slid a vanilla-icing sheet cake in front of her. For the rest of Nola's life, she'd remember the bright green letters.

WE WILL MISS YOU!

Confused, Nola glanced around. Neither of her adopted parents would look her in the eye.

"This will be your last night with the family," her dad, Walter LaPointe, said matter-of-factly.

"Wh-What's going on? Why're you doing this?"

But really, Nola knew why they were doing this.

A year and a half ago, Nola and her twin brother, Roddy, were rescued from a miserable group home in Arkansas. Barb LaPointe saw their photos on a fax and came to the house herself, expecting adorable twin three-year-olds. But Nola and her brother—with matching bowl haircuts so that predators wouldn't know Nola was a girl—were three years older than the group home had disclosed, with difficult behaviors carefully omitted.

On her first night in Texas, Nola crouched in her bedroom closet, clutching the only belonging she'd brought from the group home, a stuffed pink elephant named Ellie.

Her twin, Roddy, had matching black eyes with flecks of gold and the same honey-colored skin. But unlike somber Nola, he also came with a disarming grin, which made him more charming and likable. But also more dangerous.

Within their first week with the LaPointes, the back window of the house was broken. Neighborhood kids, the parents assumed. Then toys started disappearing. When the toys were found, they smelled like urine. Soon, the LaPointes started worrying about the safety of their own young children, a worry amplified when someone lit the living room carpet on fire.

Therapists were called, and things calmed down for a bit. But then Nola came home from school with a black eye (and a hospital bill) from a taunting boy in fifth grade, whose front teeth she'd knocked out with a steel thermos.

"Miss Nola," Walter said, lowering his voice, which only made her more uncomfortable, "it's time to go."

"N-No," she replied, tears pooling in her eyes. "No...please don't do this."

Walter grabbed her arm.

"Please don't do this!" she yelled, trying to pry herself from his grasp.

At the top of the stairs, the other kids huddled together, staring down guiltily, like they were trying to spy on Santa. At the back of the pack, no one could see her brother, Roddy, keeping his head down to hide the grin in his dark eyes.

Nola wanted to scream, *It was him! It was Roddy!*—who broke the window and peed on the toys. He was the one who picked the fight with Thermos Teeth. Roddy was about to get his ass kicked for telling the loudmouthed boy that he'd masturbated in the boy's backpack, and Nola was just coming to his aid.

True, Nola did set the carpet on fire—a hasty and poorly conceived plan to clear out the house to protect the family dog, whom Roddy was chasing with a candle—but at this point, would anyone even believe her?

They would. In truth, the LaPointes knew all of this. Both twins had problems, but it was Roddy who needed the real help. Resources were tight. With three other kids to take care of, they could help one of the twins, but not both. Barb LaPointe prayed on it for a week. A decision was made. They would find Nola a new home. She was the stronger one. Naturally, it'd be tough on her, but she was resilient. She'd be okay.

"*I'll be good! We'll both be good!*" Nola begged, bits of Oreo blacking out her teeth, crumbs spraying from her mouth. "*We'll be good!*"

Duh-duh-ding-ding-ding-ding-DING-DING. The doorbell rang. Back when Nola first came to live here, she loved that doorbell. It played "The Yellow Rose of Texas," though she never knew the name of the song.

"*No, please...*" Nola begged as Walter picked her up and carried her from the kitchen to the living room. Nola grabbed at the chairs, the phone cord, anything to get a handhold. Barb was sobbing as she followed behind them, prying Nola's grip from the threshold. "*Please, Mom—don't give me to them! Don't give me to them!*"

That's what Nola kept screaming over and over. Don't give me to *them*.

But it wasn't *them*.

It was *him*.

*   *   *

Three weeks later, Nola stood silently in a cold, tiny Oklahoma kitchen. Her chin was down—it was always down—like it was stapled to her chest. Sometimes a posture of shyness, sometimes a posture of fear. Today it was a bit of both.

Pretending to wash dishes, she was staring sideways, waiting to see his reaction to the steak.

She knew her new dad, Royall Barker—a Catholic man with a pitted face, greedy eyes, and the longest eyelashes she'd ever seen—wouldn't say anything. He rarely said anything. But Royall was particular about his steaks, and even more particular about his favorite breakfast, steak and eggs.

"You treat every steak like a prom date," Royall told her during the first week after she moved in. "You take care of it, it'll take care of you."

It made no sense to Nola, but really, neither did Royall. Why'd he even agree to take her in?

"I heard you can cook. Can you cook?" Royall had said on that night they left the LaPointes. It was the first thing he asked her when she got in the car. Actually, it was the second thing. The first was: "You part nigger?"

Nola stayed silent, confused.

"You know, part nigger...part dark...black," he explained, pointing to her honey-colored skin.

Nola shook her head. She didn't think so, though she didn't have many memories before the group home. What happened to her birth mom? Why did she leave? Was she dead? On Nola's sixth birthday, a caseworker said that her mom had been murdered, but Nola knew that wasn't true. You'd feel such a thing.

"Too bad. I heard niggers cook better," Royall said, then quickly added, "Your seat belt on?"

It took three hours to reach Royall's house in Oklahoma. He showed Nola the kitchen first, then her bedroom, which had a mattress with pale blue sheets, a knotty pine dresser covered in major league baseball stickers, and bare walls. There were a few toys— G.I. Joes, a crusty Nerf football, even a half-dressed Barbie— scattered across the tan carpet, like children had lived here before, though there were no signs of them now.

Nola was too young to ask where the social workers were, but even if she had, no one was coming. This was a "rehoming."

To adopt a child requires thousands of dollars, stacks of paperwork, and countless home visits by caseworkers. If something goes wrong and the child isn't a good fit for the family, well, kids aren't like used cars. They don't come with warranties; you can't return them. Indeed, if a family tries to bring a child back to the adoption agency, the state will label them unfit parents and force them to pay child support until the child is eighteen. The LaPointes certainly couldn't afford that.

But to simply hand off a child to someone else? All it takes is a signed letter, assigning temporary guardianship. It happened every day. If someone's going through hard financial times or a personal crisis, the government wants to make it easy for them to give the child to a relative or other responsible person until they get back on their feet.

But rehoming wasn't always temporary—and it created the perfect opportunity for people like Royall Barker, who would never make it through the adoption screening process, to get a child. The LaPointes listed Nola on an adoption website called Brand New Chance. Royall picked her the first night her picture went up.

"Maybe you're just a spic. Spics can cook too," Royall said when she came downstairs that first morning. From the refrigerator, he took out a wrapper with a raw steak in it. Rib eye. Bone in. "I like 'em medium rare," he said. "Only way. Medium rare. Got it?"

Nola got it.

When she burned her first steak, Royall pounded the counter, but otherwise did his best to stay calm. Told her she could do better. When she undercooked the next one, he pushed her aside, knocking the wind from her chest, and cooked it himself.

Nola had been here three weeks now. In any adoption, honeymoons don't last long. They're even shorter when Child Services has no idea what's going on. Nola put great care into this morning's steak and eggs.

"Okay. Smells promising for once," Royall said, taking a long sniff of the plate as Nola put it down in front of him. He had a fork in one fist, a knife in the other, like a hungry husband in an old comic strip.

Royall didn't just grip his fork with a closed fist. Nola noticed that, good mood or bad, he always talked with a closed fist too.

"By the way, your teacher called. Said you were fighting again," Royall said, cutting into the steak, its juices seeping toward the eggs, turning everything bloody and red. "That true? You fighting?"

It was true. Being the new kid always came with a price, especially when a sixth-grade boy found out about Nola's rehoming and spit in her hair, calling her a throwaway.

Yet right now, as Nola stood at the sink pretending to wash dishes, she didn't care about a schoolyard fight or the punishment that might come with it. No. As Royall raised the steak to his lips, her only concern was whether this sizzling piece of meat was a perfect medium rare.

Hot steam rose off the steak as Royall took the first bite into his mouth.

In the back pocket of Nola's jeans was a folded greeting card that the LaPointes had hidden in her luggage the night she left. A handwritten note inside read: *This will make you stronger.* She carried the note with her everywhere, like a totem, thinking of its promise of strength when she needed it most. Like right now.

The steak sat on Royall's tongue, and he still hadn't taken a bite.

He was sucking on it, savoring the juices. Then, slowly…chew…chew…chew.

How is it? Nola wanted to ask, though she knew better.

She noticed the shift in his posture. Shoulders back. Elbows off the table.

Royall cut himself another piece, then another. He was rocking slightly now, like his whole body was nodding.

Mmm. Mmmmm.

Nola flashed a smile—a real smile—and took a deep breath, thinking she was happy. She was too young to realize she was just relieved.

This was good. I did good, she told herself.

Then Royall took a bite of his eggs.

There was a small crunch.

Royall stopped, mid-chew, his long eyelashes blinking. His jaw shifted as his tongue probed for—

Pttt.

He spit it into his palm: a tiny jagged shard of eggshell, no bigger than a sunflower seed. Without a word, Royall wiped it on the corner of the kitchen table. His fists tightened, his whole body reclenched. The knife was still in his hand.

Nola took a half step back, bumping into the sink.

Royall squeezed the knife tighter, slowly looking over his shoulder and shooting Nola a dark, brutal glare.

It was in that frozen moment—here in this kitchen that smelled of grease and meat—that Nola, the girl who noticed things, noticed something she'd never seen before.

"I-I can make new eggs," Nola promised.

Royall didn't answer. He turned back to his steak.

For weeks now, Royall had appeared to be a man of strength. A man of forcefulness. But now, to see this man so bothered, so physically enraged by…*what*? A stray shard of eggshell? Right there, it made sense. Nola Brown understood.

It was no different than speaking with a closed fist.

Or gripping a knife to scare a young girl.

Those weren't signs of strength. They were signs of *weakness*.

That's what Nola noticed, better than anyone. She thought about Barbara LaPointe checking her reflection in a kitchen faucet, and Walter moving his lips when he read. Nola Brown was the girl who could spot weakness.

One day, it would save her life. And end seven others.

6

Dover Port Mortuary
Today

They called it the AttaBoy wall. It was a chalkboard really, with curvy edges to make it look playful, like something from kindergarten. In the upper right-hand corner, a big sign read:

THANKS FROM THE FAMILIES

On the chalkboard were dozens of handwritten notes:

We saw our son in a pristine uniform, looking cared for and respected. I have always been grateful that he looked handsome and at peace.

AttaBoy, you did it again.

Zig knew why the wall existed. When you're surrounded by death, you have to make sure you don't get swallowed by it. Over the years, Zig had taken great comfort from the letters here. But right now, at 5:15 a.m., he was really just standing at the blackboard, pretending to read, and scanning the hallway to make sure he was alone.

All clear. Zig darted ahead, eyeing the door on his—

They collided just as she turned the corner. Zig was moving so fast, he barely saw her before they hit.

She was a full head shorter and a hundred pounds lighter, but Colonel Agatha Hsu—Dover's wing commander—barely stepped back at the impact. Hsu hadn't gotten to be the first Asian American woman to run Dover by being a pushover.

"Apologies, ma'am. I was trying t—"

She raised a hand. *Keep quiet.* As a young Air Force lieutenant, Hsu had been shot down while flying supplies into Kirkuk, Iraq. Even the best pilots would've panicked, but Hsu, following protocol, destroyed her own aircraft, along with her supplies and computer equipment, so they wouldn't fall into enemy hands. All the while, she didn't even notice the six-inch gash in her leg. So in the question of *Heart or no heart?* she definitely had heart.

She also had ego. After the crash, she took a short leave from active duty and ran for Congress. When she lost, she signed up for the job here. Hsu didn't care about Dover's mission; she took the job because every colonel who'd ever run the place (except for one) had gone on to become a general. That made her a politician first, and one with a temper. Zig braced himself, but to his surprise, he got...

"I didn't realize you were such an early bird, Zig."

"With six bodies coming, I like to be ready."

"Today's definitely a big day."

"Every day's a big day," Zig countered with a grin.

"Agreed," Colonel Hsu said, glancing down at her phone, then looking up. Even from here, Zig could tell she was checking the Board. She wasn't tracking the plane bringing the bodies. She was tracking Marine One. Zig mentally rolled his eyes. Politician.

"Zig, have you seen Dr. Sinclair?"

Zig made a mental note. Last night, before Zig got the body, Sinclair was the one who had done the autopsy—he had to sign off on Nola's faked fingerprints and all the other nonsense they hoped no one would notice.

"He's not in his office?" Zig asked, gesturing over his shoulder to the medical examiner's suite. He waited for Hsu to head there. She stayed where she was, planted like a tree.

"I'll look. Oh, and Zig—they said you did a beautiful job with the girl who came in yesterday. The sergeant..."

"Nola Brown."

"Exactly. Sergeant Brown. She was burned pretty badly, but I heard you worked until almost midnight. I checked the schedule this morning and saw you didn't put in for overtime."

Zig gave her a small grin.

"When I first started here, they warned me you all were morticians, not magicians. You might be the exception. We're lucky to have you, Zig," the colonel added, heading for the suite without looking back. "And so is Sergeant Brown."

As the swinging metal doors closed behind her, Zig tried to tell himself that was true. But for all he knew, Nola was the one who caused all this. Maybe Master Guns had it right. Maybe Nola had crashed the plane, survived the ordeal—a parachute?—then planted a different body so she could get away. But as Zig thought about that night at the campfire— He stopped himself. Just because Nola did something good a decade ago didn't mean she's a saint. Still, as Zig pictured those burns last night, as he thought about that note—*Nola, you were right. Keep running*—he knew that whoever that body really belonged to, the woman who swallowed the note... She wasn't Nola's enemy.

Checking the hallway, Zig headed for his own destination, the one place he hoped would fill in a few new puzzle pieces. Room 115.

PERSONAL EFFECTS

At the door scanner, he swiped an ID card with a muscular black man on it. Zig didn't have this kind of clearance. Fortunately, Master Guns did. Once Zig had told him the President was coming, Guns wanted to know what was going on too.

Zig waited for the *thunk* of the lock, but it never came. The door was already unlocked. As he pushed, it slowly slid open.

7

Hello...? It's your favorite mortician..." Zig called out, elbowing the door and craning his neck so he could see into the long, narrow room that smelled like fresh dirt, wet hair, and his cousin's basement.

The only answer came from the glow of a swivel lamp that was on the desk in the corner. The lamp was on.

"Moke, it's Zig," he added, calling the name of the muscular Hawaiian Marine who regularly staffed this place.

Still no response.

Glancing around, he checked the wooden storage shelves that jutted out from the walls like bunk beds stacked five high. The deeper Zig went into the room, the more he felt the old lump in his throat—like a stuck pill—that he'd felt for nearly a full year after his daughter died and everything fell apart. During meals, all through those months, Zig could barely swallow. Going to bed, he couldn't breathe. The doctors had a name for it: a *globus*. Someone else called it a "grief lump." They saw it in those who suffered wrenching heartache. After a year, the lump faded, but in this room, it always came back.

"Moke, if you're here—"

There was a ping—new email arrived—from the computer on the desk.

Zig didn't believe in ghosts. Or an afterlife. To him, a body was a shell. He worked with those shells on a daily basis. He didn't do it for the dead; he did it for those left behind. This room was the same: It preserved what remained.

When a soldier died in the field, the body came to Dover. All the things found with the fallen came to this room. The dog tags, medical bracelets, sunglasses, wallets, medals, caps, military coins, cell phones, and especially the "sentimental effects," the first things sent back to a family—wedding rings, crosses or religious items worn around necks, photos of kids that were in pockets, and the most heartbreaking to Zig, half-written letters that would never get finished. Zig knew all too well: We all have unfinished business.

Slowly, he took another step into the room. On a nearby shelf, a light blue prep mat held a digital watch, a gold pinkie ring, barely worn boots, a scratch-off lottery ticket, an engraved money clip, and the pocket diary of a middle-aged major who'd had a heart attack last week and was still waiting to be buried at Arlington. Fallen #2,352.

There was another shelf below that one for a nineteen-year-old sailor who'd died racing his motorcycle on a base in Germany three days ago. His helmet sat there, scraped raw, like a museum piece. Next to it was a photo of his one-year-old son's Elmo birthday cake. Fallen #2,355.

The knot in Zig's throat swelled. He spent nearly every day embalming corpses, but as his favorite professor had taught him at mortuary school: "Gore you get used to. Shattered lives you don't." The professor was right. During 9/11, Zig held it together as the first dozen bodies were wheeled in. He stood there strong when they followed with a box of unsorted human arms and another of unsorted legs. But nothing undid him like seeing, in the midst of all the carnage, a boy's single sneaker that had somehow flown free from the blast. At just the sight of it, the tears finally came.

Which led Zig to the lowest tray on the shelf, labeled 14-2678—the physical equivalent of her last will and testament—the personal effects of Sergeant First Class Nola Brown.

8

Knollesville, South Carolina
Eighteen years ago

This was Nola when she was eight.

"Why're you—?" She was in pain; he was hurting her.

"I-I thought it was trash."

"*Trash?*" Royall shouted. "*THIS. IS. NOT. TRASH!*" He was gripping her under her armpits, tugging so hard she was up on her toes, which scraped across the kitchen linoleum.

Tonight was supposed to be a special night, to celebrate their move to the new and nicer house. Nola had made fish—fresh bass, prepared it perfectly, lemons and everything—even cleaned it up ahead of time.

But when she'd tipped Royall's plate into the trash, he spotted the head of the fish, eyes staring up at them. That was it.

Royall licked the corner of his mouth. He did it two other times during dinner. Nola knew that sign. Drunk.

"*You think I'm made of frikkin' money!?*" he exploded.

Nola shook her head, confused.

"*That head . . . the tail too . . . you can use it for soup! Use it to make broth!*" He started cursing at her. "*I bust my ass every day! I bust my ass, and you throw it away!?*"

And now, here she was, up on her toes, being dragged by her armpits.

Kicking the back door open, Royall gave her a final shove, practically tossing her into the backyard, a balding patch of browned grass littered with an empty bottle of Jack Daniel's, an upside-down plastic kiddie pool, and some brand-new wicker patio furniture that Royall had bid on at a local foreclosure sale and sold to furniture stores in three nearby states.

Royall didn't say a word. Nola knew what the punishment was.

At the center of the yard was a hole in the lawn.

Nola grabbed a nearby shovel and stabbed it into the earth.

It was a tradition from Royall's own father. When you dig yourself into a hole, you gotta dig yourself out. Otherwise, you dig your own grave. For Nola, this punishment had started on that night she'd stayed late at a new friend's house, eating dinner there without calling home. Royall burst through the friend's front door screaming, pulling her out of there and making a scene that would keep future friends away. That night, Royall handed her a shovel and told her, "Fifteen minutes. No stopping."

He did it again when Nola accidentally knocked the cable box from the top of the TV. And when she sneezed during dinner without covering her mouth. And even when she laughed too loudly at a stupid insurance commercial.

She expected the punishment when she mixed a red shirt in with the whites and turned half their laundry pink. But lately, it was the randomness of Royall, the arbitrariness of his explosions, that had her so on edge. It was like Royall had no rules to live by. Indeed, there were few things Nola could do where she knew how he'd react.

"*Twenty minutes tonight! No damn stopping!*" he barked, throwing the fish head at her. It wasn't until it hit her in the back—*THWAP!*—and landed in the dirt, that she realized he'd pulled it from the trash.

"*And don't you cry! Show strength! Not a tear!*" Royall added.

Nola stared down at the fish, cursing herself for cleaning

up dinner so quickly. And then this thought: *I'll never cry. Not for you.*

"You're thinking something now, aren't you?" Royall challenged. He could read people fast, a skill he used to make a massive profit on that wicker furniture, as well as the two hundred odd-lot mattresses he bought at auction last week. He was smart, almost brilliant in the way he could find what people wanted. The problem was his temper and the poor choice of friends that came with it, which explained the three hundred mini-refrigerators, all of them broken, that he got stuck with last month. Royall licked the corner of his mouth, licked it again. "You got something to say, say it. C'mon, my little nigger! Say it!"

For a moment, Nola stood there, shovel in hand. *Don't say it,* she told herself. But she couldn't help it. "Today's my birthday."

If Royall was surprised, he didn't show it. "So what do you want, a cake? Presents?"

Nola waited a minute, weighing whether she should just stay quiet. "The phone," she finally said, against her better judgment. "If the LaPointes call—"

"The LaPointes threw you away. They're not calling."

"But my brother—"

"I bought you those stamps. Has your brother written back? Has anyone written back? They're not calling you."

"Maybe they don't have our new number."

"They have it. They're not calling."

"But if they do, I can speak to them, right?"

"Just dig the damn hole," Royall said. Heading back toward the house, he added, "Happy damn birthday." The door slammed shut behind him.

Out in the yard, Nola stood there, alone, stabbing the point of the shovel into the head of the fish. "*It's my biiiirthday!*" she said in a high voice, mimicking herself and hating the fact she'd mentioned it. And really, that was the cruelest cut of Royall's punishment: Nola's developing belief that this was *her* doing, *her* fault. *I should dig another hole just for that.*

Fifteen minutes later, her hands were on fire, and a bead of sweat hung from her nose. Stomping the blade into the soil, she scooped out a mound of dirt. Then another. As she'd learned months ago, it was hard to dig a hole, or at least to get down very deep. During winter, it's even harder.

A phone started ringing in the distance. Nola turned at the sound coming from the house. Naturally, her first thought was of the LaPointes. *Could it be them?* Not likely.

It rang again, sounding louder on the second ring.

Probably one of those surveys. They always called at dinnertime. Or maybe it was one of Royall's girlfriends, the one who touched her clothes a lot. Or the fat one with the cigarette breath and the honey skin. Like Nola's.

The phone rang again. Royall still didn't pick up.

Their cordless phone had Caller ID. If Royall wasn't picking up... No. He wasn't that cruel, was he? She shook her head. He wouldn't do that. Even to her.

The phone rang again. And again.

Please... just pick up.

The phone went silent. Thank God. He picked up. He actually—

Riiiiiiing.

He hadn't picked up. They were calling back.

Nola wanted to run inside, wanted to rip the phone from the wall, see who was there. But if she left her spot... if she stopped digging the hole...

Riiiiiiing.

She was breathing heavily now, panicking, like her lungs were filled with crushed glass. Gripping the shovel, she looked around for help—

That's when she spotted the tree. On her left, past the new wicker furniture, a pecan tree, thick as a manhole, though starting to bow like a parenthesis. But what Nola noticed immediately was a dark patch at its base. To most, it looked like a knot, a small burl, even a bruise. But Nola saw it for what it was. Rot.

Later tonight, when she was lying in bed, she'd have no logical explanation for what she did next. But out in the backyard, as the phone let out another loud shriek, all she knew was that she wanted to hit something.

Storming toward the withered tree, she cocked back the shovel like a baseball bat, eyed the oval mark, and swung wildly.

Direct hit.

Riiiiiiing.

She swung again. And again.

With each impact, the metal spade bit into the bark, splintering the black rot. With each chop, fragments of wood flew through the air. But a shovel isn't an axe.

Still, Nola kept swinging, faster and faster. A piece of skin tore open on her palm. She didn't feel it, didn't feel anything, including the tears that were skating down her cheeks.

Riiiiing.

"*Y-You don't give children away! Why would you give me away!?*" she sobbed, winding up once more and swinging at—

Krrrrrrk.

The old tree flinched. Then it was moving, falling, bending really, as it tumbled straight at her.

"NOLA, MOVE!" Royall shouted behind her.

She was frozen, the tree just a few inches away.

"I SAID...MOVE!" Royall yelled, tackling her at full speed. Her head snapped to the right, both of them falling to the left as the tree toppled. She was still holding the shovel, which got slapped from her hand as the tree hit it.

They fell to the ground together, crashing into the dirt, his arms around her.

Her first thought was of Royall. He saved her.

But then she thought of the tree itself. At a height of over twenty feet, it was taller than she was, stronger than she was. She shouldn't have been able to take it down. But by going for that spot, that black decaying rot, she'd felled it.

She always knew she had a gift for finding weakness. But tonight was the first time Nola Brown had used that gift to find her strength.

9

Dover Port Mortuary
Today

Kneeling to get closer, Zig felt his age in his knees and his back. On the baby blue prep mat, most of the items were singed from the fire: a Keith Haring wristwatch, two charred boots, and half a dozen small pieces of Nola's Army uniform where they'd cut away the burnt edges. There were also a set of silver cuff earrings, a toe ring with a sun design, and a pair of aviator sunglasses missing such a big triangular chunk that the left lens looked like Pac-Man.

As Zig pulled the tray toward him, a faded black hair tie brought back the memory of his Maggie's red hair tie, which sat there, stranded, next to his toaster, for the better part of two years now.

Crouching down farther, he checked the shelf below to make sure he wasn't missing anything. Nope, this was all of it. But as Zig scanned the items one last time, what stood out most was what *wasn't* there: No phone. No wallet. But most of all: No dog tags.

Zig shook his head; he should've seen this one coming. When the Army issues dog tags, you get two sets. At least one tag goes around your neck; the other, in case your head is separated from your body, usually gets threaded into the laces of your boots. It's rare to lose both—unless someone takes them on purpose.

Pulling her boots from the shelf, Zig saw that the laces on the left boot had been sliced. Based on the nylon bootlace shavings sprinkled across the mat, it was recently too.

Another ping came from the computer desk behind Zig. Yet another email. He turned to double-check. The door was still shut. No one was there. But with all of Nola's IDs missing, he had to wonder: Was someone trying to convince the world Nola was dead? Or was the real goal to hide the identity of whomever that burned body really belonged to?

As Zig placed the boots back on the shelf, he noticed a small pile of uniform remnants and— No. They weren't just scraps of fabric. From the pile, Zig pulled out—

At first, he thought it was another folded note, like the one he found last night. But as he touched it... This wasn't paper. It was thicker and textured. Canvas.

Zig carefully unfolded it; it was the size of a sheet of paper. It was also damp, like it had been in the snow or a puddle. That's why it had survived without getting burned.

As Zig peeled the canvas open, colors jumped out. Rich purples, muted shades of orange, and camouflage olive and brown. This was more than a simple picture; it was a painting. A portrait, in thick pastels, of a woman in army greens staring straight at Zig, her head tilted. She had sad, hollow eyes, a flat nose, and her earrings... Zig glanced back at the shelf. They were the same silver cuffs.

The knot in Zig's throat felt like he'd swallowed a stapler. He knew this woman. He knew her instantly. He'd spent six hours stitching her back together last night. But what caught his attention now was the signature at the bottom of the painting, in white block letters: *NBrown.*

Nola, you painted this?

Behind him, he heard another ping. Zig assumed it was another email. He couldn't have been more wrong.

As he turned, all he saw was a blur. Then a burst of stars.

10

"—ou hear me, sir?" a hot voice blasted in Zig's face. "Sir, you okay!?"

Zig nodded, blinking awake. Whoever was yelling, his breath smelled like maple syrup. As the world came back into focus, Zig looked around. He'd had a dream about his daughter. A good one. He relished the good ones. Now he was on his back. *How'd I get on my back?*

"Sir, we need you to stay where you are," Maple Syrup told him. He was a soldier, a young one with big nostrils. Full fatigues. Early twenties. Uniform told Zig the kid was Army, last name Zager. "You passed out."

"I didn't pass out."

He put a hand on Zig's chest. "Please, sir, stay where you are," he insisted. He wasn't trying to help Zig up. He was trying to keep him down.

Zig pushed the kid's hand aside and tried to sit up. A stab of pain shot through him like a spear. Zig touched his own jaw, just below his ear. It was swollen but not bleeding. Whoever had done this knew their anatomy—and also knew that when a boxer gets punched in the face, it's a mini-stroke. Pick the right spot and you get a knockou—

Wait. The painting... *Where's the painting?*

Zig checked the floor, then the shelves. The burnt army boots, the cuff earrings, the Pac-Man sunglasses—they were all on the blue prep mat, exactly where he first found them. Even the scraps of her uniform were back in a neat stack. But the painting of the woman, the one signed by Nola...

Mothertrucker.

Zig closed his eyes, trying to picture the painting in his head. It was a portrait—a surprisingly good one—but nothing more than that. Still, for someone to sneak in here and crack him in the head to swipe it... You don't take a risk like that unless it's a risk worth taking.

Zig turned back to Maple Syrup. "How'd you get in here?" he barked.

"In *where?*" Maple Syrup asked.

"In here. The door was closed. Who let you in?"

"The door was open," he insisted as Zig replayed that too. The door was closed. Zig could swear it was closed. Behind him, the desk lamp was still on.

"Why'd you come in here?" Zig said. "This room—Personal Effects—it's off-limits."

"The colonel... She asked me to take them around—"

"Take *who* around?"

The kid pointed over his shoulder. There was a German shepherd out in the hallway, followed by two men in suits. Nonmilitary. They weren't from Dover. One of them had an earpiece.

Secret Service, Zig realized. He studied the dog. If they were already sniffing for bombs...

"What time is it?" Zig asked. Climbing to his feet and searching for balance, Zig scrambled for the door, pulled out his phone, and opened the web browser to— According to the Board, Marine One had landed six minutes ago.

The President of the United States was already here. Fortunately, Zig knew exactly where he was going.

11

This was the hardest part of Zig's job.

He was standing in the hold of a cargo plane, a massive C-17 transport that felt like a flying warehouse, even as it was parked on the flight line just behind his building. On most days, the plane could carry three SuperCobra helicopters or even an Abrams tank. Today, as the December wind tore through the back of the plane, its payload was far more precious: six American-flag-covered caskets—they were actually called *transfer cases*—each filled with a body bag covered in ice to preserve the contents. All six were lined up side by side on the back loading ramp like red, white, and blue piano keys.

Hup-hup-hup-hup.

Zig heard them before he saw them, out on the runway. The six-man carry team in camouflage fatigues and bright white gloves, marching in perfect precision, two by two, with their team leader behind them. They headed straight toward Zig.

Hup-hup-hup-hup.

From Zig's angle in the back of the plane, he spotted the maestro himself, President Orson Wallace, standing down on the runway in his black overcoat. His eyes were focused straight ahead, his arms were flat at his sides, and his salt-and-pepper hair was neatly trimmed as the carry team marched past him.

Hup-hup-hup-hup.

Zig had seen President Wallace and his perfect hair before. Ever since Obama opened Dover to the press, every commander in chief had felt the need to make a visit. But this wasn't a typical presidential visit. Wallace was here to see a friend, which meant Zig needed to keep his eyes open and get in close.

Within the last twenty minutes, someone had attacked Zig in Personal Effects and stolen Nola's painting. Whoever it was, they were probably still here somewhere.

It didn't hurt that, as always, Zig was the first one signed up to be on today's mortuary advance team. In his pocket were two dozen loose threads he'd pulled from the six American flags draped over the transfer cases that served as caskets. Zig had just re-ironed every flag, replacing the ones from the plane with new flags that had elastic borders, like a fitted bedsheet, to make sure that when it came to the bodies of the six fallen soldiers on this plane, every detail was perfect. Now all he had to do was wait.

Hup-hup-hup-hup.

Across from Zig, tucked into the opposite corner of the plane, was Master Guns. Master Guns shot Zig a look, then glanced meaningfully at the VIPs who were lined up on the runway, next to the President. The attorney general was there, along with the commander of the Army Special Forces, two brigadier generals, and of course, their boss, Colonel Hsu herself.

Master Guns didn't have to say it. Over the past six months, they'd held dignified transfers for over two hundred fallen soldiers. Colonel Hsu hadn't shown up for a single one of them. Until today, when the President arrived.

She should be here for them all, Zig said with a dirty look. *No heart.*

Click-click-click-click-click-click-click-click-click-click-click-click-click!

Below the left wing of the plane, a dozen photographers in the press pool snapped a few hundred photos of the President just standing at attention, shoulder to shoulder with the other VIPs. When the President visits, everyone comes running. No way was Hsu missing this. But considering she was the last person who'd seen Zig before he got cracked in the head, Zig was eyeing her even more closely.

Look who else, Master Guns said with a glance. At the end of the VIP line, there was a muscular, dark-skinned black man in a pinstripe suit and round vintage glasses that softened his face. Master Guns mouthed a single word: *"Riestra."*

Leonard Riestra, director of the Secret Service.

Hup-hup-hup-hup.

A metal thumping echoed through the hull as the carry team stepped onto the loading ramp and marched up toward the flag-covered cases.

"Secret Service?" Zig mouthed, cocking an eyebrow. Master Guns nodded imperceptibly.

Last year, when a Georgetown professor was killed in Qatar, the head of the CIA showed up at Dover to pay his respects. Clearly, "professor" wasn't quite the right description. At Dover, secret squirrels were here all the time. Zig and Master Guns had seen the heads of the FBI, Department of Defense, and even FEMA. But in all their years, they'd never seen the head of the Secret Service.

Kuuunk.

The carry team stopped on cue and stood at attention inside the plane, surrounding the flag-covered cases. Behind them, up the loading ramp, the chaplain followed. Since the back of the plane was open to the winter air, everyone was freezing. No one complained—not when there were six men and women who'd just lost their lives.

"Let us pray," the chaplain offered as all heads bowed toward the six bodies. No one said a word. No one moved. "Almighty God, we th—"

Th-thunk. Th-thunk.

At the sound, the chaplain looked up. Zig and Master Guns

turned. Up the metal loading ramp, the most powerful man on the planet—President Orson Wallace—surprised everyone by walking calmly toward the bodies, his long black overcoat billowing behind him like a magician's cape.

Master Guns threw a quizzical look at Zig.

Zig had no idea what the President was doing. No one did.

Click-click-click-click-click-click-click-click-click-click-click-click-click, came the cameras.

The carry team stayed where they were. So did their team leader, who knew never to break protocol. All of them stood there in the back of the plane, Zig off on the side. The only one who moved was the chaplain, who shifted slightly to the left to make room at the top of the ramp for the one person no one could say no to.

"Mr. President..." the chaplain said, though it came out like a question.

"Which one?" Wallace asked, motioning with his chin at the cases.

The chaplain looked at Zig.

"*Where's my friend?*" the President of the United States whispered, his voice catching. His head was tilted and his gray eyes sagged. Everyone knows what the President looks like, but Zig had never seen him look like this.

"He's—" The chaplain pointed to the left. *There.*

The President glanced down at the case.

According to every news article about the plane crash, Nelson Rookstool wasn't just a law school pal. When Wallace initially ran for governor, Rookstool held one of the first political fundraisers for him. Wallace eventually appointed him to lead the Library of Congress. But it wasn't until this moment, as the President of the United States pressed his lips together and fought to stand perfectly still, that Zig actually believed these two men were friends. Zig didn't know Wallace personally. But Zig knew grief.

"My apologies, father," the President said to the chaplain. "I didn't mean to interrupt."

The chaplain nodded. "Almighty God," he began for the second time, "we thank you for the freedom we enjoy in our nation as we welcome our fallen home this morning..."

Within seconds, the President straightened his shoulders, his barriers already back in place.

"Amen," Zig said in unison with the other voices as the carry team lined up, facing each other on opposite sides of the first flag-covered case, the one with a small bar code that read *Lt. Anthony Trudeau*, a twenty-five-year-old kid from Boone, Colorado, with a six-month-old daughter.

"Ready...*lift*," the team leader called out as everyone, including the President, again held their breath. In slow, perfect synchrony, each member bent down, his white gloves gripping a handle on Trudeau's case.

In addition to Librarian Rookstool, there were three Library of Congress staffers, an Army lieutenant, and an Air Force pilot who also went down with the plane. The woman identified as Nola had jumped out of the plane early, so her body got here yesterday. Everyone else had to be individually removed from the wreckage, so their bodies were just arriving now.

"Ready...*up*," the team leader said as they lifted the remains of Lieutenant Trudeau. With the body itself, plus the ice, each case weighed over four hundred pounds. Since Trudeau was Army, the oldest service, he came off the plane first.

"Ready...*face*," the leader added as the team turned sideways, facing the back ramp. Down on the runway were the open back doors of a white van, which looked more like an ice cream truck, that would transport the bodies to the mortuary for the medical examiners. After the autopsies, Zig and his crew would clean them up for official burial.

As the carry team headed down the ramp, the photographers took a quick set of shots—*click-click-click-click-click-click*—and went silent.

It was so unnaturally quiet that Zig could hear the popping of ice cubes inside the metal cases. He heard the President breathing through his nose. Then, as Lieutenant Trudeau finally left the plane, he heard a low heart-wrenching sob.

Ahhhuhhh.

Master Guns looked at Zig, who stood at perfect attention, staring straight ahead. They both knew where it was coming from. On their far right, under the opposite wing from the press, the families of the victims were roped off in a small area, getting their first good look at their children's coffins.

It wasn't a loud outburst. Military families were too tough for that. But there was no hiding that sound—the sound that haunts every funeral—hollow, shaking gasps that reach down so deep, they come from the mourner's soul.

When you lose a parent, you're an orphan. When you lose a husband, you're a widow. But as Zig had learned fourteen years ago, when you lose a child, they don't have a name for that.

Uhhuhhuhh, a family member sobbed. Master Guns again glanced Zig's way. Zig kept his stance, eyes facing front. It was freezing in the plane, but he felt a bead of sweat rolling down his armpit, toward his ribcage.

"Present *arms!*" the leader called out from the runway. On cue, the carry team marched forward, and all the VIPs in line raised their hands in a salute. This was the moment when mothers and fathers saw it . . . and finally believed it.

There was another high-pitched gasp in the distance. Zig could feel Master Guns staring at him, just like he could feel the bead of sweat. For the first few years after Zig's daughter died, every ceremony at Dover brought a ferocious flood of his own worst memories: the sound of shoveled dirt as it landed on her casket . . . his own toes like rocks as he stood there in the grass . . . the endless round of back-pats from mourners who didn't want to disturb him at the graveside. *Back-pats!*

These days, those memories were buried, dulled by repetition. It was a good thing, Zig told himself, a benefit of being at Dover

and attending over a thousand funerals. Replication brought accli-
mation; he'd been through this before.

Zig stared straight ahead. The bead of sweat was gone. Now
he could focus on Nola. Just Nola. Whatever it took, he would
do right by her—not just for him, but for his daughter. He owed
Nola—and Maggie—forever.

Down on the runway, the carry team stopped, marched in place,
and turned toward each other at the back of the white van.

"Ready...*step!*" the leader announced as they all slid the flag-
covered case into the van and onto the metal rollers that spun
and clanked. A high-pitched whimper—a howl, really, that could
only come from a mother deprived of her duties—echoed across
the runway. Zig was so focused on the sound that he didn't
even realize how hard he was clenching his jaw. He never broke
stance.

One by one, the team repeated the process, transferring each
flag-covered case from the plane into the van. Soon, there were
only four cases left, the four civilians.

Now it made sense. The President didn't say a word. He didn't
have to. Stepping toward the flag-covered case, he shot a look at
one of the uniformed carry-team members, who was smart enough
to get out of the way. Here's why the President came. This had
nothing to do with a photo op. Wallace wanted to be a pallbearer
for his friend.

"Ready...*lift*," the team leader announced as the President—
now part of the carry team—bent down, grabbing the metal carry-
bar. "Ready...*up*."

The leader of the free world didn't hold back, tugging hard on
the back left corner of the case. He wasn't wearing white gloves.
From the weight, his knuckles went pale. Even if his hands were
bleeding, he wasn't letting go.

"Ready...*face*."

The President turned and marched down the back of the plane,
he and five soldiers carrying his dead friend.

Click-click-click-click-click-click-click-click-click-click-click-click-click-click.

Colonel Hsu stood straighter than ever. She knew this was the pic.

Zig rolled his eyes, catching the attention of Master Guns, who motioned down at the President, or more specifically, at who the President himself was looking at. It happened in a split second, but Zig couldn't miss it. As the carry team filed past the VIPs and toward the van, President Wallace shot a quick look to the head of the Secret Service, who shifted uncomfortably in mid-salute. Maybe it was nothing—there were a thousand reasons these two men would look at each other. But in the back of his head, Zig kept seeing the note—*Keep running*—which begged the question: Running from who?

"Ready...*step!*" the leader barked as the President pushed his friend's body onto the rollers and into the van.

"Order...*arms!*" he added as they all lowered their salutes, slowly, over a long three seconds.

Click-click.

It was a moment made for the history books, or at least as clickbait for tomorrow's websites. But what caught Zig's eye was what else the President was glancing at. As the carry team finished their salutes, President Wallace turned away from the van, looking back at something below the wing of the plane. Or some*one*, Zig realized.

Ziggy, don't, Master Guns warned with a glare.

Zig was already moving, sliding subtly to his right, toward the far side of the ramp, which gave him a perfect view of the spectators in the crowd.

Diagonally down, sticking out from under the wing of the plane, was an area for Dover employees. In front was his sixty-year-old, egg-shaped supervisor, Samuel Goodrich, as well as Lou, short for

Louisa, the one female mortician, who had lost both parents when she was young and grew up playing Funeral with her Barbie dolls.

Next to them, and held back by an actual velvet rope, were staffers from every Dover department: Accounting, the Chaplain's Office, Behavioral Health Care, Legal, even Mrs. Howell from Veteran Affairs, all of them craning their necks to see the President.

Mixed into the crowd, Zig even spotted Dr. Sinclair, the slender, meticulously dressed medical examiner who had done Nola's autopsy last night—and had to sign off on those fake fingerprints.

Was it really so terrible for the President to be looking into the crowd? Probably not. In fact, the more Zig considered it, it seemed almost absurd to think of the President of the United States as having some sort of personal hand in this. The Librarian of Congress was his friend. Why would Wallace be here, or link himself to this, if his whole goal was to do harm? Unless, of course, Zig had it wrong. Maybe instead of searching through the crowd, what if the President suddenly saw someone down there—someone he recognized—someone who shouldn't be showing his or her face?

From this height, Zig was three stories up, making it feel like he was watching an NFL game. It was hard to read expressions, but from this angle... Wallace wasn't focused on Dover's staff. He was eyeing a different group—the group that was even closer to him on the runway—in front of the staff, in front of the VIPs, in front of everyone. The families.

Of course.

He almost forgot. All the victims' families were here, which meant...

Zig turned back to Master Guns.

Master Guns scowled at him: *No.*

Zig nodded *yes*. He had an idea. A really bad idea.

12

S orry, Mr. Zigarowski," said the twentysomething private with short blond hair that was wispy, like a baby's, "I don't have anyone checked in for a Nola Brown."

The kid was telling the truth, or at least the truth that was currently on his computer screen. "What about tomorrow?" Zig asked, leaning with both palms on the welcome desk of what looked like a fancy bed-and-breakfast and smelled like one too. Fresh potpourri; leather reading chairs; logs burning in the fireplace. "Anyone checking in tomorrow?"

"Not that I see," Blond Hair answered, scanning the reservations for what was known as Fisher House, a plush and serene eight-thousand-square-foot "hotel" with nine beautifully decorated suites. Anywhere else, it'd be a perfect vacation spot—a sprawling one-story stone getaway complete with white columns out front—but every military family understands that Fisher House is the last place you want to be invited.

Years ago, if a family member died and you came to Dover for the ceremony, you'd spend one of the worst nights of your life in a cheap motel. Until Fisher House opened. Billed as a "home away from home" and built on the base itself, Fisher House offered a free place to stay in a tasteful environment, staffed by grief counselors, supervised by a full-time chaplain, and stocked with toys for little kids whose twenty-three-year-old fathers were never coming home again.

"You sure her family was checking in?" the private asked again, using that soft, hushed voice that people reserve for hotels and funerals. Here, they specialized in both.

"Maybe they canceled? Can you see cancellations?" Zig asked, slowing his own voice down and turning on the charm. Yesterday, the body identified as Nola had arrived at Dover. If Zig wanted to know more about her, his best bet was tracking down whichever family members cared enough to make the trip.

"Sorry, sir," Blond Hair replied. "I don't have any visitors for her. Or cancellations."

"What about her PADD?" Zig asked.

The private looked up from his computer screen, forcing a nervous grin. "Sir, you know I don't have access to that."

Now Zig was the one forcing a grin. This was what he was really after. When you enlist in the military, one of the first things the government makes you do is pick out a PADD—a Person Authorized to Direct Disposition—a loved one who'll decide whether you're buried in your uniform or civilian clothes, or if you want a metal casket or a wooden one. Most people designate a parent or a spouse. Special Ops folks tend to pick a close friend. Nola was still alive and out there. Whoever she picked, it's someone she's close to, someone she might even be reaching out to right now.

"Son, how long you been with us here?" Zig asked.

"Since the summer."

That sounded right. Every few months, new recruits rotated through Dover. Most kids couldn't handle being around bodies for longer than that.

"On the night of my fortieth birthday, I celebrated here on base," Zig said. "Same with my fiftieth. So Private Grunbeck," he added, reading Grunbeck's name tag, "I know you've got Nola's PADD."

"That doesn't mean you get to change the rules. *Sir.*"

Zig was reminded why the dead were so often better company than the living: They don't lie, they don't complain, and they don't talk back.

"I appreciate the help," Zig said, thinking he could still get what he needed from Grunbeck's supervisor.

"And if you're looking for Captain Harmon, he's in a private ceremony with all the visiting families. He can't be disturbed," Grunbeck said.

Zig scratched at the scar on his chin, remembering the bar in Pennsylvania where he got it. He was nineteen then, fighting to impress a girl. Now he was older, and fighting for something far more important. Grin firmly in place, Zig leaned forward, palms down on the kid's desk. "Son, I believe it's time you learned some lessons in—"

"—JUST WANT TO SEE HIS BODY!" a female voice sobbed as the automatic doors to Fisher House slid open. Behind Zig, a woman in her late forties, with graying black hair, dressed in an old, deflated, black winter coat, stumbled in. Zig recognized her from the presidential ceremony, the family right in front. Her son was the first body off the plane. Now she was shouting at the sky, like she was yelling at God Himself. "WHY WOULD THEY—!? HE'S MY ONLY—! WHY CAN'T I SEE HIS BODY!?"

Every staffer in Fisher House trains for this moment. Grunbeck had trained for it too. But the private just stood there, frozen, behind the welcome desk. Indeed, the only one moving was—

"Ma'am, let me help you," Zig said, striding toward her. "I can help you."

"YOU CAN'T!" she screamed, shoving Zig back. "YOU DON'T KNOW ANYTH—!"

"I know your son is named Anthony. Can you tell me about Anthony?"

The woman stopped at her son's name. Her eyes flicked back and forth, hollowed and dead. The Dover look, they called it.

"Julie, what in the holy hell you doin'?" a big man with a square face and a camouflage US Army baseball cap called out. He turned to Zig. "Get away from my wife!" He was tall—at least six foot three—but the way he was hunched...and slurring his words...he nearly crashed into one of the oversized leather chairs in the lobby. *Drunk*, though Zig couldn't blame him for that.

"Sir, I was just talking about your son, Anth—"

"Don't you say his name! You got no right!"

"Sir, if you just slow down, we can help you."

"By what? By giving me more of *these*?" the man shouted, reaching into his pocket and pulling out a fistful of crumpled pamphlets with titles like *The Weight of Grief* and *Tragedy Assistance*. "This is paper! It makes nothing better!" he screamed, tossing the pamphlets in Zig's face.

Zig kept silent. Morticians may ease some pain, but they don't make anyone happy. Finally, he said, "Tell me about Anthony."

"Don't you—! I want to see my son! Why can't we see him!? It's like they're hiding something! We didn't even know he was *in* Alaska—and now they want an autopsy!?" the father blurted, swaying in place, his eyes glazed.

"I promise, you will get to see him. When the autopsy's done, we'll clean him up and—"

"*NOW! I want to see him now!*" the man exploded through tears of rage.

His wife was crying now too, sobbing as she took a seat on a nearby glass coffee table. "T-Today...it's our anniversary. Anthony was flying home to celebrate," she whispered, her voice so soft it was drowned out by a pop and crackle from the fireplace.

"*You take us to see our son!*" the dad added, reaching into his other pocket and pulling out a...

"*Gun!*" Grunbeck shouted.

"Stuart...*no!*" the woman yelled. "*Don't...!*"

Too late. Stuart pointed the barrel of the .38 straight at Zig's face. "You take me to see my son! *Now!*"

Zig didn't move, didn't even raise his hands. Instead, he stayed locked on Stuart's eyes, which were different than his wife's. Not just lost. Desperate.

"Sir, I promise you one thing. That won't get you what you want. This is a military installation. People who pull guns here get shot. Now if you could please put the gun down—"

"*DON'T TELL ME WHAT TO DO!*"

Behind the welcome desk, the panicked young private started to run. Stuart followed him with his gun, tracking Grunbeck across the lobby.

Grunbeck froze mid-step, hands in the air.

The man kept his gun on Grunbeck, his finger now gripping the trigger.

"Listen to me," Zig said. "That boy you're aiming at...he's twenty-five years old. That's the same age as your son, isn't it? Twenty-five?" The man didn't reply. "Sir, I know you're in pain—"

"You know nothing about my pain!"

"You're wrong. I know all too well how—" Zig heard his own words, wondering where they were coming from. He had a rule: He didn't talk about her at work. But here he was... "I lost my daughter too."

"You're lying."

"Fourteen years ago. Five thousand two hundred twenty-seven days."

For a moment, the drunk man stood there. His body, his arm, the gun in his hand all started to shake. Zig knew that look too. No one loved God and hated God as much as a mourner.

"Sir, just please put the gun down," Zig said.

The man shook his head over and over, snot running from his nose. "Please, Lord, forgive me for doing this..." He raised the gun—and pointed it at his own head. "Don't tell my father what happened."

He pulled the trigger.

Zig barreled forward, straight into the man, as the gun exploded. Stuart's arm jerked. His gun was now pointing straight ahead. A shot was fired.

"*STUART!*" his wife yelled, running toward them as the bullet zipped across the room.

Zig's momentum knocked the man backward and both of them tumbled to the floor. They hit the ground together, Zig facedown on top of the man. Stuart's head banged backward and the gun went flying, falling, skipping across the carpet.

Flat on his back, the man sobbed, snot and tears pouring toward his ears. He wouldn't open his eyes, wouldn't look at Zig, who was still on top of him.

"You're okay...we'll get through this...we'll be okay," his wife insisted, though Zig knew that was the biggest lie of all.

Climbing to his feet, Zig grabbed the gun, still looking where the bullet—

There. On his left. Across the lobby. There was a smoking round hole in the front desk.

Oh, God. Grunbeck.

"Kid! You okay!? You hit!?" Zig yelled, darting across the lobby.

As Zig reached the other side of the desk, he found Grunbeck down on the ground. There wasn't a mark on him.

"Y-Y'know I'm not twenty-five years old," Grunbeck said, his eyes wide, clearly in shock.

Zig nodded.

"You saved my life."

Zig was already dialing base security, letting them know all was okay. "Yeah, well, how 'bout you give me Nola's PADD and we call it even?" Zig asked with a grin.

Grunbeck stumbled to his feet, pulled his chair up to the desk. Took a breath. Took another breath.

"Do it again. Deep breath. Through your nose. You'll be okay," Zig said, a strong arm on Grunbeck's shoulder.

Ten minutes and a few keystrokes later, Nola's forms were on-screen. Grunbeck skimmed through them first, looking confused.

"What's wrong? She filled it out, didn't she?" Zig asked.

"You have to fill it out. As you know, they won't give you your dog tags until you pick your next of kin and who gets say over your burial."

"So who'd Nola pick?"

"That's the thing. According to this, Sergeant Brown signed into her account and changed her designee last night."

"*Last night?*"

"That's what I'm telling you. Nola...Sergeant Brown...she changed it *after* she died."

13

"Okay, Ziggy, on a scale of one to ten—one being a normal day, and ten being the final season of *Lost*—you're officially a nineteen."

"Dino, this isn't a joke," Zig said.

"You think I'm joking? This is that moment where they tell the babysitter the call's coming from inside the house—and you're the babysitter," Dino said, keeping his voice down as he rolled a hand truck filled with boxes across the carpet of Eagle Lanes, the bowling alley located directly on base.

His real name was Andy Kanalz, though Zig had been calling him "Dino" since they were in third grade. Big kid, little arms, like a T. rex. Today, Dino's arms had caught up with the rest of him, and now his round face and middle-aged gut made him bigger in every way.

"Can we just cut to the gruesome third act?" Dino added, pointing to the paperwork Zig was holding. "If that's Nola's file...where's her body going next?"

Zig looked around the empty bowling lanes, then checked the small grill known as the Kingpin Café in the corner. Lunch rush was over. The place was empty. As for Dino... *Heart or no heart?* It wasn't even a question.

"Up until yesterday, Nola's body was supposed to go to Arlington," Zig explained, referring to the national cemetery where so many in the military asked to be buried. "Then last night, she picked—"

"*Last night?*"

"I know. Stay with me. Then last night, she picked a brand-new designee. Someone named Archie Crowe. Name sound familiar?"

"Never heard of him. Though I pity any man named Archie," Dino said, hitting the brakes on the hand truck as he reached the vending machine in back. From his pocket, he pulled out a key ring, flipped to a tubular key, and slipped it into the vending machine's lock.

Back in ninth grade, when Zig bagged groceries at Brian Quinn's supermarket and there was an opening for a new bag boy, Zig got Dino the job. During community college, when Zig worked as a valet, he did the same, and the two of them raced Porsches in the parking lot of the best hotel in town. So back when Zig had just started at Dover, and Dino was failing in his latest career as manager of a health club, Zig got him hired to stock all the vending machines on base. He was still doing it, along with running the bowling alley and the café.

"Can I just be honest? Until the day I die, I will never ever tire of *this*," Dino said, pulling open the glass front of the vending machine and flashing a wide smile that revealed the gap between his two front teeth. "Snickers or Twix?" he asked, though he didn't have to.

Down on one knee, he handed Zig a Twix, then pulled a plain M&M's for himself. "One day, I'm gonna free those poor breath mints from their coiled solitude in the bottom corner. Maybe the Life Savers too."

"Just don't ever eat the apple pie toaster pastry. I don't think I could respect anyone who put their teeth on that." The joke came easy for Zig. Far too easy, Dino realized.

"C'mon, Ziggy. You came here for a reason. The guy Nola picked—Archie Crowe—is he someone you recognize?"

"Never heard of him. But according to the paperwork, he works at Longwood Funeral Home."

Dino turned at the name. "Longwood? As in *Longwood* Longwood?"

"I know. Little odd, right?"

"*Little?* Ziggy, this is— Longwood's where you first trained as a mortician—and now you're telling me Nola's sending her supposed body to the exact same place? You know what they call coincidences like that? Nothing. Because things like that aren't coincidence. Especially in Ekron," Dino added, referring to their small hometown in Pennsylvania.

"I'm not disagreeing, but let's not forget, Nola grew up there too."

"For barely a year. Then she moved away."

"I know. But what Nola did for my Maggie—"

"That was a nice thing. A beautiful thing. But that doesn't mean you put your life at risk for her."

"Why not? She put her life at risk for my daughter. She did right by us! How can I not do right by her?"

Dino didn't answer.

"You know you agree. This isn't some stranger. Nola's earned this. She's tied to our town, tied to me—and then there's this: In a two-hundred-mile radius, you know how many funeral homes there are for her to choose from? Three. And one of them only serves the Amish in New Holland. That doesn't give her too many options."

"Still, why change it from Arlington at all?"

"That's the question, isn't it? Maybe it was Nola, maybe it was whoever's looking for Nola, but either way, someone changed Nola's dying wishes...hours after she was supposedly dead."

Dino thought about that and threw back a few M&M's. "Listen, I know you love playing Humpty Dumpty and putting all the pieces back together again. But have you stopped and thought about the fact that maybe you were *meant* to find this body?"

Zig shook his head. "There's no way anyone could've known I'd personally step in to work on Nola's case."

"Agreed. I'm just saying, well, maybe this is exactly what Maureen Zigarowski's favorite son really needs."

"So what...now this is all fate? The universe is sending me a message?"

"You tell me. How many days until the anniversary?"

Zig didn't answer. He stared down at the still-unopened Twix he was gripping, which he could feel softening in its wrapper.

"I can look it up," Dino added, pulling out his phone. "I know it's always close for you. How many days?"

"Two hundred forty-six."

"There you go. Two hundred and forty-six days from now. And do you remember what you did this past year on the anniversary? Lemme remind you. You asked your ex-wife, Charmaine, who you still pine for—"

"I don't pine for her."

"Ziggy, to mark the day that your beautiful daughter, Maggie, left this planet, you invited Charmaine to Nellie Bly, the crappiest old amusement park in all of western Pennsylvania. Then you both spent the day walking around eating cotton candy and telling old stories about Maggie."

"There's nothing wrong with remembering her."

"You're right. But what happened when the day was done? Charmaine went back to her new fiancé and future stepson, while you came back to Dover and the dead."

"Her Facebook profile still says *Single*."

"That's because she's worried you'll slit your wrists if you see the word *Engaged*."

Zig didn't say anything, his eyes back on the faded roll of breath mints in the bottom corner of the vending machine.

"Holy Prozac, Batman—you look even sadder than when Charmaine had you go as California Raisins for Halloween."

Zig gave a faint nod. "I'll never forgive her for that costume."

"I forgive the costume. What I couldn't forgive was the gold chain and Rerun from *What's Happening!!* hat that she made you wear with it. Like a pimped Hefty bag."

Zig fought back a smile. He knew Dino's tricks. After a child dies, life is loud at first—everyone calls; everyone packs into the crowded funeral. But in time, most friends fade away, even your best friends. It's too sad for them. Luckily, there's usually one good soul who stays in your life no matter how bad it gets. Back then, it was Dino. And for so many of the hardest days since.

"Ziggy, most of your coworkers would've already finished this case and moved on to the next. Shadowy classified missions come through here all the time—your job isn't to dig around in them. But the fact this girl knew your daughter...that she saved her...that's what's got your blood pumping, isn't it? I saw it the moment you walked in here, even the way you first talked about her. Nola's not the only one alive again."

"I'm just trying to pay back a debt—and help someone in trouble."

"Or maybe she's the *cause* of the trouble. You have no idea, do you? But it's not slowing you down. All I'm saying is, even if nothing fishy's going on, maybe this case is something you *need*."

Zig's phone started vibrating and he pulled it out. He knew that number.

"Please tell me you found something?" he asked, picking up.

"That's your greeting? What're you, a millennial? Learn how to say hello," FBI fingerprint expert Amy Waggs scolded.

Zig took a breath, sliding into a seat at one of the bowling-alley scorer's tables. "Nice to hear your voice, Waggs. How are you?"

"That's better," she said. "Did that kill you?"

"Wait, that's Waggs?" Dino asked, still down on one knee at the vending machine. "Say hi for me!"

Zig waved him off. Two years ago, he'd set up Dino and Waggs on a disastrous blind date. They hadn't let him live it down since. "Waggs, I'm sorry—it's just— It's been a bit of a morning here."

"I saw," she said. "We have Fox News here too, y'know. So imagine my surprise when on my TV, the President of the United States is standing there at Dover, carrying a casket for what appears to be the very same case my pal Zig has asked me to look into. Makes me start thinking, *Hey, maybe there's more going on there than good ole Ziggy was saying.*"

"I swear, I didn't know Wallace was coming until late last night."

"I don't care when it was. If you want my help, I need to know this stuff. So the fact you didn't mention it means you're being careless or reckless, both of which you never are."

Zig grabbed one of the half pencils from the top of the scorer's table, tapping the point of it against his now-mushy Twix. "I was just trying to be careful."

"You sure about that? Because when this plane crashed in Alaska, whatever the hell this girl Nola was up to there, well...y'know that part where Goldilocks is eating the porridge and you quickly realize it's all a bear trap? Based on what I'm finding, Ziggy, you're poking at something far bigger than a bear."

"What're you talking about?"

"That body that's sitting in your morgue right now—the one who everyone insists is Nola—guess what I found when I put her fingerprints in the system?"

"Clearance issues."

"Of course clearance issues," Waggs replied.

Zig expected as much. When you enlist in the military, your fingerprints go straight into the government's database. But as Zig had learned when he started working on the bodies of agents from the CIA, NSA, and every other acronym, when it came to spies, high-level informants, or anyone else whose identity the government wanted to keep secret, their fingerprints got "X-ed out," meaning that only someone with the appropriate clearance could see who they actually were.

"This is where you tell me you've got clearance," Zig said.

"I'm working on it. It'll take a few days. Fortunately for you, I'm an impatient person. And a nosy one."

Zig knew that tone. He stopped tapping his pencil. "Waggs, what'd you find?"

"Just listen. Remember all those years ago—back when Bill Clinton was President, and his secretary of commerce went down in a plane crash?"

"Ron Brown."

"There you go," Waggs said. "Thirty-five people died that night, but all the newspapers cared about was one person: VIP and presidential best friend Ron Brown. So. Go back to today's bodies and the Alaska crash that took them down. Who's everyone currently focused on?"

"The VIP and presidential best friend."

"Bingo. Librarian of Congress Nelson Rookstool. But..."

"There were half a dozen other people on that flight," Zig said.

"Correct again. Including your friend Nola, who, well... Did you happen to see where she was stationed?"

"Sergeant First Class at Fort Belvoir. In Virginia."

"Okay, but what'd she *do* at Belvoir? What was her title there?"

"Nola was the Artist-in-Residence," Zig said.

Waggs paused. She shouldn't have been surprised. Based on what Zig said last night, he knew the girl. "You looked her up," Waggs said.

"I'd never heard of it before. Apparently, since World War I, the Army has assigned one person—an actual artist—who they send out in the field to, well...paint what couldn't otherwise be seen."

"So instead of guns, they get brushes," Waggs agreed, making Zig again think of the canvas, the portrait that was taken from Nola's belongings. "What else you find?"

"It's apparently one of the greatest traditions in our military— they call them *war artists*," Zig said. "They go, they see, they paint, cataloguing every victory and mistake, from the dead on D-day, to the injured at Mogadishu, to the sandbag pilers who were at Hurricane Katrina. In fact, when 9/11 hit, Nola's predecessor was the only artist let inside the security perimeter. And y'know why that matters?" Zig asked. "It means Nola is someone with access."

"She's not the only one. You take a peek at the names of the other victims who were on her flight?"

"There was a young soldier. Anthony Trudeau," Zig said, still seeing Anthony's mom with the dead look in her eyes, his dad lying on the Fisher House carpet. "There were others too—at least one Air Force. I'm guessing that was the pilot."

"Pilot for sure. That's three soldiers total when you include Nola. And who else?"

Zig didn't even hear the question. He was still thinking of Anthony's parents. He needed to go by later, make sure they were okay.

"C'mon, Zig," Waggs added. "There were three other people on that plane—the last three bodies carried off this morning."

"The civilians," Dino whispered, still kneeling at the vending machine.

Zig turned to his friend. He didn't realize Dino had been listening, and could hear everything, the entire time.

"Civilians," Zig repeated, focusing back on the phone. "There were three other civilians on board."

"Exactly," Waggs said. "Rookstool was the head of the Library of Congress. Of course he had staff with him. Three aides. You catch their names?"

That smelled to Zig too. Their names still hadn't been released. "They said they hadn't been able to reach the families yet, if you believe it."

"Now you're seeing how the magic trick works. Everyone's so busy mourning presidential pal Rookstool, no one bothers to see who was sitting in the two rows behind him. Lucky for me, I work for the FBI, which gave me access to the plane's full manifest."

"Waggs, this is my solemn vow to you. Next time I see you, I have a hug with your name on it."

"Save your hugs. You're assuming this is good news," she said.

"According to the manifest, one of Rookstool's staffers was a woman named Rose Mackenberg. Then there were two men. Clifford Eddy Jr. and Amedeo Vacca."

"Interesting names."

"I thought the same."

"And when you looked them up?" Zig asked.

"Amedeo Vacca, Clifford Eddy Jr., and Rose Mackenberg were all born in the late 1800s. From what I can tell, they've been dead for nearly half a century."

Zig went silent. Dino glanced over his shoulder. Behind them, the door to the bowling alley opened, and two men walked in. Both in uniform. Young Army cadets.

"Weird, right?" Waggs asked through the phone. "But not as weird as this. Back when Mackenberg, Eddy, and Vacca were alive, they all worked in the same field of study. You'd almost call them...experts."

"Experts in what?"

"The ancient art of coming back from the dead."

Zig was still staring at the cadets, who were just standing there, like they were waiting for someone.

"I didn't realize that was an actual field of study," Zig said.

"It was a passion of their boss," Waggs explained. "An obsession, really."

"Who was their employer? Dr. Frankenstein?"

"Close," Waggs said, her voice slowing down. "Nearly one hundred years ago, Rose Mackenberg, Clifford Eddy Jr., and Amedeo Vacca all worked for a man named Harry Houdini."

14

Y ou know I hate magic."

"This isn't magic, Ziggy. It's about understanding who these people were," Waggs said through the phone. "Rose Mackenberg. Clifford Eddy Jr. Amedeo Vac—"

"I heard you," Zig said, eyes still on the two soldiers at the entrance to the bowling alley. "They died fifty years ago and worked for Houdini, which means someone's pulling a fast one here."

"More than you even realize. I put their names in the system. At 0800 this morning, the bodies of Mackenberg, Eddy, and Vacca were delivered to Dover. But guess what else I found? They died five years ago in a helicopter crash. And four years before that not far from Stanford University, in an accident with an Army Humvee."

"Fellas," Dino called out to the two soldiers, who were still just standing there, "we're on break for an hour. Come back later?"

One soldier looked at the other and they nodded their goodbyes, leaving the bowling alley.

"Wait, it gets better," Waggs added. "All three of them also died right after 9/11, when we invaded Iraq. And then again in the early nineties, when we first went after Saddam. Every decade: seventies, eighties, nineties—they're like one of those contemporary easy-listening stations, but with dead bodies instead of James Taylor songs. I found records of them dying in Cambodia, Lebanon, even the Falkland Islands."

"Waggs, I've worked on 2,356 bodies here—and not one of them has come back to life. So if you're trying to sound all spooky, you need to do it with something less trendy than zombies."

"I'm not talking zombies. You know what this is, Ziggy. Mackenberg, Eddy, and Vacca—"

"I get it. They're cover names," Zig said, referring to the fake IDs that are used to hide the real identities of national security operatives. Zig saw them all the time. "Usually, though, they go with something more low-key, like Andrew Smith."

"Exactly. But now you're seeing the problem. If they're purposefully using specific names like these, either they've got a good reason to use those names—or maybe the names are somehow associated with a particular undercover unit. Those happen more than you think."

"But to use the *same* names over and over? Doesn't that just call attention to yourself?"

"Not over and over. They did it every half decade or so. Plus, people are committed to their code names. A few years back, I had a supervisor who named all his confidential informants after characters in Stephen King books."

"So then, *what*? If Mackenberg, Eddy, and Vacca all worked for Harry Houdini, we're looking for someone out there who's a magic fan?"

"Again, this is more than *magic*. Everyone knows Houdini was the world's greatest escape artist, but as I was Googling him just now, y'know what the number one thing was that he wanted to escape? Death. It was his obsession. On nearly every website I found, it said that when Houdini died, he was so determined to come back to life, he gave out secret code words to those closest to him. That way, if they tried to contact him during a séance, they'd know it was really him. Houdini's wife got a code, his brother too. And from what I can tell, so did Mackenberg, Eddy, and Vacca. They were the ones who were supposed to help him communicate from the great beyond."

"Sounds like a hell of a trick."

"Of course it's a trick. Everything with Houdini was for show. But his obsession with death? That was *real*. It started when his mother passed away. It wrecked him to his core. From that day forward, he became a walking corpse, putting on the biggest and best shows for the world, but deep down, he was so wounded by the loss, he pulled away from everyone around him. It was the one thing that the man with no fear was afraid of: opening himself up and risking pain like that again. Until the day he died, he would've given anything—truly anything—for one more chance to tell her that he loved her. Sound like anyone else you know?"

For a moment, Zig sat there motionless in the plastic bowling-alley seat, staring at the polished pins at the end of the lane.

"She's not very subtle, is she?" Dino asked from the vending machine, pretending to straighten a row of cookies but still clearly eavesdropping.

"Tell Dino I'm being *honest*," Waggs shot back. "Pay attention, Zig. Whatever's going on here, those other bodies—Mackenberg, Eddy, and Vacca...they weren't sightseeing on a teen tour. This was a plane full of secrets."

"I don't care about secrets. What I care about is Nola, which is why top priority right now is seeing who comes to claim her body."

"You mean *came*."

"Excuse me?"

"I'm looking at the big board right now. According to this, they just moved Nola's body—or whoever's body it is. She got picked up three minutes ago."

15

They called this area *Departures*. Like it was an airport lounge and everyone was sitting around, scrolling through their cell phones, waiting to take off to some exotic locale. Really, though, it was a warehouse, clean as a hospital, and long and wide enough to hold an eighteen-wheeler. On good days, it was mostly empty, except for a few caskets on display—metal or wood, the government made you choose—and a large yellow sign with red letters:

CASKETED REMAINS MUST BE
FLAG DRAPED BEYOND THIS POINT

Sure enough, as Zig burst into the room, there was a lone coffin wrapped in a freshly pressed American flag. From the lower handle, a newly minted dog tag read:

BROWN
NOLA

"Don't you muss my flag," a woman in her mid-fifties warned in a flat Indiana accent.

"Who dressed her?" Zig challenged.

"Zig, I'm serious—don't muss it!" said Louisa "Lou" Falwell—thinning brown hair, stocky round build, mesmerizing sky-blue eyes—from her desk in the corner.

Too late. With a yank, Zig tugged the flag from the shiny and freshly-rubbed-with-Pledge wooden coffin. The flag whipped into the air. Zig made sure it didn't touch the floor. Normal flags were eight by five. Coffin flags were bigger, more unwieldy, which made it drape like a cape over Zig's shoulder. Around the base of the coffin, the polyester elastic braid that held the flag in place still hugged tight.

"Master Guns warned me you were getting emotional, but has your brain officially disappeared?" Louisa asked, pointing a stubby finger at Zig but still not moving from her desk. As the head of Departures—the final stop before each body got shipped back to its family—Louisa was well accustomed to dealing with people at their worst. As Dover's only female mortician—the one who played Funeral with her Barbies—she also had a PhD in stubborn men.

"I want to know who dressed her," Zig insisted.

Before Louisa could answer, Zig flipped the latches at the head and foot of the casket. He knew which side was which—the stars of the flag always covered the soldier's heart.

Tunk. Tunk.

"Is she a relative?" Louisa asked.

"Not a relative. Family friend," Zig replied as he lifted the lid of the casket.

Inside, the woman ID'd as Nola—the woman from the painting, the woman Zig had worked on so painstakingly last night—was flat on her back, in perfect prayer pose, her face tranquil. A clear plastic sheet protected her blue Class-A dress uniform—with white gloves and dark socks—from any stray makeup that might rub off during the transfer to the funeral home.

"Robby did a good job," Louisa said, though she knew, when it came to the final dressing of the dead, nothing was good enough for Zig.

Reaching into the casket, Zig pulled aside the plastic, scanning Nola's uniform and each of her badges and cords.

"You think we didn't do the full checklist?" Louisa asked.

At Dover, there was a twenty-six-item inspection list just for each *casket*. That didn't include the body, or the checklist Zig himself had written. He focused on Nola's face, knowing how vital it was to get it right. Every parent, including Zig, needs to see the face to believe it's real. Now, her makeup was holding up nice. Her hair too. Last night, Zig had washed it himself, then washed it again. As one of his predecessors put it: The mother of the deceased is the first to wash a soldier's hair; you get to be the last one to wash it.

From his pocket, Zig pulled out the small six-inch ruler he carried with him every day on the job. He measured from the seam of her shoulder down to the tip of the chevron stripes that marked her years of service. Five inches. Perfect. Then the ribbon rack on her chest. No more than an eighth of an inch between each ribbon. Perfect. He even lifted her jacket, making sure the side of her belt buckle lined up with the zipper of her pants and the flap of her shirt. A perfect gig line.

"How do you really know her, Ziggy?"

"I told you, family friend. Like that Marine a few years back who went to your church in your hometown. You wouldn't let anyone work on that body. Cleaning, embalming, dressing...you did it all," Zig said, pulling a stray thread from the shoulder of the uniform, then another a few inches down. Then another, and another. Fourteen loose threads in total. Would anyone have noticed? That wasn't the point. Even when someone requested cremation, Zig made sure every detail was perfect.

"This was *my* job, Lou. Not Robby's. Not yours," Zig said. "Besides, we've barely had her twenty-four hours. Since when do we rush people out so fast?"

"Hsu said she wanted to make room for the six new fallen who came in today."

It made sense. Yet as Zig turned back to Louisa, he noticed she was still at her desk, like she was glued there. "You okay?" he asked.

"Of course. Why?"

Zig headed toward her, scanning her desk. "Who gave you the bag?"

"The what?"

"The bag," Zig said, pointing to the plastic baggie on her desk, tucked under her arm. "Those dog tags?"

"These? Yeah, they just came in," Louisa said, holding them up like she'd forgotten they were there. Sure enough, in the baggie were two beat-up dog tags, both labeled:

BROWN

NOLA

Just like the ones missing from the Personal Effects room—including the one that was cut from "Nola's" bootlaces.

"Where'd you get those?" Zig asked.

"Colonel Hsu brought them in a little bit ago. Said they arrived on this morning's flight with the six other fallen. Apparently, someone found them at the crash scene. She wanted me to make sure the family got them."

Zig stared at Louisa, who'd still barely moved in her seat. He'd worked with her for over a decade. He knew she was tough—from that case where a young female soldier was murdered by an officer in Iraq, and it was Louisa, as she put the woman's organs back into her body and sewed her up, who figured out the woman was pregnant. Even the male morticians couldn't handle that one.

Zig also knew how twisted and funny she was, remembering the story Louisa always told about how she got into this line of work: Her friend was dating a mortician who insisted that being an undertaker was a man's field, which made Louisa think that's where the money was. It certainly *was*—and still *is*—a man's field. But it wasn't until Louisa enrolled in mortuary school in Oklahoma that she realized how crap the pay was.

Heart or no heart? Louisa had heart. Always. *Didn't she?*

"Don't look at me like that," Louisa said, finally getting up from her seat. She was still holding the baggie with the dog tags. "You think I don't know why Hsu is suddenly showing interest? All she wants is another excuse to brief the White House and maybe get a thank-you from the President. I wanted to barf on her when I saw her out on the flight line this morning."

At a nearby table, Louisa slid the dog tags into a larger plastic pouch that held other personal effects, including the burned boots with the sliced laces.

"Can you help me get her ready? We need to close her up," Louisa said, motioning to the casket.

Before Zig could answer, there was a loud buzz, the doorbell from the outdoor loading dock. Louisa pushed a button on the wall, and the roll-top door at the far end of the room began to rise, revealing a shiny black hearse—Cadillac, brand-new—that was here for the casket. Zig knew where it was headed: Longwood Funeral Home. The only question was, who'd be waiting at Longwood for it?

"*All available personnel, report to the front for a send-off,*" a voice announced through the PA system.

Peering into the casket, Zig took one last look at this dead woman's face, at the thick makeup that made her so bronzed and beautiful. Still, as he did with every send-off, he couldn't help but imagine the pale gray skin that was lying just underneath. And now, for the first time in years, he was thinking of his last moments with—

"Zig, little help here?" Louisa said, fighting to spread the protective plastic sheet back over the body.

As Zig grabbed a corner of the sheet and tucked it over the dead woman's uniform, he noticed the brand-new name tag on her chest, black with white letters. *Brown.*

Like so much in this case, it was, of course, a lie.

Somewhere right now, Nola was out there. And somewhere right now, there's a family who has no idea their daughter is never coming home again.

"Wanna talk about it?" Louisa asked.

Zig stayed silent.

"I heard she's from your hometown. That she knew your daughter," Louisa added. "That must be—"

"I appreciate it, Lou. I really do," Zig said, taking one last scan of the casket and noticing... *There.*

With his pointer finger and thumb, he tweezed a single stray hair from the white satin coffin liner.

"I think there's actually a molecule out of place if you look close enough," Louisa teased.

"Shh, I'm checking the protons and neutrons first," Zig teased back, though he was still studying the stray hair. Short and frizzy. An Afro. The mortuary wasn't a big place. Only one man around here had hair like that. Master Guns.

It made no sense. Master Guns did investigations; he didn't get involved with prepping and shipping bodies.

"If it helps, Sergeant Brown's lucky she had you working on her," Louisa said, shutting the casket. It took a few more minutes to re-drape the flag. In most cases, when a casket went out of state, it was put in an "air tray"—a massive container that would keep it protected on a plane. But Nola's—and Zig's—Pennsylvania hometown was only a short drive away.

Unlocking the wheels of the metal casket cart, they pushed the flag-covered coffin toward the waiting hearse.

"Here for a pickup. Sergeant Nola Brown," the driver called out. He was a kid. Late twenties, military buzz cut and build, same as half the people here. "I'll take good care of her," he promised, helping them navigate the coffin into the back, where it slid easily across the car's rolling rack.

Buzz Cut slammed the back door shut.

"Meet you around front?" Louisa said to the driver, who nodded as the hearse took off.

"Zig, you coming?" Louisa added, heading back inside. Right now, on the front side of the building, a young cadet assigned to serve as a military escort was waiting to join the hearse. Fellow Dover employees were also lining up along the circular driveway for a final goodbye—and the final salute—that they gave every departing body. No one left the mortuary without a proper show of respect.

"Be right there," Zig said, still standing in the threshold of the open warehouse.

He waited for the hearse to disappear—and for Louisa to leave—then he pulled out his phone and started to—

"*Here for a pickup!*" a voice called out.

On Zig's right, a new hearse pulled up—a silver Buick with a black top—driven by a man with a bumpy nose and a mustache to offset it. The words *Longwood Funeral Home* were written in script on the driver's door.

Zig felt a pressure on his chest; his arms went numb. "Don't tell me you're here for—"

"Sergeant Nola Brown," Mustache said. He looked over Zig's shoulder, at the now-empty warehouse. "Everything okay, sir? I don't see Sergeant Brown's coffin."

16

W e're gonna go to hell for this, aren't we?" Dino whispered.

"You're already in hell. You work in a bowling alley," Zig whispered as they approached the back of the hearse.

"Yeah, says the guy who works in the morgue. By choice. Also, do I even want to know whose coffin this is?"

Zig shot him a look, gripping the corner of the shiny wooden casket, which smelled like lemon-fresh Pledge. Someone already came and took Nola's casket; Dover had plenty of extras. No one would miss this one. Or realize what Zig was up to.

"Okay, on three," the driver with the mustache called out. He was crouched down on his knees inside the back of the hearse. "One...two..."

With a single heave, Zig and Dino shoved the flag-covered casket into the car. The driver tugged from inside, then used the nearby straps to lock it in place.

"That was lighter than I thought it'd be," Dino whispered.

Zig shot him another look. Wooden caskets weighed more than metal ones. But not when they're empty.

It wasn't hard to pull off. With a phone call, Dino came running. He was the perfect distraction for the driver. From there, Zig reprinted Nola's paperwork, grabbed a new casket, and carefully affixed a freshly pressed American flag. He even added metal ID tags to the handles at the head and foot of the casket. Each one read:

BROWN

NOLA

"And here are her personal effects," Dino said, handing the driver a pouch filled with a set of keys, a cigarette lighter, and an old BlackBerry from the bowling alley's lost and found.

"Got it. Great," the driver said, marking it off on his own check-list and sliding into the front seat. "So I pick up the military escort around front?" he added.

"Actually, I'll be escorting today," Zig said, tightening his tie and pulling his blue blazer from a nearby chair.

"I thought the escorts had to be soldiers," the driver said.

"Or someone from Dover," Zig shot back. "In this case, I knew the deceased. She's a friend of the family."

There was a loud *thunk* as Zig slammed the trunk shut. Before he could reach the passenger seat, Dino grabbed him by the arm. "You know we can just follow the hearse in your car," Dino whispered.

"And tip off the people we're actually looking for? In case you didn't notice, they stole Nola's body."

"Then you should report that!" Dino hissed.

"To whom? Colonel Hsu? Master Guns? No offense, but for Nola to be rushed out of Dover that quickly, both of them had to've okayed it—or at least known about it. Just like they did on the night she came in."

"Then track that other hearse—the one that took the body. When they drove off base, Dover cameras should've gotten a shot of their license plate."

"Do you really think anyone will give me access to that footage? Pay attention, Dino. Whoever pulled this off, they're the same peo-ple who faked the fingerprints and rushed Nola's supposed corpse so quickly through the system. And they're the same ones who made sure her body was dressed early this morning and whisked it off an hour ago. And you know the only people who can pull that off?"

"The people who run this place," Dino whispered, staring through the hearse's back window, at the empty casket marked *Brown, Nola.*

"Believe me, we may not know the *why* yet, but someone wants this body."

"We don't have a body!"

"They don't know that! Whoever was in that other hearse, they're driving around with a casket. So when the Dover big board lights up and says that we just left the base with another casket that has another Nola body, trust me, they'll start wondering if they're the ones who got the fake. Someone's gonna come running. At the very least, by the time we get to Longwood, we'll see who's waiting for us at the funeral home."

"*If…*" Dino said.

Zig knew what he meant. *If* Zig made it to the funeral home.

For the better part of his professional life, Zig spent his days with the dead. He cleaned them, scrubbed them, cut their nails, and lovingly rebuilt them. But here, with Nola, a woman who was very much alive, it was Zig's first chance to actually save someone. Someone who once saved and helped him—and who he'd tried to help too. Back then, he'd failed. Right now, she was definitely in trouble. He wouldn't fail her again.

"You sure this girl's worth it?" Dino finally asked.

Zig locked eyes with his old friend. He didn't have to say it.

"All set?" Zig finally called out to the driver, sliding into the passenger seat and checking the side mirror to see if anyone was watching.

All clear. For now.

"Next stop, Longwood Funeral Home," the driver from Longwood said, turning the ignition.

Zig took another look at the side-view mirror. Still clear.

From this angle, he had no idea what was coming.

17

Zig thought he was prepared. For nearly two hours now, as they headed up DE-1, he'd been sitting there, fidgeting with his tie, counting the highway exit signs, bracing for this return to Ekron, his hometown. He knew so many memories were about to be stirred up, memories of his younger life, his married life . . . and of course, memories of his Magpie.

Ekron was where his daughter was born. Where she learned to ride a bike. Where she crashed. Broke her arm. Broke her other arm in dance class. Where she hid in a tree for four hours during hide-and-seek—Zig actually called the sheriff—until Magpie revealed herself as the best of hiders. Where she threw up in The Luncheonette—that was its name, *The Luncheonette*—the first time she ever tried eggs.

During the first few years after the funeral, Zig saw his daughter everywhere, whether he wanted to or not. These days, the opposite was true. Magpie was still there, he could always feel her there, but she was elsewhere too, off in the ether, until a conscious thought, a memory, a song, brought her instantly back.

He could feel it right now . . . her coming back, slowly, as they left the highway, as four lanes became two, as rural Delaware gave way to rural Pennsylvania—separated by a rusty mobile home on the Delaware side—and the scenery turned familiar.

"Maybe we should take Third Street," Zig offered. But it was too late, and there they were, rolling toward the one place he was hoping to avoid: the white headstones of Octavius Cemetery, where all those years ago, Zig buried his daughter.

"How old was she?" the driver with the mustache—his name was Stevie—asked.

"Excuse me?"

"*Her*," Stevie said, pointing a thumb over his own shoulder, toward the casket in back. "Sergeant Brown. What was she, twenty-six?" Stevie was in his thirties, thick fingers, crow's-feet around the eyes. Even in a small-town funeral home, there were plenty of things to squint away from. "I don't know how you do it."

"What're you talking about? You drive a hearse," Zig said. "Don't you see the same every day?"

"No, here at Longwood, we get people in their eighties, their nineties. People who know it's coming. Sometimes we get a few like Walter Harris, who was fifty-one when he had his heart attack—and a few years back, we had this young boy who went swimming and..." Stevie stopped himself. "What a horror."

It was no different when Maggie was mentioned. People felt the need to editorialize with the same useless words. *A horror. A tragedy. Can't imagine.*

"Regardless, cases like that are one in a million," Stevie added. "But to do what you do at Dover—twenty-year-old soldiers...just kids...every day..." He tried to finish the sentence, but again never got there.

Zig nodded, now eyeing the passing headstones of the cemetery, all of them blurring together in a jagged line. He wondered if the groundskeepers put out the fresh flowers he paid for each month. He should check. He wanted to check. Wanted to see her. Usually, he dreaded coming here. But that was the real secret about loss in the long term.

After Maggie's death, it tore Zig apart to visit places like the Jersey Shore, where they used to take their daughter on vacation.

Years later, though, a new trip to the Shore brought back the best of memories—flying a giant butterfly kite, finding her stealthily tucked away under a lounge chair during yet another game of hide-and-seek, and eating bad pizza and fantastic soft ice cream, a rainbow-sprinkles mustache on her face—returning small pieces of her, like a reward. It was the same here today, Zig now flush with thoughts of the fall trees, all orange and yellow, when Maggie was born. Indeed, memories that once ripped his heart open in the early days of loss were, years later, what eventually came back and comforted him. Zig was, for this moment, happy.

It wouldn't last.

"Final stop," the driver announced as they turned down Legion Drive and headed for the wide one-story gray building directly next to the firehouse. The sign was new, but the green-and-white script was exactly the same: *Longwood Funeral Home.* "Welcome back," Stevie said.

Zig turned. "How'd you know that?"

"Know what?"

"That I'm from here. You said, *welcome back.* But I never told you that I lived here...that I worked here."

"I looked you up."

"Why?"

Stevie pushed a button on the overhead console. The garage door of the funeral home slowly rose as the hearse rolled inside.

"I asked you a question," Zig insisted, reaching for his knife.

Inside, an automatic light popped on. There were stacks of orange traffic cones, a neatly wrapped rubber hose, and gallons of detergent for washing the hearse, which always needed to be spotless. On Zig's right were two metal coffins, both of them on steel casket carts.

Stevie cut the engine, finally turning toward Zig. His eyes were two bricks of coal. "You should go inside."

"What're you talking about?" Zig asked.

"Someone's waiting for you."

18

Zig knew that smell. Stale potpourri and Carpet Fresh. It was a trick of his old boss, a way to convince people they were coming to a real house as opposed to a house of death. As with nearly everything in a funeral home, it was another lie.

"Anybody here...?" Zig called out, heading slowly down the wide hallway that connected the garage with the rest of the house. His hand was in his pocket, on his knife. "Hello?"

No one answered.

Zig kicked himself for not seeing this coming. When the bodies of fallen soldiers were returned to their hometowns, the local funeral home was usually covered in flowers and American flags. People came out. Police cars and fire trucks greeted the hearse like it was a parade. Here at Longwood, though, everything was silent. When they first drove up, Zig assumed it was because Nola hadn't lived here in years, or that she'd changed her arrangements so recently. But now, it finally made sense. Someone here kept it quiet on purpose.

"I'm here. You got what you want," Zig said, passing the stairs to the basement, where the embalming room was.

He felt the old lump in his throat at the sight of the basement. He'd seen his first dead body down in that room. Actually, that wasn't true. At eleven years old, he'd found his grandmother dead in the big yellow easy chair in their living room, her skin porcelain white, her eye shadow bright blue, her perfume as potent as ever.

Years later, Zig learned his trade in this basement. He worked on bodies in this basement, learned where to inject the embalming fluid in someone's cheeks so their smile was just right—never too big of a smile, no one wanted a clown—just enough for the "pleasant look," his boss, Raymond, used to call it. And one day, in this same basement, Zig stood there, staring down at a zipped vinyl body bag, the corpse inside so small, it nearly looked empty.

He'd told everyone he wanted to work on Maggie himself. The damage was so bad. His wife fought him on it, begged him, but he told her this was his privilege, that there was no greater honor than putting to rest those you love.

It was, simply put, a disaster.

As Zig unzipped the bag, just the sight of his daughter's light brown curls... That was it. When you lose someone close—someone who was bound to your soul—there's a moment when the tears come. Not the standard tears, where you cry and hug, and then the funeral's over and you go back to work thinking, *I really need to make some changes and appreciate life more.*

No, these are the tears that sneak up on you, that catch you off guard and quickly swirl into a vortex in your throat and chest, robbing your breath and bringing on a cry like you've never cried before, a gasping, wrenching sob that rips at your belly, your core, at every belief you've ever held about the universe. Forget sadness. This was despair.

Zig, on that August night, had that cry right here, down those stairs in that basement, standing over his daughter's body. It was a moment he was reliving now as he pushed through a closed door and found himself in the back of the reception room.

There was a quiet *click* behind him. Someone holding a gun.

Zig turned.

She was tall and had pointy features. Beautiful and sharp. Her hair was straight, white with a dyed single black streak. On closer glance, her white hair wasn't the color of things old; it was more silver, the color of the moon. She looked nothing like her old self. But there was no mistaking those black eyes with flecks of gold, no mistaking that scar on her ear.

"Hands. *Now*," Nola Brown said, aiming her gun at Zig's face.

19

This was Nola when she was twenty-six.

"Empty your pockets," she insisted.

"You think I'm armed?" he asked, flashing a grin.

"Stop talking." Nola didn't know this man. Had no idea his name was Zig. But she knew this: She didn't like charmers—and she didn't like him.

"Your knife," she said, pointing her gun toward his hip. "Right pocket."

Zig paused, looking confused.

Nola saw it the moment Zig entered the room. At the first sign of panic, his hands didn't go to his waist, his chest, or even his ankle—all places for a gun. He went for his pants pocket. Pepper spray? No, he was too old, probably too proud. Had to be a knife.

On a nearby podium, Zig dumped his keys and his folding knife. A SOG Trident Elite. Big blade. Typical military machoness—though the way his shoulders sagged, she wasn't convinced he was military. As for the knife, it was modified with a deep groove in the top of the blade so it could be opened as it was removed from his pocket. It also did extra damage, adding a puncture to every slice. Maybe he used it at work. Nola made a mental note.

"What about the key?" she added.

"I gave you my keys. They're right—"

"The other key. The *real* one." She raised her gun to Zig's chest, but he barely stepped back, barely even reacted. Like he hadn't even heard the words.

She took a closer look at him. Fifty years old. No wedding band, but still good-looking, a fact he was keenly aware of, based on the way he jutted his chin, like he led with his face. Still, he had hair on his ears, plus a few strays in his eyebrows. Signs of a man living alone, or at least someone dating around so much, every girl was too new to pluck them for him yet.

What Nola noticed most were the dark circles under his eyes, like half-moons on his face. There was a twinkle in his gaze, but also an eerie sadness. And the way he was looking at her... *No. Not just looking. Scrutinizing. Recognizing.*

"Nola," he finally said.

She stayed silent, gun still on him, finger tightening on the trigger.

"Nola, it's me. I know you from when you're little." He stepped toward her. He had a stillness about him, even as he moved. *A leader, but also a liar.*

"I've never seen you before in my life." She pulled the slide back, cocking the gun and pointing it at his neck. "Now gimme the key."

"I don't understand. The key for what?"

"For the coffin."

"You mean the coffin you're supposed to *be in*? Wooden coffins don't have keys. There's just a latch," he explained. "Besides, the coffin's empty. The body's gone."

Nola studied him. He did this thing before he spoke, touching his tongue to his right incisor. Sign of the truth or sign of a lie. "Tell me what you want," she said.

No tongue, no incisor. "I want to know what's going on—and what happened to those people on the plane." Had to be truth. And then, tongue to incisor: "Tell me that and I'll show you where the body is."

Nola stood there a moment, motioning him toward her. As Zig got close, her hand shot out in a blur, palm up, her four long fingers straight like a spear, which she drove under his ribcage, aiming for—

There. His liver.

"What in the f—?"

The vomit came so quickly, he never got the words out.

"*Huuuuch!*"

Gasping for air, Zig collapsed on his knees as hunks of his morning toast sprayed across the carpet. Nola learned that one from her dad, who once kicked her so hard in the liver, she tasted blood.

Stuffing her gun in the back of her pants, Nola stormed out of the room, back toward the garage.

Zig yelled something behind her. She didn't care.

Reaching the hearse, she ripped open the back door, revealing the flag-covered casket. At the foot of it was a metal nameplate:

BROWN

NOLA

She stared at it, reading her own name twice, then tore the flag off the casket and yanked the casket toward her. Just from the weight, she knew. But still . . . she had to see for herself.

She gave the casket another yank, then another, which, like a see-saw tipping, sent the casket falling to the ground. There was a dull thud as the foot of it hit the concrete.

Kllk. Kllk.

The latches were easy to find. The casket lid was heavy, but as she pried it open and saw the first hints of the satin liner inside . . .

Empty.

Enraged, Nola slammed the lid shut, ramming it so hard, it let out a thunderclap that echoed off the garage door and vibrated against her chest. Still, she never said a word, never screamed, never yelled. Silent Nola learned that long ago. It never did any good. Especially when someone was watching.

Mongol...Faber...Staedtler...Ticonderoga...Swan. Nola mentally rolled through the list, using the meditation technique the psychologists gave her. For when the rage got to be too much. *Mongol... Faber...Staedtler...Ticonderoga...Swan.* It wasn't helping.

"You lied to me before," she growled. "You have no idea where her body is."

"Y'know, for someone who just made me spew all over the carpet in a funeral home, you really have an awkward way of saying 'I'm sorry,'" Zig said, standing in the threshold that led back into the house.

"That wasn't an apology."

"So I gathered. I'm not your enemy here, Nola. I actually came to help."

Nola stayed silent, staring into the back of the hearse. *Mongol...Faber...Staedtler—*

"Are you listening?" Zig asked. "You obviously paid the hearse driver to pick up the casket, which was a bust. Someone else took the body you're looking for. I'm offering assistance and you've got nothing else to say?"

Nola kept her back to him, like he wasn't there. She was still staring into the hearse, at the metal rollers, at the straps, at the nicks in the leather, at the front seats, at the two cups of coffee in the cup holders. She pulled out a small notepad and pencil from her pocket.

"What're you doing, taking notes?" Zig asked.

She was drawing. Always drawing, sketching, visually capturing the moment. Nola learned long ago, this was how her brain worked. *Mongol...Faber...Staedtler...Ticonderoga...Swan.*

"I'm guessing the woman from the plane crash...the one everyone thinks is you," Zig said, "I take it she was a friend?"

Nola didn't answer, still sketching, recreating in fuzzy pencil lines the open back door of the hearse and the coffin that was sticking out from it like a wooden tongue.

"I worked on her, y'know. In the mortuary, I took care of her," Zig added, approaching the car.

Nola whipped around, holding the pencil like a knife.

"Easy," Zig said. "I just—" He crouched, picking up the American flag that was on the ground. He started folding it carefully.

"Sorry about the flag," she offered. She meant it. Her whole life, Nola knew she wasn't like most people, didn't even *like* most people. It was no different in the military, where during her first few weeks, she was quickly singled out for stabbing a key into the hand of a fellow private who touched her ass. Still, in the Army she found a consistency, a regularity, that had been missing from her own uncertain life. Plus, they let her kill those who did harm in this world, and man, did Nola excel at that.

"Can I ask you another question?" Zig said, though he didn't wait for an answer. "How come you haven't asked how I know you?"

Again, no response. Apparently, he wasn't as stupid as she first thought.

"Nola, back in the room...when you first saw me...you recognized me, didn't you?"

Nola kept sketching, head down. *Mongol...Faber...Staedtler... Ticonderoga...Swan.* "Maggie's dad. The mortician."

Zig stood up straight.

Right there, Nola saw it. A flash of light in this desperate old man's face. He hadn't heard those words in so long, he'd forgotten how good they felt. *Maggie's dad.*

"Call me Zig," he said far too excitedly as he extended a handshake.

Nola ignored it, still focused on her sketching. She had finished drawing the hearse and the coffin. She flipped the page, sketching something new. Sketching Zig himself.

"You remember saving her, don't you? My daughter?"

Again, silence.

"Listen, I meant what I said," he added. "If you tell me what happened, I can help you."

Nola stayed quiet, her pencil a blur.

"Can you at least tell me her name? Your friend... To be here, you obviously care about her," Zig said.

More silence; more sketching. The likeness was okay, a serviceable first draft. But as usual, her art—the actual process of drawing—it always showed her something...more. She could see it in her rendering of Zig's eyes. Not just sadness. Loneliness.

"Nola, you do realize someone took this woman's body—and if they don't know you're alive already, it's not gonna take them long to figure ou—"

"Where's her body now?"

"I don't know. They took it."

"Who's *they*?"

"No idea. We were waiting for the Longwood hearse to show up, but another hearse came in first, pretended to be Longwood, and swiped it."

"So why'd you come here?"

"You switched to Longwood last night. I figured there had to be a reason why. At the very least, whoever was behind this, if they thought we had the body, maybe they would come running. I can tell you this, though—whoever's doing this, I'm assuming it's the same people who faked your friend's fingerpri—"

"I need to go," Nola interrupted, flipping her notepad shut. She hit the garage opener with her palm. The door yawned open. "My apologies again about the flag."

"Nola..."

No response.

"Nola, please wait!"

Still nothing. She was already outside.

"Nola, she left you a message. Your friend...in her stomach...I found a message for you."

Nola stopped mid-step. "What kind of message?"

20

A nd this was in her stomach?"

"Found it myself," Zig said as they stood there in the closed garage. Nola looked at him. This was truth. "She must've swallowed it when she knew that the plane was, well... y'know."

Nola nodded. She knew all too well. For three days now, she'd been replaying those final moments in Alaska, when she was leaving the small airfield and suddenly, people were yelling, crying, the wave of emotion so strong, she felt it across the parking lot before she even heard it. People were pointing. Sobbing. In the far distance, across the plain of snow, was a twirl of faint black smoke.

"And that was all the note said?" Nola asked, staring down at the picture on Zig's phone. She read the words, then read them again.

Nola, you were right.
Keep running.

"I assume that means something to you?" Zig asked.

On-screen, Nola enlarged the photo with her fingertips, studying the shaky handwriting and the bumpy stippling that comes from writing on an airplane's plastic tray table. She couldn't help but think about the moment these words were written, about the terror that propelled them.

Nola had faced death before, most recently in a helicopter that was forced to make a crash landing in a qat field in Yemen. At the time, as the pilot was screaming things no one could understand, Nola's thoughts were about how she somehow expected a . . . better death for herself, something more meaningful than an inconvenient electrical short.

Today, she wondered if her friend had a similar feeling as the plane went down in Alaska. Yet as Nola reread the note, a sadder truth emerged: In those final frantic moments, her friend wasn't worrying about her own death, or even herself. She was worrying about Nola.

"Kamille," Nola blurted.

"Excuse me?" Zig asked.

"Kamille. That's her name. The woman on the plane—the body everyone thinks is me. Kamille Williams. Staff sergeant assigned to Army Special Ops. Twenty-seven years old. From Iowa."

"She was a friend?"

Nola turned toward Zig, giving him a good long look. But she said nothing.

"Nola, when you're on a plane that's about to crash, do you know the number one factor when it comes to who survives?"

"Be near the exit door," Nola shot back.

"No. That's number two. Number one is: Be a male. Yes, proximity to the exit door will decide who survives. But when the plane is going down and everyone rushes for that door? We become animals. We're always animals. To survive the crash, be a male," he said, his voice slowing down. "Kamille somehow got out. I'm wagering she was not a pushover. Now do you want to tell me more about her?"

Nola stayed silent, again hitting the button for the garage door, which again rolled open. She was leaving.

"I know you painted her," Zig called out as Nola headed outside. "I saw the canvas in Kamille's personal effects." It didn't slow Nola down. "I also looked up your job—Artist-in-Residence—that's what they call you, right? The Army lets you travel the world, painting soldiers in Afghanistan or relief workers in Bangladesh. You can go anywhere, can't you?" Zig added. "Yet what I can't understand is what you were doing out there in Alaska. Did you go just to paint Kamille, or was there something else going on there?"

Nola kept walking. She didn't like Zig, didn't like the subtle tone of accusation in his voice.

"Can you at least tell me why Kamille was flying under your name? You switched spots with her, right? Was that her idea or yours?"

Nola was outside, scanning the block and heading for the car that she'd hidden around the corner.

"What about Houdini?" Zig said.

Right there, Nola stopped.

"You think you're the only one who found the names of the other victims?" Zig asked. "Rose Mackenberg. Clifford Eddy. Amedeo Vacca—they were all on the plane with your friend Kamille. But all three of them died fifty years ago."

Nola stared down at the driveway, at a thin crack that zigzagged across the concrete. Not enough water in the cement mix. Such an avoidable error. "They were cover names," Nola finally said.

"I know what cover names are. What I want to know is what they were covering. To be that far out in Alaska, this was a group that clearly didn't want anyone else around, yet there you were, right at the center of it with your paintbrushes. So why don't we start over, Nola? You saw something out there in Alaska—something that I'm guessing made you stay off that plane. So. What was it?"

Up the block, an old man was walking a far too small dog. The kind of dog that no one in their right mind would put on a leash. "This doesn't concern you, Mr. Zigarowski. Have a nice life."

"No. Don't *Mr. Zigarowski* me. That note Kamille left...whoever took that plane down, if they were aiming for you—"

"I had no idea they were aiming for me. I still don't know."

"But you've got a feeling. If you didn't, you wouldn't still be hiding like this—or scanning the street like the bogeyman's coming."

Nola looked away from the street, away from the man and his little dog. Zig was staring straight at her.

"Nola, whatever's going on, you owe it to Kamille to find the truth. I can help you with that."

"I'm not twelve anymore. I don't need your help."

"You sure about that? You're officially deceased. That means your IDs won't work, and neither will whatever classified security clearances you once had. At least with me, whatever doors you're planning to bang on next, you keep the element of surprise, which, far as I can tell, is the only thing you've got going in your favor right now."

Nola glanced back down at the crack in the cement. "Why're you doing this, Mr. Zigarowski?"

"The same reason you changed your PADD and tried to bring Kamille's body here instead of sending it to Arlington Cemetery. You wanted to get Kamille to her family, didn't you?"

"That doesn't tell me why you're doing this."

"Nola, I put people to rest. That's my job. So your friend Kamille..."

"You keep calling her my friend. She wasn't my friend."

"Either way, she's someone's daughter. She's a member of our military." He looked Nola deep in the eyes, firing up the charm. With a quick lick of his lips, he touched his tongue to his right incisor. "I need to put Kamille to rest."

Nola knew it was a lie. Or at least a half-truth. No way was Zig risking all this just to help some girl from his old neighborhood. No one would. So was this about what Nola did all those years ago at the campfire?—tackling Maggie?—was he doing this out of guilt or to repay some perceived debt? If so, he was more reckless, and more wounded, than she thought. But Zig was right about one thing: Nola's movements were definitely limited. If she wanted to figure things out, she'd need someone who could move around in the light of day, especially considering where she was going next.

Nola thought about the pencil sketch she just drew of Zig...of the loneliness on his face. Did she like Zig? No. Did she trust him? No. But that didn't mean she couldn't use him.

"How'd you like to go to Washington, DC?" Nola asked.

21

I D," the soldier insisted.

Leaning an elbow out of the driver's side window, Zig teed up a grin and handed over his Dover mortuary ID.

"I have an appointment," Zig said, eyeing the guard—and the second guard behind him, both of them armed with MP5 assault weapons.

At the front gate of most stateside military bases—including here at Fort Belvoir—the guards carried M9s. Standard handguns. *For them to have MP5s, they're on alert, looking for something. Or someone.*

"You in yet?" Nola asked in Zig's ear, through one of those Bluetooth earpieces that made him look part robot, part business-traveler-from-2006.

"Busy day, huh?" Zig called out to the guards.

Neither responded. The taller one, whose teeth were perfectly white but crooked like toppled buildings, was still studying Zig's ID.

The other guard pulled out a long pole with a round mirror at the end of it, and ran it under Zig's car. Even from here, Zig could see the Airborne patch on his uniform with the sword and three lightning bolts. Forget military police. These were Special Forces.

"Two years ago, my sister-in-law came through Dover," Crooked Teeth finally said, handing back Zig's ID. He pushed a button, raising the arm for the security gate. "Thanks for what you do. Welcome to Fort Belvoir."

Zig nodded his thanks and hit the gas.

"Told you the Dover ID would work," Zig said to Nola.

She didn't respond. No surprise. The entire ride here, Silent Nola barely said a word. Was it smart for him to be here? Of course not. But was he breaking the law? Not yet.

"Drive straight," Nola said as Zig weaved through the tidy streets, past the base's long white warehouses and redbrick buildings.

Located half an hour outside of Washington, DC, Fort Belvoir may look like a typical Army base, but it housed some of the Defense Department's top secret-keepers. The Army Intelligence and Security Command was headquartered here. So was the real-life Big Brother, the National Geospatial-Intelligence Agency. To put it in context, Fort Belvoir had almost twice as many employees as the Pentagon. And in that final scene of *Raiders of the Lost Ark*, where they put the Ark in the massive warehouse with the rest of the government's unmentionables? That's what they call this place right here on base, in the exact location Zig was now headed—the nondescript beige building with a sign out front that read:

MUSEUM SUPPORT CENTER
CENTER OF MILITARY HISTORY

Inside this wide government building was the cleanest air in the Washington, DC, area, filtered down to the particulate level and kept at a perfect 70 degrees. To protect the treasures hidden inside, they even charged the air with positive static energy, so that contaminants would be pushed out rather than stay inside.

"Last space on the right has a blind spot," Nola said as Zig pulled into the parking lot and glanced up at the pole camera that apparently couldn't see him.

Keeping his head down as he got out of the car, Zig headed quickly for the building's glass front doors.

"1083," Nola added in his ear as Zig picked up the black telephone on the wall and entered the number into the intercom. It rang three times before—

"Barton here," a voice answered with a Kentucky drawl.

"We spoke earlier. I'm the investigator," Zig said. It was a lie, but not too far off. "From Dover—"

Click. That was all it took.

There was a loud buzz. Zig shoved the door open. It was late now—almost 7 p.m.—the wide atrium was dark, everyone gone for the day.

"What's with the car?" Zig whispered to Nola.

In front of him, in the center of the lobby, was an antique automobile, complete with fancy spare tires on the side, like you see in old movies and Scrooge McDuck comics.

"General Pershing's limousine from World War I. His Locomobile," Nola said, even though she couldn't see him. The car was clearly a museum highlight.

Zig cocked an eyebrow at her sudden helpfulness. The whole ride here, she barely said a word, Silent Nola in full effect—though it wasn't just silence. Zig watched her carefully. *Heart or no heart?* Jury was still out. There was an impatience about her, a hidden rage. If she was now suddenly being talkative, she wanted something.

"I need to ask you a question," she added.

"Do it quickly. Your pal Barton is almost here."

"How badly was she burned?"

Who? Zig almost asked. But he knew. The woman whose body he worked on yesterday—the body that was now missing—and that Nola was chasing. Kamille.

"She was flash-burned. Charred her skin," Zig explained.

"Were they chemical burns or—?"

"Not chemical." Zig knew what she was getting at. When a missile hits a plane, people's skin will have chemical burns, caused by caustic fuel. If it's a bomb, the body comes apart, creating fragments. "Kamille was intact. Broken legs. Burned on her right side only."

"You think she jumped," Nola said.

"That would explain her legs. And with no signs of chemical burns or fragmentation—"

"No bomb, no missile," Nola said. "She knew what was coming. That's why she ate the note. Soon after takeoff—maybe even during it—she knew the plane was going down."

Zig nodded. "Can I ask *you* a question now?" he said, approaching the front grille of the limousine. Up the hallway, a figure turned the corner. Zig didn't have much time, but with Nola suddenly being talkative… "Tell me something about Maggie," Zig blurted. "My daughter."

There was a pause. "Mr. Zigarowski—"

"Zig," he insisted, forcing a laugh. "You have to call me Zig."

"I didn't know her well. I only lived in Ekron a year."

"Still, you did Girl Scouts together…and at the campfire, you saved her—"

"I knocked her out of the way. That doesn't mean I—"

"Who knows what would've happened if you weren't there. Thankfully, though, you were. And after that, you and Maggie… you walked the same halls…sat in the same classes. You had to've seen each other somewhere. Just tell me one thing—anything you remember about her."

For a solid five seconds, Nola was silent. Until… "I remember her being in the car when you took me to the hospital. She kept saying *thank you* over and over. Otherwise, we really didn't spend any time together."

"C'mon, even just something stupid you might remember. Anything," Zig said, fighting hard to keep the pep in his voice. "Anything at all."

Another five seconds. Zig was listening so hard, he started leaning forward, his shins pressing against the shiny front bumper of the limousine.

"It was a long time ago, Mr. Zigarowski. I'm sorry. I didn't know her that well."

Zig stared down at his own warped reflection in the chrome bumper, kicking himself for even asking. He wasn't new to this, wasn't a recent mourner. Maggie died over a decade ago. His wounds had scarred over. *No*, he thought, *had healed*. His life was good now. And fulfilling. He was healed.

"You must be Zig," a voice called out.

Fluorescent lights popped on in the distance—motion sensors kicking in—lighting the hallway and revealing a paunchy little man folded like a dumpling. His plodding walk and bow tie said he wasn't military, but the way he was twirling his key ring like a gunslinger... *Administrator*, Zig thought.

"*Barton Hudson*," Nola whispered in Zig's ear.

"Barton Hudson," the man said, offering a damp handshake. Through his gold-framed glasses, he had desperate eyes, eager for attention. "You like the Locomobile, yes? Have you seen our Napoleon cannon?"

Before Zig could argue, Barton led him back up the hallway, toward a massive antique cannon that was nearly as big as Pershing's limo.

"Named for its killing power—which explains why Uncle Sammy brought it here for the Civil War. Beautiful, yes?" he said, Zig realizing he was one of those people who added "yes?" at the end of his sentences to get people to agree with him.

"*His wife died last year. Cancer in her kidney. He's got no one to go home to*," Nola said in Zig's ear. "*Keep him on track, or he'll talk your ear off all night.*"

"I really do appreciate you staying late," Zig said, glancing down the long cinder-block hallway that had all the charm of a prison. Nearly half a football field down, the hallway dead-ended at a set of sealed metal doors. Even from here, there was no missing the white sign with bright red letters:

RESTRICTED AREA

WARNING

"So about Sergeant Brown..." Zig added.

"Of course. So sad. So sad," Barton said, giving another twirl to his key ring and heading deeper into the building. Every twenty steps or so, more motion sensors clicked, lighting the hall with bright fluorescents. "Everyone here—we're all heartbroken."

"He's a liar and a petty man," Nola said in Zig's ear. *"Tried to get me transferred every year since he first met me."*

"Such a tragedy," Barton added.

"Cameras on your right and left," Nola warned as Zig counted no fewer than four ceiling cameras, as well as a temperature alarm, chemical reader, even a moisture monitor, like you see in the world's top museums.

For well over a decade, the Army has been trying to open its own Army Museum. Until the funding came through, this enormous warehouse, tucked away at Fort Belvoir, was where they stored their best weapons and treasures, from thousands of antique and modern guns, cannons, bazookas, and every other armament, to flags flown in the Revolutionary War, to a rifle used at the Boston Tea Party, to frock coats worn at Gettysburg, to Ulysses S. Grant's Civil War cap, to the drum that the 3rd US Infantry—the Old Guard—played at JFK's funeral.

"He also fidgets when he's nervous: touches the arm of his glasses, twirls his key ring," Nola added.

"So when was the last time you saw Nola?" Zig asked, watching Barton smooth his thumb against the length of a hunk of keys.

"I guess...last Thursday, yes? The day she left for Alaska," Barton replied, weaving off the main hallway, toward a door that looked like the entrance to a bank vault.

There were doors like this all around the building. Some protected military artifacts, others secured the Army's sixteen thousand pieces of fine art, from propaganda paintings by Norman Rockwell to watercolors done by Adolf Hitler himself, captured by US troops during raids at the end of World War II. But of all the treasure-filled rooms in the building, *this* was the one he most wanted to see.

"To be honest, I haven't been here since she—since everything—Well, you know..." Barton said, unlocking the door, shoving it open, and revealing a long rectangular room that smelled like paint and turpentine. The sign read: *Room 176—Artist Studio.*

"Here you go. Nola's office," Barton added.

"*Tell him to leave,*" Nola said in Zig's ear. "*Remind him you're investigating my death and that y—*"

Zig reached for his earpiece. *Click.*

Call ended.

A few minutes from now, Zig would tell Nola that there was no signal in the building, that his phone dropped the call.

Would she believe him? Maybe.

Did he care? Not at all.

An hour ago, Nola asked him to go to her office to grab something she couldn't grab. But considering how many bodies had already shown up—and that Nola was the only one who somehow escaped the plane crash—Zig wasn't putting his life at risk without first investigating the one person who required the most investigation: Nola herself. Zig needed to repay her, and he might be sentimental, but he wasn't stupid. *Heart or no heart?* He needed that answer.

"Best I get out of your way, yes?" Barton asked.

"Actually, before you go..." Zig said. "Can I ask you a few questions about Sergeant Brown?"

"Sure. Of course."

Two hours from now, when they were cleaning up the blood,

this is the moment Barton would remember. He'd wonder why he was so helpful to Zig, and why he let him in in the first place. He'd ask it over and over: Would things have turned out differently if he didn't? But the truth was, nothing would've changed at all. The blood was always coming.

22

"Nola is— Or rather . . . she *was*—" Barton took a breath and shifted his weight, his whole round body wobbling. "Nola's an artist."

Zig knew that tone. No one likes speaking ill of the dead. "That bad, huh?" Zig said, adding a warm smile to keep him talking.

"She was just—" Standing in the doorway, Barton stopped himself again. "Nola was . . . *interesting*."

"Sir—"

"Call me Barton. I'm civilian, just like you."

"Barton, then. Nice to meet you, Barton," Zig said, flashing a new grin, the grin he learned in his old life, when his job was to put people at ease so they wouldn't stiff him when they saw the final price of the casket and burial. "Barton, at the start of my career, I used to be a funeral director—and I can tell you: people only use the word *interesting* when the deceased was a pain in the ass. Now I know it's tough, but this investigation—"

"What're you investigating? According to the news, the plane went down because of mechanical failure, yes?"

"Absolutely," Zig said, kicking himself for being careless. He hadn't looked to see what the news was reporting. Mechanical failure. "That's our belief too," Zig added, not even realizing how easily the lies came. "But back at Dover—you know the job—we check every box, make sure we're not missing anything. So. Whatever you think about your coworker Nola, your candor would be greatly appreciated—even if she *was* a pain in the rear."

Barton twirled his key ring, letting out a little chuckle and glancing around Nola's office. Behind them, back in the hallway, the lights went out—*pooomp*—the idle motion sensors returning everything to darkness. "They tell you what Nola's job was here?" Barton asked.

"I know she was a war painter."

"Not just a painter. She's the Artist-in-Residence. It's one of the Army's most prestigious honors; dates back to World War I and runs through every battle since—Normandy, Vietnam, Cambodia, Iraq, you name it. Anywhere we've stormed the beaches, we've had a painter there. You know why?"

"So we can document it?"

"No. Documenting is easy. You want to document something, send photographers and videographers. The reason we send a painter, it's not for documentation. It's so we can *learn*. Painters can— Look. Here… *Look…*" Barton said, taking out his phone and pulling up a painting of a soldier, an oil on canvas.

"Like *this*," Barton said, shoving the screen toward Zig's face. The painting was of a soldier from the chest up, in full army fatigues, standing in the clearing of a jungle.

"This was painted in 1944 when we invaded the island of Peleliu," Barton explained. "It's called *The 2,000 Yard Stare*. But you can see what the artist does here, yes? The soldier is looking right at us, but his eyes are wide, vacant . . . his cheeks hollow and covered in the grime of war. He doesn't even see the giant tank and the slumped body that's behind him. So what's the effect?"

Zig studied the painting, mesmerized. He'd seen looks like that before, on Dover's young cadets, every time they'd see their first decapitated body. Zig used to have that look too. But it came from something entirely different, something that he thought he'd put away—that is, until Nola showed up and ripped his old scars open. "This soldier looks shell-shocked."

"Not just shell-shocked. Horrified," Barton said. "*This* is how you show people horror. Artists can make knapsacks and rucksacks bigger, can add sweat to worried brows. No photo would ever capture this moment, because this isn't just a painting. It's a *story*."

Zig was still staring down, hypnotized by the young soldier's faraway gaze. "What's this have to do with Nola?"

"To create a painting like that—that's not just something whipped up by a kid with some crayons. The last Artist-in-Residence was forty-two years old. A sergeant first class. The one before that was forty-three. Nola Brown was twenty-five—just a private when they brought her in. So ask yourself: How does a twenty-five-year-old get a job that's always been held by people almost twice her age?"

"I take it it's not because she's a really great painter?"

Barton was still standing in the doorway, like he was afraid to step inside. "You never heard what Nola did in Iraq, did you?"

23

It started nearly two and a half...maybe three years ago, yes?" Barton began. "I didn't even know Nola at the time. Her Army unit was in Northern Iraq, tracking an ISIS electronics supplier who was using old phones to build detonators. Somehow, the trail led to a little town called Tel Asqof."

Zig knew Tel Asqof. Last year, he'd worked on the body of an Army Ranger—thirty-one years old, from the same town in Arizona where Zig's college roommate lived. Fallen #2,286. Shot from the side, through the esophagus.

"When they arrived, Nola's unit spent hours kicking in doors, looking for the supplier," Barton said. "At the time, Nola was stationed up on the roof, providing cover. Then the unit got a call to lift and shift. Apparently, they had bad intel—the supplier was spotted in another nearby town. 'Stand down,' their unit leader said, telling them to eat some lunch as they waited for the Humvees and trucks to arrive. So what do most soldiers do in that moment?"

"They eat lunch."

"Of course they eat lunch. Everyone eats, smokes, writes a letter, whatever. And then there's Nola," Barton said with a brand-new coldness in his voice. "Up there on the roof, Nola pulls out her sketch pad and starts drawing. From her high perch, the street, the houses, they look almost mystical. So there she is, drawing away, her pencil scribbling as she adds the details you see on every poorly paved street in Iraq: trash and rubble, a burned-out car, a rat the size of a small cat...she even draws the manhole cover at the center of the road," Barton says, pausing for effect. "And then it hits her. Why would there be a manhole cover when Iraq doesn't have a defined sewer system?"

"Oh crap."

"*Oh crap* is right. Dropping her pencil, Nola grabs her rifle, looks through the scope, and...there it is—a copper wire running out from the manhole. '*Clear out!*' she yells to everyone. '*Clear out!*' As the last person evacuates, Nola leans over the side of the roof, shoots once with the rifle, and misses. She shoots again and misses. Then with her third shot, she hits the wire and..."

"Boom," Zig says.

"Like you wouldn't believe. The whole damn street exploded, then collapsed on one side as a volcano of fire erupted into the air. From what they could tell, there was a massive weapons cache hidden underground. Our troops had been through there over two dozen times, but no one ever saw it...until Nola drew her picture and realized that this street with a manhole shouldn't have a manhole."

"I'm surprised they didn't give her a medal," Zig said.

"They should've. But then her commanding officer came running up to the roof, screaming at her for firing her weapon without first being fired upon. That's a violation of the rules of engagement. Could've gotten everyone killed."

"But she saved the day."

"She thought the same. So before her commander knew what was happening, Nola hit him in the chest, ripped his captain's patch off his uniform, and tossed it off the side of the building, down into the flames. 'Sir, see you back at camp, sir,' she told him, giving him the eff you of a full sir sandwich."

Zig couldn't help but laugh. The motion sensor lights in the hallway popped on again. *Pooomp.*

"Janitor," Barton reassured him, pointing out into the hallway.

"As for Nola," Barton continued, "she was confined to her barracks for nearly a month, which apparently was something that happened a lot. A few weeks later, they transferred her to a new unit—now they had her doing supplies—shipping clean water to all the other nearby units. And then she does it again."

"Does what again?"

"Painting," Barton said. "When she draws— I know it sounds kinda whackadoo, but I'm telling you...Nola can—" He tapped the temple of his glasses with his pointer finger. "She sees things."

"So now she's got superpowers? Like she got stabbed with a radioactive paintbrush?"

"I know what you're thinking. But one night in the back of a Humvee, Nola's unit was heading to this tiny Iraqi town called Rawa. As she's peering out the window, she starts sketching the landscape, drawing the sunset as it hits the fresh hay in the field. Here's the thing: years ago, Rawa was bombed to devastation. Nothing grows out there; all the hay should be brown and dead. Nola of course starts shouting—*Stop the truck! The hay's the wrong color!*—but her captain, he knows Nola's a headache even on her best day. So maybe he pretends not to hear, maybe he doesn't give a crap since his orders are in Rawa. Regardless, the Humvee keeps going. So Nola opens the door. And jumps out."

"Now the truck has to stop."

"From the report I read, she never even looked back. She was storming toward the field. And there it was. Hidden underneath the hay, they found two hundred stolen AK-47s—guns that would've killed countless of our sons and daughters."

"Okay, so she's good at finding things that're out of place. That doesn't mean—"

"Have you ever seen the report that was done on spotting explosive devices?" Barton asked. "Back in Afghanistan, the Army actually studied it. And y'know who was best at spotting IEDs?

Redneck kids with hunting backgrounds, and poor urban kids who knew how to spot which gang controlled which block."

"What's your point?"

"That's who was best at it. But Nola crushed them all. Two years ago, in an Iraqi slum where we'd never sent troops before, she spotted a green Mountain Dew bottle. How'd it get there? Behind one of the mud huts, she found a false wall that hid two ISIS chemical engineers, storing enough fertilizer, ammonia, and tanks of nitrogen to take out a small city. A few weeks after that, a large oil spot in a field led her to a stash of stolen Navy uniforms that ISIS was using to smuggle their people across borders. A month after that—"

"I get it. She's a bloodhound for finding stuff."

"I'm not sure you're grasping the full picture here," Barton said, not even noticing that out in the hallway, the "janitor" had gone silent. "Nola has an exceptional visual memory; she can absorb and recreate a crime scene in a moment. When she starts painting, details leap out at her, details no one else sees. But what she excels at more than anything"—he took a breath through his nose—"is pissing people off."

Zig thought about that, glancing into the office at the desk in the corner. Even from here, he could see there were no personal photos. "Is that why they stationed her here? When a disaster happens, you ship her out on a mission, then she can come back and keep painting without everyone trying to take her head off?"

"They still wanted to take her head off. In six months, she went through six units. Seven different reprimands. It's a personal record—and that doesn't include all the captains and other commanding officers who looked so inept by what she found, they didn't report her. From what I heard, a Marine gunnery sergeant took a swing at her. Nola's reaction? She jammed a colored pencil into his elbow. But it's not until he starts howling and ripping his jacket off that they see she stabbed him in the exact spot he had elbow surgery years earlier. Right in the scar.

Like she could see through his uniform and knew the wound was there."

Zig nodded, replaying his and Nola's near-silent ride over the past hour. Throughout the trip, Zig felt her stare. Even as a child, Nola's black eyes looked through him. But now...he wondered what she saw in him today.

"Eventually," Barton added, "one of the Army bigwigs got smart and asked, 'Why don't we make her the Artist-in-Residence?' So for the past few years, she's been here, working out of our studio. As the artist, she can go anywhere, painting whatever she wants. If the Army needs her for something specific, they can send her in too—and take her out once she finds what we're searching for."

"So she's the Army's bloodhound."

"Bloodhound?" There was a hitch in Barton's voice. He shook his head. "Call her whatever you want, but trust me on this: Nola Brown isn't a pet. She's a gun. A weapon. You point her at something and you'll get what you want—but just know it may also come back in pieces."

"You saying this plane crash—?"

"I got no comment on the plane. All I know is what's on the TV. But whether it was a faulty engine or anything else, there's no shock she eventually went down in flames."

Zig thought about that, thought about how many of Nola's fellow soldiers had their careers ruined by her brashness, or lack of social skills, or whatever you wanted to call it. It was a hell of a suspect list.

In his pocket, his phone began to vibrate. Had to be Nola calling back. Zig didn't pick up. Not yet. "Can I ask you one last question? Nola's final trip—this one to Alaska... Was this *her* mission or an Army one?"

"I think it was hers, but with Nola..." Barton glanced over Zig's shoulder, into Nola's office. "The Army doesn't tell me every secret. You should look for yourself."

"Weren't you her supervisor?"

Barton readjusted his glasses, forcing a fake laugh. "There was no *supervising* Nola. Even on assignments, she didn't listen. Didn't engage or even argue. Nola just *did*. You want to know what she was chasing in Alaska?" He motioned again toward her office. "Have at it. God knows what you'll find."

24

The first thing Zig noticed were the walls. They were covered, floor to ceiling, with overlapping posters that made Nola's office feel like an indie record store, but with old Army propaganda prints from World War II (*"It Can Happen Here!"*), painted covers from old *Life* magazines (*"Vietnam—Why We'll Win!"*), psyops pamphlets that were dropped in Kuwait (*"Leave!"* in seven languages), all of them mashed together—Soldiers! Guns! The American flag!—a bright kaleidoscope of red, white, and blue. There was also a postcard of TV host Bob Ross, painting his happy little trees.

"You hung up on me," Nola said in his ear.

"The call dropped," Zig shot back. "Coverage is crap in this building." Truth was, he almost didn't pick up when she called back. But that would've led to even more problems. "By the way, you're welcome. I got rid of your coworker Barton."

"I knew he'd leave. Even when I'm dead, he's afraid of me."

Zig nodded, knowing she wasn't joking.

"Make sure the door's locked behind you," Nola added.

Zig didn't even hear the words. He was moving fast, too busy looking at the wall on his right with its inspiration corkboard filled with dozens of photographs—big 8x10s, standard snapshots, even some Polaroids—all of them of soldiers: soldiers shaving, soldiers eating, soldiers texting, soldiers playing basketball on a makeshift court with a desert backdrop. There were no weapons, no fighting. These were normal scenes. There was even a black-and-white photo of an Iraqi kid dancing, his arms twisted in an old-school hip-hop move as a group of soldiers crowded around, cheering him on. *Downtime*, Zig decided, thinking it was probably something Nola had a hard time comprehending.

"Tell me what you see," Nola said in Zig's ear. "Before Barton comes back. You find the desk?"

There was no missing it. On Zig's left was an oversized drafting table, angled like a pinball machine. Unlike the walls, which were covered in chaos, the desk was neat: file folders in one pile, notebooks in another, opened mail in another, each pile in perfect size order. Even Nola's colored pencils, in a nearby pencil tray, were lined up shortest to tallest and in perfect roy-g-biv rainbow order: red, orange, yellow, green, blue, indigo, and violet.

Pooomp. The noise came from out in the hallway. Zig glanced over his shoulder. Idle motion sensors again blinked off. Barton was gone. *Good. All alone*, Zig told himself.

"Tell me what's there," Nola said.

"They nabbed your computer."

"What?"

"Your computer," Zig said, eyeing the metal government-issue desk that held an old PC keyboard and bulky monitor. Underneath, though… "Your hard drive's gone. Someone grabbed the whole tower." Zig took another scan of the office. Everything else was still in place. Nothing looked messy or torn apart. Whoever took the computer, they were in and out immediately. Professional job. Or someone who knew exactly what they were looking for.

Nola made a noise, a grunt that said she wasn't surprised. "Get what you came for. The canvases—"

"I see them," Zig said, heading for a dozen or so painted canvases leaning against the back wall, one against the other, like oversized dominos stacked too close.

"Pull them forward," Nola said.

Zig grabbed the pastel painting in front. It was mostly camouflage olive and muddy brown, a portrait of a black female soldier from the chest up, head cocked with a ghostly sadness, like someone who just heard that her dog was sick. Zig knew this painting—he'd seen another just like it back at Dover, in Personal Effects, right before he was hit in the head. The soldier was different, but it was the same pose, same artist. The signature at the bottom confirmed the rest. *NBrown.*

Zig flipped to the next canvas, then the one after that. They were all similar, focused on a single soldier—black, white, Hispanic, all heights and body types—staring straight at you. Some looked angry and intense. One had a strained smile. But all of them had that same *look*—that emptiness in their faces like they were somehow... broken.

"Who are these people?" Zig asked.

Nola didn't answer.

Zig flipped to another painting. Then another, realizing that the broken looks on their faces...it reminded him of the look that Nola herself had.

Flipping to the next canvas, he noticed something on the back of it. Tiny block letters in a perfect handwriting. He squinted to read it:

DANIEL GRAFF—MONTEREY, CA

Zig flipped to the next one. On the back it said:

SGT. DENISE MADIGAN—KUWAIT

Pulling out his phone, Zig flipped through the next few—there had to be twenty or more in total—taking a picture of each name.

Pooomp. Another sound from the hallway. This one more faint. Like the motion sensor lights had popped on in the distance.

"Your pal Barton might be headed back," Zig said, frantically tilting all the paintings forward until he revealed...

There. Behind the final painting.

The canvases were so big, at first you couldn't see it, which was the point. The best hiding spots were the places no one would look. But with the paintings all tipped forward, there it was, solid and gray, complete with a blast-resistant combination lock.

A steel-reinforced safe.

"Exactly where you said it was," Zig said, reading the warning sticker on the front. In bright red letters were the words: *Flammable Items Inside!* "Now what's the combination?"

25

Twenty-seven right, nineteen left, seven right," Zig repeated, turning the lock on the waist-high safe.

Kuunk.

The lock popped. He was still staring at the warning sticker: *Flammable Items Inside!*

Zig grabbed the latch and gave it a twist. As he tugged the door open, there were two metal shelves. The smell of turpentine hit him.

"Tell me what's there," Nola said, her voice flat and measured. She hadn't lost her cool yet. But she was getting close.

"You got some serious stuff in here."

There was a bowie knife, an old World War II Ka-Bar Marine fighting knife, and even a broken Strider SMF Special Forces knife where the blade was snapped. There was also ammunition—all shapes and sizes: empty rusted shells for rifles, handguns, machine guns, and some ordnance Zig didn't even recognize. Plus two rusty grenades. None of it was live. If anything, it looked like the same collection most soldiers kept, war toys from bases they visited.

"It's up top," Nola said.

On the top shelf, Zig shoved aside four cans of spray paint, a bottle of turpentine, another of brush cleaner, and yet another of something called Oil Mediums. Nola's building was a museum-level facility that held the Army's entire collection of art and antiquities. Of course anything flammable had to be stored in a bombproof safe.

"I'm still not seeing it," Zig insisted, stretching his arm into the safe and patting around.

"In the back. It should be—"

"Got it," Zig said, feeling a rectangular box. "I got it."

He pulled out from the safe an antique metal tin, like an Altoids container but bigger and far older. The pale green logo had a man wearing a cap and gown while smoking a pipe. *Yale Mixture Smoking Tobacco—A Gentleman's Smoke*, read the vintage label. Five different rubber bands held the tin shut.

"Go. Get out of there," Nola said in his ear.

Zig didn't hesitate. There was a *ting-ting-ting* as he shoved the metal tin in his pocket, like there were dice or keys—something small—inside.

As he quickly cleaned up and darted for the door, he spotted—

There. Under the door. The lights in the hallway were on. With the motion sensors . . . shouldn't they be off? Maybe not. Barton left only a few minutes ago.

Slowly, Zig opened the door and stuck his head out. The hallway was clear. It didn't make him feel any better. For twenty years, Zig had worked on and studied nearly every part of the human anatomy. But there were some things even science couldn't explain. Like the ability to know when you're being watched.

"You have the box?" Nola asked.

Zig didn't answer. Weaving back to the main hallway, he was tempted to run, but instead he walked with purpose, holding tight to the metal tin in his pocket. *Stay calm. Don't call attention.* Up ahead, he eyed another set of cameras he'd missed on the way in. Still no one in sight.

"You have it or not?" Nola added.

Zig barely heard the question, suddenly all too aware of how quiet the hallway was. His shoes squeaked against the floor. He could hear his own breathing. And then—

Ka-tang.

There. Straight ahead. A high-pitched sound, like something hitting metal. Zig cocked his head toward the only thing in sight: General Pershing's limousine.

It was after hours. Everyone was gone. As Zig slowly approached the limo, he eyed its open windows. Were they open on the way in? He thought so.

Slowly getting closer, he peered inside the car. Empty. But that feeling of being watched? There was no ignoring it.

"Get out of there," Nola insisted.

Picking up speed, Zig plowed for the front glass door, ramming it with his shoulder. The door flew wide and a snap of cold air had him sweating and freezing all in the same moment. Without slowing down, he headed left, to the far corner of the parking lot.

Reaching the gray rental, he was out of camera sight. He glanced over his shoulder. No one there.

"You in the car?" Nola asked.

"Yes," Zig said. It was a lie. From his pocket, he pulled out the metal tin with the green tobacco label. When Nola first asked him, their plan was simple:

1. Get inside
2. Get the tin
3. Get out of there

Sometimes, though, even the best plans had to change. Nola wouldn't tell him what was in the tin, but since he was the one who took the risk and pulled it from the safe...

4. Time to see what was so important

Zig yanked the rubber bands from the tin. It didn't feel heavy, but it felt full. Maybe a cell phone was in there?

With his thumb, he popped the lid, squinting down and seeing...

Crayons. A dozen fancy crayons. Oil pastels.

He broke a few in half, wondering if there was something hidden in them.

No. Just...crayons.

Zig raised an eyebrow. It made no sense. Why would she have him come all this way for something as useless as—?

There was a noise behind Zig. A skittering of stray gravel.

Zig turned just in time to see the punch coming. Zig had been in enough fights. He knew to roll with it, but it still hit like a pool cue to his face. A burst of bright stars detonated in his eyes. The tin tumbled to the ground, near the front tire. Zig was still on his feet, determined to get a better look at—

"*Where is she!?*" a man's voice exploded. "*Tell me where Nola is!*"

26

Zig stumbled backward, crashing into the gray car in the corner of the lot. *Stupid old man*, Zig cursed himself. *You let him pin you in a corner.*

His attacker wasn't tall; he was wide like a garage door. And fast. Short blond hair, wide-set eyes, thin nose. But no uniform. From his fighting stance, definitely military training. Recent too—he was in his late twenties. Half Zig's age. A kid, really. In his hand was a telescoping baton. Zig made note of that. Standard issue for the Secret Service.

"We know you were with her," Wide Eyes said.

We. Zig made note of that too, even as he lurched sideways. Zig held on to the car for balance. He was still blinking stars from his eyes. Could he take another hit? It was Zig's one advantage. He could always handle pain. *Catch your breath*, he told himself. *Make a plan. Get your knife.*

"And don't even think of going for that knife," Wide Eyes said. Kid was young but well trained. "Last chance," the kid warned, cocking the baton back. "Where's Nola?"

"Nola *who*? I just—"

Fwwsssh. With a ruthless swipe, Wide Eyes slashed down, nailing Zig in the meat of his left calf.

Crumpling to one knee, Zig made a noise, like a grumble, but refused to cry out. Hunched over, he reached into his pocket, pulled out the knife and—

Whaaap. The baton hit like a baseball bat. There was a crunch of fingers. The knife went flying, skittering into the nearby grass. The impact tore open Zig's skin in a thin red line.

Down on both knees and gripping his bloody hand, Zig shook his head. "Y-You do realize...I'm gonna shove that baton—"

Wide Eyes wound up again, this time smashing Zig in the shoulder. Then again in Zig's lower back. The world went blurry at the edges, then black, and then there Zig was, down on all fours, suddenly seeing his mother, watching as she used to beat Zig's brothers with an ironing cord. But never Zig. Zig was the one she always protected.

"—even know who Nola is!?" Wide Eyes shouted as the world again blurred at the edges and shrunk down to a tight pinhole. "You got any idea what she's done? What kinda monster she is?"

Still down on all fours, Zig was thinking about what Master Guns would say about Nola—that she set Zig up, that he didn't owe her anything.

"Don't let Nola fool you—she put that plane in the ground!" Wide Eyes insisted. "If you keep hiding her..." He raised his baton for another hit.

"S-Stop...I-I'm not hiding her...I know where she is..." Zig sputtered. He could barely move.

Wide Eyes kept his baton cocked, leaning down as Zig whispered two words.

"Suprasternal notch."

"*Wha?*" Wide Eyes asked, leaning even closer.

Zig didn't like violence. Every day, he saw the damage it did. But after years of rebuilding broken soldiers, Zig also saw which parts of the human body were most resilient. And most vulnerable.

"Suprasternal notch," Zig repeated, thrusting his thumb—like a spear—straight into the small hole—the suprasternal notch—below Wide Eyes's Adam's apple. "That little pocket right...

there?" Zig said, driving his thumb even deeper, then gripping the man's neck. "Your collarbone doesn't protect it, so that pain you're now feeling? That's me crushing your trachea."

Wide Eyes was gasping, grabbing at Zig, who wouldn't let go. The color ran from Wide Eyes's face. He was wheezing now, choking, dropping the baton. Zig still held tight.

We all have truths we don't admit about ourselves. As Zig tightened his grip, he felt that embarrassing flush of adrenaline that comes from having power over another person. Every day, Zig told himself he hated violence. But deep down, he knew one thing: He was good at it.

Would Zig kill him? He'd never kill. He made that promise long ago. Death already had enough helping hands.

Zig studied the sudden whiteness on Wide Eyes's face, watched his eyes roll back in his head, the first sign of flaccid paralysis: when the brain stops sending signals to the muscles and the body goes limp. Wide Eyes crumpled like a sack of batteries. It was a victory, but Zig took no joy in it.

"You could've knocked him out faster by blocking his venous return," a voice said behind him.

Zig turned just in time to see Nola standing there. With a shove, she planted the heel of her palm into Zig's forehead. On her hand was a black insulated glove with metal pins—just a centimeter long—at the thumb and pinkie.

Gripping Zig's forehead, she pressed the pins into Zig's temples, squeezing tight.

"*Nola, don't*—!" he started to yell, but his body was already convulsing, vibrating with more electricity than a military-grade stun gun.

As the world once again went black, the last thought in Zig's head was a curse word, directed at himself, for not seeing this coming.

27

Ekron, Pennsylvania
Fifteen years ago

This was Nola when she was eleven.

She was in the back of a car, the big willow-green '65 Chevy that her dad Royall bought at foreclosure to fix up and resell, though eventually, he wouldn't part with it. Royall traded a doctored passport that he'd worked on for weeks for the car's original hubcaps, then bartered an expensive set of hearing aids to get the front grille, its chrome still pristine. Royall waxed it every other weekend, even gave the car a name. *Teri*.

It was parked in the driveway, and Nola was in the backseat, curled on her side, trying to sleep.

This was where she slept every Tuesday and Saturday. Those were Royall's drinking days. He was strict about that, learned it in a book about success. But she learned early on: better to stay away on those nights.

Shifting from her side to her back, she readjusted her pillow, then made sure her blanket was tucked just right to protect her from the cold seat belt. Truth was, she didn't mind sleeping in the car. In fact, on September nights like this, when a cool wind was blowing, she preferred it.

It was quiet out here. The sound of the wind was soothing. And most important, it was safe.

Tonight, though, Nola could feel it—something was wrong, like the wind was blowing the wrong way. A storm was coming.

She'd been living with Royall for four years now, and unlike those first few months, most days now were incident free. Were there blowups? She was eleven. Of course there were, like the night she walked into the living room and scared off a buyer of something that Royall was hoping to sell.

A storm came that night. A storm Nola had never seen before.

But again, nights like that were rare. By now, Nola was an expert in Royall. Or at least an expert in avoiding him.

There was a scratch against the pavement outside. Nola sat up in the backseat. The block was empty. She checked the house. The lights were off. An hour ago, she saw Royall come back from the bar, stumbling inside. He should be asleep by now.

The lights were off. TV was off too. Definitely asleep.

Lying back down, Nola pulled up the covers and checked her digital watch, a gift from Royall after a particularly good week. He was making money now. It started a few years ago when Royall began creating and selling counterfeit driver's licenses. Then he added fake electric bills, phone bills, and the other paperwork that documents a person's life. Royall was good at it too. A master, like Picasso. His specialty wasn't just *creating* the documents; he'd make them look worn, match them to torn-down buildings that no one could check. For a price, Royall would build you more than a fake ID; he'd truly create a new identity.

His first real client was an old pal from junior high, an ex-con who wanted to restart his life from scratch. But then Royall found a real market for his talents in an immigrant community outside of Philadelphia. And of course, he used that skill for Nola, putting together a fake birth certificate so she could enroll in school.

In the backseat, Nola took another look at her digital watch. Almost 2 a.m. She could feel the exhaustion pressing heavily on her brain. But try as she might, sleep still wouldn't come.

A half hour later, Nola pulled a worn, folded wad of paper from her pocket. She carried it everywhere, for years now, though she rarely used it. It was faded and fraying, like homework left in the wash, but there was no mistaking it—the old greeting card the LaPointes had put in her luggage. The message inside read: *This will make you stronger.* But as Nola peeled it open and reread it for the first time in at least a year, it did nothing of the sort.

For another hour, Nola tossed and turned, fighting with the seat belt in her back, then sitting up to again recheck the house.

It was still dark, completely quiet. Royall was unconscious.

By morning, Nola would realize she was wrong. There was no storm coming.

Sometimes, when you're eleven years old, it's just hard to sleep in the backseat of a car.

28

Fort Belvoir, Virginia
Today

Zig woke up in a car. Head ringing.

Where'm I?

He licked his teeth and looked around. Driver's seat. Alone. The world was blurry, like he was peering at it through gauze. He kicked open the door, not even realizing he was doing it.

The car...it was the gray car, the one he drove onto the military base. Behind him...the museum where...it was like Indiana Jones in there and—

Nola.

Nola did this. Attacked him with a...what in the hell was it?...some sort of Taser glove. She was supposed to be hiding outside the base, waiting for Zig to open—

Mothertrucker. The safe— The green tin—

Zig patted his chest, then his front pockets, like someone searching for his keys. Then he remembered.

He spun around. There. Down near the tire and the blood, on the pavement. There was the green tin. It was open, but still mostly filled with fancy oil crayons. A few were scattered nearby. But like before, nothing else was in there.

The tin was untouched. Nola didn't care about it.

And now, Zig had that feeling he'd get when he was putting the finishing touches—the uniform and all the medals—on a corpse, when the minor problems were gone and you finally got to see the full picture.

Stupid old man. Nola wasn't after the metal tin...or even the crayons inside. So why'd she send Zig to break into her office safe?

To see who else would show up. Zig was nothing more than bait. And now, thanks to his naivety—and his eagerness to pay his debts...to come to the rescue...whatever it was—Nola had what she needed.

Zig did too. What was the word Wide Eyes called her? A *monster*. He said Nola was the one who put that plane in the ground.

Did Zig believe it? He didn't *want* to believe it, and the truth was, there was no logic in that statement. Nola had gone to Alaska for a reason... She saw something out there...or found something...something that kept her off that plane. So why'd he even care whether Nola was innocent? Why was he still chasing her? Why'd he even come here?

He told himself he wanted the truth. Then he told himself that he owed Nola for what she did to protect his daughter. Then he told himself what he told himself every day. He pictured those dead young soldiers—innocent souls—being carried in their flag-draped caskets this morning...their sobbing parents...plus the Librarian of Congress and that young woman whose body Zig worked on last night. Kamille Williams. Twenty-seven years old. From Iowa. Her body was taken—by someone—this afternoon, someone who knew their way around Dover, someone with access to the highest levels of military security. Wasn't that what this was about? Or was this all just a way for Zig to protect his own past, that as long as he saw Nola as innocent and undamaged—as the hero who saved the day—he could also keep his own daughter preserved in whatever perfect memory vault he'd been storing her in for the past decade?

Zig didn't have the time to sort through it all right now. All he knew was that he had to see this through—he *needed* these answers, needed to repay this debt. That was the right word now. *Need.* Regardless of how personal it was all becoming, someone put that plane down in Alaska, murdering seven people. And as far as Zig could tell, there was only one person who seemed to know why.

Now he just had to find her.

From his pocket, Zig pulled out his phone and swiped to an app called *RFTrack*.

On-screen, a small red triangle appeared, then a single word:

Scanning...

Back at Dover, when a new fallen arrives, the very first order of business is to attach state-of-the-art RFID tags so that each body can be catalogued and tracked. Especially with mass fatalities, Dover's top priority was to make sure that no bodies would ever be lost or misplaced. That's what Zig was counting on when, during the drive to Nola's office, he slipped a spare RFID tag into the pocket of her winter coat. C'mon. She'd asked him to sneak into a guarded military base. Zig was stupid, but he wasn't that stupid.

Connecting...

The red triangle blinked. A map appeared on-screen.

Location Identified.

Zig squinted at the map, remembering the days when he didn't need reading glasses. He knew those streets. Washington, DC. And that five-sided building.

The Pentagon.

Nola—what the hell are you up to now?

29

Washington, DC

Wide Eyes was unconscious. Then he was awake.

"H-How'd...?" He looked around, blinking, still lost. "Wh-What is this?"

Nola was sitting across from him—sketching in a notepad, legs crisscrossed Indian style—in a leather recliner that was bolted to the floor.

"M-My clothes..." Wide Eyes looked down, realized he was naked. "Why'd you—? You took my—" He looked around some more. "Is this a boat?"

It was. Nola didn't like boats, didn't trust them. But she understood their benefits. Back during World War II, FDR used to have his most secret meetings on a boat—called "the floating White House"—that used to sail around the Potomac. Why? Back then, being on a boat was one of the best ways to guarantee no one else was listening.

It was no different today. In downtown DC, when the military brought in high-ranking officials, they didn't put them up in hotel rooms. Hotels in DC had eyes and ears everywhere—even in the bathrooms, despite what people think. Instead, Uncle Sam owned apartments in Crystal City, townhomes near the Capitol, and yes, even a few boats, which they stored at a little-known dock off the Pentagon Lagoon known as the Columbia Island Marina.

"I know the tricks...taking my clothes...you think this'll intimidate me?" Wide Eyes asked, now realizing his hands were tied to his armchair. He took a breath. He was a pro. Knew enough to not lose his cool. "Nola, I'm not your enemy."

"Now you're lying, Markus," she said, calling him the name she found on his CAC, the common access card that all military use as ID. No driver's license. No credit cards. No insurance papers. Nothing else in his wallet.

He sat up straight as she said *Markus*. *That's his real name.* He was still trying to play cool, but Nola saw the way he was tugging against his restraints, favoring one arm. *Left-handed.* She looked down at her sketch pad, back at him, then back down to add a few more lines. He was built—wide like an elephant—but one of his arms was thicker, more muscular than the other. *Undisciplined.* As she sketched his legs, they weren't nearly as bulky as his upper body; he was skipping leg days in the gym, focusing on his chest, arms—the parts people notice. *Vain.*

"Okay, I get it, you got my wallet. Probably my phone too."

Right about that. Burner phone. No calls or contacts in it.

"I also found your gun, Markus. Beretta M9. Spec Ops favorite," Nola said, happy to have his gun in her pocket. After zapping Zig with the electroshock glove she made by hand, it was fried, its wires burnt. Better to have a real weapon.

On her sketch pad, Nola added shading along Markus's cheeks. He had beautiful cheekbones—like Zig's—though now Nola was cursing herself for still thinking about Zig, much less his facial features.

She didn't like Zig, found him sentimental and self-important. Like a dad who, at his daughter's graduation, shouted her name louder than all the other dads, thinking that it's all for his daughter, not realizing it's all about himself. People like that? Assholes. Nola knew that. But if that was the case, why was she spending so much mental energy thinking about him? Indeed, since the moment Zig got roped into this, she couldn't get him or his daughter, who, yes, she did right by that night, out of her brain. It was, she realized, her own weakness—some leftover memory from her childhood bringing out the most maudlin version of herself.

"Nola, you listening?" Markus interrupted. "If you think I'm answering your questions—" He cut himself off, angled his legs to hide his private parts. "You understand this is torture?"

She understood.

Nola often found herself contemplating the concept of torture. How could she not? At its core, wasn't it just a way of exploiting other people's weaknesses? The problem was, Hollywood movies and overcaffeinated novels always got it wrong. Today, most people thought torture relied on pliers, hacksaws, and a metal tray full of dental tools. In reality, the simpler methods were far more effective. Like taking someone's clothes.

"I told you, I know how it works," Markus added, licking sweat from the dimple of his top lip. "You put on the heat, didn't you?"

Right again. Nola had cranked the thermostat up to 85. Markus was damp and sweaty, his body now convincing his brain that maybe it was time to start panicking. There were other methods too, honed over the past century, like injecting salt water into someone's veins and watching them find new levels of pain. Or making them drink a mix of water and benzene—found in any cigarette lighter—which caused stomach cramps, an onset of the shits, and delirium. Pre–World War II, before we knew about amphetamines, nothing was more effective. Even the operatives with the highest threshold for pain—the Russians, Mexicans, the Vietnamese—it was the only thing they feared. Truth serum was a lie. But with a shot of lighter fluid...once delirium hit? That's when you'd get your answer.

"Think this scares me?" Markus challenged, taking another lick of sweat from his lip. Big as he was—as big as an elephant—he didn't look so fearsome now.

"Markus, I'm not good at talking to people. It's why people don't like me. Why they're afraid of me. But some days...it's smart to be afraid."

Markus shook his head, forcing a grin. "I was in Yemen...in Libya! I was pulling out our boys who got their hands chopped off. You make it as hot as you want! I ain't answering none of your questions!"

He was right about that too. Or at least partly right. But like any good interrogator, Nola knew that once the pain starts sinking in, you can't ask dozens of questions. However. You *can* get a shot at one. With the right lever, you can move anything. Including an elephant.

"That was smart, Markus, carrying this burner phone," Nola said, pulling out the cheap flip phone that she found in Markus's pocket. "What was dumb, though, was parking your car behind the dumpsters and leaving your *real* phone under your floor mats, thinking no one would find it."

Markus stiffened. The dimple in his top lip filled with a brand-new pool of sweat.

"I work at Fort Belvoir. It's my home, Markus. If you really wanted to stay out of sight, you should've hopped the wall. When you bring your car on base, people can see you coming. And see what you brought with you."

From her opposite pocket, Nola pulled out a second phone—also a flip phone, though this one was older, with real wear on it.

Markus's face, his chest, his thin arm and thick one—everything went white. "That's not mine," he stuttered.

"This isn't a court of law, Markus. It's a truth factory." She headed toward him. "So tell me: How do you think your boss will react when he hears that you blew all his security protocols and stupidly left the phone that you last called him on sitting in your car, ripe for the taking? In fact..."—she flipped open the phone, her finger ready to hit the *Send* button—"maybe I should just tell him myself."

"DON'T! *Please!* He would— I got a kid—"

"You don't have a kid. I looked you up. You're about to be kicked out of the truth factory."

"If he finds out— You don't understand!"

"I think we can both agree I very much understand. So answer me," Nola said, leaning in so close they were nose-to-nose. "I need a name. His real name. Tell me who Houdini is."

30

"here's she now?"

"Pentagon. At their marina," Zig said, holding the steering wheel with one hand, his phone with the other. On-screen, he studied the red triangle. "She's moving now. Fast. I think she got into a car."

"Maybe she's leaving," Master Guns said through the speakerphone, his deep baritone echoing through Zig's car. Zig hadn't called him; Master Guns called on his own. But he was still clearly lost. "You think she's meeting someone?"

"I think they already met," Zig said, hitting the gas and steering toward the highway exit. He was less than a mile away, his body pressed against the driver's door as he veered around a loop that led him onto the George Washington Parkway. On his left, the Potomac was a pool of black ink with the Washington Monument in the distance, a tiny exclamation point.

"Ziggy, we don't need you confronting her."

"Who's *we?*"

"Me. *I* don't want you confronting her."

"Then why're you saying *we?*"

"Don't start, Ziggy. I'm trying to keep you safe. And y'know how I know you're not safe? Because we just got a call from Nola's boss..."

"There you go using *we* again."

"You're not listening. Her boss—Barton—he called to check your credentials, Ziggy. Said the parking lot was filled with blood. Said you went to Nola's workplace. Introduced yourself as an investigator. That's *my* job. Not yours."

With his foot still on the gas, Zig headed for the first exit, which dumped him into the parking lot of the marina. On-screen, the red triangle was on his far left. Zig looked out his window. It was late. Dark. He didn't see any cars moving. The lot was as big as a football field. Still too far away.

"You told me you were just going to your old funeral home, the one in Ekron," Master Guns added.

"I know how this looks, but when I got there, when I saw her—I'm telling you, I don't think Nola's our enemy here."

"What'd she say to you, Ziggy—something about your daughter?"

"She didn't." That was the truth, though Zig was now replaying those moments with Nola, the way she was sketching so furiously, the anger that seeped off her...and her clear determination to put her hands around the neck of whoever was behind this. "I'm not wrong about her."

"She put a Taser to your head!"

"If she wanted me dead, I'd be dead. She knew someone was watching. She just needed me to lure him out."

"Oh, to lure him—that's much better!" Master Guns took a breath, like a wolf about to blow Zig's house down. "Y'know what else her boss at the museum said about her? He said Nola was dangerous, that everywhere she went, she brought destruction, which is exactly what we're seeing here. She's making you emotional, Ziggy—and you're putting your life at risk in the process."

"*You tell him we need him now! That's an order!*" a female voice interrupted through the phone, yelling in the background.

Zig knew that voice. Colonel Hsu. Top commander at Dover. And top of the list of people who would have his head if she knew what he was up to.

"You let Hsu listen this entire time?"

"Do you have any idea what's going on here? We're getting hourly calls from the Secret Service, plus half-hourly calls from some Ivy League snot whose first name is Galen. You know who Galen is?"

"I assume someone from the White House."

"He's chief of staff. To the President. And according to him, the leader of the free world wants personal updates on why one of his best friends went down in a plane crash—and apparently also wants to see the body when it's ready for burial. On top of all that, we've got half a dozen fallen service members that need your skills. So yes, get back here. Now."

"Francis, you said you wouldn't— How could you tell Hsu about Nola?"

"*I didn't tell her anything,*" Master Guns whisper-hissed. "*She just walked in. She wants her best mortician on these bodies.*" He said something else, but Zig was barely listening, plowing through the parking lot, which was shaped like an H turned sideways. Zig was on the middle bar of the H, headed straight toward the poorly lit docks.

Once again, Zig glanced to his left, toward the side of the H, which ran parallel to the water. Still nothing.

Maybe Nola stopped or turned around. Zig glanced back at his phone, at the red triangle. The RFID tags never failed, but that didn't mean they were perfect. Especially at high speeds, they could be a few seconds behind.

On-screen, Nola's car was still on his far left, at the top corner of the H, half a football field down, but now it was moving—and picking up speed.

Zig made a quick left, into that same row.

Nola's car appeared from nowhere, flying toward him. Full speed. Her headlights were off.

Skrrrrrrrch!

Zig slammed the brakes. So did Nola. Tires screamed across the asphalt. Zig's car skidded to the right, Nola skidded the other way.

There was a dull thud as Zig plowed over an orange safety py-lon. His car was still moving, still turning, lost in momentum as it spun toward the boats and the water.

"*Ziggy! Ziggy, you okay!?*" Master Guns shouted through the speakerphone.

Zig's car bucked to a stop, his front tires on the dock. Zig kicked his door open. If he lost her again—

"*Nola, don't move!*" Zig shouted, pulling his knife, ready for—

The window of the car—an old outdated Subaru—slowly rolled down. "Y-You came out of nowhere!" an elderly man with thinning black hair insisted.

"Randall!" a female voice scolded. "Ask him how he is! *You okay, sir?*" an older woman added from the passenger seat. Zig saw her smeared lipstick—and the old man fiddling with his pants. "I told him—put your lights on!"

Zig looked into the backseat. No one there. He glanced at his phone. The red triangle was at dead center. Nola should be here. Right here.

Then Zig saw it. Tucked under the Subaru's windshield wiper. A square piece of plastic, no bigger than a postage stamp. The RFID tag.

Nola found it. Of course she found it. And got rid of it.

"Maybe we can avoid calling the authorities. Y'know, for insur-ance purposes," the older man said.

"Yeah, no . . . of course," Zig said, the older woman giving him a thankful wave. "Drive . . . uh . . . drive safely."

"*Ziggy, talk to me! You there!?*" Master Guns shouted through the phone. "*What the hell's going on? You find her?*"

Zig didn't say anything. Not for a long while.

31

At 2 a.m., walking up his front porch, Zig thought he'd be exhausted. But he wasn't. He felt... good, which should've been a sign. If life taught Zig anything, it's that the universe saves its best punches for when you least expect it.

Sure enough, as Zig twisted his key in the lock, he saw a flicker of light under his door. His mouth went dry.

Someone was inside.

Slowly, Zig edged open the door. He heard noise. A woman's voice.

Nola...? he thought, though he quickly heard... in his living room...

The TV was on—some mindless sitcom about how men and women were so different. Zig didn't think he'd left the TV on, but maybe he did. God knows he needed it to sleep. These past few years, silence was a crappy friend.

It was one of the main reasons Zig loved his job. When he was on a case, he was fixing things. He didn't have problems, or at least he wasn't thinking of them. The undertow of loss was coming for other people. Not him.

Upstairs, there were three rooms, Zig's bedroom being the smallest—a private punishment he imposed upon himself that only he knew about.

Two minutes later, Zig was in his backyard, his ritual beer in his hand to help nurse the pain in his head and legs from today's attacks.

"Evening, ladies. Everyone okay?" he called out to his bees.

"*Mmmmmmmmmmmmmm*," the bees sang as Zig sat in his rusty lawn chair, curled in his winter coat, replaying the day's events. For a few minutes, he thought about Nola's friend Kamille and the other victims on the plane, about the scolding he got from Master Guns, about Colonel Hsu's sudden interest in the case, about the President and the Librarian of Congress, and about what the hell this all had to do with cover names that somehow traced back to Harry Houdini.

But more than that, Zig was thinking about today's visit to Ekron, his hometown. His synapses were flooding with old memories stirred awake by the sights and smells where he trained as a mortician, where he buried his dad, where he fell in and out of love, and where he became a husband, a father, and eventually, a mourner. More than anything, he was thinking about how it felt good—or at least felt right—to be so close to Magpie's grave—and how reassuring it felt just to feel that. Still, throughout it all, no matter what path he took down memory lane, he was also thinking of Nola. Not the little girl from years ago, cowering in his backseat. The Nola from today. Here. In the present.

Ten minutes from now, Zig would be upstairs, head on his pillow, hands on his chest, sleeping in that same *at-rest* pose he put people in every day. It wouldn't be until that exact moment, right as sleep tightened its grip, that he'd realize he'd forgotten one ritual—he forgot to check Facebook, forgot to take a look at his ex-wife, forgot to see all the beautiful things happening in her life today. And then Zig would head downstairs, take a quick Facebook look, and think, *What's the harm in that?*

32

Ekron, Pennsylvania
Fifteen years ago

This was Nola when she was twelve.

It was the night of the Girl Scout campout when the can of orange soda exploded.

Royall had pulled her from the hospital in a fiery rage, but over the long drive home, he calmed down.

In the backseat, Nola was curled in a ball, like it was her bed. Silent as ever, she had a white bandage covering her ear, with dried blood splattered across her Girl Scout T-shirt.

"Quick bump," Royall barked as their '65 Chevy turned into the front driveway.

Nola lifted her head off the seat, as if the bump itself might undo her forty new stitches.

"Omigod! LookAtHer! NolaLookAtYou!" cried a heavyset woman with brown hair pulled back in a strict ponytail. The car still hadn't stopped, but she was running with it, practically bursting through the side window. Lydia Konnikova. The troop mom who did car pool for Nola so Royall wouldn't have to drive her to school or to her meetings, which really was the only reason he let her join Girl Scouts. Too bad Lydia was also the town's most notorious gossip.

"How's she doing? I heard stitches!" Lydia said, still dressed in her blue troop vest, her blue-and-white Girl Scout bandanna tied around her neck. Nola noticed that Lydia always answered her own questions. "We sent everyone home. I had to come over. Y'know she saved another scout, right? She saved Maggie! We're going to nominate her for the Scouts' Medal of Honor!" Lydia got her first good look at the bandage. "Was it bad? It looked so bad," she said to Royall. Then to Nola: "You look great, sweetie. Just great!"

The car stopped and Lydia opened the door, extending a hand. "Here, lemme get you inside, hon."

From the front seat, Royall glanced back at Nola with his eyebrows raised.

Nola shot him a look, shaking her head without really moving.

"C'mon, sweetie, gimme your hand," Lydia offered, still leaning into the car.

"I got her," Royall said, opening the car's back door on the driver's side. In one quick scoop, he lifted Nola out of the car and cradled her, carrying her to the door.

"Here, hon, let me—"

"*I got her*," Royall repeated, working hard to keep Lydia at his back, curling Nola close to his chest.

He let the front door slam behind him and carried Nola upstairs, placing her gently on her bed. Then he pulled the covers up to her chin and gave her more medicine, just like the doctors instructed.

33

Dover Air Force Base, Delaware
Today

The following morning, Zig was covered in brain matter and blood.

It was on his plastic face shield; it was on his gloves, which were pulled up to his elbows; it was spattered all across his white, zipped-up Tyvek jumpsuit.

"How's he coming?" fellow mortician Louisa asked.

Zig shook his head. There were five of them in the medical suite, each at their own gurney, each with a different fallen. Overhead, Prince played from the old iPod speaker, swearing he never meant to cause you any sorrow, never meant to cause you any pain. All the morticians knew when it was Louisa's day for music, she played nothing but the sad Prince songs, plus her favorite fun ones.

Usually Zig got the hardest case. Or the most important. Today, he had both.

For three hours, he'd been at it, but even by Dover standards, presidential best friend and Librarian of Congress Nelson Rookstool was a mess. Fallen #2,357.

The hardest part was aligning his head back onto his broken spine, so he wouldn't look like an abandoned marionette. Set the head wrong, and nothing else looks right.

"We'll get you there," Zig whispered to Rookstool's lifeless corpse.

The back of Rookstool's neck, the back of his arms, all of it was burned, though not as charred as Kamille's body was two nights ago. Whatever caused the fire on the plane, Rookstool was farther away from it, sitting in the front row.

According to the medical examiners, Rookstool's cause of death was a broken neck (pretty standard for a plane crash). But as Zig looked inside the interior wall of the ribcage, he found a shard of pointed plastic—beige—the size of a pen cap.

Zig yanked it out. It was jagged. A stray piece of the fold-down tray table, which shattered on impact, stabbing Rookstool in his seat. Happened all the time. When you free-fall four hundred feet from the sky, nothing lands gracefully.

"Broken tray table?" a voice asked behind him—one of the other morticians, Wil with one L. Zig never liked people with misspelled common names. Jayson with a Y. Zakk with two Ks. It was the same here. Wil always left work at 4 p.m. and still sometimes referred to the fallen as "stiffs." *No heart.* "How bad'd it get him?" Wil added.

"Bad as it gets," Zig said, still staring at the shard of plastic.

"Same result either way," Wil said, forcing a dark laugh.

Zig didn't laugh back. For the past few hours, he'd been focused on the big picture—setting Rookstool's head, cleaning out his chest—but as with any jigsaw puzzle, once the main border's done, you finally start looking at the rest of the pieces: the creases on Rookstool's face, the crow's-feet around his eyes, even the width of his fit-but-not-as-fit-as-they-used-to-be biceps. Middle age always took a toll. For Zig, it was far too familiar.

Turning toward the medical rolling cart, Zig eyed Rookstool's ID, which was clipped to the side of the cart as a visual guide. Round face. Tired eyes. The gray hair made him look older, but— Zig rechecked the date of birth. October. Same year as Zig.

Same age.

Zig shouldn't be surprised. These days, so many of the senior officers that Zig worked on were close to his age. But every once in a while, a body type hit a bit too close to home, leaving Zig with the same feeling you get when you find out a friend has cancer: *I'm gonna start eating better, taking better care of myself.* Today, though, Zig felt the opposite. Despite the throbbing in his head and the pain in his legs from yesterday's attacks—or perhaps because of them—Zig felt *younger* today, younger than he'd felt in a long time.

"Ziggy, you got a moment?" Louisa interrupted.

"Yeah, no, sure." Heading for Louisa's gurney, he asked, "You have Vacca?" though he knew the answer. Since the moment Zig arrived, he'd been waiting to take a peek at all three of the so-called Houdini assistants: Rose Mackenberg, Clifford Eddy, and Amedeo Vacca. According to their files, they all supposedly worked at the Library of Congress. Time to learn the real story.

"Nose collapsed, everything collapsed. I hate plane crashes," Louisa said, handing Zig a metal tool that looked like a coat hanger. In fact, it *was* a coat hanger, cut down to just the curve at the top. "He's supposed to have a bump on his nose, but when I—" She stopped herself, never one to complain. On the table, Vacca's face was pretty much intact, though his nose looked like a deflated balloon. "His parents were there today. Two sisters too. Just want to get this right."

Zig nodded, taking a look at the ID photo of Vacca that Louisa had clipped to her own rolling cart. Vacca was a baby, late twenties at the most. Looked like a young Stallone. Hangdog eyes. Meaty face. And sure enough, crooked nose.

"You made the bump too low," Zig said, carefully re-bending the coat hanger. On a corpse, rebuilding an arm, a leg, even a shoulder is easy as long as you have enough modeling clay. Noses and faces required a subtle touch—and to get it just right, it took an artist.

"Now you're just showing off," Louisa said.

"Only if it works," Zig replied, scanning the rest of the body. Unlike Rookstool, Vacca was big, with a wide chest and muscles like a wrestler. Or a Navy SEAL. On the medical cart, Vacca's ID photo listed him as *Aide to Librarian Rookstool.* Zig made a mental note. Since when were librarian aides built like bodyguards?

"What're you staring at?" Louisa asked.

"I'm not."

Louisa made a noise underneath her filter mask. "Seems pretty beefy for a librarian."

"I hadn't noticed."

"Well, y'know who did notice? Your pal Master Guns. Was here first thing this morning, making sure everything was just right."

Zig twisted the coat hanger tighter around his finger. Prince was singing a new song, about how life was just a party and parties weren't meant to last.

"Ziggy, I know you've got personal ties to this case—"

"That's not even—"

"Please don't lie to me. When it comes to caring about a case, it's not a bad thing. In fact, it might even be a good thing."

With an artful push of his thumb, Zig inserted the re-bent coat hanger into Vacca's nostril, where its wire frame added new structure and lifted his deflated nose like a circus tent.

"I take back what I said. *Now* you're showing off," Louisa added. "You could've just—"

"*Psst.*"

The sound came from their left. The doors to the medical suite were closed, but even through the translucent glass, Zig knew that round silhouette anywhere.

"I think your friend who runs the vending machines is trying to be subtle," Louisa said.

"Are you playing *Prince* in there?" Dino called out through the door. "I feel like that's somehow ruining Prince for me."

Hitting a button, Zig opened the automated doors and pulled the O2 mask from his face, but never stepped into the actual hallway. The embalming fluids had to stay in the sterilized suite. "Dino, what're you doing here?"

"*Jiminy Christmas!*" Dino instinctively recoiled from the smell, holding his nose and stepping back from the threshold. "No matter how many times I'm here— Good God, man, it's on your mask—

that was by your *mouth*! You're wearing glops of dead by your mouth!"

"Dino, this better be an emergency."

"She said it was."

She? Zig asked with a look.

Dino nodded, still holding his nose. "Your friend. From the FBI."

Zig knew who he meant. Waggs.

"She tried calling you. I told her you don't carry your phone while you're working."

Zig glanced back over his shoulder, checking to see who else was listening. Louisa, Wil, and the other morticians were turned the other way, focused back on their respective fallen.

"She find something?" Zig whispered.

Dino gave him that look he had on that night when they met those twins at the bar.

"I need at least another hour in here," Zig said.

"Don't you think this might be more impor—?"

"I need another hour," Zig insisted, pointing a thumb back into the medical suite. Dino knew better than to argue. Rookstool had a wife; two little grandkids. Zig would never leave a deceased while a family was waiting for closure. "Tell her I'll call her in an hour."

There was a pneumatic hiss as the doors swung shut, and Dino headed up the hallway, already dialing Waggs's number.

"Mr. Kanalz . . . ?" a female voice called out as Dino turned the corner.

Dino looked up, spotting an Asian woman in full officer uniform. She had the most penetrating gaze he'd ever seen.

"You have a moment?" Colonel Hsu said.

"Actually, I'm—"

"It wasn't a question. This way, Mr. Kanalz."

Dino stuffed his phone in his pocket and headed hesitantly to her office. "Can you tell me what this is about?" Dino asked.

"Don't play stupid. It just insults both of us."

34

Homestead, Florida
Eleven years ago

This was Nola when she was fifteen.

"Pencils down," the teacher warned.

Nola kept scribbling.

"Pencils down."

Nola lifted her chin, her eyes narrowing and disappearing in a black hole of dark eyeliner that only a fifteen-year-old could think was acceptable. She was in her usual spot, in the back row, in her usual uniform: wifebeater tank, boy jeans (secondhand, which her dad hated), and Doc Martens (brand-new, which her dad hated even more). *"Me?"* she asked.

The teacher made a face. There were only three other kids in the room, all of them boys. Nola was the one girl, which is how it usually was in the unfortunately acronymed CSI, the Center for School Improvement, the place for students who got kicked out of class, which is exactly what happened when Damien D'Abruzzo burped in his hand and threw it at Nola, who immediately socked him in the face.

Years ago, both would've been suspended, or forced to do community service, like washing jeeps at Homestead's local military base. These days, educators were convinced that the only way to help a student was to keep them *off* the streets. Hence CSI—locking kids up in daylong detention.

"So I'm supposed to just sit here and do nothing?" Nola challenged.

"Blame *The Breakfast Club*," said the teacher, Ms. Sable, a stubby fiftysomething woman with three hidden tattoos, wary green eyes, and dyed black hair that was supposed to be Bettie Page but looked more like Betty Rubble. She hated using her free period to staff CSI, but it paid time and a half, which was the only way to afford the aide who watched her Alzheimer's-stricken mother. "Nola, I'm not saying it makes sense to me either, but rules are rules. Now. Pencils. *Down.*"

"Or what?"

Ms. Sable rolled her eyes. She had three older kids. All boys, and boys were animals. She didn't take their crap; she certainly wasn't taking this crap. She moved closer. "Nola, see me after class."

"I don't have class. I'm locked in here with you all d—"

In a blur, Ms. Sable yanked Nola's notebook from her desk.

"Hey—! That's mine!"

"Was. See me after class," Sable said, heading back to her desk and flipping through the pages of the book, more out of habit than anything else. Then she saw what was actually inside. Ms. Sable stopped, turning back to Nola. "Nola. Is this *your* book?"

Nola went silent. Had she left something in the notebook?

"Nola, did you draw this?" Sable asked, holding the notebook open, like a *Playboy* centerfold. Across two pages was an elaborate pencil drawing of a fat drooling goblin with leathery wings and a rusty broadsword. The goblin was feasting on a human arm, and below it were the words:

HOMESTEAD'S LOUDEST THRASH METAL BAND!!
THE ONE!! THE ONLY!!
PRETENTIOUS CRITICS!!!!

"Nola, did you draw this or not?"

It'd been eight years since Nola was abandoned by her adoptive family and handed over to Royall. Eight years of his screaming. Eight years of his mood swings. Eight years of digging holes hidden by different-sized kiddie pools in different-sized backyards. And eight years of sleeping in the car on Tuesdays and Saturdays.

But of all the damage Royall had done, the worst was simply this: She got used to it. It was commonplace. Faced with that tone of questioning—Royall's primary tone in all conversations—Nola's years of conditioning gave her only one logical response.

"What'd I do wrong?"

Ms. Sable was still staring down at the goblin drawing, barely hearing the question. Nola noticed her posture shift.

"Nola, this is beautiful."

Confused, Nola searched the teacher's face, looking for the lie, the tell, the flaw in her words. Ms. Sable's nails were a mess (she bit them); her lower teeth were crooked (needed braces, couldn't afford them); and just above her earrings were two other holes, long since closed (why would someone let an earring-hole close?). Still, try as she might... It made no sense—there had to be a tell in there somewhere. But Nola couldn't find it.

"Nola, do you know what I teach here?"

"Video production."

"And art. I teach art. Y'know what that means?"

Nola shook her head.

"It means I know what I'm talking about. You have a real knack for this, girl."

Nola said nothing. And then, "I take woodshop. I don't have art."

"You do now. Sixth period. Same smelly room as woodshop. Be there tomorrow." Ms. Sable tossed the notebook back. It slapped against Nola's desk.

At the front of the class, the three boys were turned in their seats, staring. Nola lowered her chin quickly, closing her notebook and hating them for witnessing this feeling she was feeling, this feeling that was twisting her stomach in a grip of confusion, nausea, and . . . something else, something lighter, something she didn't have a word for. For the rest of Nola's life, she'd carry this moment with her, for when she needed it. And she'd never forget the five words she suddenly noticed, carved into the desk: *Ms. Sable sux donkey dicks*. She would've laughed, but no way was she letting the boys see that.

This was Nola at fifteen—the very first time someone told her she was good at something.

35

M arkus was naked. He was inside, on a boat. He was tied to an armchair and blindfolded.

"W-Who's there? Can— Is someone there?" Markus sat up in his seat. There was a muffled creak. He listened intently. On his right, by the door.

Another creak. Outside.

"Hey! *Hey, I'm in here!* I need help! *Can you hear me!?*"

Markus thrashed, his naked legs sticking to the chair from his own dried urine. He was groggy, still in pain from what that girl— Nola—from what Nola had done to him. Shoved something in his throat. Knocked him out.

"I'm in here! Please! Help! I need—!"

There was a pop in the air. On his right. The door opened.

"Thank God!" Markus shouted. He'd never been more wrong.

"I-I thought I'd be stuck here until the morning," Markus said as someone arrived. "I was worried th— Thank God you're here."

Sitting up like a star pupil, Markus stuck out his chin, waiting for his rescuer to pull off his blindfold.

On his face, the black bandanna stayed where it was.

Confused, Markus bent his head back, trying to peek underneath. It was still too dark, but Markus could feel a shift in the air. Someone slowly moving toward him.

"Whoever you are, I hear y—!"

Something swiped at Markus's face, slicing his blindfold as it fell away.

Markus blinked a few times, his eyes adjusting to the light. But his expression fell when he saw...

"You gave us a scare there, Markus," said a broad-shouldered Native American woman with jet black hair pulled tight in a ponytail. Her crimson brown skin came from her father's Shoshone side; ice blue eyes came from her mother.

Markus hadn't seen her in nearly a year, not since that fiasco in Montana.

"Teresa, please..." Markus begged, smart enough to call her by her real name rather than the one they used behind her back. *The Curtain.* As in, when The Curtain comes... it's all over.

"I-I swear on my life, Teresa... I didn't say anything!" he insisted, again using her real name and again thinking he was smart. If he were really smart, he'd know that when it came to being called *The Curtain*, she relished it.

"Your friends are worried about you," The Curtain said, standing perfectly still, shoulders back, even with the sway of the boat. Her father taught her the benefits of good posture, just like he taught her how to pitch a good curve, tie a proper fishing knot, even how to skin a rabbit without a knife. Growing up, The Curtain knew her dad wanted a boy and got a girl. But when her mom's drug use got worse and turned her into something they no longer recognized, Dad kept his daughter right by his side, storming off the reservation so she'd never be "one of them Indians that sits around with gambling money and sucks off the tit of the tribe."

It was The Curtain's earliest memory—at seven years old, ducking down in the back of Dad's truck, escaping in the middle of the night. It wasn't until years later that she finally learned what Dad did before they ran off that night. But to this day, it was her father's most potent lesson: The world eats the weak; hit the hyenas before they feast.

"Markus, remember that restaurant we ate at in Montana? The place with those wonderful buffalo burgers?"

"Teresa, please... You know I didn't say anything."

"What was the name of that place?" The Curtain tapped her palm against her thigh, her hand turned so he couldn't see the ancient weapon she was holding. It was called a *bagh nakh*, also known as a tiger's claw, made of four curved metal blades that are fixed to a crossbar that you grip in your palm. The Curtain used it to slice Markus's blindfold, though it also ripped open a cut on his cheek.

"It had one of those kooky names, like *Tequila Mockingbird*, but not that."

"I-I swear on my nieces...not a word...I didn't say a word!" Markus insisted, finally seeing two drops of his own blood as they hit his lap, dripping from his cheek. He tried to wipe them away, but his hands were still tied to the chair.

"Remember that corn with the goat cheese in it? That was divine," The Curtain added, picking up Markus's clothes from the floor. The pockets of his jeans were empty. He knew not to carry a wallet. His burner phone was on a nearby counter. But as she checked the other pockets...

"Markus, where's your other phone?"

"I'd never— She asked me all these questions... I didn't tell her anything!"

"Your real phone, Markus. Where's your real phone?"

"I-I left it in my car. I swear. It's not here." He was sweating now, the backs of his thighs again sticking to the chair.

"This girl. Nola. I know she found your car. Now she has your phone, doesn't she?" The Curtain said as she scanned the rest of the cabin. On the bar was an empty glass and a small plastic lid, like you'd see on a prescription bottle. "She drugged you."

"She asked questions. But I didn't answer her! She knew about Houdini. Asked for him by name! But I didn't say nothin'! Not a word! You know I wouldn't do that, right?"

The Curtain stared at Markus, her body still, like she wasn't even breathing.

"Teresa, *please!*"

She took a slow step toward him.

Tears flooded his eyes; snot ran from his nose. "*Please* tell me you believe me!"

"I believe you, Markus."

Exhaling, Markus tipped his head back in relief—at which point, Teresa's hand swiped at the air, her tiger's claw slicing a deep gash into Markus's throat, severing his carotid artery.

In the movies, blood sprays everywhere when you slit someone's throat. In reality, it follows the beat of your heart, pumping out and raining down in a slow waterfall. Markus tried to get out a few final words. But he couldn't.

Pulling out her own burner phone, The Curtain dialed a number, never taking her eyes off Markus's now-lifeless body. It was another of her dad's best lessons—and an army lesson too. Make sure the job is done.

There was a click as someone picked up. They didn't say a word.

Neither did The Curtain. Message sent.

Then, to The Curtain's surprise...

"It was the girl, yes? Nola Brown?" asked the man with a voice like a woodchipper.

"Don't worry," The Curtain said. "I'm on her."

More silence. Another message sent. *You better be.* Without another word, both hung up.

Riverhouse Grill, The Curtain thought to herself as she headed for the door of the boat. That was the restaurant in Montana. Fantastic barbeque.

36

Mr. Kanalz, I understand you stock our candy machines?"

"And manage the Kingpin Café, where the soup of the day is always cheese fries," Dino said.

Colonel Hsu didn't laugh. Didn't smile. Didn't even blink as she sat there, both hands clamped together on her desk, which held a stack of pamphlets about depression in the military and a gold watch engraved "Hsu 2028," a gag gift from her staff for her eventual run for President. "I've been to the Kingpin."

"I've never seen you there, Colonel. What's your order?"

"I send my assistant."

"Wait. Are you the person who, every few weeks, orders the flatbread with just loads of olives, extra ketchup on top? That person *worries* me."

"That person *should* worry you. I'm grilled cheese with tomato and avocado on whole wheat bread."

"That's a reasonable order."

"I'm a reasonable person, Mr. Kanalz. More reasonable than you might realize."

Dino shifted in his seat. If she was playing nice—

"My assistant told me they call you the Candyman around here. That's a great name. *Candyman.*"

"Colonel, if there's something you want to ask me—"

"Mr. Kanalz, I'm sure you're aware that there's only one set of candy machines here in our particular building. In the breakroom. Just that room," Hsu said. "And yet, over the past day and a half, security shows that you've been here nearly half a dozen times."

Before Dino could say a word, she added, "In fact, when I looked closer at it, yesterday, Mr. Kanalz—when the Secret Service was scanning this place before the President's arrival—*you* were one of the few people swiped in. That was pretty early in the morning."

"That's my job description: *Stock the machines pretty early in the morning.*"

"What also caught my eye is that, according to those security records, you were in this building around the same time your friend Zig got knocked in the head."

Dino sat up straight, annoyed. "Are you accusing me of something?"

"I'm just pointing out facts."

"Zig *got me* this job. He's a brother to me."

"I'm thrilled to hear that, Mr. Kanalz—especially because we've all been worried about our friend Zig lately."

"You should tell him that."

"I'd love to. But that's the problem. I tried calling him yesterday afternoon, and he wouldn't pick up. We even sent someone to his house. No one could find him. It was like he just disappeared."

"So talk to him now."

"I'd love that as well, but as you saw, he's been in the embalming room for nearly four hours. And here I am with so many questions about where Zig was once Sergeant Brown's body shipped out of here yesterday."

For the first time, Dino just sat there, saying nothing. Hsu's hands were still clamped together. Like someone praying.

"You've heard her name before, haven't you, Mr. Kanalz? *Nola Brown?*"

Again, Dino just sat there.

"What about the name Markus Romita? Ever hear of him?"

"I don't know what you're talking about."

"Markus Romita. From Tucson, Arizona. Trained as Special Forces, then got discharged. For a preexisting personality disorder."

"That usually means someone was an asshole."

"Maybe. But imagine our surprise when Markus was found dead two hours ago on a boat...one that was docked in the Pentagon marina. Throat slit. Perfect carotid neck cut. Like a pro—or someone who knows their anatomy. Any morticians come to mind?"

"Ma'am, you really think Zig would—?"

"I'm not accusing anyone of anything. I just want to know where Zig was last night."

"He wasn't slaughtering people on a boat, I can tell you that."

"And I want to believe you, Mr. Kanalz. But according to some grainy security footage that we're just starting to sift through, a driver who looks a lot like Zig was spotted in that same marina last night."

Dino again went silent.

"Mr. Kanalz, I pulled your employment records. Every month, half your check gets garnished to the IRS. Unpaid taxes for nearly three years, with foreclosures on...looks like, one, two, three, four different homes."

"That has nothing to do with— Those were legitimate investments!"

"I understand how the housing bubble worked. When it burst, my sister-in-law made the same exact mess, meaning my brother is still pulling extra night shifts as a dispatcher in the fire station. What I'm driving at, Mr. Kanalz, is I know how important this job is to you. So if you know anything about Zig...or Nola Brown...or about anything that's going on...we're just trying to help."

"By what? By calling me in here and gripping your hands together like some finicky villain in a straight-to-video Nickelodeon movie? You realize I'm gonna tell him everything you've said, right? Zig's my family."

"I'm not questioning his commitment to you. I'm questioning his commitment to *us*."

"Then you know nothing about him. So if you want to fire me for paying back taxes, fire me. Otherwise, if you've got any problems with my work, report me to the contracting officer's rep. Otherwise, I've got a lunch rush to prepare for," Dino said. "Oh, and putting avocado on grilled cheese? You're turning a good sandwich into a shitty one. Show the grilled cheese some respect."

Without another word, Dino headed for the door, slamming it as he left.

At her desk, Colonel Hsu stared down at her watch, at the words *Hsu 2028*. For a moment, she sat there, hands still clasped. Then she pulled out her phone and texted two words to a number that was unlisted.

Your turn.

37

Y ou alone or not?" Waggs asked.

Approaching the door scanner, Zig swiped his ID, the lock clicked, and he pushed his way into Room 028. *Uniform Prep.*

"All alone," Zig said, eyeing four faceless, stark white mannequins at the center of the room. Each wore a different uniform: Army, Navy, Air Force, Marines, like you'd see in a department store. On Zig's right were dark wood display cases filled with every military badge, ribbon, and medal you can imagine—Purple Hearts, Silver Stars, Distinguished Service Crosses—each encased in plastic, each hanging on its own wire hook, reminding Zig of when he was little, on a trip to Hershey Park, flipping through a display rack of kid-sized personalized license plates, searching the alphabet for his own name. Back then, his mom was still strong and healthy.

"You in your office?" Waggs asked.

"Uniforms," Zig said, scanning the single sheet of paper he was holding in his other hand. At Dover, it was called a rip sheet— a printout of all the medals and badges a fallen service member would wear in their casket. In this room, uniform specialists would assemble and iron the uniform, collect and polish the medals, and get everything ready to dress the corpse. Today, though, Zig decided to give it a little personal touch.

At the top of the rip sheet was one name:

ROOKSTOOL, NELSON
VIP/LIBRARIAN OF CONGRESS

1. Superior Civilian Service Award
No surprise, Zig thought, pulling a bright silver medal with a crimson ribbon from its wire hook. Presidential friends always got good hardware.

2. President's Award for Distinguished Federal Civilian Service
Also no surprise. Eisenhower established the award so Presidents could single out government service. But the third and final medal on the list...

3. Secretary of the Army Award for Valor
Zig paused, reaching the wire rack and pulling out the gold medal with its red-and-blue ribbon. "Waggs, did Rookstool ever serve?"

"Pardon?"

"Nelson Rookstool. Librarian of Congress. Yesterday, when his body came off the plane, he was received as a civilian, but was he a vet? Afghanistan? Iraq? I don't know, even National Guard or something?"

Through the phone came the hushed clicking of a keyboard. "Nope. Never in the military," Waggs finally said. "Nothing in the Bureau, CIA, or other agencies either. He's full muggle his whole life. Why you asking?"

Zig pulled the gold medal close, eyeing the engraved five-pointed star. Above it was the word *VALOR.* "They're awarding Rookstool a medal for valor."

Waggs didn't say a word. She didn't have to. Even in the world of secret squirrels, medals for valor were for bravery, which usually meant combat—or at least for doing something in the field.

"You think when Rookstool was on that plane," Waggs began,

"whatever he was doing in Alaska—he wasn't just there as a librarian?"

"That's the question. Maybe he really *was* bringing literacy to rural Eskimo communities. Or maybe, considering the names of the dead Houdini assistants who were staffing him on the plane, he was on a mission we still haven't figured out yet."

"Speak for yourself," Waggs shot back.

"Wait. You found the Houdini folks?"

"And I found Markus Romita."

"Who?"

"Last night at Fort Belvoir. The guy who attacked you outside Nola's office. Wide eyes. Hit you with a telescoping baton."

"How'd you—?"

"His CAC," Waggs explained, referring to his military ID. "He had to swipe it to get into Fort Belvoir. But when I checked their records, Markus was the only visitor on base who didn't hand his guest pass back at the end of the night. Find him and you'll have your best shot for figuring out who's really doing these Houdini tricks."

"Waggs, you're getting sneakier in your old age, y'know that?"

"You said Nola ambushed him. I'm guessing she dumped him in his trunk and drove off base."

"Any idea where he might be now?"

Waggs paused. "Would you be surprised if I said, 'A morgue in Virginia'?"

"Oh no."

"Oh yes. Police found Markus dead early this morning—tied to a chair on a boat..."

"...in the Pentagon marina. I was there last night."

"Which probably means that when they run their security tapes, cops are going to be knocking on your door, anxious to ask a few questions."

"I never touched him...didn't even know he was there..."

"Said the man who drove there alone and therefore has no alibi.

I told you from the start, Ziggy, you're headfirst in quicksand. Nola slit his throat."

"No way. She wouldn't—"

"Do *not* tell me this girl is innocent. Everywhere she goes, she brings one thing with her: Death. Death on a plane. Death on a boat. She's like a walking Agatha Christie novel, and you're playing the part of the plucky and well-meaning investigator who dies right before the ending because he's too blind to see the noose that's wrapping around his neck."

Staring down at Rookstool's shiny medal for valor, Zig watched his own face twist and shift in its reflection. Did he think that Nola was innocent, incapable of any harm? Of course not. His head was still ringing from that zapping she gave him. Plus Nola's boss's words: *She's a gun. A weapon.* But ever since Zig saw her back in Ekron—at the funeral home—the way Nola reacted to the note and the plane crash... Some things can't be lied about. Whatever else was going on, no way did Nola put that plane down. *Nola, you were right. Keep running.* Deep down, he knew it now more than ever. That was a warning.

Right there, Zig felt an old thought coming back. Previously, he called it a *need*. But now he saw it more clearly, recognizing it from so many mourners. When it came to Nola, Zig didn't just have a need to know what happened. He had a need to see her in her best light, a need to prove her innocent, a need to prove he was right about her that night at the campfire. It was, he knew, a blind spot. But that didn't mean it was wrong.

"She knew what she was doing after Markus's attack," Zig added. "If Nola wanted me dead, I'd be dead already."

"And that makes her a hero? That she slit *his* throat but not *yours*?"

"For all we know, Markus is the one who put the plane down!"

At that, Waggs went silent.

"Oh, Waggs, you looked Markus up, didn't you? If you found something—"

"What I found is he's no pushover. Markus was Special Forces, spent some time at Fort Lewis, then an ugly discharge—though he was clearly still working for someone since as of yesterday, he had an active ID card."

"And if he had an active ID..."

"...then we can see his last assignment. Took me a while, but apparently, he was working on something called Operation Bluebook."

"Never heard of it."

"No one had. I checked every database—JWICS, JIANT, even Room 11," she added, referencing the cyberwarriors who hacked for the NSA, CIA, and a few secret others. "This was clearly above what's usually above top secret. All I was able to find was an address in Washington, DC. 278 H Street SW."

"Sounds like a storefront."

"It is. It's a business that's been around since the early 1960s."

"And it has something to do with Houdini?"

"You tell me. 278 H Street is home of the Conjuring Arts Eclectic Studio."

"Alakazam."

"The last place your attacker was stationed? It's an antique magic shop."

38

Homestead, Florida
Eleven years ago

This was Nola when she was fifteen.

Once again, she was sitting in the back—in the art room—on a three-legged stool that wobbled.

"Take one, pass them back," Ms. Sable said, handing a stack of index cards to Sophie Michone, the smiley student government treasurer who would one day grow up to be the person in her office who, when everyone played Powerball together, would be the one who got left out.

"Pass 'em back," Smiling Sophie repeated to the other students at her four-person workbench. Then her best friend, Missy F., passed them to Harold at his four-person workbench, who passed them to Lazy Eye Justin at his four-person workbench, who walked them to Nola, sitting at her own four-person workbench all by herself.

"Don't even try to touch me, Scuzzy," Justin whispered as he handed Nola the stack of index cards, then flinched as she reached for them. "I heard they put you here to keep you from fighting."

"Eat a fart," Nola growled.

This wasn't the first time Nola had been singled out for her art. When she was five, her kindergarten teacher told the LaPointes that she was coloring "too hard," breaking all the crayons, especially the purples. But even then, Nola was determined. *If it's purple, it's gonna be <u>purple</u>.*

"Everyone have one? Good," Ms. Sable said, waving her own index card like a white flag. "On this card, I want you to write down the most important thing in your life. For some of you that will be your family; others—I know—you're teenagers, you hate your family. It can be something different: A boyfriend. Girlfriend. Your dog. A grandparent. A prized possession. The. Most. Important. Thing," she reiterated. "Also, there's no judgment here. It can be a personal philosophy, it can be something you love—*Harold, don't look at Sophie for help. Write your own answer.* And I know, this is high school—your favorite thing can be sex for all I care," she added as the room let out a few nervous giggles. "Or it can just be the one item in your house that you'd grab if everything caught fire."

"Can I ask a question?" Smiling Sophie said, Nola noticing that Sophie always prefaced her questions with permission for those questions. "Will anyone else see what we write?"

"Glad you asked," Ms. Sable said, her arms now crossed, her card tucked into her armpit. "No. You will never show *me* what's on your card. You will never show *anyone* what's on your card. If it makes you feel better, you can shred it and throw it in the trash for all I care."

"Then why even bother writing it down?" Missy F. asked.

"Because this is *art*! Art doesn't exist in your head. It exists when you express it, when you let it out—when your pencil hits paper; when your brush hits the canvas. But to create good art, well . . . whatever you write on this little index card? The most important thing in your life? That's your *point of view.*"

Ms. Sable stopped, letting the words sink in, something that Nola noticed she did a lot, using silence to make you think. In Nola's own house, sudden silence meant one thing. Anger. And an imminent explosion.

"Whatever you draw," Ms. Sable continued, "it *must* relate to what's on this card. Your point of view is what makes you special, it's what makes your art special. Only *you* can view the world your way. That sounds like a yoga quote, but it's gospel. Does that make sense?"

Nola watched the other students shift in their seats. It didn't make sense to most of them. Nola wasn't sure it made sense to her either.

"*For example*," Ms. Sable added, "when I did this same exercise in art school, I was about to get married. On my card, I wrote: *Being Married*. Don't judge," she warned as the class again nervously laughed. "God forgive me, but back then, all my art had two of everything in it. Two palm trees, two rivers, once I even painted two full moons, which doesn't even make scientific sense—especially when you consider how quickly that marriage fell apart. However! *That* was my point of view."

Missy F.'s hand shot into the air. "So it has to be something you love?"

"It absolutely does *not* have to be something you love. It can be something you want, something you dream of, something you can't stop thinking about. The only requirement is that it is *what you care about most* on a daily basis."

Waste of time, Nola thought, glancing to her left, where Justin the jerkwad was rolling his eyes, shooting a look at one of his friends.

"Waste of time," Justin whispered to Sophie.

For a moment, Nola sat there, realizing just how powerful her own spite of Justin's spite was. She stared down at her index card, tempted to doodle a picture of Justin, maybe with a few knives stuffed into his eyes. Instead . . . she looked up at Ms. Sable, who quickly made eye contact.

Just try it, her teacher pleaded with a glance.

Justin snickered, whispering something to his friends.

Grabbing the card, Nola scribbled something quick, then folded it up and stuffed it in her pocket.

Thank you, Ms. Sable said with another glance. "Everyone else, when your card's filled out, take one of these," she added, handing out 9x12 pieces of sketch paper. "Whatever you wrote, here's where you put it to work. Make some art."

For the next forty minutes, Nola kept her head down, hunched over her paper as she sketched, stippled, and colored her newest creation.

At the front of the room, Ms. Sable took the teacher's stroll that all teachers take, pausing over a few students, offering silent nods, but never coming near the back of the room, never coming near Nola.

As the bell rang, Nola was still drawing, her pencil moving at hyperspeed.

Driiiiiiing.

Nola looked up. Ms. Sable wasn't at the front. She was behind her, staring down. Unreadable.

"It's not done yet," Nola insisted.

"Nola..." Ms. Sable said, and already Nola could hear the insults, the mistakes, everything bad that was about to be mentioned. "... I don't know what to say. Nice work. Beautiful start."

"*Beautiful?*" Nola stuttered, not even realizing she said it out loud, like it was a word she didn't understand, or from another language.

On the page was a glorious sky, wide and inviting, with ethereal clouds that were rendered with such uncanny, photorealistic detail, they looked like you could touch them. On the far right, so small you barely noticed it, was a lone bird.

"Blackbird?" Ms. Sable asked.

"Raven."

Ms. Sable nodded. Cliché for sure, but c'mon. Nola was fifteen and a goth. Also, there was something familiar about the raven, something elegant. It was in mid-flight, its wings wide as it arced up through the sky, like nothing could stop it.

"Okay, I kinda want to salute this," Ms. Sable said, putting a hand on Nola's back and adding a squeeze that was the closest thing to a hug that Nola could remember.

"Toldja you have a knack," Ms. Sable said.

Nola felt a smile lift her cheeks. In the coming months, especially when things went bad, Ms. Sable would become the most important person in young Nola's life.

But of all the things she'd find out about Nola, Ms. Sable would never learn about the six words that were written on the index card stuffed in Nola's pocket:

He watches me when I sleep.

39

Washington, DC
Today

Y ou look lost," a female voice called out.

"No, I was just—" Zig paused, looking around. "Okay, I'm definitely lost," he said, scanning the pockmarked street that dead-ended here—in a parking lot for a beat-up soccer field. "You don't happen to know where 278 H Street is?"

"Store or apartment?" asked a young African American girl, thirteen years old, earbuds still in her ears as she walked off the field.

"Store. The Conjuring Arts."

"Wha?"

"It's a magic shop."

"Yesyesyes...the place where all those white people got jumped."

Zig turned, cocking his head.

"I'm kidding. I'm funny," the girl said, pretending to laugh at her own joke, but really still laughing at Zig. "This isn't a bad neighborhood, y'know."

She was right about that. A decade ago, this area was dominated by drug dealers, gangs, and vacant lots. But when Major League Baseball announced Nationals Park five blocks away, a neighborhood sprouted from nowhere, filling the Ballpark District with new apartment buildings, shops, and even a five-acre waterfront park with views to rival Georgetown. Nevertheless, that didn't mean there weren't a few back alleys and side streets that should still be avoided as the sun started to fade, including this one, on the back of the junior high school.

"That your school?" Zig asked, wondering if Hsu had finally realized he snuck off base.

"I go to private school," the girl said dryly. "St. Peter." For a moment, she stood there, twirling her earbuds like she was enjoying herself. "You still looking for that magic shop?"

"More than I can possibly express right now."

She laughed and pointed to her left. "Head toward Third Street. Between the tall apartment buildings, there's a little side alley. It's sorta smushed in there, next to the old pawnshop that no one ever goes to."

Two blocks later, Zig spotted a hand-painted sign bolted to a lamppost: *Pawn by Yolanda 2—This Way!*

The sun was fading, the sky a gray purple, but even from here, Zig could see what was waiting for him. Down the narrow street was a line of painted white brick storefronts, all at the base of two-story row houses, like old five-and-dimes. Two were closed, protected by metal roll-down grates. But the third . . .

Zig headed straight for it. In the front window was a vintage neon sign shaped like a fanned deck of cards showing an ace of spades. The neon was dusty, like it hadn't been lit in years. Same with the faded *Open* sign that looked like it hadn't been touched since Nixon was President, which Zig was starting to realize was probably the point.

Some places were designed to make sure you look right past them.

The *Conjuring Arts Eclectic Studio* was one of them.

"You ready?" Zig asked into his phone after dialing a quick number.

"Listening and recording," Dino said on the other line. "Just say the word *parachute*. I'll call the cops."

Nodding to himself, Zig slid his phone into his breast pocket and stepped inside the magic shop.

40

Arlington, Virginia

Nola knew this parking lot was safe. Overhead, she didn't need to check for surveillance cameras. There weren't any. It was a detail of pride for the owners of the restaurant. But also one of necessity.

Sandwiched between a 7-Eleven and a takeout Chinese place, the Crystal City Restaurant was named like a restaurant. It was built like a restaurant, complete with its brick facade and Christmas wreaths on its trendy outdoor barn lights. It even showed up on credit cards and company receipts like a restaurant. But really, the Crystal City Restaurant in Arlington, Virginia, was a strip club—the nearest one to the Pentagon and therefore one of the least videotaped blocks this close to our nation's capital.

For nearly two hours, Nola had been parked outside, sitting in her car as she went through Markus's phone. She'd made a list of every incoming number, every dialed number, every missed call. There were nearly a hundred in total, most of them coming up as *No Caller ID—Unknown*. Those were the burner phones, or at least those who were smart enough to shut off their tracking. Another two dozen gave her "...the number you have dialed has been disconnected or is no longer in service..."

It used to be to track a phone number to a name, you had to have someone inside the phone company, or at least do what private eyes do and pay seven bucks a pop to a place like Intelius. Today, all you needed was the right website, which is what Nola was counting on as she opened a browser on her phone.

One by one, she entered each number. A few were traceable to a carrier—all to MetroPCS, though they weren't attached to names.

"*Cellular,*" it read on-screen. More burner phones. She then noticed three phone numbers that were in a near-identical sequence. Yet more burner phones, all bought at the same time. She knew this was the tricky part. On the boat, Markus had given her Houdini's real name, but before she went hunting, she needed to know who else she was up against.

Outside, a chubby bald man in an *Elliot in the Morning* baseball hat kept his head down as he entered the strip club. His left hand was fidgeting in his pocket. Took off his wedding band and still wasn't used to it. *Putz.* He shot a quick look at Nola as she entered yet another phone number into the online site. It was a number that hadn't been called in over a month.

240 area code. Western Maryland.

Seconds after hitting *Search*, the details appeared on her phone screen. Nola's eyes narrowed. So far, every single hit came up the same: "*Cellular.*" Never linked to a name, always a burner. But there it was—rare as a dodo. An actual landline.

Corporate account. Registered to something called *Powell Rock Inc.* Established 1987.

Most important? The very best thing that comes with every landline.

An address.

41

Washington, DC

The shop had a metallic smell, like a used bookstore filled with old pennies.

As the door closed behind him, puffs of dust cartwheeled through the air. Zig didn't say a word. Better to get a lay of the land.

The magic shop was a time machine straight from the 1960s, cluttered with rusty spinner racks and vintage bookcases filled with magic wands, exploding pens, X-ray specs, and everything else that used to be sold in the ads in the back of old comic books.

Then Zig's eye caught the stainless-steel surveillance camera up on the ceiling. A round lens at the center, with seven little lenses circling it. Thermal imaging. Military hardware. In a decrepit magic shop.

"Anybody home?" Zig called out, approaching the L-shaped glass counter.

No one answered. Next to the antique cash register was a dirty ashtray and an open can of cream soda. Someone was—

"Hope you're not here for the bathroom," a man in his late eighties called out in a Southern twang. With a big barrel chest, buzzed gray hair, and a long nose that had outgrown his face, he hobbled out from the back room, the sound of a toilet still flushing behind him. "Because if you are, I apologize for what I just did in there."

"Sounds like my ex-wife," Zig teased, determined to keep things light.

"You look like you got something on your mind," the man said as Zig eyed a pale yellow business license underneath the glass counter. *Registered to Joe Januszewski.*

"Januszewski?" Zig asked, feigning excitement. "My whole family's Polish, though that just gives me lots of vowels in my name."

"Haven't been called that in years," the old man said, pointing to a business card taped to the front register:

THE AMAZING CAESAR

GREATEST MAGICIAN IN DC

(EXCEPT FOR THE LIARS IN CONGRESS)

"I take it you're the owner?" Zig asked.

"For the past few years. Original owner is *there...*" He pointed at a Bozo the Clown head, up on the wall, stuffed and displayed like a wild animal. Bozo had a perma-smile. It was meant to be a gag.

Zig wasn't laughing.

"Clown jokes don't seem to land the way they used to—but at least it keeps the little kids outta here," the old man jested, though again, it didn't feel like much of a joke. "So what kinda magic can I help you with?"

"Just looking for a few supplies. Some mouth coils, a new squeaker...plus I'm due for a new thumb tip," Zig said, recalling the list he memorized from a magic website.

The old man nodded, taking a sip of his cream soda. He had an elderly warmth about him, but dark, doubting eyes, the color of dirt. His hands were big like manhole covers, and though his posture was no longer at its peak, no question...former military. In the field, not behind a desk. An old bruiser.

"What size for the thumb tip?" The Amazing Caesar asked.

"Usually a medium."

"Even though thumb tips are individually measured and don't come in small, medium, or large?"

Zig just stood there, feeling the stare of Bozo the Clown—and that thermal camera.

"Wanna start again? Maybe without all the horse manure this time?" the old magician challenged.

"I'd like to ask a few questions."

"About what?"

At this point, it made no sense to hold back. "Harry Houdini. And Operation Bluebook."

"I think you have the wrong person."

"Sir, I'm not insulting you, so please don't insult me. I'm guessing this is a shop-and-drop, yes?" Zig asked. The government had them all over the world. People came in and gave a password; if it was right, the shop would give them something they needed. "Whatever the case, I know that a man named Markus Romita came in here before he—"

"You're not listening to what I'm saying." Stepping out from behind the main display case, Caesar lumbered toward Zig, putting a hand on his shoulder and shooing him toward the door. "I don't know what you're talking about, I don't know who Markus is, and if you—"

"I'm not your enemy here," Zig said, hands in the air.

Caesar kept pushing. He was stronger than he looked.

"Sir, if you'll just listen—"

"I don't like liars. Even worse, I don't like people pretending to be magicians so they can case my place. That's disingenuous bullshit," Caesar said, reaching the door and pulling it open.

"Listen to me! My name is Jim Zigarowski—"

"I don't care if you're Elvis Aaron Presley—and I'm from Tennessee, where that still matters—if you don't get outta my shop—"

"The crash! Please...the plane that crashed. I know you saw the news...the plane that went down in Alaska..." Zig's voice was racing, pleading as he stood there in the threshold, Caesar about to slam the door in his face. "Seven people died on that flight! The pilot was twenty-nine. An Army lieutenant, Anthony Trudeau, was twenty-five. They all died. And one of them..." Zig felt that pill in his neck. The globus. He swallowed, but it still wouldn't go away. "I'm just asking for two minutes of your time. Please...two minutes."

Caesar looked down his long nose, his dirt eyes unreadable. "I hate watching cable news; it makes you dumber. So I guess I missed it. You have a good day, Mr. Zigarowski."

With a slam, The Amazing Caesar was gone, leaving Zig alone in the street, watching the puffs of his own breath.

"Okay, so that went crappily," Dino said through the phone as Zig headed back up the block. "That's the very last time I'm buying any saw-a-girl-in-half boxes from *that* magic shop."

"He knows who Markus is. I could see it in his face."

"You knew that two hours ago."

"Yeah, but now we have his name. The Amazing Caesar," Zig said, reaching for his car keys and—

"Ziggy, you there? You okay?"

In his pocket, Zig felt his car keys...and something else. A small, folded-up sheet of paper. Zig pulled it out, confused. *How did...?*

Unfolding the paper, he read the handwritten message.

Capitol Skyline Hotel
I Street
Ten minutes

Zig looked over his shoulder, back at the shop. Show-off magicians.

42

Dover Air Force Base, Delaware

There are plenty of places to hold a private meeting at Dover: staff offices, conference rooms, the clean break-room, the medical examiner's room, the chaplain's office, or even the casket storage room. There's also the embalming room and the viscera prep room, which don't allow cameras.

But when Master Guns heard that someone wanted to see him *here*—in *this* room, accessible only from the back of the building? He knew he wouldn't leave here without some bruises.

Lifting a roll-top metal door, Master Guns revealed a long concrete hallway. There were a few doors along the sides—a mop closet and a contamination shower—but Master Guns's attention was focused straight ahead, at the dead end: a set of double metal doors reinforced with five inches of steel. There was no room number out front, no door handles either. These doors opened only from the inside. Master Guns knew better than to knock. They'd be expecting him.

Sure enough, as he approached, the steel door rumbled open.

"I'm here to see—"

"Not out here," warned a man with a dark suit and a heart-shaped face. He scanned the hallway as he led Master Guns inside.

The room was dark. There were no windows. It took a moment

for Master Guns's eyes to adjust. People called it a room, but it was really a bunker, its bare walls built with steel-reinforced concrete that was at least a foot thick.

"Metal on the belt," the man said, pointing Master Guns to one of two Rapiscan metal detectors. Now they were just trying to intimidate.

"You're kidding, right?"

"On the belt," said a second man, also in a dark suit.

When fallen service members are carried off the plane at Dover, this is actually their first stop. One by one, each body is run through the scanner to check for unexploded ordnance, concealed IEDs, and any other booby traps that might be hidden on a body. The reinforced walls can withstand just about any blast. Except for maybe the one that was coming.

"Let's go," Heart-Shaped Face added, motioning to the plastic bin by the metal detector.

Master Guns unloaded his homicide badge, a pen, a Leatherman combo knife and pliers, and his Beretta 9mm. He then reluctantly pulled off his dog tags and dropped them into the plastic bin.

There was a high-pitched beep. A green light went off as he stepped through the scanner.

Master Guns was close enough now that he saw the five-pointed star pin on Heart-Shaped Face's lapel. Secret Service.

There were plenty of private places at Dover. But none as private as this.

The agent handed Master Guns a thin cell phone that looked like nothing else on the market.

"*Hello?*" Master Guns said.

"Please hold for the President," a female voice announced.

43

Washington, DC

The Capitol Skyline Hotel sat on a corner, across the street from a construction lot on one side, a homeless shelter on the other, and diagonally from a McDonald's, which was where Zig parked.

For two minutes, Zig stared out his front windshield, fighting off the smell of french fries and scanning the hotel for anyone who might be watching.

All clear. At least from here.

Zig didn't want to be early. He pulled out his phone, looking again at the photos he took yesterday at Nola's office. The painted canvases. He'd forgotten about them until now, but here he was, again staring at the haunting portraits that Nola had done. He swiped left, enlarging the photos of the names on the back.

DANIEL GRAFF—MONTEREY, CA.

SGT. DENISE MADIGAN—KUWAIT.

A quick Google search told him the rest. They had one thing in common.

"*Huh,*" Zig muttered, making a mental note. He put his phone away and stepped outside. Something to deal with later.

Keeping his head down as he walked across the street, Zig

entered through a side door, which was marked with its own warning.

DOORS LOCK AT NIGHT.

Designed by an architect in the futuristic modular style of 1960s Miami Beach, the Capitol Skyline Hotel aged into one of those outdated concrete behemoths that people hated about downtown DC—until the family of one of the Studio 54 developers threw millions into the interior, declared it *retro*, and suddenly, poof, it was chic.

Sure enough, as Zig reached the modernist lobby, with its chocolate-brown leather Barcelona chairs and hip Deco wallpaper, the place felt more South Beach than Southwest DC.

"Anything I can help you with?" called a male desk clerk who was a little too handsome for his own good.

"Meeting a friend," Zig said, eyeing a nearby couple, two men who could both give the desk clerk a run in the handsome contest. In a place like this, The Amazing Caesar should stick out like a turd in a fishbowl. But there was no sign of him.

Same in the fancy restaurant. Same when Zig checked the poolside lounge in back.

"Nothing, huh?" Dino whispered through the phone as Zig returned to the lobby.

"Maybe he got scared," Zig said as two sliding doors opened on his left. Outside, idling in front, was a two-tone eighties-era Lincoln Continental.

"Dino, what kind of car did your grandfather drive?"

"Same as every Pop-Pop. His trusty Lincoln, why?"

Zig nodded to himself, heading straight for the car. The perfect accessory for an eighty-year-old magician.

Yet as Zig stepped outside, the car started moving, a slow easy roll out to the street. Through the window, Zig spotted the driver, a young woman with cat's-eye glasses and those stretch earlobe things that the military would never allow. Just another hipster who didn't realize her trend was over.

"Need a cab?" one of the valets called out.

"Thanks, I'm set," Zig said, watching the car disappear up the street.

"Maybe our shuttle, then?"

"No, I'm—" Zig turned to the valet, a lanky kid with acne scars. The valet kept staring, shooting Zig a look. It wasn't a question.

"*Maybe you'd really like our shuttle,*" the valet repeated, pointing far too long at the boxy airport shuttle bus with the bright red stripe.

"Yeah, no . . . that's a good idea," Zig said, heading for the shuttle.

As he got closer, the shuttle doors didn't open. He tapped the glass with his knuckles. Still nothing. Then he gave them a push and the bifold doors gave way.

Zig climbed the carpeted steps. The driver's seat was empty. But when he looked to his left, in the very last row there was an older man in a tan trilby hat with a pinch front.

"Abracadabra, Mr. Zigarowski," The Amazing Caesar said. "I should warn you, I'm only doing this because of those people who died. They deserve better. Now would you mind shutting off your phone? Despite what you think, not all magicians love an audience."

44

This was Nola when she was fifteen.

It was after school, nearly five o'clock. Ms. Sable was grading papers as Nola cursed at the charcoal pencil in her hand.

According to the syllabus, charcoals wouldn't be introduced until next year, in Advanced Art. But Nola was ready, Ms. Sable insisted, teaching Nola that when you work with charcoals, you have to grip them differently than a pencil.

"Hold it with your thumb and pointer finger," Ms. Sable had explained, holding her own arm up and revealing a glimpse of the tiny initials tattooed on her forearm. "And keep your palm off the page. Charcoals smear."

It was that precise detail that had Nola cursing and starting again, rubbing the paper with a kneaded putty eraser that lifted the charcoal off the page. "I hate this," Nola said.

"Just draw the damn jug," Ms. Sable shot back, pointing Nola to the aquamarine water jug at the center of the table.

For the next half hour, both were silent, both lost in their work. This had been Nola's afternoon for weeks now: sketching, drafting, practicing. *Extra credit*, they called it. For Nola, although she wouldn't know it for years, this time with Ms. Sable—it wasn't a relationship that was simply about art. It was a relationship about respect.

"Great Hera. Good for you, Sophie," Ms. Sable said to herself, flipping to a new sheet of drawing paper and admiring a pencil sketch that Smiling Sophie had submitted. It was of Sophie's dog Flynn, a drooly pug with a wide bow tie that made him look like a Republican.

"That's really good," Nola said, craning her neck to admire Sophie's art.

Ms. Sable looked up. Eyebrows furrowed. *"What'd you just say?"* Ms. Sable asked.

"Sophie's art," Nola explained, wondering what she did wrong. "I was just— I thought it was . . . good."

"Good?" Ms. Sable asked. "You don't know enough to know what's *good.* If you want, you can say you *like it,* or that you like how it makes you feel, or even say that you *love it.* But if you *ever* say that something is *good* again, you'll be cleaning paintbrushes for the next month. You don't know what *good* is. After college— after you study form, color theory, perpetual presence, and negative space—then you can tell me what *good* is. Or when you get a fine arts degree and study the difference between intention and execution, then you'll know what's *good.* But until then, *I'm* the teacher. I'll tell you what's good. We clear on that?"

Nola nodded, though from the look on her face, she was still clearly confused.

"What?" Ms. Sable asked.

"I just—" Nola paused, as long a pause as she'd ever done before. "What's *college?"*

45

Washington, DC
Today

My phone's not on."

"At the Conjuring Arts, you had it on. And it's on right now," The Amazing Caesar said, sliding into the driver's seat, starting the shuttle, and steering the small bus out of the driveway. "You get three lies. That's one, Mr. Zigarowski."

"Zig. Friends call me Zig."

Caesar's eyes slid to his right. Zig was sitting in the very first seat of the shuttle, holding the pole like an umbrella.

"You tell me two more lies, Mr. Zigarowski, this conversation's over."

Reaching into his breast pocket, Zig took out his phone. "I'll call you back," he whispered to Dino. "Yeah, no, don't worry. I'm okay." With a tap, the phone was off.

"You lost someone in that plane crash, huh?" Caesar asked.

Zig didn't answer.

"For what it's worth, it's the one thing I thought you weren't bullshitting about," Caesar added. "When it comes to real loss, it never leaves someone's face."

Zig glanced upward at the bubble-shaped escape hatch in the shuttle's roof. Bright red letters read: *Emergency Exit*.

Hitting the gas, Caesar spent the next two minutes hunched in the driver's seat, his pointer and middle fingers on the steering wheel at the five and seven o'clock positions. Old man out for a casual ride.

"You said you felt bad those people died. What do you know about it?" Zig asked.

Caesar just drove.

"Can you at least tell me where we're going?" Zig added.

"I like parks," Caesar said, turning the corner and pulling to the side of the road, in front of a large abandoned lot with a state-of-the-art construction trailer on it. The shuttle lurched and shuddered, Caesar not yet used to the hard clench of its brakes. "Plus, I like knowing who's sniffing after me."

Zig looked out the side window of the bus. This part of the neighborhood was far less developed, a scattering of open lots with no restaurants or buildings nearby. If anyone was following, they'd be impossible to miss.

"Pretty soon, the corporate bomb will hit, and this block'll be covered in Starbucks and Paneras—but no matter how much money they pour in, this town *still* won't be able to produce a proper slice of pizza," Caesar said. "By the by, guess how much that valet kid wanted from me to borrow his shuttle?"

Zig was still staring out the side window. From this distance, the sixties-era hotel, lit up at night and dotted with its TV-shaped windows, looked like a tiny concrete beehive, which brought an odd sense of calm to Zig, something safe from home right here in a spot where he felt so uniquely off-balance.

"I'd like to know about Operation Bluebook," Zig insisted.

"Do me a favor first—watch the key," The Amazing Caesar said, pulling the key from the ignition. The shuttle went dark, the only light now coming from a shattered street lamp with an exposed bulb. "Still see the key? Now I want you to hold it for me," Caesar said, swiveling his seat toward Zig and handing it over.

"I don't have time for a magic trick."

"Mr. Zigarowski, if there was ever time for a magic trick, this is most definitely it." His voice was deadpan, but as he started doing his act, you could see hints of the natural performer buried underneath. "Now I want you to put the key in this envelope," he added, pulling a crisp letter-sized envelope from his jacket pocket.

Humoring him, Zig took the key and slid it into the envelope.

"Seal it with a lick," Caesar said. "Don't worry. I didn't poison it."

Zig looked down at the envelope, then licked it, sealing the key inside.

"Now what do you suppose is the big ta-da of the trick?"

"I honestly don't care. I don't like magic. The only reason I'm—"

"I know why you're here, Mr. Zigarowski. Your commitment to repetition makes it nauseatingly obvious. I'm trying to illustrate a point. When it comes to magic, do you know how many tricks there are?"

"I don't know. Thousands."

"Don't let sarcasm mask frustration. There are four. That's it. Sure, there's levitation, with all the strings and wires. And there's escape stuff, which relies on gimmicked cuffs and other gaff. But for the rest of them, there are only four different magic tricks: You make something appear. You make something disappear. You make two things change place. Or you change one thing into something else. Everything in magic is a variation on those four."

"So what's that have to do with Operation Bluebook?"

Swiveling back toward the steering wheel, Caesar stared out the front window, pursing his lips, like he was trying to touch his top lip to his nose. "You military, Mr. Zigarowski?"

"Never enlisted, but I work with our troops. Mortician. Dover Air Force Base."

"Mortician? No wonder you hate magic."

"You were saying something about Bluebook."

"Just that— You were right before. My store. It's a shop-and-drop. People come in, and we do a little challenge and password. I say the prearranged phrase; if they reply with the right password, well, sometimes I make something appear, sometimes I make it disappear."

"And people pay you for that?"

"No, no, no, no, no." He shook his head, still staring out the front window. "I don't do this for profit. I do this for—" He stopped. "I've got one client. My dear old Uncle Sammy."

"So you do work for the government?"

Again, he tried to touch his top lip to his nose. "How old are you, Mr. Zigarowski? Late forties?"

"Fifty-two."

"Mhmm. You got lucky with that head of hair. Lady Time picks her lovers with care."

"You were saying about the government..."

"When I enlisted, I was seventeen. World War II was long done, but even then, to see how our troops were treated... Someone gave my older brother a car—a used 1938 Ford Prefect! And that got him a wife, so...I gave Uncle Sammy a fake age, I wanted in so bad. The Marines said no, but the Navy put me in a wet suit and let me be a frogman, long before there were SEALs. When they saw I could read, they sent me to officers' school. But in military life, y'know, you turn forty—if you're lucky, you turn fifty—and then..."

"No one gets old in the military," Zig said.

"No, you can get old. You just get less useful," The Amazing Caesar said, staring out the front windshield like he was looking at something he couldn't quite bring into focus. "It's the hardest part of aging—you don't even notice it at first, but boy does that phone stop ringing. So when a colonel called me up one day and asked me if I could take a shipment for him in the magic shop? Mr. Zigarowski, it was like being at the prom and having the prettiest girl ask you to dance and then whisper in your ear that she wants to—"

"I think I got it."

"I'm not sure you do. My job at the Conjuring Arts... I take pride in my shop. I built the wooden bookshelves, built the awning out front, I built it all with my own hands. And I was happy with it. But when that colonel called up and asked for help—the shock of adrenaline—the electricity shooting through me—that's the real magic of life. That's what feeds us—that need to be needed. You say you're fifty-two, Mr. Zigarowski? You're telling me you never got a charge from a need like that?"

For a moment, Zig stared out his window, focusing on the beehive-shaped hotel, his tongue tapping against his sharp incisor. "Not really."

Caesar made a noise, part laugh and part *humpf*. "You say you're a mortician? You should know better than anyone. Just because you're not dead doesn't mean you're alive."

"I appreciate the advice—but I know that's not the reason you brought me out here in the middle of—"

"I brought you out here because people were killed," Caesar snapped, his voice showing its first hint of . . . not just anger. Guilt. "Seven people, yes? I need to make that right."

"I appreciate that, sir. So if we can get back to the colonel . . . What kinda shipments was he asking you to take?"

"You're assuming I'm a bad person, Mr. Zigarowski. This isn't some crooked underground operation. It's a necessity of military life. In the old days, when our SEALs needed a dozen clean laptops, they went through Acquisitions. Today, with WikiLeaks dumping every battle plan on the Internet, if there's an above–top secret mission in Yemen that no one can ever find out about, well, Acquisitions can't be trusted—and you certainly can't head over to the Best Buy with a shipping address that says *The Pentagon*. So all across the country, there are places like mine, shops run by nostalgic old vets who miss their old lives so much, they're happy to take delivery on whatever Uncle Sammy needs to keep quiet. And y'know how we do it? The same way as those four magic tricks."

"Sleight of hand."

"Sleight of hand is the end result, but when it comes to selling a sleight, do you know the trick to the trick itself?" Caesar paused, ever the showman, then pumped his overgrown eyebrows and cupped his hands together. "The big motion covers the small motion. Like this..." Shaking his still-cupped hands, he did a quick three-count, then lifted one hand away, revealing a familiar gold Seiko.

"Is that my watch?" Zig asked.

"That's what you get for looking so hard at that envelope with the key," Caesar said, dangling the watch off his crooked finger and handing it back. "You asked about Houdini before—he used to do the same. He'd have you check his mouth for lockpicks and other files, but while you were doing that, no one would notice that good ole Harry had six fingers—he'd wear a fake hollow pinkie, where he'd store metal picks and a thin bendable Gigli saw that could slice through anything. Or he'd hook a lockpick on the back of your shirt while you examined him, then pull it off when you were done." He pantomimed his left hand moving high in the air—"The *big* motion..."—then closed the fist of his right hand, like he had something in it—"covers the *small* motion."

"So in this metaphor, the Conjuring Arts—?"

"These days, every country in the world, every enemy we have, has a team of computer nerds on staff. They watch the Pentagon—what we order, our supply lines. They watch the big moves. And while they're watching those big moves..."

"...they don't see the small ones being funneled through your little magic shop." Zig nodded. That part made sense. "But what's that have to do with Operation Bluebook? You said you needed to make something right."

Caesar cupped his hands again. One, two, three. Then revealed: A shiny silver dollar. He cupped his hands again. One, two, three. *Clink.* Another silver dollar. Then, *clink*, another. Slowly, though, his expression changed, and—one, two, three—as a new silver dollar clinked against the others, his features fell, looking despondent.

"Caesar, if you know something—"

"I'm a good person. A good American," Caesar insisted as—
clink—he lifted his hand and another silver dollar appeared. "I
served our country my entire adult life. And when they needed
me to do a little more by helping with these shipments, I served
again. In the beginning, it wasn't much. A new delivery would show
up every six months or so. After 9/11, of course, more shipments
started coming in—during the heyday, I signed for so many laptops, printers, flip phones, and chargers, I swear to Moses, our
government was single-handedly keeping the CDW computer cat-
alogue in business. But again, that's the job, right? At least I'm in
the game. I'm alive. Back from the dead! The Amazing Caesar feels
amazing again—so amazing that I didn't even realize they were
about to play me for a sucker. It started a few months ago, when
I got the kind of delivery you never want to sign for. No packag-
ing. Just a briefcase. Military issue. Bombproof. They told me not
to look inside."

Zig sat there, silent.

"What was I supposed to do? I'm a breathing human, and they
were stupid enough to leave it with someone who's a master at
picking locks. I had to take a peek."

"And inside...?"

"There it was—the deadliest weapon of all. Neat stacks of cash.
Two hundred thousand dollars."

"You never moved cash before?"

"This is Uncle Sammy. Half the time, I assumed I was moving
cash. For this one, though, they said my contact would be someone
named *Houdini*, which I thought was just their way of making fun
of my store, like ha-ha, you eighty-year-old fool, you're spending
your retirement in a magic shop. Then they told me the code name.
Operation Bluebook."

46

"You're looking at me like I'm supposed to know what that means," Zig said.

"Even I don't know what their current operation is—but I know the history," The Amazing Caesar said. "You never heard the stories? Houdini and his Blue Book?"

"I looked online. Said it was some sort of codebook."

"Not just a book. It was part of Houdini's act. At the peak of his fame, his shows had three parts: First, there was the magic..." In the palm of Caesar's hand, he squeezed the silver dollars. He opened his hand; now they were gone. "Second, he'd do his escapes—from handcuffs, straitjackets, and of course the Chinese water torture one. But during the final years of his life, the best part of every show was when he'd expose the fraud of local mediums."

"Y'mean like fortune-tellers?"

"Back then they were called spiritualists. They even had their own religion—Spiritualism—based on the idea that you could talk to the dead. Today, of course, it makes you think of palm readers and crystal balls, but in those days, this so-called religion was big business."

"And people believed it?"

"It was right after World War I. Families who lost their sons in battle got preyed upon by hucksters offering séances. To Houdini, whose heart was broken by the death of—"

"His mom," Zig said, remembering what Waggs said, which he'd confirmed online.

"Exactly. Houdini felt that pain personally from the loss of his mother. From there, he made it his mission to go after spiritualists. He saw it as the most hurtful crime of all—ripping open old wounds and taking advantage of someone's lost family member, or lost child. I mean, can you imagine?"

Zig could. He'd been imagining it since the moment he thought it was Nola in the morgue, since the moment she returned to his life. The worst of it was last night, when she manipulated him into going to her office just to see who would follow. Zig could live with the maneuverings; indeed, he had to respect her for a smart play like that. No, for Zig, the real pain came from what it showed him about himself.

A decade since the funeral, he wasn't a novice mourner. Zig knew where his scars were; he was used to living with them on a daily basis. Plus, he worked in death, spending years using it to inoculate himself against the shattered feeling that came with the loss of Maggie. To be around so many young fallen took away the greatest weapon in death's arsenal—just being with other mourners, Zig no longer felt alone.

And then, Nola appeared—this girl who saved his daughter— and in an eyeblink, all that protective work was unraveled, tearing his skin off in sheets and reminding him of the one thing he'd worked so hard to overcome: The deepest wounds—the ones that pierce you to your core—they heal, but they never disappear.

"Can you please tell me what this has to do with the Blu—"

"I already did. It was the secret of Houdini's trick—the secret behind all his tricks. Big motion covers the small motion, right?" Caesar asked. "Erik Weisz, aka Harry Houdini, was the big motion, the star of the show. But while everyone was focused on him, the real work was being done by Houdini's secret service."

"His what?"

"That's what he called them. They were his closest confidants: his wife, his brother, an assistant named Amedeo—"

"Vacca," Zig blurted.

"You know him?"

Zig shook his head, noticing a dim light outside. In the distance, up the block, a car came to a stop, its headlights glowing. It was parallel with the shuttle, still debating whether to turn. "Vacca's name was listed as one of the passengers on board the plane that crashed in Alaska. Same with Rose Mackenberg and Clifford Eddy Jr."

"Both were also members of Houdini's secret service," Caesar said. "So someone's using old Houdini names?"

"That's our theory."

Caesar took a long look at Zig, who was still studying the headlights outside. Even from here, there was no mistaking the siren on the roof. Police car. "Mr. Zigarowski, those three names you just mentioned…they weren't the only people on the plane, were they? Please help me make this right. Was someone you care about on there too?"

"It's a long story."

"I'm eighty-seven. I've got time."

"I'm not sure *we* do, though," Zig said, motioning to the police car in the distance.

"I see 'em. Rental cops. We hire them for the neighborhood. They've passed us twice now," Caesar said as the car started moving, disappearing to their left. "Anyhoo, you were saying—?"

"No. *You* were saying. About Houdini's secret service."

"Right. Before Harry got to a town—Vacca, Mackenberg, Eddy, and the others—they would come a few days early and do the recon work, figuring out everything from what brand of handcuffs the local police used—so Houdini would have a key when he challenged them to lock him up—to what kind of locks were on the jail cells. But their number one mission was to help Houdini prepare for the big finale of the act."

"Exposing mediums and fake fortune-tellers."

"It was Houdini at his sneakiest. Back then, whenever a medium would travel to a new town, they'd establish themselves by approaching someone in a prominent family and saying, *I have a message for you from your dead brother*—or dead mother, or whoever it was. Then they'd ID the person, by name, like: *Someone named Maggie is in great pain.*"

"What'd you just say?"

"Back at my shop, you gave me your name, Mr. Zigarowski. You think I didn't do a quick Google search? I found the obituary. I'm sorry you lost your daughter."

"That's not—"

"You're proving my point. Today, the Internet makes it easy. Back then, though, it would blow people's minds. *How'd this stranger know all those details about me?* But no one realized that the mediums themselves had their own underground network— they called it the Blue Book. In every town, they'd write down all the details of everyone who lived there. *Mr. Montgomery recently buried his wife Abigail after she fell from a horse; Mrs. Addison is blind in one eye and lost a sister named Gertie.*"

"That's what it said online. That it was like a Hobo Code."

"With more details and info. Think of it as Google .01. They'd hide the Blue Book in a known spot—somewhere by the train station—and when different mediums would come to town, they'd study the book and immediately be ready to show off their amazing powers. In Houdini's act, he'd grab the Blue Book first, call the local mediums onstage, and show everyone what frauds they were."

"So when you opened that briefcase full of cash and saw the paperwork for Operation Bluebook—"

"Whoever's pulling the strings here, they're obviously Houdini superfans. They're using his old tricks, the names of his old agents—but what set me off wasn't the bombproof suitcase, or even the cash inside it. It was the pickup man who came for it."

"The one they called *Houdini.*"

"Like I said, I been doing this since Nixon was cursing in the White House. Every six months or so, Uncle Sammy sends someone to my shop. We make small talk, they mention the code name, I give them a package. No one's perfect, but most people are generally nice. This guy, Houdini, though... Y'ever give your car keys to a valet and start worrying about your house keys being on that key ring too?"

Zig nodded, noticing that through the front windshield, a few blocks away, there was another set of headlights. A new car was slowly coming toward them. Nothing to worry about. At least, not yet.

"For most of my pickups, they send me Marines or SEALs. They're kids...messengers...but they're solid, like hammers," Caesar explained. "This so-called Houdini, he was older. In his forties, at least—and when you spot a colonel suddenly doing a corporal's job, you know something's not right. That's why I popped the locks on his suitcase. Then, after his first pickup, my phone rings again. And rings even more. Deliveries start coming more frequently. Every other month, then once a month, then every two weeks. And the suitcase? It's getting heavier. Whoever Houdini is, he's not just moving a few shekels. He's moving *cash*—more and more with each visit, all of it peaking four days ago, when my phone rings and there he is, telling me that something big is coming. That I need to keep an eye out. And guess where that shipment was from?"

"Alaska."

"Every time he came in, I swear, I had that bad feeling. But I'm a good American, Mr. Zigarowski. My orders were clear: Accept the cash and hand it over. Yet when I saw the news of that plane, I swear, I had that same bad feeling, praying it was just coincidence. But for you to show up now... Sacred Mary, if I caused those people's deaths...!"

"Caesar, you couldn't have—"

"I *knew*! Deep in my belly, I could feel it! Every time he came in, I knew something was off. And then for him to start calling me personally, checking to see exactly when his suitcase would arrive? *No one does that.* It was like he had a personal stake in it."

"Hold on. Back up. He called you personally? So you know how to reach him?"

"Yeah. Sure. For emergencies only. Why?"

Zig thought about that. Then, right there, Zig had a brand-new idea.

47

Dover Air Force Base, Delaware

W hat can I do for you, Mr. President?"

"Let me first say, I appreciate what you do there at Dover. We all do, Francis," President Wallace said, using Master Guns's first name. Even with admirals, most Presidents do away with titles and keep things informal.

"Thank you, sir."

"To that end, I know you're busy. I'll keep this quick. We were wondering..." He stopped himself, taking a moment. The concrete bunker was silent. "I was wondering...about that plane that went down in Alaska..." He stopped again. "I'd like to know how the investigation is going."

Master Guns glanced at the two Secret Service agents, both of whom were now pretending to look down at the metal detector. It wasn't uncommon for White House staff to contact Dover; this week, they were calling at all hours. But in nineteen years, this was the first and only time a President had called directly. "We're just getting started, sir," Master Guns said. "I will say, I think we're proceeding along nicely."

"I'm glad to hear that, Francis, because as I understand it, you're our chief homicide investigator there, correct?"

Master Guns paused, sensing a trap. He'd never met President Wallace, but he knew all politicians were natural-born liars. Especially the world's top politician. "I'm not sure what you're getting at, sir."

"What I'm *getting at* is that as chief investigator, you're the one who goes out in the field. Last month, when that helicopter with four of our soldiers went down in the Philippines, you immediately flew to the Philippines. When that corporal went on a shooting spree at our base in Turkey, you flew to Turkey the next day. You interviewed everyone, examined it up close, and made a determination. But here we are with a plane down in Alaska—an entire crime scene out in the snow—and you're still sitting there at Dover four days later."

His dog tags clinked around his neck as he put them back on. Master Guns chose his next words carefully. "Sir, if you're accusing me of someth—"

"Francis, do you know what's on my schedule after I hang up with you?"

"Pardon me, sir?"

"It's late in the day. At this hour, I usually get my final briefing from my national security team. After that, I return phone calls, like the one I have to make to Senator Castronovo, who's been busting my chops on every damn cable show over the rehaul I proposed for the post office system. But tonight, do you know what I'll be doing instead? Writing a eulogy."

"I know you and Mr. Rookstool were close," Master Guns said, referring to the Librarian of Congress. "I'm sorry you have t—"

"Don't be sorry. This is my honor. Nelson was in my wedding party. On the night my son was born, he brought a Wiffle ball bat to the hospital. If he were just a friend, I'd have our top speechwriter write his eulogy—she'd do a beautiful job too. But for Nelson..." The President made a noise, a grunt that sounded like *nuh-uh*. "When I stand there at his funeral on Friday—when I look down at Nelson's son and two daughters...at his ten-year-old grandson... *this* is a story only I can tell. So once again, Francis, tell me why you're sitting on your thumbs in Delaware rather than sitting on a plane heading to Alaska?"

"Because it's my job, sir."

"No, your job is to find out why that plane went down!"

"No," Master Guns said as both Secret Service agents turned at his tone. Master Guns stared back, still gripping the phone. "With all due respect, sir, my job is to *investigate*. And as we both well know, a few hours after that plane crashed in Alaska, two men in suits were waiting in my office, demanding Sergeant Brown's body. Do you know what that did to the investigator in me? It told me to start investigating anyone who's interested in that body or, more importantly, this case. To my surprise, sir, that person is now you."

The phone went silent. Not for long, though. The President's voice stayed calm and steady. Like yesterday out on the runway, no matter how hard the wind blew, Wallace didn't let a hair on his head get out of place. "I'm glad to hear that, Francis, because the very last thing I want is for you to go easy on this."

"I can assure you, I never go easy, Mr. President. Honesty is my true north."

"Funny you should mention that," Wallace said—and right then, Master Guns realized the trap wasn't coming. It had already been sprung. "Earlier today, Francis, the Service took a look at Dover's security records. And y'know what they found? According to the card swipe systems in your building, an ID with your name on it was used to access a room called Personal Effects. But when they cross-checked their other reports, they realized that a mortician named Jim Zigarowski was attacked in that exact room at that exact time."

Master Guns stood at full attention, replaying how he let Zig use his ID to take a quick look in the room. "I would never hurt Zig."

"That's the right answer, Francis. And I assume that if we look at all the photos that were taken out on the runway, we'll find one with you on the back of the plane at the same time you were supposedly in that Personal Effects room. But the fact re-mains that even if you weren't the one who personally attacked

Mr. Zigarowski, the person who did it was someone who knew that he would be there at that time. And as far as my people can tell, you're one of the few who fit that bill. In fact, Francis, you're the only one who fits that bill."

"Zig is my friend."

"And Nelson Rookstool is *my* friend," the most powerful man in the world said. "Do your job, Francis—because I promise you, we'll be doing ours."

Before Master Guns could say a word, there was a click. The President of the United States was gone.

The agent with the heart-shaped face pointed to the door. "This is the easiest way—"

"I know how to get out," Master Guns said, plowing toward the exit.

In the hallway, he waited for the steel door to slam behind him. Then he pulled out his phone—the one his wife didn't know about.

Master Guns sent a quick text.

We need to talk.

48

Nola was cold. She was hungry too, with nothing but a scattering of granola-bar wrappers tossed across the passenger seat. Granola bars were never a proper meal, no matter how many you ate.

She'd been sitting in the car for hours now, her notepad propped against the steering wheel as she drew another sketch in green pencil of the old storefront diagonally down the street. She liked using green in winter. Made everything seem serene. According to phone records, this was the one landline Markus called from his cell, squeezed between a check-cashing place and a liquor store. *Powell Rock Inc.*

It was an insurance agency. Prudential. The front glass window had the old eighties logo that built the Rock of Gibraltar out of a few slanted lines, with these words underneath: *Get a Piece of the Rock with Benjamin R. Powell.* Prudential updated the logo years ago. The same wasn't true of the storefront. With its peeling sign and tattered blue-striped awning, it was decades past its golden days.

As Nola continued to draw, new details popped out: The pattern of zigzagging cracks in the storefront's wood paneling. *Rotting underneath.* The rust streaks below the gutters. *Definitely a leak there.* And the subtle sag of the roofline that made the front sign look slightly higher on the right than the left? *Foundation problems for sure.*

Yet of all the details in Nola's sketches, the most noticeable was what *wasn't* there. People.

For hours now, no one went in the place, no one came out. Not a big deal for most insurance agencies. Walk-ins had to be rare. But here, there were no customers, no employees, no deliveries, nothing. Even after lunch, when the rest of the street swelled with locals, Powell Insurance was lifeless.

Only one way to find out what's going on.

Readjusting the mesh baseball cap that she'd bought at a gas station, Nola picked up her new disposable phone and started to dial. But as she entered the number—

Across the street, in front of the coffee shop, a quick movement caught her eye. A fluffy white dog—a bichon...no, a Havanese—was being yanked on his leash, back toward his owner, a heavy man with a beard. Middle-aged. Expensive shoes, expensive gloves. *Likes to be noticed.*

He was talking, leaning in toward a younger woman. Late thirties. No lipstick. No wedding ring. *Still deciding if she's buying his bullshit.*

The dog let out a high-pitched whine, trying to get to a nearby tree in front of the coffee shop. The dog had to pee.

The man yanked the pup back. Then yanked him again, still focused on the woman.

The dog was begging now, whining and pleading. Like he was in pain. *Yank.*

Nola was tempted to get out, tempted to have a few words about the way this man was treating his dog. But now wasn't the time. *Stay focused,* she thought, entering the final digits of the phone number. But just as she did...

The man gave another yank, a hard one that, as the dog was in mid-jump, sent the furry animal crashing on its back, scrambling to right itself.

Shutting her phone and tossing her sketch pad aside, Nola kicked open the car door. *Dammit*, she cursed herself, knowing she was being stupid. But as the dog let out a yelp— *Screw it.* She headed straight toward the man. The dog was rattled now and skittish, looking up as Nola got closer.

She walked up to the man. His lower teeth slanted sideways, like half-fallen Towers of Pisa. No braces when he was young. *To afford those shoes and gloves, he worked for it.*

"You got something to say?" the man challenged, turning toward Nola, expecting her to back up.

She stayed where she was. "Your dog's trying to tell you something."

"You fucking kidding me?"

"Mason, not here," the woman warned. This wasn't the first time he lost his temper.

Nola turned to Mason, so close that her elbow was now touching the woman he was talking to, edging her out of the way. "I have a thing about animals," Nola said. She glared at him and let him take a good long look at her black eyes with flecks of gold. Let him see the depth of the hole he was about to step into.

In her pocket, she was still holding the green pencil she'd been sketching with. She eyed fourteen places to impale him, six of them deadly.

This close to the man, she saw the hair-plug divots along his forehead, the edge of the contact lenses in his slowly widening eyes, and even the one stray thread sticking up at the collar of his designer wool overcoat.

Over his shoulder, people in the coffee shop were starting to stare, including a Native American woman with a long black ponytail, dressed casually, sipping her latte and looking up from her newspaper.

"*Nn, nnn, nnnn,*" the white dog continued to whimper.

"Go potty, Crackerjack. That's it. Go potty," the man said, letting the dog drag him toward the tree, where Crackerjack quickly relieved himself.

"Happy now?" the man asked.

Nola ignored him, locking eyes with the man's girlfriend. "You can tell a lot about a person by how they treat their dog."

Leaving them behind, Nola headed back to her car as she pulled out her phone and quickly redialed the number for Powell Insurance.

Time to get some answers.

49

The Amazing Caesar had a throbbing pain in his hip. The doctors blamed it on the way he carried his weight, always leaning to one side as osteoporosis compressed his spine. They told him he should *take it easy*, whatever that meant. But as Caesar began dialing the phone number from the back of his magic shop, he was still leaning on his left side. At a certain age, you can't change who you are.

"*Hello?* You there?" Caesar asked into the phone as someone picked up.

It was quiet on the other end, and Caesar could feel an unnerving silence seeping through the large room, a long rectangular space almost as big as the public part of the shop, though far less cluttered. There was an old oak desk, tall and short mismatched file cabinets, but really, most of the room was empty, facing the huge metal roll-up door that led to the alley. This wasn't an office; it was a shipping and receiving area.

"Everything okay?" asked the man known as Houdini. He sounded annoyed, but there was something else in his voice—concern—and a real sense of charm. Like he was worried about Caesar.

"Something came in today," Caesar offered. "A package. For you."

Houdini went silent. "No one mentioned any shipments."

"I'm just relaying what's here. And from the smell that's leaking from it, I think you may have a problem."

"The smell?"

"It actually smells. *Bad*," Caesar insisted.

Houdini knew what that meant. Counterfeit money had its own odor, from the printing. It made no sense. The government wouldn't use phony money, which meant this was from someone else. So now Houdini was curious. "Any idea who sent it?" Houdini asked.

"I just sign for deliveries. If you want, I can send it back."

"No, it's fine. It's good. I'll be right over," Houdini said. "You'll stay late, yes?"

"Sign outside says *Closed*, but I'm in back."

That's all Houdini needed to hear. With a click, he was gone.

Caesar hung up the phone and sat back in his chair, leaning to the left. Seven people were dead. This was his chance to make it right.

"He's on his way?" Zig asked behind Caesar.

"You put meat in the trap, you'll get the lion," Caesar said. "Now you just have to figure out what to do with him."

50

Homestead, Florida
Ten years ago

This was Nola when she was sixteen.

"*Get...over here,*" Royall growled, grabbing Nola hard by the arm. Breakfast was finished, and she was in the kitchen, doing dishes. The water was running, Nola reaching back to shut the faucet even as Royall tugged her to the door. If it kept running, she'd pay for that too.

"What'd I do?" Nola asked, replaying the last few hours. Saturday laundry had already started; yesterday's shopping was done; she'd put all his change by his wallet, except for the few quarters she always stole. *Was this about the quarters?*

"*Move your ass!*" he insisted, kicking open the screen door and pulling her into the backyard.

She tripped over one of their new but crooked patio stones as they headed for the overturned kiddie pool. Nola knew what the pool covered: the hole underneath, a new one that Nola had been digging since they moved to this new house.

"You see this?" Royall asked.

She was off-balance, her hands still wet with dishwashing soap, tiny sudsy bubbles popping along her fingertips. Next to the kiddie pool, she eyed the nearby shovel with the pointy spade.

"Dummy! *Look!*" He was pointing straight up, at the sky.

It was morning, but the moon was floating there, a faint half circle visible in the pale blue sky. Like a chalk drawing, Nola thought.

"Pick one," Royall said.

"The *what?*"

"Pick one. The sun or the moon?" He pointed up at both, though the sun was mostly out of sight. "Pick."

Nola paused, thinking it was a trick. Royall was too calm, the bounce in his voice too...happy.

"C'mon, Nola, pick. Sun or moon?"

"I don't get it."

He rolled his eyes, now annoyed. "Listen, I know I'm not a good dad, okay? I don't buy you stuff; with the business," he said, referring to the passport and other forgeries he was now doing on an even bigger scale, "I need to put our cash into printers and laminators, rather than wasting it on useless toys or presents. It lets us have a nice life, this new house," he explained. "But someone told me this story—I think it's from a movie or book. This dad tells his kids to pick a star in the sky. That way, when all the wealthy kids' presents are gone, his kids will always have that star, y'know? I just figured...I dunno...if stars are good, the sun or the moon's better. I mean, today's your birthday, right?"

Nola nodded. He never remembered her birthday. Not for years. And he rarely bought her anything, not when he could make more cash upgrading his ever-expanding *document business*, which had recently caught the attention of Royall's new boss, Mr. Quentin Wesley.

From the bus ads she'd seen around town (*Got a Mess? Call Wes!*), Wesley was a local immigration lawyer. He was also a crook, Nola decided, considering how many fake social security cards, phone bills, and driver's licenses (complete with magnetic strips) Royall was churning out in their back bedroom for seemingly hundreds of Wesley's undocumented clients. Wesley told Royall from the start, "Your work is truly masterful."

According to the bus benches, Wesley also did a little criminal law, which brought an influx of ex-cons. Royall didn't mind convicts—everyone deserved a fresh start—but when Wesley asked Royall to build a top-shelf "wallet" for a fifty-year-old pedophile who was tired of everyone knowing his business? Royall refused.

"Now you're suddenly a snob? Peds pay top dollar," Wesley had told him.

"Don't care," Royall had shot back. Every man has a line. Even Royall wouldn't do that.

"So there's my gift," Royall told Nola. "Your choice. The sun or the moon. Just fucking pick one, alright?"

Nola looked up toward the sky. Her voice was soft. "The moon."

"Yeah," Royall said, craning his neck and looking up with her. "Me too."

For a minute, the two of them stood there in the backyard, both of them staring up at Nola's new—and only—birthday present.

Finally, Royall headed toward the house, glancing back at Nola over his shoulder. "I'm not a total asshole, y'know."

51

The Curtain wasn't happy with her coffee.

It was supposed to be an artisanal Indonesian blend, a mix of toffee, citrus, and tangy herbs. But the bitter taste told her the beans were too finely ground. Typical. You need them coarser to get the full flavor, which made her think of that luscious cold brew she had in Kyoto, Japan, on the night she tracked down and opened the wrists of that German snitch who always smelled like cough drops.

"You still see her?" a voice asked through her phone.

"You have to ask?" The Curtain shot back, glancing outside, where Nola had just gotten out of her car.

"You're lucky you found her."

It wasn't luck. Once The Curtain realized Nola had grabbed Markus's phone, it was only a matter of time until Nola went through the records and tracked the landline for Powell's Insurance. No different than what The Curtain would've done herself.

"You sure she hasn't seen you?"

"Stop talking," The Curtain was about to say, but to her surprise, Nola was now storming straight toward the coffee shop.

The Curtain slid her hand in her pocket, readying her blade. That is, until Nola stopped short, approaching a fat man outside who seemed to be strangling his hyperactive dog.

"What's she doing now?" the voice asked in The Curtain's ear.

"Picking a fight."

"What? With who?"

"Not important. I'll call you back," she said, hanging up.

Cradling her coffee cup, but never drinking from it, The Curtain turned her attention outside, watching through the plate glass as Nola stepped into the fat man's personal space.

Rash, The Curtain thought. Calling attention to herself. Plus, not taking the time to assess who this guy might be? Nola was fighting angry now. Fighting dumb. And for what?

At the end of the leash, a little white pup was whimpering, fighting to relieve itself.

A dog? Really?

The Curtain made a mental note. She'd been told Nola was disciplined. Unemotional. That's what made her so dangerous. But here it was—proof that she could be stirred up, just like every other slob in the world. It was a detail The Curtain wouldn't soon forget.

Outside, as Nola argued with the man, she suddenly glanced up. For a picosecond, she and The Curtain made eye contact, twenty feet apart, separated only by the front window of the coffee shop. Nola quickly turned back to the fat man, glowering at him until he finally realized this wasn't the kind of fight he'd be walking away from.

The Curtain made a mental note of that too. Everyone thought Nola Brown was a wild card, but if you watch anyone long enough, even the wildest of cards gets played with its own predictability.

"How's the coffee?" a young barista called out. He was cute. Trendy but edgy beard. Someone The Curtain would hit on if it were another day.

"Perfect," The Curtain said, taking a fake sip.

Outside, Nola headed back to the car, her back turned.

52

Y ou look like death," the man known as Houdini called out.
"It's called old age," The Amazing Caesar said as the
roll-top back door rose upward, revealing his guest, a forty-
something man with thinning black hair who was chewing gum so
aggressively, you'd think it was an Olympic event. "What's your excuse?"

"You're funny for someone from the Great Depression," Houdini shot back, stepping inside, hiding his gum in his cheek, and
flashing his toothy grin. It was a natural smile, one he used to his
advantage to offset the intensity of his pointy fox face and skeptical
brown eyes. "Really, though, you don't look so good."

"Yeah, well, see how you're looking when every time you sneeze,
you piss a little puddle in your pants," Caesar said, hitting a button
and lowering the door.

Houdini forced a fake laugh as he shook hands with the old
man. He didn't mind the chitchat with Caesar. To be over eighty
years old and still in the game, still feeling your blood flowing? Isn't
that what everyone wants? Yet as the door rolled down, Houdini
was again chew, chew, chewing—checking over his shoulder, making sure no one was following. He didn't mind talking with Caesar,
but that didn't mean he trusted him.

"So I hear you've got a new rabbit in your hat," Houdini said, motioning with his chin at the soft leather briefcase on the nearby desk.

"Came in a few hours ago. Same as always," the old magician said, meaning it was addressed to Caesar but with an H as his middle initial, for *Houdini*.

Chewing his gum even harder, Houdini stared at the case. Most of his deliveries came in a bombproof attaché. This was cheap, faux leather, like something from an Office Depot. "No return address?"

Caesar shook his head.

Chew, chew, chew. "You try the lock?" Houdini asked, eyeing the small padlock on the main zipper.

"I'm just a messenger."

Chew, chew, chew. Houdini could smell the briefcase from here, or at least what was in it. That sweet and sulfury stench. Printer's ink, which meant counterfeit money, which meant someone new was at the table . . . or even worse, that someone had found out what Houdini and his partner were really up to. Either way, whoever that someone was, they were trying to get Houdini's attention. And right now, it was most definitely working.

"You okay?" Caesar asked, adding a final verbal shove. The people who died on that plane deserved his very best.

"Absolutely." Houdini grabbed the briefcase. It felt light; there wasn't much in it. Chew, chew, chew. "By the way, last time, that magic trick you gave me for my nephew . . . ?"

"The Teleporting Key? With the metal key that comes free from the key ring? He like it?"

"It was too hard for him. He's fourteen and lazy. Maybe you got something simpler, like that plastic box where you put the quarter in, then turn it around and the quarter disappears?"

Caesar rolled his eyes. "Magic Money," he said, leaving the back room and heading into the main part of the store. "It comes in a starter set," he explained as he reached a bookshelf and grabbed a box labeled *Ages 5 & up*.

"That's the one. I know it's easy, but he's a stupid kid—he'll love it," Houdini said, standing just behind Caesar. "You mind opening it up?"

As the old magician pulled the toy from the box, he was thinking so much about the Alaska victims, he didn't even feel the gun that was now pressed to the back of his head.

Pffft.

A spray of blood hit the bookshelf. Caesar swayed a moment, then crumbled, his legs first, then his upper body, plummeting to the wood floor like all his bones suddenly disappeared at once.

Thuuump.

The Amazing Caesar took his final bow, his body convulsing as a small red puddle widened below him.

"I humbly apologize to your family, wherever they may be," Houdini whispered. He meant it. He liked the old man—and certainly appreciated all the help he'd been over these past months. But there was a reason they called him Houdini. The man who made all problems disappear.

Caesar's body continued to jerk.

Houdini kept his head down, away from the video cameras, then stepped over the body and leaned down, grabbing the plastic magic trick for his nephew. Then he figured, what the heck, and snatched the entire starter set, stuffing the small box in his coat pocket. It was nearly Christmas, for chrissakes.

Within a minute, briefcase in hand, Houdini was out the back door, weaving through the alleys behind the magic shop. His first stop?

Same as always.

*   *   *

A few blocks away, Houdini turned the corner and checked over his shoulder. No one there. On his left and right, he scanned every parked car. All looked empty. There were plenty of people scattered across the sidewalk, most of them headed to or from the brand-new Safeway supermarket on the next block.

This block, though, was a relic of the past. Which is why Houdini picked it. Across the street was a run-down storefront with a sagging striped awning. The front glass was covered in a giant peeling *Prudential Insurance* sticker that had these words in a smiley-face curve below the logo: *Get a Piece of the Rock with Benjamin R. Powell.*

Crossing the street and approaching the thick glass door, Houdini smelled the stale cigarettes inside. For the money they were paying, couldn't they clean up the place a bit?

Glancing over his shoulder one last time, he again scanned all the parked cars and every nearby storefront window.

Convinced he was alone, Houdini opened the front door.

It closed silently behind him.

53

Six minutes ago

P owell Insurance," a woman answered.

"I want to buy insurance," Nola blurted into her phone, sitting in the driver's seat, once again sketching in her notepad with the green pencil. She was drawing the woman on the phone, based solely on her voice. *Curt.* Trying to sound nice, but subtly annoyed. Someone who had no problem lying.

"I'm sorry, all our agents are really busy right now. Can I take your number?"

"I can hold," Nola said, looking out the front windshield and down the block at the storefront that clearly had a light on, but no movement inside. "I'm a friend of Benjamin's," she added, reading the name from the front window. *Get a Piece of the Rock with Benjamin R. Powell.*

The receptionist went silent. "Ben passed away in 2003."

"Did I say *Benjamin*? I think I had the wrong guy," Nola said, noticing just how many people were headed to the nearby Safeway supermarket now that work was over. This late in the day, like any commercial block in Washington, it was a mix of faces—whites, blacks, Asians—the usual professionals in their usual professional wear. Underneath their coats was a fashion range that, for women, stretched from Banana Republic to Ann Taylor, and for men, Joseph A. Bank to Brooks Brothers. Still sketching away, she started drawing the coffee shop across the street, suddenly recalling the Native American woman with the long black ponytail. Nola looked for her. She was gone.

"What'd you say your name was again?" the receptionist challenged, a bit too aggressively.

"I didn't," Nola replied, her green pencil no longer moving. She turned her attention down the block, to the insurance agency. "I appreciate the help. I'll call back later."

"Ma'am, if you just tell me your na—"

Nola shut the phone, eyes still on the storefront. Whatever was happening inside, there was only one way to find out. Time to go in.

On the front dashboard was an open pencil tin. Nola tossed her green pencil inside and snapped the tin shut. From her waistband, she pulled out her gun, sliding it in her coat pocket.

Nola started to elbow open the car door, and then—

Up on the next block, a man darted across the street. Balding. Close-cropped black hair. Fox-shaped face. Nola thought he looked familiar. He was carrying a briefcase, chewing gum like a teenager... and heading straight for Powell's Insurance.

Taking out her phone, Nola pulled up a photo. LinkedIn headshot. Same receding hairline. Same fox face. This was him. Perfect match.

Last night on the boat, as Markus begged for his life and pissed all over himself, he finally gave up his boss, or at least who he reported to. And now, here he was—Foxface with the briefcase. Real name, Rowan Johansson—also known as Houdini—one of the few people who knew what Operation Bluebook really was—and who no question had a hand in putting down the Alaskan plane that took Kamille's life.

Mongol... Faber... Staedtler... Ticonderoga... Swan, Nola said to herself. She clenched her jaw so hard, her teeth made an audible crack. Out the front windshield, Nola watched as Houdini glanced over his shoulder, taking one last look around. For a second, it looked like he was staring right at her.

Mongol...Faber...Staedtler...Ticonderoga...Swan.

Deep down, Nola secretly hoped she'd been spotted. Then her next move would be easy. But the way the bill of her cap was blocking her face, plus the fading light, no way could he know she was here.

Down the block, convinced he was alone, Houdini switched his briefcase to his left hand and used his right to tug open the front door of the insurance place. *Right-handed.*

The door was old. Heavy. It slapped shut behind Houdini as he disappeared inside. Nola counted to herself.

One...two...

Kicking open her car door, Nola crossed the street at mid-block. In her pocket, she gripped her gun. *Mongol...Faber...Staedtler... Ticonderoga...Swan.*

Like before, it wasn't helping. Though sometimes that wasn't a bad thing.

54

Six minutes ago

Y ou still see him?"

"He's there. I see him," Zig whispered, ducking down by the steering wheel as Houdini turned the corner diagonally across the street. He was heading away from Zig.

"I assume he can't see you?" Dino asked through the phone.

It was an absurd question, making Zig wonder if looping Dino in was a mistake. Naturally, Zig tried Waggs first, but for the past half hour, Waggs was nowhere to be found. At least with Dino, Zig had extra eyes and ears—as well as someone to pull the emergency cord if it all went bad.

"What about the old magician?" Dino asked. "Any word from The Amazing Caesar?"

"I called. He didn't pick up," Zig whispered.

"You sure he's okay?"

"I told you, he didn't pick up."

"You should still check in on him. Even if he was feeling guilty, this guy Caesar put his life at risk for you. Make sure he's okay."

"I will. After we—" Zig cut himself off.

Diagonally across the street, Houdini paused at the front door of an insurance shop, checking over his shoulder. Zig scooched down slightly, but otherwise didn't move. Didn't say a word.

Houdini tugged on the door and stepped inside, disappearing.

"I gotta go," Zig said.

"Stop. Tell me where Houdini is."

"Insurance place. Prudential. I need you to look it up. See who owns it."

"Ziggy, don't be stupid. Stay where you are. You have no idea what you're walking into."

"This guy knows what Operation Bluebook is. He's the one—That's the reason the plane crashed in Alaska. Whatever this Bluebook thing is—"

"You don't even know if this is part of it!"

"He took seven lives, Dino! *Innocent lives!*" Zig hissed with a guttural roar, spit flying from his lips.

Dino went silent, knowing that tone in his friend's voice—a tone last heard on that night when Zig made the poor choice of taking on a six-foot-four Marine who was screaming in the parking lot and gripping the arm of his sobbing girlfriend. When Zig jumped in, even the girlfriend turned on Zig, shouting that he should mind his own damn business. The Marine did far more damage, fracturing Zig's eye socket. Still, Zig wouldn't stop swinging, even as the blood turned the sclera of his eye completely red. Only later, in the emergency room, did Dino realize it was the night of what would've been Zig's twentieth wedding anniversary.

"Ziggy, you're picking the wrong fight here. Let me call the cops."

Zig barely heard the words. Reaching for the door handle of the car, he looked outside and—

"*Mothertrucker,*" Zig muttered.

Down the street, a new person got out of their own car as Houdini entered the insurance place. Her head was down, but even under whatever baseball cap she was wearing, there was no mistaking her stark white hair.

"Nola," Zig blurted.

"*Nola?* Where?" Dino asked though the phone. "She's *there?*"

"Mhmm," Zig said, his hand still on the door handle. Staring through the windshield, he felt like he was watching her on TV. Her head was down and her back was to Zig, so she couldn't see him. But the way she was moving, like the best soldiers on a sneak—small steps, each one slow and careful—she knew exactly where she was going.

She wasn't the only one.

In a single smooth movement, Nola pulled open the door and stepped into the insurance place. Yet as the door swung shut, a brand-new figure stepped out of the crowd. Just outside the Safeway, across from the coffee shop.

Another woman. Native American. Wore a hunting jacket, a black one with loads of pockets. Even from here, her walk stood out—the same slow and careful steps. Military training for sure.

"What the crap is going on?" Zig whispered. He had no idea she was called The Curtain. But he knew a threat when he saw one.

The woman stopped near the corner, still a block and a half away. Zig squinted through the dark. Unlike Nola, who was small and compact, this woman was wide-shouldered.

"*Ziggy, tell me what the hell is happening!*" Dino insisted.

"I'm still trying to figure it out."

Taking her time as she crossed the street, the big Native American woman looked around, scanning every inch of the grid that soldiers are trained to examine.

Zig leaned forward even more in his seat, squinting as she crossed the street and made her way toward the insurance agency. No question, her posture was perfect—but the way her left shoulder looked higher than her right one... She was carrying something under her field coat.

"She's wearing a strap. For a gun. Or something worse," Zig blurted.

"*You don't know that.*"

The woman approached the front door of the insurance agency. Unlike Nola, she paused, standing there in the cold, scanning the block one final time. Then she disappeared inside.

"They're ambushing her!" Zig said.

"This isn't your fight. Don't do something stupid!"

Kicking open the car door, Zig hopped outside. The wind was cold, scratching at his face.

"Ziggy, I'm calling the cops! They'll be there in minutes!"

"She'll be dead by then," Zig barked, already across the street. He stuffed his phone in his pocket, though he didn't hang up. If things went upside down, at least Dino could be a witness.

"Ziggy, you haven't seen this girl for years!" Dino shouted, though Zig couldn't hear it.

Running full speed, Zig darted for the insurance shop. *Get a Piece of the Rock with Benjamin R. Powell,* he read to himself as he caught his breath.

His right hand gripped the knife in his pocket. His left gripped the door handle.

Swallowing hard, Zig gave the door a tug and stepped inside.

55

Six minutes ago

Houdini hated it here. Hated the way the whole insurance agency reeked of stale cigarettes, Carpet Fresh, and mediocrity, but hated even more that it reminded him of his grandparents' place.

"Evening, darlin'. How can I—?" the middle-aged receptionist called out, cutting herself off. She had braces, and a tattoo that read *Cha-Cha* vertically down her forearm. Looking up from her cell phone, she spotted Houdini, then looked right back down. Just like she was paid to.

"You got scissors?" Houdini asked, approaching her desk.

"P-Pardon?"

"Scissors? You know...*scissors?*"

From a neon orange pencil cup, the woman pulled out a pair of scissors, keeping her eyes down as she handed it over.

"*Muchas gracias,*" Houdini said, standing there and chewing his gum for an extra half a second, as if he were waiting for her to say something back. She knew better than that.

Picking up speed as he headed for the back of the office, Houdini made a quick left, then right, navigating a small hub of cubicles, all of them empty.

For months now, after each package pickup, Houdini came here—to the back of Powell Insurance—to this frosted glass door and its big eighties-era half-moon door handle that looked like a frown. Yanking it open, he revealed a wide conference room with a Formica oval table at the center and a built-in kitchen along the left-hand wall. The refrigerator door was propped open; it was clearly unplugged, filled with file boxes.

On the oval table were two dirty ashtrays as well as the most valuable thing in this entire shithole: an ancient corded telephone.

Time to tell the man in charge.

In the current world of high-tech surveillance, where the government can access everything from your Internet-connected doorbell to the microphone in your Wi-Fi-enabled cable box, it's not that hard to trace a cell phone. So the safest way to make a private call these days is to use the one technology even the government doesn't have the manpower to check anymore: a plain, old-fashioned landline.

"Malvina, I dial a nine first, then a one?" Houdini shouted at the wall, which was covered with awful landscape paintings in gaudy gold frames. At the head of the table were four wall clocks, all in a row, labeled London, Tokyo, Los Angeles, and Washington, DC, though they were all now stopped, showing four incorrect times.

"Nine, then one," the receptionist shouted back.

Letting the phone ring, Houdini tossed the briefcase on the conference table. The padlock was still in place; the zipper wouldn't budge. Time to find out what was inside.

Cradling the receiver with his chin, Houdini gripped the scissors like a knife and plunged it into the side of the soft leather briefcase. Slicing down, he made the hole wider and wider until—

Click.

Someone picked up.

"Talk," a man with a woodchipper of a voice insisted through the phone.

Houdini rolled his eyes. "I'm not hired help."

"You sure about that?"

"You're a dick."

"Spit your gum out. Makes you sound like a child."

Houdini made a *ptooo* noise, though he didn't spit the gum out. "Our magician friend," he finally said, referring to The Amazing Caesar, "is not feeling so good."

"What about the most recent present?"

"He's a clueless old dinosaur—had no idea where it came from. But I'm telling you, someone's stepping in our shit. We need to— *ruhhhh*," Houdini said, wedging his fingers into the side of the cheap leather briefcase and tearing the small hole wider.

Inside, as always, was money. Bundles of cash. But instead of being green, it looked... royal blue, almost purple. Across the front was a picture of Muhammad Ali Jinnah, the founder of Pakistan. These weren't dollars. They were...

"Rupees," Houdini said.

"Pakistani money?"

It made no sense. Their deliveries were always in US dollars, one or two times in Iraqi dinars. If someone was sending new currency—

"Bitch of a bitch," Houdini blurted, pulling out a stack of cash and flipping through it. A 1,000 Pakistani rupee bill was on top, but the rest of the pile was... All of it was blank. "It's blue construction paper," Houdini said. He flipped through the rest. All three stacks were the same. All of it worthless. This wasn't a delivery. It was a trap.

"You need to get out of there."

Houdini glanced over his shoulder. Through the frosted glass, the secretary went to stand up, then sat back down. Like she was talking to someone who just arrived.

"You need to get out of there," the man repeated.

"Lemme just—"

"Get out of there. *Now.*"

Houdini slammed the receiver down, but just as he turned— *Phoom.*

The glass door flew open.

Nola stormed inside, her gun pointed at Houdini's head. "You must be Rowan."

"Whoawhoawhoa. You have the wrong—"

"They call you Houdini. Your real name is Rowan Johansson. You're from Scottsbluff, Nebraska."

"I don't know what you're talking abou—"

Nola pulled back the hammer on her gun, aiming it at his forehead. "I'm now going to shoot you in your face. You have three seconds to prevent it. Your boss—"

"I don't have a boss."

"Call him whatever you want. You're too stupid to do this yourself—so that person you were just talking to," she said, her finger tightening around the trigger. "Tell me where he is."

56

He was too calm. That was Nola's first thought.

"Take a breath. I'm not your enemy," Houdini said, chewing his gum, his hands raised casually in the air.

He wasn't sweating. *Seemed unafraid. Maybe just dumb.*

"You know who I am?" Nola challenged, her gun still pointed at his face.

"Nola. The one who died."

"The one you tried to *kill*."

"Not me. Wrong guy," Houdini said, lowering his chin and offering a conspiratorial grin, like they were on the same side.

He was a charmer, a natural salesman—like a lawyer but with less polish. She eyed his gum chewing. *More street-smart than book-smart.* He wasn't a dummy, though. Deep crow's-feet were in the corner of his right eye; his left eye was clean. That's his aiming eye. *A hunter. Definitely right-handed.*

He chewed some more, short quick bites. *Impatient? Annoyed? Anxious?* No. He kept on chewing, his grin never leaving his eyes. *In control.* Like he knew what was coming.

Nola glanced over her shoulder, turning toward the door. Too late.

"*Gkkk.*"

She never saw the person behind her. An arm wrapped around

her neck as four metal blades—like a metal paw—pressed hard against her throat.

"Your day's about to take a noticeable turn for the worse," the tall Native American woman whispered.

"Nola Brown..." Houdini said, still chewing his gum as he stood there on the carpet/linoleum border between the conference room and kitchenette. "I want you to meet our dear friend, The Cur—"

In a burst, the glass door to the conference room shattered, bits of aqua shards spraying everywhere. A metal rolling chair was still in midair, thrown through the door by—

Zig raced into the room as the metal chair somersaulted, colliding into The Curtain, catching her off-balance.

"*Don't move—she goes down, you go down!*" Zig shouted, jamming the tip of his knife into the back of The Curtain's neck. She started to turn, but he wedged it in there, through her black field jacket. "This is your C7," he told her, pushing his knife between her sixth and seventh vertebrae. "That's what protects your spinal cord. If you ever want to move your arms, or walk again, you need to let go of her."

"Tell Nola to drop her gun," The Curtain challenged, her claw weapon still at Nola's throat.

Nola didn't budge, her gun still aimed at Houdini.

"Everyone, take a breath," Zig said.

"Nola, listen to the man," Houdini warned, amping up the charm as he backed up a few steps into the kitchenette. "Put your gun down, or you're gonna get your throat slit."

"No one's slitting anyone's throat!" Zig insisted.

"Put the gun down, Nola," Houdini repeated, chewing his—

Blam.

Nola pulled the trigger, shooting Houdini directly in the throat.

57

Homestead, Florida
Ten years ago

This was Nola when she was sixteen.

"What's wrong?" Nola asked, clearly anxious.

Ms. Sable laughed. "Can you just close your eyes and stop worrying?"

Sitting across from Ms. Sable at the wide art table, Nola closed her eyes, but she couldn't stop worrying. Not after that night a few years back when Royall covered her eyes.

"They closed?" Ms. Sable asked.

Nola nodded, hearing her teacher rummage through her purse. *Fwap.*

Something hit the wooden table.

"Open."

Nola opened her eyes, staring down at a rectangular box, the size of a brick. It was covered in Muppet wrapping paper that featured Fozzie, Miss Piggy, and of course Kermit, in the middle of a celebratory Kermit-flail. A present.

"I'm a crappy wrapper. The paper is all we had left. From when Dominic was little," Ms. Sable explained, referring to her son.

Nola looked at it like someone took a dump on the desk. *Why would—?* "What's this for?"

"This weekend was your birthday, wasn't it? I believe that entitles some of us to say, *Happy birthday.*"

Nola fidgeted with the cuffs on the jean jacket she'd bought at Goodwill on Ms. Sable's recommendation. *Girls shouldn't be walking around in wifebeater tank tops.* Nola still wore the tank underneath. But every day, she wore the jacket.

"Ms. Sable—"

"When someone gives you a present, say *thank you.*"

"But you—"

"Try it, okay? *Thank you.*"

"Thank you," Nola repeated, unable to look up at her teacher. Ms. Sable opened her mouth, ready to lecture her about eye contact, but it was her birthday.

Tearing at the wrapping paper and opening the narrow box, Nola was hit by the smell first—her favorite smell over these past few months. Freshly sharpened...

"Pencils. Cool," Nola said, revealing half a dozen professional-quality pencils, each in its own pristine plastic case.

"It's not much. Teacher's salary," Ms. Sable said. "But y'know...for sketching."

Nola nodded, flashing a hint of the ruined smile that always broke Ms. Sable's heart. Like Nola was afraid to commit to a full grin, or didn't know how. "They're all different," Nola said.

"That's the point. As you know, the number on the side is their lead grade, and a 4B is softer than a 2B. Each has a different touch, like a different brush. When I bought Dominic his first baseball mitt, this handsome guy at the Sports Authority told me it all started with the right equipment. That's how he got me wasting fifty bucks for a glove for a kid who hated baseball. Anyway, there you go. Now you have it. The right equipment."

For the rest of her life, Nola would come back to this moment, relishing it, thinking about it, replaying it in her head. In the next few months, when Nola's life imploded and her soul was ripped to shreds, she'd need this day more than ever.

Leaning down toward the box, she'd never seen anything so...beautiful. She hesitated on the word, but that was the right one. *Beautiful.* Over and over, she reread the names of all the different pencils.

Mongol, Faber, Staedtler, Ticonderoga, and Swan.

"Just you wait. You haven't even seen Part Two yet," Ms. Sable said, darting to her office, a small closet in the back corner of the art room. She ran like an athlete, Nola thought, realizing for the very first time how little she knew about Ms. Sable's life outside of school.

There was some whispering, like Ms. Sable was talking to someone.

"*Close your eyes!*" Ms. Sable called out.

This time, Nola didn't hesitate.

"Nola, just so you know, this is a *potential* gift. You don't have to take it, okay? Only if your dad says it's fine."

Nola nodded, eyes still shut and so excited, she didn't even hear the mention of Royall.

"Okay. Open. Look."

On the art table was a cardboard box, big enough that it could hold an old computer monitor. The box wasn't wrapped, wasn't even closed. Something moved inside, scratching wildly. Something alive.

"I'm warning you, you don't have to take this. It's my son's, and he's leaving for— He enlisted in the Army, God bless him. They're gonna pay for his college. He says he'll eventually ask to be stationed at the base here," she said, referring to the nearby Homestead Air Reserve Base. "Anyway, he's my different one, never on the conventional path. So when he said he couldn't take pets with him, well...Happy Birthday Part Two," Ms. Sable said, quickly adding, "*if you want it.*"

Nola lunged forward, ruined smile on her face.

"Here, let me introduce you," Ms. Sable said, reaching into the box and pulling out... It had elegant black fur and a red bow taped to its collar. It looked like a cat, but as the light hit it—

"A skunk?"

"Before you judge, it's been de-scented," Ms. Sable explained. "So no stink bombs, no rotten smell. Don't ask how we got him; my son's idea. But he's been with us for four years now. They act like cats, though. Eat cat food, use a litter box, they just look like, well...like this."

Nola stared at the skunk as it gracefully prowled across the art desk, cocking its head sideways at Nola. A skunk. Even Nola knew this was weird. Another thing for her classmates to point at. Another thing to make fun of. Another thing to make her different.

"Does she have a name?"

"El Duque—I think it's the name of an old baseball player— though we call him Dooch. She's a he."

Nola stood there a moment. "I want him," she decided, pulling Dooch close, into a hug.

Dooch relished the touch, rubbing his cheek against Nola's arm. He didn't smell at all, and he moved just like a cat.

"Nola, there's something in everyone that's beautiful. Your job is to unlock it. That sounds like a yoga quote, but it's gospel."

Nola nodded, not realizing how soon she'd need those words. It would be one of the most important lessons of her life.

"I'm glad this is gonna work out," Ms. Sable added. "Just make sure it's okay with your dad."

58

The bullet hit Houdini in the center of his esophagus.

"*Hgkkkk!*"

He was still in mid-chew, still grinning at Nola—as a small black bullet hole appeared in his neck. He tried clearing his throat. It was filled with blood.

He grabbed his own neck, his body lurching backward against the sink in the kitchenette. It helped him keep his balance until his eyes went wide, then rolled backward too. His legs buckled.

Nola knew what came next.

He hit the linoleum like a discarded marionette, blood pouring from his throat.

"*Nola, are you nuts!?*" Zig yelled. "*How could you—?*"

The Curtain spun backward, her claw no longer at Nola's neck as she elbowed Zig in the face, just like Nola gambled she would.

Whoever The Curtain was, she was a pro. Her top priority would always be self-preservation. It was a risk Nola had to take; if she didn't shoot Houdini, she and Zig would already be—

"*Fuh!*" Zig groaned, stumbling sideways, slipping on the shattered glass, blood pouring from his nose.

The Curtain didn't let up. Storming toward Zig, she sliced at his hand, her metal claws tearing his skin and sending his knife flying. But as The Curtain was about to learn, there's a cost to turning your back on Nola.

Without a breath of hesitation, Nola raised her gun, aimed it at the back of The Curtain's head, and pulled the trigger.

Blam!

A tall panel of frosted glass—next to where the door used to be—shattered from the stray bullet. Nola was surprised by her own miss. The Curtain was fast, especially for someone her size.

Nola raised her gun again. Same spot. Back of The Curtain's head.

In a blur, The Curtain spun with a roundhouse kick aimed at Nola's gun.

Nola saw it coming, but she had to give The Curtain credit. Whoever this woman was, she was a brawler. Well trained too. The roundhouse kick wasn't karate or tae kwon do. *Jeet Kune Do*, Nola decided, noticing the way The Curtain's leg swept like a hook. She was going for speed, not power. Not that it'd help The Curtain here.

Nola put up a blocking elbow. She had to use her shooting hand, had to move her gun.

The Curtain grinned, snapping her kick. Nola stood her ground, absorbing the impact and realizing half a second too late that the hook kick was just a distraction, a setup for The Curtain to get close enough to—

With a swipe of her hand, The Curtain sank her metal claws deep into the inside of Nola's wrist, slicing it open.

Nola made a noise, a groan, but she wouldn't cry out, even as the blood trickled toward her elbow.

Dumb, Nola cursed herself. *Should've seen that coming.*

In the distance, she heard the faint sound of sirens. The police were still blocks away. But as Nola felt her own heartbeat pulsing in her ears, she could hear...*everything*, like every noise in the universe was suddenly isolated and— *There*. Another sound. Coming from the front of the office. Someone sobbing. The receptionist

was under her desk, crying. When the world sounds like this...
Nola knew she was going into shock.

Nola tried holding tight to her gun—*Don't let it go!*—but the
pain... *Forget the pain. Put it away.* She'd been in worse fights.
She thought of Royall and the friends he brought home, the things
they'd say. She put the pain of those nights away. She'd bury
this too.

Looking down, Nola clutched the gun with everything she had.
But there was nothing in her hand. The gun had fallen to the floor.
Barely three seconds had passed. Gripping her own bleeding wrist,
Nola fought to stay on her feet.

A few feet away, Zig was still on the ground, bleeding from his
nose and finally getting his bearings. Barely three more seconds
had passed.

"You have about four minutes before you pass out," The Curtain
said, picking up Nola's gun, admiring the weight. "Approximately
six minutes until you hemorrhage." Pressing her lips together, The
Curtain grinned at her own victory, then aimed the gun at Nola's
chest and gripped the trigger. "This is for making me drink that
shitty coffee."

"*No!*" Zig screamed, fighting to get up.

Blam!

Nola intentionally turned toward the bullet.

Instead of hitting Nola in the chest, the bullet burrowed just below her collarbone. She was still clutching her own wrist, the blood
seeping between her fingers as the world went blurry, then black.

Her last thought was about the color of her own blood and how
it looked in this green fluorescent light. It gave the crimson a hint
of purple. There was a color just like that on the color wheel. It was
called... *Carmine*, she finally remembered as she fell to the floor,
just shy of the conference table.

Storming toward her, The Curtain leaned down over Nola's unconscious body and pressed the barrel of the gun to the side of
Nola's head. Her finger tightened around the trigger and—

"*Fuuh!*" The Curtain roared in pain as Zig plunged his knife through her field jacket and deep into the back of The Curtain's shoulder blade.

The knife was halfway in when it hit bone. Zig gave it a sharp twist, widening the wound, which made The Curtain drop her gun. It was a move he learned from the dozens of fallen service members who'd been ambushed in hand-to-hand attacks—and whose rounded gashes he'd stitched up so many times.

Zig thought the pain would make her pass out. He couldn't be more wrong.

"*You're fucking dead!*" The Curtain boomed, still on her feet, her back to him, as she thrashed and swung wildly.

To protect himself, Zig had to let go of the knife, which was still in her shoulder. Thrusting her elbow, then a backward headbutt, she clipped him in the gut, then the chin. Her metal claw scratched at his leg. It was like he was standing behind a wild bull and trying to hold it in a headlock.

"*Enough!*" Zig said, still directly behind her. His chest bumped into her back as he gripped her neck and dug his fingers above the hollow of her throat. The more he pressed into her larynx, the harder it was for her to breathe.

"*Hhh,*" The Curtain gasped, still violently thrashing, still trying to stab him with her claw. He held his arms straight out to keep her away. Outside, in the distance, the sirens were getting louder.

Zig squeezed even harder. The knife was still sticking out of The Curtain's shoulder. She tried to reach for it, tried to grab at him. Zig tightened his grip as she shoved herself backward. Her ponytail hit Zig in the face. Zig squeezed even tighter. Within seconds, The Curtain's movements slowed down, her arms sagging to her sides.

No.

Not to her sides. She reached for something in her army coat, in the lower left pocket. A gun? Another claw?

Tung.

The round metal object hit the floor, rolling like a wobbly egg toward Nola's lifeless body.

It was a grenade.

Dangling from The Curtain's middle finger was the pin.

59

Oh, shit.

The Curtain slumped sideways, nearly unconscious. The trigger—the metal lever on the side of the grenade—was at Zig's feet. No question... it was live.

Oh, shit.

Outside, the sirens were shrieking loudly. The police— If they ran in now—

"Nola, get up!" Zig shouted.

She didn't move. Didn't look like she was even breathing. She was turned on her side in a puddle of glass shards and blood, still lifelessly holding her own wrist.

Zig dropped to his knees next to her, looking for a pulse. Her skin was gray, but her chest... She was breathing.

He tried to lift her. There wasn't time. Back at Dover, grenade injuries were a regular occurrence. Once the pin was pulled and the trigger got loose, the delay fuse on a grenade was barely five seconds.

Four... three...

The sirens were screaming. The police were pulling up.

Behind Zig, someone was coughing. The Curtain. She was awake, hunched over and down on all fours, air now filling her lungs. The knife was still sticking out of her back, reminding Zig of the sword in the stone.

The Curtain turned toward him. "Now…" she coughed, her dark eyes on Zig, "we all die together."

"No, asshole," Zig said. "Just you."

Springing to his feet, he kicked the grenade back toward The Curtain, then threw all of his weight onto the wide side of the conference table, tipping it toward himself and Nola.

The table landed on its side with a *chomp*. Zig gave it another tug, letting momentum do the rest. As the table flipped upside down and toward them, Zig pounced on Nola, covering her body with his own. The table slammed him from behind, sandwiching them together.

Zig shut his eyes and started praying, the same prayer he'd been saying far too often lately. *Magpie, I hope I'm wrong about the afterlife, because I really can't wait to see you.*

Two…one…

Zig's final thought was a fleeting one, about how grenades work—by projecting bits of metal into vital organs—and hoping that if his body got sent to Dover, Louisa would be the one to embalm him rather than Wil. Because Wil was a jerkoff.

Zig shut his eyes, holding tight to Nola and pressing his forehead against hers. And then…

Nothing.

Silence.

He gave it another few seconds.

Still nothing.

Opening his eyes, Zig glanced over his shoulder. From his angle down on the ground, the slanted table gave him only a small triangular view of the conference room, which was covered in glass. He shoved the table slightly so he—

There. On the floor. Right where he kicked it.

The grenade.

It was just sitting there, fully intact.

Confused, Zig gave the heavy table a shove, pushing it aside. The Curtain and Houdini…both of them…gone.

Mothertrucker. The grenade…it was fake. *Dumb old man,* he scolded himself. *So stupid to fall for such an easy distraction.*

Along the floor, there was a trail of blood that led to the back of the office, past the kitchenette. There was a *click* as the fire door slapped shut. When The Curtain left, she was carrying Houdini's body.

Maybe Zig could still catch her. Certainly he could. But only if he left Nola.

If Zig were smart, he'd run right now—leave Nola to the cops. They'd get her the medical attention she needed. And they'd also start asking questions, which would cause a brand-new set of problems.

Zig thought back to the magic shop, to what the old magician Caesar had said about the big move covering the small one. Whatever Operation Bluebook was doing with those suitcases full of money, someone in the military was making really big moves to keep this all quiet. It was the same with—who was that woman? The Native American? No rank, ribbons, or name tag on her army jacket. That's how Uncle Sam goes in when they don't want to risk being traced to a particular mission. If she's active military… Big moves were definitely happening. That's why Colonel Hsu, Master Guns, and everyone else at Dover were suddenly working double time to see why Zig was so interested in this case.

So why *was* Zig so interested?

He stared down at Nola on the ground, her head awkwardly sagging sideways. To the untrained eye, she looked like a corpse— but Zig knew, the dead have a stillness and weight that can't be replicated. Nola was alive. And if everyone on the other side was active military, there was only one way to keep her that way.

"I got you," he whispered, scooping Nola into his arms. He grabbed her gun too, just in case. As he lifted Nola, her white hair flowed away from her face, revealing the scarred and jagged edge of her left ear. Zig was embarrassed by how good it made him feel.

"*G-Get...Get off me...!*" Nola growled, her words slurring, her eyes still closed. "*I...I don't need your help...*"

Zig ignored her, eyeing the wound below her collarbone. Clean hit. Even if the bullet was still inside, that was good—meant it could be stitched.

The sirens outside were deafening. There was a screech of brakes. The cops were arriving.

Zig headed toward the back door, cradling her as he kicked it open and darted out into the cold. He glanced around. The alley was wide—big enough for a truck—but completely empty. Thank God it was dark.

"*Mongol...F-Faber...Staedtler...Ticonderoga...*" Nola mumbled.

"*Ticonderoga?* That a person or a place?"

Nola shook her head, blinking herself awake and wincing in pain. "Y-You better be able to stitch me together," she muttered.

60

aesar, we got problems!"

No one answered.

"Caesar, get out here—I need help!" Zig shouted, bursting into the magic shop. He had left Nola lying across the backseat of his car, floating in and out of consciousness. *"I need a first aid kit! And a sewing kit if you've got it!"*

Zig made it all the way to the front counter before he noticed the smell—the smell he knew so well from Dover—the coppery stench from when a body was still fresh. The smell of blood.

"Caesar, if you're about to jump out wearing a gorilla mask, please do it n—"

On Zig's right, down one of the aisles, he spotted a small dark puddle seeping from the foot of one of the bookcases, coming from the aisle behind it.

Zig's chest felt like it was hollowed out with a metal rake.

He ran to the next aisle. The puddle was larger there. At eye level, a shelf filled with bendable magic wands and rubbery pencils was sprayed with bits of meat and bone. The words *Kids Section* were handwritten on a laminated index card that was taped to the top.

Along the floor, a long smear of blood ran down the aisle and turned the corner, like someone had dragged the body away. Or was still dragging it.

Zig reached into his pocket, putting his hand on Nola's gun. He was tempted to yell a warning—something to scare them off—but the truth was, whoever was here, Zig didn't want to scare them off.

Cocking the gun and gripping the trigger, Zig walked quickly down the aisle, sticking to the left to keep himself off the overhead camera. On the opposite side of the store, the mounted Bozo the Clown head kept watch.

The smear of blood across the tile veered around the corner, then beelined toward the store's back room, where the door was propped open.

Zig looked up, eyeing the ceiling. He could still see the mounted Bozo the Clown. But unlike the front of the store, there were no cameras back here. Whatever business Caesar did in the back room, he didn't want records of it. More important, whoever was back here now, they wouldn't see Zig coming.

On three, Zig told himself, pausing just outside the threshold. He held his breath and gripped the trigger. *One...two...*

Darting inside, Zig pointed his gun. The wide storage room was just as he had left it. Stacks of cardboard boxes, egg-crates filled with old magic tricks, but otherwise empty.

Along the floor, the smear of blood veered to the left, to Caesar's tiny office. Sticking out of the open doorway were the legs of an old man dressed in slacks and orthopedic black shoes—

"*Nonono*," Zig muttered.

Zig raced to The Amazing Caesar's side. The back of his head was a wet mess of hair and exposed bone. He was facedown in a pool of his own— The blood was everywhere...on his chair, on the handles of the desk drawers...there was even a perfect red handprint, like a kindergarten painting, on the leather blotter on his desk.

Caesar wasn't dragged here. He crawled on his own.

At Dover, Zig had seen it dozens of times: on the battlefield, a soldier with a missing jaw and no legs crawling two miles back to his base, just so he could die in his own bed. No one fights harder for life than the dying.

Zig reexamined the blood on the chair, the desk, even the blotter. So what made Caesar crawl all the way here?

Zig turned the body over. A spit bubble, tinted red with blood, popped at Caesar's lips. He was breathing.

"*Caesar . . . Caesar, can you hear me!?*"

The old magician didn't move, though his eyes were still open, dilating in the light. His skin was gray, like an elephant. He didn't have long.

"*Caesar, if you hear me, blink!*"

He didn't blink. He just stared up at Zig, peaceful as could be. There was no fear on his face. He knew what was coming.

Zig went to say something, then noticed . . .

Caesar was clutching something in his hand. It was square and silver. A picture frame. He was holding it to his chest. This is what Caesar crawled back for.

"Who's this? This *you*?" Zig asked, tugging on the frame. Caesar nodded with his eyes, but wouldn't let go.

The frame was smeared in blood, but Zig could still make out the image: a muted color photograph from the eighties—of an elderly couple on a cruise ship. The man's hair was thicker and darker, but it was clearly Caesar, his arm draped around the woman's waist.

It was the pose from every cruise ship photo, right down to them standing in front of a round life preserver with the name of the ship on it. S.S. *SeaDream*. From the looks of it, Caesar was a bruiser back then, a rhino stuffed into a Hawaiian shirt. But God, the way his mouth was open in mid-laugh . . . did he look happy.

"Your wife?" Zig asked, now picturing his own ex-wife, in a similar photo she and Zig took decades ago, on a riverboat in New Orleans for his thirtieth birthday. Would Zig crawl back through his house just to get one last look at the photo? He knew the answer.

"T-The plane . . ." Caesar sputtered, his face ruled by sadness.

"That wasn't your fault. You couldn't have known."

Caesar shook his head. "I-I-I...I knew he was..." He fought to get the words out. "T-Toldja Houdini was a...was a shitbag."

"This is because of me. I had you give him the bag. This is my fault, Caesar. I'm so sorry!"

Caesar shook his head again. He tried to say something, but the words wouldn't come. He looked angry now. No, not angry. Frustrated. Then irritated, then terrified, then full of despair, his emotions galloping. It reminded Zig of the hospital all those years ago. When someone's dying, their face betrays every thought, their filter gone, their eyes like a flip-book of passions and sentiments, each fully formed thought a bolt of electricity whistling through their synapses. On your deathbed, life may very well pass before your eyes, and so does your reaction to it.

Caesar's breathing slowed. His skin was grayer, looking like putty. And then...he started to smile. Began to laugh.

Another bubble formed at Caesar's lips. "B-Before he shot me...the...he..." Caesar swallowed hard. "I-I saw it had GPS."

"What had GPS? I don't understand."

"S-Special Forces...they all have— So...so they can track...I saw it on him when he took the bag," the old magician insisted, reaching into his pocket. His hand was shaking as he pulled it out and revealed what would be his final magic trick. The item dangled from his crooked finger. "I...I stole the fucker's watch."

61

This was Nola when she was sixteen.

"You're shitting me. A damn skunk?" Royall asked.

"It's de-scented. He's like a cat."

"It's a fuckin' skunk!"

"Look at him. It's like a cat. *Like a cat*," Nola said as the skunk did infinity loops around her legs, its tail lingering in the air.

"I thought you liked cats," Nola added.

Royall did like cats. He'd never admit it, but Nola saw the way he'd kneel down and do kissy lips whenever their neighbor's pet—a fat and snooty ginger cat named Tubbs—sauntered into their front yard.

"He's cute," Royall blurted.

"I know, right!?"

Royall was down on one knee, rubbing his fingers together to call the skunk close. "When I was little, I wanted a cat so bad," he explained, the skunk now nuzzling against his fingers. "My mother would never let me have one."

"What about your dad?"

Royall looked up, flashing Nola a—she'd never seen this look before. More than sadness, there was sorrow on his face, profound sorrow. That was the last time she'd ever ask Royall about his dad.

They both turned back to the skunk.

"Where will it poop?"

Nola held up the litter box that Ms. Sable gave her. "In here. Like a cat," Nola said for the fourth time. "His name is Dooch."

Royall eyed the litter box, then Dooch. He was unreadable, even to Nola. "I'm not calling him that."

"You don't have to."

"And I'm not saying we're keeping it—"

Nola nodded, far too excitedly.

"—but until we decide what's what, I've got kitty litter in the garage. In the bookcase, by the hoop."

"Why do you have kitty li—?"

"For the grease. C'mon, I taught you that! It gets grease stains out of the driveway."

Nola took off for the garage, her sudden movement startling Dooch, whose rear end spiked in the air, armed with blanks.

In the garage, Nola headed for the basketball hoop that Royall got as payment for a fake Canadian passport. It leaned on a rickety wire shelving unit that bent like a palm tree in a hurricane.

Nola thought the kitty litter was on the lowest shelf. But when she got there, it was gone. Confused, she checked the other shelves, then checked below the brand-new workbench Royall had just bought himself. She even checked behind the stolen stop sign that Royall had illegally taken down at the end of the block since no way did they need a four-way stop there, what kinda dumbass rule is that?

Still no kitty litter.

Glancing around the garage, Nola noticed a few folding chairs and two four-hundred-dollar vacuum cleaners (another trade from an immigrant family) that were blocking the bottom shelves of the white particleboard bookcase that Royall used to store industrial packs of laminating sheets. Maybe that was the bookcase he was talking about.

With a tug, Nola pulled away the vacuum cleaners. There! Kitty litter! But as she stepped in to pull it off the lower shelf, her foot kicked the bookcase and—

Tunk.

The toe kick of the bookcase fell forward. Nola knelt to pick it up. Behind it, though—in the narrow space behind the toe kick—there was something back there. Something hidden. Papers. No, not papers. Envelopes. A small stack of them.

Nola pulled out the stack, which was covered in ancient dust and held together by a green rubber band. They were all addressed to Royall, but the handwriting...the return address... Nola's throat tightened, her windpipe feeling like it was filled with sand.

B. LAPOINTE

GUIDRY, TX

Barb LaPointe. Nola's old family. The ones who gave her away, gave her to Royall.

Nola tore off the rubber band, flipping through the stack and scanning postdates. Nine years ago, eight years ago, even one from seven years ago...these were right after Nola left, after Royall took her. All these years, she thought the LaPointes abandoned her, but they were reaching out! *They were writing!*

Nola's heart punched inside her chest, like it was about to burst through her ribcage.

Ripping open the first envelope—a bright red one, like a Valentine—Nola pulled out...it wasn't a card. It was a note, handwritten, on white loose-leaf paper. Nola tried reading it, but her eyes...her brain...just seeing the tidy loops of Barb's old handwriting...everything was moving too fast. None of the words made sense.

She started again.

Dear Royall...so nice meeting you face to face...with such a difficult decision...we know you'll take care of Nola, but...

But? Why was there a *but?*

...realized we forgot *to collect payment.*

Payment?

Nola tore open the next letter.

*...I'm sure it was just an oversight, but Christmas is coming, so
if you could send a check...*

She tore open another. And another. And another. Each letter
growing more insistent.

Expect you to keep your promise, Royall. Check. Cash. Money.
And that one word Barb used over and over:

Payment.

Nola's head was spinning, and her heart was deflated, sagging
over her lungs, making it impossible to breathe.

All these years, Nola thought the LaPointes gave her away
so...so they could give her an improved life...so they were in
a better position to help her brother...but now, to read these...
They didn't just give her away.

They *sold* her.

And worse, Royall bought her. Like property. And apparently, he
thought so little of her, he never even made the payment, not that
the LaPointes could tell that to anyone. All they had was Royall's
word. They could never enforce an illegal agreement like that.

"Nola, you find the cat litter, or not?" Royall called out, his voice
close.

Nola stuffed the letters back into place, quickly closing the toe
kick and sliding the vacuum cleaners back, just like it was. But as
she grabbed the kitty litter—

Behind her, there was a sharp creak of moving floorboards.

Nola looked over her shoulder. The doorway was empty. Motes
of dust floated in the air—but she could tell, sometimes you just
know—Royall had been standing there.

Did he see? Did he know what she'd found?

Nola had no idea, until later that night, when she decided that her best course of action was to go back and grab the old letters.

She sat awake half the night, staring up at the ceiling, her new pet, Dooch, curled in a ball at her feet. Nola wasn't moving until she was sure Royall was asleep.

At 2:30 a.m., she finally got out of bed, Dooch raising his head at full alert. Quietly as she could, she snuck back to the garage, pulled the vacuum cleaners aside, and once again kneeled at the toe kick.

Wedging her fingers in there, she pulled the toe kick down, revealing Royall's secret hideaway.

A ball of dust bunnies rolled toward her. But the letters—the proof of what he and the LaPointes had done—all of it was gone.

Royall knew. He knew what she'd found. The only question now was: What was he planning as a punishment?

62

Maryland
Today

Tampons and nasal spray. Oh, and a water bottle. And scissors. And duct tape. That's what he needed.

An hour ago, after tying a quick tourniquet in the car, Zig raced out of DC, not stopping until he reached a small town called Mitchellville, Maryland. From there, he picked a CVS a few towns over—and the Mi Casa Motel, chosen because its rooms led out to an exterior walkway right next to the parking lot.

Cradling Nola, Zig kicked open the door and was hit by the motel smell of stale cigarettes, sweat, and whatever that Rorschach-shaped stain on the carpet was. With Mi Casa's Southwestern theme, every piece of furniture was blond Formica.

As Zig pulled down the patchwork top sheets and carefully lowered Nola onto one of the sagging twin beds, she was still in and out of consciousness. At one point, she insisted she was fine, though she was clearly unaware that sudden blood loss caused a rush of the same hormones and endorphins that produce second winds during marathons. Within a minute, she was out cold.

"Doesn't even look that bad...you can barely see it," Zig said, whispering the same lies he told all the fallen service members who came through Dover. Back in mortuary school, Zig's professor warned him not to keep speaking to the dead. *The closer you get, the harder it gets*, as they say in the funeral industry. But for Zig, there was no other way.

"I'm right here. Y'hear me? Right here," he said, cutting off her shirt to get a better look at the deep puncture wound below her clavicle. The blood was dark red. Good. The darker it was, the less likely it was coming fresh from an artery. Over the years, in the process of cleaning out and rebuilding over two thousand fallen service members, Zig had become well trained in every makeshift trick our medics use on the battlefield—and the results that came with them. Puncturing a water bottle with the scissors, he sprayed a jet stream at the wound.

"Just cleaning it out. Best way to stop infection."

Leaning in, he saw that the blood coming from her wound wasn't pumping in a steady heartbeat. It was oozing slowly. Even better. Meant her subclavian artery was intact. He checked the pulse in the radial arteries of both her wrists. Perfect match. Good sign. Blood pressure okay too. No signs of internal bleeding.

"Lucky girl," he told Nola, who just lay there, unconscious.

Gently, Zig turned her on her side to check her back. There were faded scars there, old ones, crisscrossing up her spinal column. These were from years ago, when she was a kid. The only good news was...at the top of her shoulder...no exit wound. The bullet was still inside her. Lucky for that too. If the bullet had burst out, there'd be a far bigger and bloodier mess to deal with. Plus, with bits of bullet inside her...

"TSA is gonna love you at airport metal detectors," Zig said, tearing open the bag of tampons. This would be the hard part.

Cutting a tampon in half, he sprayed it with the Afrin nasal spray, then aimed it directly at the soupy, bloody hole below Nola's collarbone. No anesthetic. Pain was coming.

"If it helps, squeeze my fingers," he said, taking her limp hand in his own. On three...two...one...

He shoved the tampon deep into Nola's wound. The tampon

expanded, instantly absorbing—while the nasal spray did its job, tightening the blood vessels to prevent further bleeding.

Nola's whole body shook, like she was jolted from a dream, her eyes still closed.

Zig jumped back, so lost in the moment—so used to being around corpses—he forgot she was alive. In that moment, for the very first time and in the very worst way, it hit Zig that he'd become more accustomed to the dead than the living. It was a thought he wouldn't shake for days.

Using his thumbs to stuff the rest of the tampon into place, he sealed the wound with duct tape, then turned his attention to treating (and sealing—more duct tape) the cut on Nola's wrist. As he looked closer, he realized that wasn't the only cut there.

"Oh, Nola, what'd you do?" he muttered, eyeing at least three other faded pink scars across her wrist. Unlike the ones on her back, they all ran in the same direction. *How old was she when she got these? Sixteen? Seventeen?*

There were so many questions he wanted to ask: about her, about the plane crash, about Operation Bluebook, and especially about Houdini—my God, she shot and killed Houdini!—but as Zig moved her to the clean bed and pulled the covers up to her chin, one question stood out above all others. *Why?* Why the hell did that plane go down? Which of course led to *what*. What could possibly be so important about Nola that people were suddenly committing murder? Which naturally led to... *Who?*

From his pocket, Zig pulled out the bulky military watch that The Amazing Caesar had stolen from Houdini. Zig had seen watches like this before, back at Dover, on fallen Special Forces soldiers. The more macho the man, the bigger the watch—but big watches like this? Made by a company called Suunto.

Special Forces loved Suuntos because they had built-in MGRS—the Military Grid Reference System—which, like a high-octane GPS, allowed troops to input digital grid coordinates and find locations to within a few meters as they were moving through the theater of war. Efficient? Absolutely. Safe? That was the issue. Once something had GPS, everyone could learn where you—

"Oh, Caesar, you cruel old mastermind."

Grabbing the landline from the nightstand, Zig started dialing Waggs's number. Somewhere in this watch were coordinates— coordinates that would show every place Houdini had been today. And also, presumably, every other place he'd visited in the last month.

"*Don't*—" a voice called out.

Behind him, Nola fought to sit up in bed, her color pale.

"D-Don't do it," she whispered. "Whoever you're calling… they'll know where we are."

Zig kept dialing. "This is someone I trust."

"You don't know that."

He turned, still mid-dial. "What're you talking about?"

Nola sat up, wearing just her bra. She glanced down at her duct tape bandage, eyeing it with approval. "You're supposed to be a smart person, Mr. Zigarowski. Have you really not noticed that everywhere you go, Houdini and his crew somehow always know you're coming?"

"That's not—"

"Back at Dover, they shipped out Kamille's body before you could figure out what was happening. When you went to my old office, they were waiting for you there too—"

"They were waiting for *you*, not me."

"What about now? Back in the car, I heard you call 911. You said there was an old magician—Caesar. They killed him, didn't they? You called the paramedics so someone would find him. Don't be blind, Mr. Zigarowski—"

"I told you, call me Zig."

"Stop with the bullshit charm and pay attention, Mr. Zigarowski. Whatever dumb trap you were planning in that magic shop, Houdini *knew*. He came there with every intent to put a bullet in that old man's brain. The only thing that didn't go his way was that he thought he'd find you there too."

With a clang, Zig hung up the phone. For a moment, he just stood there, staring down at the Suunto watch. Was Nola right?

Only one way to find out. He held up the watch. "We still need to get someone who can read the grid coordinates in here."

"Gimme the watch," Nola insisted.

"What?"

"Give it to me. Now."

For the next two minutes, Nola held the Suunto like a stopwatch, clicking the chronograph buttons, the watch beeping like a droid. As Nola scrolled through its on-screen menu, Zig was hit by that same feeling every dad gets when their child grabs their phone or remote control and displays a clear superiority over new technology.

"Get a pen," Nola said, still focused on the watch. "Write this down."

Zig didn't move fast enough. Nola grabbed the Mi Casa pen and matching pad of paper from the nightstand. Quickly jotting down some letters and a ten-digit number, she clicked back through the watch's menu, reentering the digits.

A map appeared on-screen. There was another beep, then...

Nola made a face.

"*What?* What's it say?" Zig asked.

She looked over at the notepad, then back at the watch, rechecking to make sure she had it right. "According to GPS, this is where Houdini was yesterday."

"Is it someplace we know?"

"I'd say you definitely know it. Based on the time, he landed there last night."

"So it's an airport?"

"Not an airport."

"I don't understand. Where do you land that's not an airport?"

"The one place where he clearly had a friend who could help him get inside. *That's* how Houdini stayed out of sight..." she said, holding up the watch toward Zig.

Zig's eyes went wide. At the bottom of the screen were the letters DE. *Delaware*. "N-No. That can't be."

But it was.

"Houdini arrived last night—hid there right under your nose," Nola explained.

On-screen, Zig eyed the familiar outline on the map. The mortuary.

"He was in your building, Mr. Zigarowski—at Dover Air Force Base."

63

In the man's ear, the phone rang three times. Voicemail.

Annoyed, he hung up and dialed again. New number this time.

Riiiing . . . riiiing . . . riiii—

"What're you doing!?" his associate hissed on the other line. *"This is my work line!"*

"You ignored my call on your cell phone," the man with the woodchipper of a voice said. "Don't do that."

"Will you get over yourself! You and Houdini told me to be smart; I'm being smart! Unless you want me picking up your call in front of half of Dover?"

There was an announcement from the intercom. People bustled back and forth through the waiting area, most of them with their heads down, scrolling through their phones. It made the man think how much he hated the damn Internet.

"Where are you anyway? Sounds like an airport," his associate said.

"You promised an update," the man with the woodchipper voice shot back. He had gray hair, the color of smoke, and kept his back to the crowd so no one could get a good look at the fleshy white scar that split his lower lip and ran down to his jaw. "I need to know where Zig is."

"That's our first problem. I haven't heard from him in hours."

"Then let me give you a hint. Houdini's dead. Zig and Nola are gone. You missed an entire firefight. We sent cleanup in, but it's still a hot damn mess."

"You have no idea. Remember when you said your magician friend Caesar was all taken care of? He was more hearty than you thought."

"He's alive?" Woodchipper asked.

"Not anymore. But someone placed a 911 call. Everyone here's saying it sounds a lot like our friend Zig. Did Caesar know anything about you?"

The man with the woodchipper voice went silent.

"*Now boarding on Track 29,*" the intercom announced overhead.

A small crowd of travelers surged for the gate marked *Track 29.* The man with the woodchipper voice barely moved, gripping his phone, his back to them all.

"Train station, huh? What, you don't like flying?"

His associate was perceptive. Even more than he thought. "Just do what we asked," the man growled. "I know this isn't easy for you, but if you don't help us find Zig soon, we'll all be—"

"I know the damn consequences, okay? I'm on it. I'll call you back."

Without a word, the man with the woodchipper voice hung up the phone and headed for the train. He chose the silent car because, God, he'd had enough slobs barking into their cell phones, clueless to the volume of their own voices.

As he finally found a seat, his own phone buzzed with a text message. Six words.

Spotted. At a CVS in Maryland.

A small grin twisted the fleshy white scar along the man's lip.

With a few taps, he composed a new text message to a brand-new recipient.

We got him.

64

Zig gripped the corner of the motel's thick TV, like he was using it to stand. What Nola said, did he believe her? Did it make sense? Part of it did. Back at Dover, someone made sure the body was switched. Someone purposely rushed the wrong fingerprints and dental records through the system. Someone even knocked Zig out on the morning when the other bodies arrived. Houdini was a stranger—a fast-talking thug—no way could he pull all that off. Not without help.

"Whoever snuck Houdini into our building..." Zig paused, rerunning the logic. "It could've been anyone. There're thousands of people on base."

Nola didn't say anything, still focused on the watch.

"Don't give me that look. My friends...Dino...Master Guns... even Amy Waggs...they wouldn't do that," Zig added, now pacing. "It could've been *anyone*."

Nola sat there in the bed, hitting buttons, the watch beeping.

"Colonel Hsu... Her, I'd believe," Zig continued, carefully watching Nola's reaction. "But it's gotta be someone who knows about the ways we ID people."

She still didn't say a word.

Heading for the nightstand, Zig picked up the landline.

"Who're you calling?" Nola challenged.

He put the phone back down. He wasn't even sure.

"What do you want, Mr. Zigarowski?"

"In alphabetical order? I want to know what the hell is going on. I want to know every single person who's chasing us. Who was that Native American woman...the one who shot you and tried to murder us?"

"The Curtain."

"That's her name? *The Curtain*?"

"That's what he called her. Never seen her until today. I'm guessing she's a hired gun."

"Hired by who?"

Nola went quiet, letting out a low deep breath. "Houdini."

At just the name, Zig's brain flipped back to what Caesar said about Houdini's old Blue Book...about the three aliases on the plane...a small group that no one ever realized was there. Zig could feel the pieces starting to fit together at the far edges. But even so, the way Nola said his name... There was newfound anger in her voice. "So you know him," Zig said.

"I didn't say that."

"You haven't said *anything*. In case you didn't notice, I saved your life."

"I didn't ask for your help."

"And yet I still gave it. According to most dictionaries, that's called *generosity*. Or *kindness*. Some might see it as *stupidity*, but I prefer something a bit more benevolent."

Nola sat there, silent, now sketching something on the motel notepad. She didn't look mad. She looked...lost in her thoughts.

"That's how you process, isn't it? By drawing?" Zig asked.

Still no response.

"I had a coworker who used to do that. He'd have to draw a picture of how the deceased would eventually look before he could start working on them."

"Liar. You just made that up."

Zig nodded. It was a lie. A white one, designed to gain some trust. But once again, she'd seen right through it. He wanted to be annoyed, but he was actually impressed.

"Nola, if I were working against you, we wouldn't even be having this conversation right now."

Back to silence. Back to her sketching.

"Okay, let's try it this way," Zig added. "Let me tell you what I know—and then, you sit there and draw whatever it is you're drawing, and we'll see where it gets us. Okay. First: I know, for sure, you had a seat on a military plane in Alaska. I know, for sure, you didn't get on that plane—maybe you saw something and had a quick thought; maybe someone saw you and you took off. However it happened, you gave that seat to a woman named Kamille. Maybe Kamille was a longtime friend, or maybe someone you recently met."

"I told you, I didn't know her well."

"You knew her well enough to paint her portrait."

Nola again went quiet.

"Regardless, from the way you came looking for Kamille's body—you didn't know that plane was going down. Neither did Kamille, until it was too late. And that also tells me, for sure, that Kamille had some idea of what you were worried about, because during her last moments on a plane that was falling from the sky, Kamille ate a sheet of paper with a warning message for you.

"So if all that's true—which I believe it is—that means that whatever brought you to Alaska, while you were there, you uncovered something—something that I'm wagering is called Operation Bluebook."

"If I knew what Bluebook was, I wouldn't be hiding in a motel."

"But you know who *Houdini* is. Is he the one in charge?"

Nola shook her head. "He's just a paying agent."

"A what?"

"Paying agents. They make payments. That's the job."

"Payments to who?"

"Depends what our government needs. Sometimes an Army

unit needs a hot tip; other times, we need a toilet paper contract so our troops can wipe. Usually, though, it's just quiet money."

"I have no idea what *quiet money* means."

Still sketching, Nola explained, "Years ago in Iraq, one of our tank drivers read his map wrong and mistakenly plowed over a farmer's herd of goats. Another time, our mortar men accidentally bombed the wrong building, sending bricks flying and injuring half a dozen innocents. When disasters like that happen—and they always happen—the paying agent comes in to make restitution with the locals."

"So he's a guy with cash?"

"Again, that's the job. Most soldiers carry an M4 rifle. The paying agent carries a far more potent weapon—a briefcase full of money. He can make payments up to $30K, no questions asked. A supervisor can get him above that. To go above $100K, he needs to clear it with the Department of Defense."

"That's a lot of currency for one person."

"Consider it the cost for good PR. If we've got an Army unit sneaking into town, the last thing we need is to call attention to ourselves, or even worse, have some local farmer reveal our location while we're still in the initial stages of an operation. You can make a lot of peace with a lot of cash."

"So Houdini—"

"His real name was Rowan Johansson."

"Okay. Rowan. He was one of these paying agents?"

"One of the best. When a Humvee hits a farmer's handmade rock fence, you call for a paying agent. But when that Humvee hits something more valuable, you call Rowan."

"What's more valuable? Like hitting someone's house?"

"Like killing someone's child," Nola said, looking up.

Zig stood there, not blinking.

She continued to stare, which Zig was starting to realize she did quite often. She had the wary eyes of an old woman, and they were always *perfectly* focused, picking life apart. Indeed, even now, as she talked about the death of someone's child, she turned that focus straight toward Zig, searching him for a reaction.

For Zig, though, there wasn't one. Despite the loss of his daughter, he knew how life worked. He saw death all the time. Every week, he'd stand over a gurney, putting flesh makeup on a gray body, prepping yet another young soul who was cut down in his prime.

"I see it every day," he told her.

"No. You see it after the hurricane hits," Nola said. "Imagine the moment itself, when a Sunni mom comes running down a dirt road, yelling in Arabic that our unit just left live ordnance around, which was found by her now-dead five-year-old son. I couldn't understand the dialect, but I'll never forget that woman's screams. Anguish sounds the same worldwide."

"What's your point?"

"You asked about Rowan Johansson. That's what he does. People are horrified when you put a price on a child's life, but in a small Sunni town, for a male child—which are valued there more than females—when you calculate lifespan, add the fact they can work until they're eighty years old, then compound it all as an annual salary... That dead boy will cost Uncle Sam about seventy-two thousand dollars. Pay the poor family in cash and—*abracadabra*—the problem goes away." She paused as she said the words. "Now you understand why they call him *Houdini*? He makes the biggest mistakes..."

"*Disappear*," Zig said as Nola went back to sketching on her notepad.

To Zig, the story made sense—and matched up even more with what he'd heard back at the magic shop. Houdini seemed to be spending a great deal of time moving cash, and lately, according to The Amazing Caesar, appeared to be moving more of it than usual, including a big shipment from Alaska. Which begged the question: What was going on in Alaska that they had a sudden influx in cash? Did all the extra cash mean that someone was asking Houdini to cover up an even bigger problem? And more important, how'd this all tie in to Nola, that crashed airplane, and Operation Bluebook?

Glancing over at Nola, Zig noticed the way she was holding her pen, like she was strangling it.

"Nola, if there's anything else you know—?"

"I know Houdini, like any Special Ops paying agent, specializes in disasters. Especially the ones that the Army doesn't want anyone to hear about. That's all I know."

"So could that be what Operation Bluebook is? Maybe that's why he was in Alaska? Maybe Bluebook isn't the *process* of making big things go away—maybe instead of being a slush fund, Bluebook is its own private mission—and in the midst of it, they made a mistake that they now need to cover up?"

Still sketching, Nola didn't say anything.

"Or maybe someone accidentally found out that Houdini was covering Bluebook up? Or..." Zig said, still letting the facts tumble through his brain, "maybe when Houdini saw all the cash he was being sent, maybe he started taking his own private cut? Is that possible? How much did you say a paying agent carries around with them?"

More silence.

"Y'know, Nola, if you want to figure out what's going on, it might be helpful to actually speak to each other."

She continued to sketch. Zig wanted to be mad, but he knew silence like that was trained into her.

Zig cleared his throat and craned his neck, trying to get a look at what Nola was drawing. She turned away, just slightly, making it clear she wasn't sharing.

"Nola, if it makes you feel better, I figured out your art. That's what brought you to Alaska, right? I know why you went there."

Nola glanced up, but not for long. She was about to say the word, *Liar*.

"I saw them," Zig interrupted. "In your office, all those portraits you painted...the canvases that were leaning against each other. There were dozens of them—soldiers from the chest up. They're really beautiful when you look at them—but also pretty sad," Zig added, searching her face for a reaction. "On the back of each one, I noticed you always listed the soldier's name: *Daniel Graff—Monterey, CA. Sergeant Denise Madigan—Kuwait.*"

Nola's sketching slowed down. Not by much, but enough.

"C'mon, Nola, all it took was an Internet connection. Once I got pictures of them, did you really think I wouldn't figure out what all your paintings had in common?"

"You don't know what you're—"

"Attempted suicide," Zig blurted. "That's it, isn't it? Every Artist-in-Residence has her own motif. Years ago, during the wind-down in Afghanistan, one of the artists used to just paint landscape scenes of our troops leaving the desert. Painting after painting of piles of computers we left behind...holes where our HQs used to be...bulldozers that took our old bases apart. Other artists focused on people, painting soldiers in the field. But you? Daniel Graff. Sergeant Madigan. You paint those service members who tried to take their own lives."

Nola sat there in the bed. She was no longer sketching.

65

How much longer?" Kamille asked.

"Soon," Nola said, a pastel crayon in her hand. "Stop talking."

Kamille shifted in her seat, a plastic folding chair they took from the PX. Nola sat across from her, peeking out from behind her canvas every few seconds.

"C'mon, Sergeant Brown. Can you at least tell me how I look?"

Nola grunted, still trying to figure it out. She took another glance. Kamille squinted when she talked, like she was always asking for a favor. That was the secret. Her flat nose was easy, but for Nola, nothing was right until she captured Kamille's squint.

"So this painting thing— You've done it with other people, yeah? People who tried to...who did what I..." Kamille's voice trailed off. No one liked to say *suicide*. "You've met a lot of us, huh?"

"It's not a club," Nola shot back, using her finger to blend the beige pastel into the canvas.

"The other people you've met, Sergeant Brown. How did they do? Y'know, after they..." Again, her voice trailed off.

Nola usually despised small talk. But she liked this girl. Kamille wasn't some self-hating cloud of doom. She was sharp, funny, even teased Nola for her subject matter, saying, "Maybe next time you can paint something less depressing, like a sad clown series...a dead kitten collection... or *Still Life with Gun to Head*." Even Nola grinned at that.

"What you've been through," Nola said. "Think of it as life's second chance." She dabbed the pastel some more. "Some people come back even stronger."

Kamille sat up straight. A second chance. She liked that. "I'm gonna be one of those people."

Nola nodded, cursing her pastels for not doing what they were told. She wouldn't be happy until she finished Kamille's eyes.

"So the Army really pays you to paint?" Kamille asked.

"I'm assigned. It's a mission."

"Still...to draw like that... You're gonna make me immortal, huh?"

Nola made a face.

"I'm serious, Sergeant Brown. In a hundred years, thanks to your art, I'll still exist."

66

Maryland
Today

I'm right, aren't I?"

Nola ignored the question. Sitting there on the motel's saggy bed, she was pretending to sketch.

"You know I'm right. That's why you went to Alaska, isn't it?" Zig added. "Every morning, at that base in Virginia, you'd come into your office and scour the nightly blotter reports from each base. Then one day, you saw it in some outpost in Alaska: reports of a T14.91—attempted suicide—and you went running. That's how you met Kamille."

Nola still didn't reply.

"Usually, no one gave it much notice," Zig said. "That's the artist's job, right? You come in, paint a few pictures, and leave. That's the job. Your boss told me back at your office. The Army gives you the right to go wherever you want. But when you arrived in Alaska...maybe Kamille told you something...maybe you saw it yourself. Whatever happened, though, something just didn't seem right, did it? You realized it as you were going to leave: Something on that base was just a little bit off."

"You don't know what you're talking about."

"Actually, for the first time, I think I finally do," Zig said, his voice now racing. "What'd you see out there, Nola? A crime? Or maybe something that just caught your eye...made you dig a little bit deeper? Either way, you realized what they were up to—"

"I still have no idea what they're up to! I don't know what Blue-book is!"

"But that's why you stayed. Look at the timeline. You met Kamille and painted her picture. Your job was done. You had a seat on that plane and should've been on that flight that was leaving Alaska. But then you got that knotty feeling in your gut. It happened after you painted Kamille; maybe she said it while she was sitting for you ... Something told you there was a better story if you stuck around—maybe a better painting even. All you had to do was stay. So at the very last minute, you got off the plane, gave your seat to Kamille—"

"I didn't give her anything! She begged me for it!"

"But that's why you went to Alaska, isn't it? To paint Kamille's portrait—she's the one who tried to kill herself."

"I brought her joy! My painting— It made her happy! She loved it so much, she begged me to keep it! Then she begged me again to take my spot on the plane! She was trying to see her fiancé!"

"And the next thing you know, just as you're starting to snoop around, the plane plummets from the sky. And now you realize your gut was right." He paused, letting it sink in.

Sitting in bed, Nola stared straight ahead—refusing to look at Zig—focusing on a peeling section of Southwestern tribal-pattern wallpaper. Her pen was still in her hand. But it wasn't anywhere near the pad of paper.

"Nola, before you blame yourself—"

"Why'd you protect me before?" Nola blurted.

Zig looked at her, confused.

"Back in the insurance shop. With the grenade ... when The Curtain threw it ... you jumped on me and tipped the table to protect us."

"I thought you were unconscious."

"I was awake," she shot back, still staring straight ahead. "If that grenade went off—"

"The grenade wasn't real."

"You didn't know that. If it went off, the shrapnel would've ripped through you. I'm asking you a question, Mr. Zigarowski. Why'd you risk yourself for me?"

A long, weighty silence took the room. Zig stood there, between the two twin beds. The air was so quiet, he heard the running water through the pipes and the cycling of the toilet.

He shrugged. "Why'd you do what you did at the campfire?" He took a deep breath. "It just seemed like the right thing. I didn't want you to get hurt."

Nola paused. "Is this about your daughter, or me?" she asked.

A new silence took hold, a far deeper silence as the air itself grew heavy and thick. It was the kind of silence that came not just from a lack of sound, but a lack of movement. In his ears, Zig heard a high-pitched hum, like in the embalming room.

For a minute, Zig stood there, swaying just slightly. His voice was barely a murmur. "I don't know."

In the bed, Nola was still looking straight ahead, staring at nothing in particular. "Horatio," she announced.

"*Wha?*"

"That's him. He's the one," Nola explained. "Back on the boat, I got his name. That's who Houdini reports to—the real string-puller behind Operation Bluebook."

"So he—?"

"He's the one who hired The Curtain, ordered the plane crash, and murdered Kamille. They call him *Horatio*."

67

Am I supposed to recognize that name?" Zig asked.

"*Horatio*," Nola repeated. "It's the name of another magician."

"Like a modern magician or—?"

"From the 1800s," Nola said, climbing out of bed and standing there a moment to get her bearings. She blinked a few times, light-headed from the blood loss.

She headed for the bathroom, sat down, and peed with the door open. Zig looked away, though he still caught an unwanted glimpse of her in the mirror above one of the dressers.

"So this Horatio...?"

"Where's my gun? I saw you grab it," she said, still in her underwear and a bra as she opened and shut the shower curtain, then stepped back into the room and did the same with the closet. She ran her fingers across the top shelf as well as the headboard of each bed. Then she opened every drawer in each of the two dressers.

"No one knows we're here," Zig insisted, eyeing the way her white hair ran down, covering the scars on her upper back. But it couldn't obscure all of them. She wasn't thin; she was muscular, like a boxer. And the way she was moving—favoring her left hand—she was working hard to hide it, but she was in pain.

"Where's my gun?"

"I put it in the trunk of the car."

Nola stared at him a moment, studying his face. Then she turned to the mattress, lifting it from the box spring. Underneath was her gun, exactly where Zig had hidden it.

She shot Zig a look...and climbed back into bed. As she sat there, Indian style, Zig couldn't avoid her underwear.

"Maybe you could...cover yourself up?" he suggested.

She didn't. Instead, she was focused on her gun, quickly field-stripping the pistol. Within seconds, she ejected the magazine and pulled off the slide and guide rod, then inspected the feed ramp and the grooves inside the barrel.

"Can we please get back to Horatio?" Zig asked.

"During the Civil War, Horatio G. Cooke was a well-known rope escapist," she explained, still working on the gun. "So much so that his skills caught the attention of a man named Abraham Lincoln."

"Is this for real?"

"Look it up. President Lincoln was so impressed, he had two generals and a senator tie up young Horatio, who was just eighteen at the time. When Horatio escaped, Lincoln made him an offer, asking him to personally work for Lincoln in the war."

"So he was Lincoln's spy?"

"Officially, they called him a scout—but yes, Horatio was sneaky, a secret weapon—which is what Lincoln needed back then. Soon after, Horatio started working for the Union, and when he saved his scouting party from capture, he and Lincoln actually became friends. According to what I found online, on the night Abraham Lincoln was shot, Horatio Cooke was one of the people in Ford's Theatre...and one of the very few by Lincoln's bedside when the President died."

"I've never heard of this guy."

"Neither had I," Nola confessed, already done putting the gun back together. She racked the slide to make sure all was working. "What makes the story even more memorable is that after Lincoln died, Horatio continued to do magic, continued to work for the government, and also turned his attention to exposing fake mediums. By the time he was an old man, he even befriended an up-and-coming magician named..."

"Don't say Harry Houdini."

Nola was still staring down at the gun, like Zig wasn't even there. "I couldn't make this up if I wanted to."

"So in real life, you're telling me Houdini and Horatio were friends?" Zig asked.

"Friends and fellow magicians. And from what I can tell, they both traveled around the country exposing anyone who claimed they could talk to the dead. Apparently, they both lost people close to them—and weren't ever able to move past it."

Looking to his left, Zig studied his own warped reflection in the curve of the motel's old TV. "You said the real Horatio worked for Abraham Lincoln. Did the real Houdini have any connections to presidents?"

Nola looked up from her gun. "He knew Teddy Roosevelt. Also met with Woodrow Wilson too. Why?"

"You said Horatio was Lincoln's secret weapon. Was Houdini one too?"

"So now the White House has an army of undercover magicians? You're watching too much History Channel."

"I'm not talking about an army. I'm talking about a single magician, someone whose specialty is doing exactly what you said this guy Rowan Johansson—using the code name Houdini—was doing in the Army: making very big problems disappear."

Nola thought about that. Zig did too. A century ago, the real Horatio and real Houdini spent quality time with the most powerful men in the world. And now, today, this modern Horatio and Houdini were using them as namesakes, moving loads of cash, and were ruthlessly determined to keep a lid on whatever was really going on in Alaska. Whatever they were up to, they were definitely covering—

"*The big move covers the small one,*" Zig blurted.

Nola shot him a look.

"Just a— It's a magician saying," Zig explained, suddenly picturing President Orson Wallace barely two days ago, during his surprise visit to Dover, heading down the back of the plane and carrying the transfer case with his dead pal's remains. The whole world was watching Wallace, including every single person at Dover. But no one was watching the President's friend.

"Abracadabra," Zig muttered, thinking about his visit to the magic shop. Pulling out his phone, he opened a browser and quickly typed three words into Google: *Houdini* and *Nelson Rookstool*.

The big move covers the small one.

"What if...?" Zig started speaking before he even had the full thought. Then he saw what popped up on-screen. "I don't believe it," he added, scrolling and trying to speed-read. "They have everything...his letters, his playbills...even his—" He looked up at Nola. "When Harry Houdini died, guess what government agency got all his books and papers?"

"The Library of Congress."

"Wait. You *knew* that?"

Nola nodded. She'd looked it up days ago.

"*He owned one of the largest libraries in the world on psychic phenomena, spiritualism, magic,*" Zig read from the site, "*and returning from the dead.*"

"There is no return from the dead," Nola said.

"Not literally—but think about it. We know one magician worked for Abraham Lincoln. From there, it sounds like the real Harry Houdini also did undercover work for the government. So if you were the President and you wanted to make sure no one found out about your favorite secret program, would you put it in the White House, the Pentagon, or would you hide it in some lesser-watched government location where no one would ever look?"

Nola started sketching again as Zig stared down at the website for the Library of Congress.

"Maybe that's why Nelson Rookstool was on the plane. In fact, maybe that's why the President appointed him," Zig added, his voice at full speed. "If the leader of the free world goes to Alaska, the whole world watches. But if the Librarian of Congress goes there—"

"Stay with Horatio."

"Just listen! Houdini donated all his books to the Library of Congress for a reason. What if that's the home base for Operation Blueb—"

"*Horatio's our focus!*" Nola growled.

Zig turned. Her face was red, her fists clenched. Silent Nola was no longer silent.

Confused, Zig asked, "Don't you want to know what Bluebook is?"

"I don't give a turd. *You* give a turd. What I want are the people who put that plane down. I got Houdini, so Horatio...whoever he is... They murdered seven people! They killed Kamille! They were trying to kill *me!*"

Flicks of spit left Nola's lips as she said the words.

Zig just stood there, at the foot of the twin beds, watching her catch her breath. In all the time they'd been together, she was an expert at being quiet. Now she was smoldering.

Back at the insurance place, Zig convinced himself that when it came to killing Houdini, Nola had no choice. It was self-defense. Now he wasn't so sure.

"Nola, as you track this guy Horatio—when you finally find him—what are you planning to do to him?"

Nola didn't answer. She didn't have to.

Zig knew. Deep down, he always knew. For Nola, this wasn't about Operation Bluebook, or a government cover-up, or even the dead innocents on that plane. It was about revenge.

"I'm telling you right now," Zig added, "whoever Horatio is, killing him won't solve anything."

Nola was still silent, staring straight down at the reassembled gun in front of her.

"And just so you know, I'm not helping you commit murder," Zig said.

Still no response.

Zig thought about calling the cops, or someone at the FBI, maybe even Colonel Hsu's commanding officer, the general in charge of Dover. But at his core, Zig was all too aware of this unarguable truth: Whoever he turned Nola over to, wherever they locked her up, her real name would eventually be put in the system. Once that happened, some bad folks who were looking for her would quickly find her. And *once that happened*, wherever Nola was being hidden, that wouldn't be a place she'd be walking away from. Ever.

"If you have something to say, just say it, Mr. Zigarowski."

"Why're you still here?" Zig blurted.

Her dark eyes slid his way.

"I mean it," he said. "I stopped your shoulder from bleeding. I patched you up. I even got you a sweatshirt from the lost and found at the front desk—it's a size too big, but if you put it on, it'll do the job. Every other time I've seen you, you leave as fast as you can. Even now, you could've darted outside and stolen my car...or just slipped away while I was cleaning the blood from your coat. But for some reason, you're still sitting here, staring down at your gun, which is out of bullets. So tell me, Nola. Why're you still here, much less putting up with all my questions?"

With a clench of her feet, Nola cracked her toe knuckles. "Because you're the one who can get me on that plane."

Zig was confused. "What plane?"

In her right hand, Nola picked up the notepad she'd been drawing in. She held it up, giving Zig his first good look at what she'd been sketching: the Suunto watch. Nola had drawn it over and over, each watch showing a digital time, a few letters—and a ten-digit number.

"You did these by memory? Or did you copy them down?" Zig asked.

She didn't answer. But as Zig looked closer, he could see that all the letters and numbers were different, each representing its own grid based on latitude and longitude.

"You know where Horatio is, don't you?"

Silent Nola didn't say a word. Until. "I need you to get me on that plane, Mr. Zigarowski."

"Nola, this isn't—"

"Please. Listen. I know where Horatio's hiding. I need you to get me to Alaska."

68

This was Nola when she was sixteen.

It was the morning after she found the old letters. Royall was in the kitchen, flipping through a glossy magazine for high net worth individuals that Mr. Wesley had given him (*Dream it to live it!*) and eating his peanut butter on toast. He was up early. On a Sunday. That was her first sign something was wrong.

Nola kept her head down, cradling Dooch in her arms. At night, the skunk slept at her feet—even hesitantly followed her to the bathroom this morning, which brought Nola a silent thrill and sense of love she'd never experienced before. She tried focusing on that, hoping that maybe Royall would stay away.

"What do you want for breakfast?" Royall asked, a smile on his face.

That was her second sign. He was being nice. Wasn't licking his lips either. Not drunk, not hungover. Whatever Royall was planning—whatever punishment was coming for Nola finding those letters—he was taking his time.

"Just...I guess...cereal, I guess."

"Coming up."

Royall grabbed a box of Lucky Charms, poured it in a bowl, even took out the milk. He poured some for Nola, and some for

Dooch, who had leapt down from Nola's lap and was now walking in small but meaningful circles around the edges of the milk bowl.

"*Pwwp, pwwp, pwwp,*" Royall said, squatting down and making kissy noises, trying to draw the skunk closer. "That's for you—drink up." Dooch stayed where he was—by the milk bowl—cocking his head and adding a sour expression of judgment.

"So where you going today?" Royall asked Nola, his eyes still on the skunk.

"To a friend's." Nola knew better than to tell Royall about Ms. Sable. "She's got some toys and extra food for Dooch. A little cat bed too."

"*Oooh, you want a cat bed?*" he babytalked to the skunk. "Go . . . drink . . . yummy," he added, motioning to the milk bowl.

Dooch just stood there, not taking a sip.

"Maybe you want some cheese. *You want cheese?*" Royall said, reaching for the refrigerator.

"We should run," Nola interrupted, scooping up Dooch and heading for the door. "Be back later."

Usually, Royall couldn't muster a goodbye. But today . . .

"Enjoy the sunshine," he announced. "It's beautiful out."

He was right. Outside, the weather was gorgeous, the sky a pastel blue that reminded Nola of an iceberg. Deep down, though, Nola knew . . . she could feel it in her soul. No matter how much the sun was shining, a merciless storm was on its way.

69

Mitchellville, Maryland
Today

Nola told him she was hungry.

That was all it took. She said she wanted a hamburger, and Zig was on it, headed for the door to get them some dinner.

As Zig slid an arm into his jacket, Nola was sitting in bed, combing through the Twitter feeds of every Washington, DC, news site, looking for mentions of the shooting—or of finding Houdini's body—back at Powell Insurance.

"Still nothing?" Zig asked.

Nola shook her head, still scrolling. They both knew what was happening. For a shooting to stay this quiet, it's because, yet again, someone high up was working to *keep it* quiet.

"I'll keep looking," Nola said as Zig headed out.

Yet as the door slammed behind him, Nola opened a new browser, typed in *YellowPages.com*, and clicked on the button marked *Find People*. From there, she entered a name she hadn't thought about in years:

Lydia Konnikova
Ekron, PA

An address and number quickly appeared on-screen. *Same address*, Nola thought. No surprise.

She clicked on the number. The phone rang three times before—

"Good evening, this is Lydia," a quiet and tired female voice said.

"Mrs. Konnikova, this'll sound awkward and I'm not sure if you remember me, but my name is Nola Brown. When I was little, you were one of our Girl Scout moms. I'm the one—" She was about to say, *who got the top of her ear cut off at the campfire.*

"Nola Brown!? Whose dad loved those thin mints?" Lydia sang, the life now back in her voice.

"That's me," Nola said, remembering the fight Royall raised when, after he ate a dozen boxes of cookies, he found out how much each box cost. Naturally, he refused to pay, screaming at all involved, until one of the moms paid for the thin mints herself, just to shut him up.

"How you getting along, sweetie? *Where* you getting along? My gosh, how long's it been?" The good news was, from the sound of it, Mrs. Konnikova hadn't heard that Nola was supposedly dead.

"I'm sorry to bother you so late, ma'am," Nola said, ignoring the question. "I'm just wondering if you can help me with something. I recently ran into Jim Zigarowski . . ."

"Ziggy? How's he doing? *Where's* he doing?"

"It was at a work event, ma'am," Nola said, now wondering if Mrs. Konnikova uttered anything other than questions. "I hadn't seen him in over a decade. To my surprise, he remembered me right away. So as we were catching up, I asked him how his daughter Maggie was doing, and, well . . ."

"Oh dear, you didn't know she passed, did you?"

"I didn't, ma'am. I felt horrible, of course—but later that night, when I tried to find out what happened, the records for the *Ekron Eagle*—"

"They weren't online back then, were they?"

"That's what I'm trying to say, ma'am."

"Oh dear, so you *still* don't know? No one told you?"

"I don't mean to pry. I just didn't know who else to call."

Mrs. Konnikova let out a long aching sigh. "You have to understand, this was back when Ziggy and Charmaine were still married. It was toward the end, of course, when the fighting got heated. In fact, now that I'm saying it, this was the *real* height of it all, screaming and yelling about—" She cut herself off.

Nola made a mental note, knowing all too well why middle-aged couples scream at each other, especially before a divorce. Grabbing the notepad from the motel nightstand, she wrote the word *Affair?* She then crossed out the question mark. No shock, considering the last hoochie Zig was dating, who Nola found when she ran his phone records.

"What I'm really getting at," Mrs. Konnikova added, "is this wasn't a good night for the Zigarowski family. From what I understood, the shouting got so bad that, well... Twelve-year-old girls don't like their parents screaming at full blast. So without telling anyone, young Maggie opened her bedroom window and snuck out."

"Did Mr. Zigarowski know she ran away?"

"Not for hours. They had tucked her in—thought she was asleep—but at midnight, when they saw her bed empty... any parent would be panicked."

Nola cleared her throat, staring at the notepad, tempted to draw her old bedroom. She decided against it.

"Anyway, when they realized Maggie was gone, all it did was take the fight to DEFCON 1. Maggie had run away before—during another night of arguing. She was such a good hider, it took Ziggy and Charmaine hours to find her. One time, she was nearly a mile away, hiding on some swing set in a neighbor's backyard. So you can imagine the scene on this night: They're both running through the house, calling Maggie's name. Charmaine's blaming Ziggy for yelling so loud; Ziggy's blaming Charmaine for the same.

Then Ziggy...hoping to find her, he grabs his car keys, storming outside. He couldn't have any idea, y'understand?" Mrs. Konnikova added, her voice slowing down, filling with dread.

"He was just worried about his daughter—determined to track her down. So in a bolt of anger, Ziggy races out to the driveway and gets in his car." Mrs. Konnikova's voice cracks as she says the words. "But what he couldn't possibly know is that, on this night, young Maggie's hiding spot was underneath the car. She'd crawled under there for some quiet, and apparently, had been out there so long, she fell asleep..."

"*No,*" Nola whispered, not even realizing she said it out loud.

"Ziggy couldn't have known. He couldn't have. He was upset, in a mad panic, just a frantic father trying to find his missing daughter. So he gets into the car, throws it in reverse, and as he peels out of the driveway—"

Nola's mouth gaped open, her pen hovering inches from the paper. "Oh, God."

"It was worse than you can imagine. According to Sheriff Vaccaro, Maggie was— She was— They declared her dead on the scene. I remember getting the call that night. We all went over the next morning with candles and flowers, everyone in the troop putting plush unicorns outside the house since Maggie always loved unicorns."

For a full thirty seconds, Nola just sat there, mouth still sagging open, replaying every conversation she'd had with Zig over the past two days, every thought she had about him, rewriting and recoloring it with this new information.

"I haven't seen him for years now," Mrs. Konnikova finally said. "How's he holding up?"

This entire time, Nola thought he looked sad. Definitely lonely. But now... "He's stronger than people think."

"My gosh, I remember him as so handsome. Like a young Paul Newman with those eyes—"

"He still blames himself, though," Nola blurted.

"Can you fault him? In one terrible night, his whole life disappeared. No wife, no daughter—he lost his parents years ago. The man went from everything to nothing. No one looking out for him. *No one*, like they were erased. I mean, can you imagine?"

Nola held the phone tight, not saying a word.

"Plus, even if you can move forward after burying a child, which, let's be honest, is impossible," Mrs. Konnikova added, "but even if you could, everyone knew Ziggy still blamed himself for all of it...for Maggie being under that car...for the fight that sent her there...even for his wife sleeping around on him."

"His *wife?*" Nola asked, eyeing the word *Affair* on her notepad. "I thought Zig was the one who had the affair?"

"Ziggy? Nooo, that was Charmaine—she was sneaking off with an old high-school flame. Some big-shot finance guy in Philadelphia. Unfinished business and all that. Jacquie Segal said she just heard they're finally getting married. But Ziggy? This planet doesn't make people as stubborn and stupidly loyal as that anymore. No, even back then, when it came to his marriage, the only thing Zig did was kick himself for not seeing it coming. As a mortician here, he would get so absorbed in everyone else's losses, but there he was, completely missing his own. And then, in one foul day, his life as he knew it was gone," Konnikova said. "Truth is, I'm just happy to hear he's still standing. To live through what he lived through... Oh, gosh, if I'm being honest, I worried he might've put a gun to his own head, y'know?"

Nola glanced down at the faded old marks on her wrist—and the wound in her shoulder, which Zig spent the better part of the evening stitching and sealing. "I'm glad to report, his life is finally calming down."

"You think you'll see him again?"

Nola looked at the door. "Unclear."

"Well, if you do, do me a favor—give him a big fat hug from all of us here. I remember that last night before he moved away. There was a going-away party, all of us hiding in the Back 40 Bar, waiting to yell *surprise*. His old troop even baked a Samoa cookie cake—his favorite. Of course, Ziggy never came—again, not that I blame him. These days, I just wish he could give himself some forgiveness. He's been through enough to earn that."

Twenty minutes from now, Zig would return to the motel room with three burgers for the two of them, plus some fries and onion rings. "Everything okay?" he'd ask.

Nola would nod, barely looking up. "Just hungry."

70

Zig couldn't sleep.

No surprise. Even on a good night, in a good room, on a good bed, Zig could never sleep in a hotel. He'd stare at the ceiling, his thoughts wandering to what other celebrations and sins other ghosts had consummated there.

Tonight, though, Zig wasn't staring at the ceiling. He was eyeing Nola, who was dead asleep in the twin bed on his right. She slept on her side, her weight on her shoulder, despite the aching pain she had to be feeling. Her face was calm, however—and Zig realized it was the only time he'd ever seen her with a placid expression. When Nola was awake, her brain was working; only in sleep did she look untroubled. It made her look younger, like a child.

At 1 a.m., Zig was still awake, watching the steady rise and fall of Nola's breathing, just like he used to when Maggie was little—and now he couldn't help but wonder if Nola was right. Clearly, this wasn't just about a decade-old campfire. So was he really here just because he missed his dead daughter? Was he really that simplistic—that as long as Nola was around, it made him feel like a father again?

If he were in his own house, lost in his own head like this, Zig would be in his backyard, studying his beehive, his ritual beer in his hand. Then he'd go on Facebook, checking on his ex-wife. Rituals were good things to have in life—everyone needs something they can count on—especially when you feel like no one understands.

Just a few feet away, Nola's chest rose and fell again with another steady breath.

Some nights, Zig couldn't bear not seeing his daughter's face; other nights, there was no pain greater than actually seeing it.

A few feet away, perched on the nightstand, were the remnant wrappers from the burgers they had for dinner—and the new prepaid phone Zig bought at CVS. If he wanted, he could use it to go online, or at least get onto Facebook. Even without signing in, he could see his ex's profile photo and marital status.

If someone was watching online, they couldn't trace him. With a quick look, maybe Zig would at least get some sleep.

No, he told himself. *Don't be so—*

Zig grabbed the modern-looking flip phone. With a flip, it was open and on. All he had to do was put his ex's name into Google. Her Facebook page was the third thing that came up.

Zig glanced over at Nola. Her chest rose and fell.

Snapping the phone shut, Zig slid it back across the nightstand. *There you go. That's the right choice.* He told himself it had nothing to do with Nola. He was just tired of being so damn predictable.

Ten minutes from now, when he finally fell asleep, Zig would have an old dream that he hadn't had for decades, a dream where he was driving his first car—an old Mercury Capri that smelled like wet fur—with his grandfather sitting in the backseat, telling dirty jokes.

In just a few hours, he'd wake up feeling lighter than he'd felt in years, ready to take on anything.

The feeling wouldn't last long.

71

Homestead, Florida
Ten years ago

This was Nola when she was sixteen.

It was supposed to be a good night—or at least an easy night. It'd been a while now since the letters, making Nola think that Royall had forgotten, or at least moved on.

She was waiting by the front door as Dooch rubbed against the tufted leather ottoman like it was a conjugal visit. Months ago, Royall got pulled over by the police. He thought this was it—they'd finally tracked him down—his trunk was filled with printing supplies—they'd arrest him on the spot. But as the cop came to his window, the officer explained he'd simply been caught going forty in a school zone.

Right there, Royall said a thank-you to God and decided to make a change. He would go back to sales, use his skills to build a business he could actually be proud of. He even had the product: One of Mr. Wesley's clients was a wholesaler of snacks and granola bars. Sell them in bulk to office breakrooms and big businesses. *"If you're ambitious, there's real money."*

Royall saw it as his second chance. In his very last act making fake IDs, he got the new ottoman by trading a social security card and a set of phone and electric bills to the owner of a furniture store in Tampa. Royall thought it made the living room look fancy. Sophisticated. When potential clients came over, they needed to see that.

But as Nola was keenly aware, it had been weeks since they'd seen any clients.

Tonight, though, was different. Royall had nabbed the biggest fish of all—the supply sergeant for nearby Homestead Air Base had made an introduction to her superior. Royall had gone to the base to close the deal and, more important, collect the check. A big one. According to Royall, if things went right, maybe his biggest. Something to do with the Southern Command, covering every military base in Central America, South America, and the Caribbean, he'd told Nola last night. "Y'know how many granola bars they go through? This is change-your-life money," he'd added as Nola took those words and imagined what they looked like. *A brand-new life.*

"Maybe we move closer to the base, get our own pool!" Royall had said.

So tonight, as Royall's car pulled into the driveway, Nola was standing by the front door eagerly awaiting his arrival. She didn't care about Royall or whatever dumb military deal he was chasing. God knows, she didn't even care about the money. Sure, Royall had made a good living selling IDs over the years, but Nola never saw any of the cash. She was just excited for the Chinese food that Royall would be bringing home tonight . . . and the dry cleaning that always came with it.

That's how it always was when Royall got paid. For weeks, the dry cleaning would build up—too expensive to retrieve—but when Royall delivered on a big order of IDs and driver's licenses, and Mr. Wesley gave him his cash, Royall would return home with a big smile on his face, Chinese food in one hand and a fresh stack of plastic-covered dress shirts slung over his shoulder. All hail the conquering hero! On nights like that, Royall wasn't a better person—but he might let his viciousness go for a few hours. And on a night like this? His biggest deal *ever*? Nola wouldn't be surprised if he had bought the whole Chinese restaurant.

"Dinner's here!" Nola teasingly whispered to Dooch as Royall kicked at the front door. Of course he was kicking. His hands were

full with food and dry cleaning. Finally, Royall could get rid of Mr. Wesley and build a proper business.

"*Coming!*" Nola called out. Dooch raised his tail at attention.

Smiling hopefully, Nola undid the locks. But as the door swung open, there was Royall. Empty-handed.

A jolt of fear ran through her as she stepped out of the way.

Trudging, his shoulders sagging, Royall didn't even look at her. It seemed he wasn't even angry. He was...nothing. It was like someone had hollowed him out.

No cash. No deal. No Chinese food. And certainly, no changing your life.

As Royall reached the couch, he took off his blazer and let it fall to the floor. Then he collapsed into the cushions, his torso hunched like the letter C. Dooch leapt up next to him. For a moment, the way his body jerked as he breathed in, Nola thought Royall was about to cry. But he didn't.

Throughout her years with him, especially during his early days in sales, Nola had seen Royall *make* deals, *close* deals, and *lose* deals. But she'd never seen him...she searched for the word. *Defeated.*

"I can make dinner," Nola finally said. By now, she'd made peace with the fact that he took her in all those years ago so he'd have someone to cook and clean for him. Then, for a reason she couldn't explain, she decided to join him on the couch. She didn't get close. She just sat there on the other side of him, so Royall was between her and Dooch. The three of them sat there for a while, Nola searching for something else to say.

Finally, he spoke. "Yeah," he mumbled. "Go make dinner."

72

Dover, Delaware
Today

First, he'd need to hide her.

Zig knew where. It was barely 5 a.m., the sky still an inkwell. They'd left the motel hours ago, Nola lying down in the backseat as they weaved toward Dover's downtown historic district, not far from the courthouse. At this hour, the quaint narrow streets were empty. Even Tiffanee's bakery wasn't open yet.

"You sure there's no alarm?" Nola asked as they reached their destination.

"No alarm," Zig insisted, sneaking through the side yard of a grand 1918 white clapboard home. With its laid-back front porch and antique carriage lights, it was the kind of house you see in a movie, a romantic comedy where the characters live in a place that you know they couldn't afford in the real world, but you don't care because you'd love to live there yourself.

Nola stared at the house, cocking her head to the side. But in the past few hours, Zig had become better at reading her. She didn't like this place.

"Don't worry, we'll be quick," Zig said as he reached the old garage in back. It had vintage swinging wood doors.

"*This?* This is what we came for?" Nola asked.

Now Zig was the silent one, grabbing the padlock on the garage doors and pulling out a key.

Nola glanced back at the house, giving it one of her good, long stares. Every window was dark. There's no way she knew what she was walking into.

"No one lives here, do they?"

Zig turned. "How'd you—?" He shook his head, knowing better than to ask. With a twist of the key, the padlock popped and Zig tugged open the garage doors, revealing the back of a shiny black car that at first looked like a station wagon, but as the moonlight hit it...

"A hearse?" Nola asked.

"How'd you know no one lives here?"

"The place smells like death." Turning back toward the beautiful old house, she added, "It's a funeral home, isn't it?"

"One of Delaware's oldest. There's a sign on the other side of the house. When they're busy, I pirate here."

"Pirate?"

"Sorry... When you... When there's a big disaster—like a traffic accident with multiple deaths—a local funeral home will get so overwhelmed, they can't handle all the bodies. So they'll call in a 'pirate,'" Zig explained, using the nickname for roving embalmers. When Zig first started in the industry, it's how he got experience, floating from funeral home to funeral home, community to community. "The joke is, when you pirate around, you're kinda like Death himself."

Nola stared at him. "I always thought Death was a she."

Zig let that one sink in. "Anyway, when it's winter in the Middle East, fighting season winds down, so there are fewer casualties among our troops. When Dover gets quiet, I'll sometimes add a few hours and moonlight here after work."

Nola turned back to the garage. "Tell me why we need a hearse."

"You said Horatio's in Alaska. I checked the schedule. The flight that brought the bodies to Dover is finally headed back. If you want to be on it, we have to first get you on base."

"Dover won't stop a hearse?"

"Of course they'll stop a hearse. It's a military base. They stop everything—scan your IDs...mirror under the car...pop the trunk. But even when they search the trunk, there's one place they'll never check..."

Inside the garage, Zig pulled the string for an overhead light. In front of the hearse, up on a rolling church cart, was a seven-foot-long box. Shiny cherry veneer. Antique bronze hardware. A casket.

Nola looked like she was about to take a half step back, but she stood her ground.

"All you have to do is lay there," Zig said, raising the casket's head panel and pointing inside. Cream velvet interior.

Nola studied the coffin for a solid ten seconds. Her lips were pressed together in a thin flat line. As always, she had that blazing focus, like her eyes were microscopes, able to see down to the molecular level.

"Nola, if you don't want to do this—"

"I can do it."

Committing to the cause, she climbed inside the coffin and leaned back into resting position, as if she'd done it before. "Shut the lid, Mr. Zigarowski. I'm not missing that plane."

73

Dover Air Force Base, Delaware

They found a *what?*"

"A finger," Zig said. He kept his voice low, like he was sharing a secret. "Plus someone's femur."

Out on the runway, the young staff sergeant with cropped black hair and a triangular nose made a face. He was barely thirty. Easily fooled.

"That's what happens in a plane crash," Zig added, his voice still quiet. With a glance over his shoulder, he checked for the fourth time that they were alone. It was almost 6 a.m., the sky starting to blink awake. Like any military base, Dover was up early. But not this early. As far as he could tell, there was still no one watching. "During search and recovery, we'll be finding portions of people for days."

The staff sergeant looked at the three metal transfer cases, sitting there, each on its own industrial rolling cart. If they had been transporting fallen service members, the cases would be packed with ice and covered with American flags. These three were uncovered, looking like long silver coffins shining in the morning sun. "I don't know how you do it every day," the staff sergeant said. His name tag said *Kesel*. "But I appreciate that you do."

"Then maybe you can help me get these on board?" Zig asked, tugging on the metal cart and steering one of the metal transfer cases across the asphalt runway.

He didn't like hiding Nola like this. But forty minutes ago, as he rolled her out of the hearse and into the mortuary building—and then switched her from the casket into one of these metal shipping cases—he knew it was the only way to pull this off.

Fifty yards ahead, a mammoth C-17 transport plane was on the flight line, its back loading ramp wide open, awaiting its last few items. The four fans weren't spinning yet, but its engines were prepping, making a loud drilling sound.

"Here... you need these," Kesel said, reaching into his pocket and handing Zig what the Army called *hearing protection*. A two-dollar set of bright orange earplugs.

As Zig put them in with one hand, he used his other to rap his knuckles against the head of the metal case, right where he drilled the airholes. A single tap, loud enough that there was no missing it. Simple code. *Almost on the plane.*

Zig knew Nola was too smart to tap back. Not until she was sure they were alone.

"So you think there are more bodies in Alaska?" Kesel called out, grabbing the other two rolling carts and giving them a tug. He was used to the job. As a loadmaster, he was in charge of the plane's cargo.

"We'll certainly find out," Zig said, leading the way and checking over his shoulder for a fifth time. He scanned every window in every nearby building. On the second floor of the mortuary, a light popped on. Dr. Sinclair in the ME's office was setting his morning tea on his desk.

Even if Sinclair looked outside, there was nothing out of the ordinary, at least for Dover. Two days ago, Kesel and his crew flew the bodies here from Alaska. Today, he'd be making the return trip, the plane restocked with empty transfer cases for when the next disaster hit. For mass fatalities or something like a plane crash, a mortician would also be sent to the crash site to help with recovery and cleanup—a detail Zig took full advantage of first thing this morning when he switched with a coworker to be on this outbound flight. To keep anyone from finding out, he didn't even put it in the system. Stay out of sight. Don't let them know you're coming. The only question was: Could he do the same for Nola?

There was a metal *ch-chink* as the wheels of the rolling cart hit the base of the plane's ramp.

"Here...lemme help," Kesel called out. "The cases are light. We can just carry them on b—"

"I'm fine," Zig insisted, shoving the rolling cart and pushing it—and the metal case—up the ramp. The thick wheels on the cart were able to hold six hundred pounds. This should be an easy climb. If the casket were empty.

Zig stared down at the aluminum case. Even as it rolled, it barely rattled at all.

"You okay?" Kesel called out.

"Fine. Tweaked my back a few weeks ago," Zig said, faking a grin and taking a sixth scan of the building behind them. There was another *ch-chink* as they reached the top of the ramp.

Inside the plane, the cargo hold was pretty much bare. If a general was scheduled to be on board, they'd roll in a palette with a fully functioning executive office, complete with desks, couches, and a fancy bathroom. If there were loads of passengers, they'd add a palette filled with airline-type seats. Today, though, at the back of the cargo hold were two large supply crates strapped into place. The rest of the open space was empty, except for three other metal transfer cases, lined up side by side, their toes facing Zig, in meticulous formation.

"There should be straps—"

"I see 'em," Zig said, eyeing the black nylon straps that would hold the case in place. Inside the cargo hold, the humming of the engines echoed even louder.

In one quick movement, Zig turned the pushcart around, lowered it to the ground, and gave a tug to the handles on the aluminum transfer case. Six metal rollers sent the case sliding toward him. Momentum let it skid across the floor and roll into place so that the head of Zig's transfer case was perfectly in line with the foot of the case already on the plane.

Outside the back of the plane, at the mortuary, another light went on in another window. The blinds were closed, but Zig knew that room. Colonel Hsu. If she found out what Zig was up to...

Don't think about it. Just keep moving; get to takeoff, Zig told himself, quickly ratcheting and strapping Nola's case to the metal floor so it'd stay put during the ride.

Next to him, Kesel was doing the same, lost in his work.

Seeing Kesel distracted, Zig again gave a quick *knock-knock* to the metal case. Two taps this time. *On the plane.*

"Need some assistance?" Zig offered, turning his attention back to Kesel, who was already working on the third case. With a hard tug of the nylon straps, they ratcheted it in place and locked it to the floor. Outside the back of the plane, two more lights went on in the mortuary. Time to get this moving.

"What else you need?" Zig asked, purposefully stepping a bit too close into Kesel's personal space.

"Actually, I should get upstairs," Kesel said, heading for the ladder that led up to the cockpit. Despite the mammoth size of the plane, the flight had a tiny crew: pilot, copilot, and Kesel the loadmaster, who stopped at a large wall panel of knobs and switches. He pushed a button and, with a mechanical whirr, the loading ramp slowly closed, swallowing the morning sun from outside. Zig's eyes were still on the mortuary, which seemed to shrink as the back door shut. The interior went dark; fluorescent lights popped on.

"Ten minutes until takeoff," Kesel said as the plane began to rumble. The first of four engines started to spin up to full speed.

"Sorry I can't offer you a better seat," Kesel added, pointing to the fold-down jump seats along the wall of the hull. "Our pilot's a stickler, but once we hit ten thousand feet and level off, I'll get you up in the cockpit."

As Kesel disappeared upstairs, Zig pretended to sort through his own belongings, including the oversized army duffel he'd brought onto the plane earlier and strapped to the metal rings on the floor. Inside was Zig's winter coat, plenty of layers, plus his full mortician kit, including baggies, modeling clay, makeup, and of course scalpels and tools. He also had a guidebook on their actual destination—*Alaska's Wrangell–St. Elias Park and Preserve*—not far from where the original plane went down and all of this started.

Zig already knew the park was enormous, the largest national park in the entire country. But according to the guidebook, it was also one of the least explored, which begged the one question Zig still couldn't answer: What was the government really doing out in the Alaskan wilderness?

From what Nola said—and what Zig learned at the magic shop—Houdini's specialty was moving money, more specifically, money that was used to pay off innocents when the government accidentally plowed through their lives. So was that what happened in Alaska? A disaster took place during Operation Bluebook? Or was Bluebook itself the disaster? Whatever the case, according to Nola, only one person had the answer. The person who was pulling the strings from the start: *Horatio.*

Outside, the second engine churned to life, its fan now spinning. Wouldn't be long now. Sitting in the jump seat and pretending to flip through his guidebook, Zig opened to a page that featured the rare fauna of Alaska, including a tiny blue flower that was so poisonous, it could kill a humpback whale. Upstairs, there was a loud metal *clank*, the cockpit door slamming shut. Kesel was finally inside.

Racing across the hull, Zig slid down on his knees, nearly slamming into the farthest transfer case on his left. He gave the metal top three quick taps with his knuckles. Their final code. *All clear.*

Zig waited for a response.

Nothing.

He tapped the case again. Three taps. *All clear. Tap back that you understand.*

Still nothing.

"Nola, can you hear me? Tap back if you hear me," Zig whispered, his mouth up against the casket's airholes.

Once again, nothing but silence, Zig's brain quickly calculating just how little air was inside.

The airholes he drilled were big enough. *Weren't they?*

74

Homestead, Florida
Ten years ago

This was Nola when she was sixteen.

He threw the letters at her head, the whole stack of them. It happened midway into one of Royall's rages, one that ignited when he blamed Nola for a flat tire caused by a broken bottle of scotch in their driveway. Never mind that the bottle was left there by Royall. *"You should know to clean it up! That's your job, nigger!"* Royall screamed.

It'd been barely a week since Royall lost the military granola-bar deal. He was back to making IDs and fake paperwork for Mr. Wesley.

Nola was down on her knees, garbage bag in hand as she picked up shards of glass from the driveway.

"You know what this costs me? That was my spare!"

Whap!

She didn't even see where the letters came from. Royall reached into the car—*was he hiding them in the glove box?*—and next thing she knew, with Royall in mid-rant, his rage peaking, the full stack hit Nola in the back of the head, ancient letters from Barb LaPointe scattering along the asphalt.

"Don't you dare pick 'em up!" Royall roared, awkwardly trying to kick the letters down the driveway, most of them going nowhere.

At the sight of it, Nola almost laughed. She didn't, though, not after what he did last time he thought she laughed at him. Still, seeing the old letters, an odd relief ran over her. She knew he'd make her pay for finding the letters; at least the waiting was over.

"You think you can go through my stuff!? You think you can steal from me like that!?"

I didn't steal, Nola thought to herself.

"Don't look at me like that! You got something to say?"

Nola stared straight down, picking glass from the driveway, knowing better than to answer.

"You know how much money you cost me!? When those thieves the LaPointes... When I took you in... That wasn't a party! I was trying my fuckin' best, but it cost money! Everything costs money! Class costs money! Don't I teach you that!?" he shouted, working himself up to the next level of rage, a bonus level, where he was yelling so loud, his voice went hoarse and his nostrils went wide. The grid of veins below his eyes was now showing.

Nola knew what came next.

Hoping to buy some time, she picked up the final shards from the driveway, a web of glass held together by the scotch label, and tossed it into the trash.

"Let's go...now!" Royall growled, yanking her by the back of her neck, shoving her toward the side of the house, to the backyard.

At the center of the yard, Royall unleashed a violent kick on the upside-down kiddie pool, sending it sliding across the green grass, wobbling like a 1950s flying saucer and revealing the hole that Nola had been digging since they first moved here.

"Half hour. No stopping!" he said with a final shove, sending her crashing to her knees, into the damp dirt. "No breaks either!"

At the bottom of the hole was a shovel—a new one actually, since Nola threw the old one away, pretending it was stolen. Royall borrowed this one from a neighbor, Nola knowing he'd never give it back.

"What're you waiting for?" Royall added, even though she was already climbing into the hole, which was as long as a coffin.

It was deep now too, up to her thighs, and would've been even deeper if the frequent Florida rain didn't backfill at least half of it with each downpour. Royall didn't care. *When you dig yourself into a hole, you dig yourself out.*

For the next half hour, Nola did just that. Shovelful by shovelful. She wasn't eight anymore. She'd just turned sixteen. Each scoop of dirt was hard, but it wasn't impossible. Her hands had calloused long ago as muscle memory handled the rest.

Dig...and throw. Dig...and throw. Dig...and throw.

Twenty minutes in, she'd barely slowed down. It's not that she wasn't tired. Beads of sweat high-dived from her nose. But over her shoulder, she could feel Royall watching from the house. She wouldn't give him the satisfaction.

Dig...and throw. Dig...and throw. Dig...and throw.

Twenty-five minutes in, the sky was getting dark, and the moon was out. A half-moon. Nola wouldn't look up at it. Ever since Royall gave her the moon as a present, she hated it.

By the last few shovelfuls, sprinkles of dirt were scattered across the back of her neck, in her hair, on her arms—she was covered. But finally finished.

She looked back at the house. Royall was gone.

Tossing the shovel like a javelin into the ground, she actually felt good. In fact, as adrenaline flooded her brain, it made her wonder if, despite Royall's assholeyness, he might actually be on to something. After so much digging, her anger was gone, or if not gone, at least muted. She remembered that, taking it with her always.

Heading back to the house, she saw the kitchen lights were on—Royall had grabbed a soda. TV flickered from the living room—he was now medicating himself with sports highlights, waiting for her to make dinner. She took it as a good sign. He didn't like anything interfering with dinner.

Indeed, as the back screen door snapped shut behind her, the one thought in Nola's brain was that, maybe, tonight might even be a quiet night.

She couldn't have been more wrong.

She stopped mid-step, seeing the shadow on the orange linoleum floor that was supposed to look like terra-cotta tile.

"Dooch?"

At the center of the kitchen, her skunk was lying there, flat on his side. His four legs were awkwardly extended, like he was sleeping. But...he always slept curled up, in a ball.

"*D-Dooch*...?" Nola whispered, the dark feeling already tightening in her chest.

The skunk didn't move.

"Dooch, you okay?" she added, smacking her palms together in a single loud clap, hoping to startle him. Even before the sound hit, she knew the answer.

The skunk didn't react to the sound, didn't move. He just lay there, frozen on his side, with a weight Nola had never seen before, but instantly recognized.

"*Nononono*," Nola pleaded, sliding to her knees, fresh dirt raining off her as she scooped the lifeless skunk into her arms. His body was stiff—the stiffness caught her off guard, and she dropped him. He bounced awkwardly against the linoleum, his eyes still open, pupils wide and dilated.

She didn't care. She scooped him up again, holding him to her chest, embracing him and knowing this lifeless thing in her arms, it wasn't her pet anymore. It was just a thing, and she hated herself for thinking that.

"*I-I'm sorry...I'm so sorry*," she whispered, down on her knees, rocking back and forth, cradling Dooch's body.

In the corner, his food bowl held a few crumbs. He'd just finished eating.

Nola didn't cry. She kept that promise. There was a moment where she thought the tears would come, but it passed too fast, punctured by a far more powerful feeling—a swell of anger, of hatred, *real hatred*, that crept up from her belly, invading her on a molecular level.

There was a noise on her left. She turned.

Royall was standing there, like he'd been there all along, arms crossed at his chest, soda in his hand, on the threshold of the kitchen.

"My God. What happened?" he asked.

The world went red. At just the sight of him, Nola could feel something hardening inside her, could feel something elemental rising.

"Is Dooch okay?" he added.

On most days, Nola's specialty was finding the hidden things, the lies we hide every day. But here, in this kitchen, as she cradled her dead pet in her arms, Royall wasn't hiding anything. It was right there on his face. He had a fire behind his eyes, and an unmistakable grin.

"Nola, I feel awful for you. Is there anything I can do?"

She wanted to fight, wanted to rush at him, wanted to lace her fingers around his throat and squeeze tight until her nails pierced his windpipe and his life was gone, and he was the one who was just a stiff, empty, lifeless *thing*. But she knew what would happen in a fight like that. Today was proof of it. She wasn't fighting a man. Royall was an animal.

"God, just heartbreaking, right?" Royall asked. "The world isn't perfect. Why do folks think it is?"

She didn't respond. Years from now, an Army psychologist would make a note in Nola's file, saying she suffered from RAD— Reactive Attachment Disorder—which happens when a child can't form attachments because of early neglect.

But tonight, Silent Nola just sat there, down on her knees, cursing herself for thinking she could have anything good—and cursing herself even more for taking the pet near Royall in the first place. If she hadn't taken him home, he'd still be alive.

Lesson learned. She'd never bring anything she loved near the house again.

75

ola, we're on board. All clear," Zig whisper-hissed, leaning down to the casket's airholes. He pulled out his earplugs, so he wouldn't miss her response.

Outside, there was another loud whirr. The third engine began its high-pitched whine. One more until full power.

"Nola, you hear me?" Zig added, now louder, his mouth up against the airholes. *"You okay in—!?"*

"Final check," Kesel called out on the PA system. Two minutes to takeoff.

Silent Nola. That's her MO. Always silent, Zig told himself. He thought again about the airholes. They had to be big enough. *Right?*

Behind him, Zig heard a noise by the stairs. Kesel was coming. Racing back toward the jump seat, Zig grabbed the Alaska guidebook, pretending to read.

"Make sure to strap in," Kesel shouted over the noise, hopping off the bottom step for his final inspection.

Zig fastened his safety belt, still studying Nola's metal case. *She's fine,* he insisted, reminding himself that there's enough air in a coffin for at least four and a half hours of breathing.

Kesel made a quick loop through the hull, checking every light, every gauge, every switch, every cargo strap, plus the anchor-line cable that ran down from the ceiling.

Diagonally across from Zig, toward the back of the plane, he noticed the side door with the red and green lights above it. *Emergency Exit.* Wide enough for a casket? Zig didn't even want to think about it. *She's fine.*

There was a final loud whirr as the fourth and final engine began to whine.

"See you at ten thousand feet," Kesel called out, closing the door and heading back upstairs.

The moment Zig was alone, he raced back to the case. Forget the stupid codes. He banged hard on the metal top.

C'mon, Nola… Gimme a response.

He put his ear to the case.

Nothing.

"*Nola, if you're okay, say something!*" he shouted directly into the airholes.

Still nothing.

Could she've passed out?

Zig stuck his fingers into the airholes. All clear. Even if they weren't…there's enough air…

Zig banged the case again, harder than ever.

Maybe being in a confined space… maybe she did pass out. If she did… she'd still be okay. Unless… Zig's brain was racing now. *If she accidentally turned on her side…*

Zig shook his head, refusing to consider it. And then he replayed the familiar image that always leapt into his brain whenever he saw a news report about a child who drowned, or a little boy who was shot by a stray bullet…or a young girl who—

Zig shut his eyes, but he couldn't stop seeing it: The red siren, spinning and blinding him. He was fighting through a crowd, pushing his way to— To those doors. To the open back doors of an ambulance. The doors seemed so far away, and then suddenly so close…close enough to see— There. Dangling from the gurney—a sagging arm. His chest turned to ice. Every parent knows their child. He knew it ten minutes ago, but now…to see it again, to see it this close... That was his daughter's arm. Maggie's arm. Just from the color of it—the gray color—he knew all hope was gone.

He was still elbowing through the crowd, fighting to get closer. No one fought against him, except at the end, when he reached the tall black paramedic who had no hope of stopping him. And then Zig was standing over the gurney, gasping for breath, like his lungs would never hold air again. *Nononono.* Even now, Zig could hear himself sobbing, praying, pleading with God that Zig could trade and be the dead one instead.

"*Nola!*" Zig shouted, grabbing at the metal casket, undoing the nylon straps with one hand, the clasps along the side with the other. *She needed air! Get her out!* He flicked open the final three clasps at the foot of the case.

Ka-clack. Ka-clack. Ka-clack.

Gripping the lid of the metal case, he wedged his fingers into its seam. Zig's body swayed as the plane began moving, taxiing toward the runway. Still plenty of time to get her out, get her help.

With a yank, Zig lifted the lid and shoved it back, revealing...

Books. Nothing but books.

Confused, Zig looked over his shoulder, scanning the empty hull. He looked back at the books.

There were dozens of them—fanned in a neat stack like tumbled dominos—textbooks with titles like *Modern Military Uniforms* and *20th Century Military Regalia.* They were from the library...the tall bookshelf right next to where all the extra caskets and transfer cases were—

Mothertrucker.

That's where Zig took her— When he snuck Nola back into Dover, he backed the hearse into Departures, moving Nola out of the casket and into the metal transfer cases that were stored there. When Zig went out to check on the plane, she must've—

Again. She did it again. Zig slammed the lid shut, kicking himself for not seeing it coming, for not seeing the big move or the small one. He should've known all along. It's the one rule of Nola: Nola doesn't change.

Vrrrrrrrrrr. The plane rumbled and shook, picking up speed as it rolled toward the runway.

Zig replayed their last few hours in the motel room last night, slowly fitting each piece in place. When Nola was clicking through Houdini's watch...she found new coordinates. From there, she knew Zig's weaknesses. His guilt and sentimentality. All she had to do was ask him to team up. Make him think she wanted help.

That's all it took. Nola didn't need Zig to get on the plane, or to go anywhere near Alaska. No. The only thing she wanted from Zig was to get her here, into the one place where only he could bring her—directly into Dover. And for the third time, Zig walked right into it.

The rumble of the engines was deafening now. But as the wheels left the ground, and Zig was down on his knees, fighting for balance, he didn't know what worried him more: that somehow the digital coordinates on the watch traced back to Dover...or that whoever Nola was now searching for, they'd been hiding here all along.

76

There he is!" a female voice called out.

Master Guns rolled his eyes at his boss's favorite line. *"There he is!"* she'd say, adding a thumbs-up if she really wanted to sell it.

Sure enough, as Colonel Hsu stepped into his office, she gave him a big thumbs-up with a double pump. Hsu was a politician. If she was leading with charm, bad news was coming.

Before she even turned the corner, Master Guns shot out of his seat, standing at attention behind his desk, both hands at his side.

"Really, Francis?" Hsu asked, clutching her cell phone. She was always clutching her cell phone. "Have I ever been that formal?"

Master Guns stood there, straight as a pencil. He was a Marine. Customs and courtesies still meant something. Colonel Hsu was Air Force. Didn't mind breaking. So typical.

"At ease, okay? That make you happy?" Hsu asked.

"Just showing respect, ma'am."

Hsu waved him off, like they were the oldest of friends. But Master Guns didn't need to be Dover's chief investigator to know they weren't.

"What can I help you with, ma'am?"

"You weren't at yesterday's stand-up," Hsu said, referring to her morning senior staff meeting. "You also, considering all the bodies that arrived, didn't file a report for this morning's stand-up. Just making sure you're okay."

"Apologies, ma'am. No offense meant. I've just been busy with the Alaska investigation."

"I figured," she said, adding a smile to keep things light. She took a seat opposite his desk, glancing over at the framed antique American flag on the wall.

"Thirty-eight?" she asked, counting the stars on the flag.

"1876. From when they added Colorado. My home state." Master Guns took a deep breath through his nose. "Ma'am, if there's something you want to talk about—?"

"I got a call this morning. About the plane crash in Alaska. Mind you, I've been getting calls all week, but this one came from the White House's chief of staff—that little bug—what's his name—?"

"Galen Gibbs."

"Galen Gibbs. He calls me every few hours, looking for details."

"He calls me every few *minutes*."

Hsu laughed at that, her eyes no longer on the flag. "So you can imagine my surprise when Gibbs called me at five thirty this morning and asked me when the final autopsy report would be filed. Not just for the Librarian of Congress, but for the other victims on the plane: Clifford Eddy. Rose Mackenberg. Amedeo Vacca. He wanted all of them, said they weren't filed yet. So odd, right? Our medical examiners are usually meticulous about that. Those should've been filed immediately. But they weren't."

Master Guns sat there silent, his hands gripped together on his desk in a little church and steeple.

"Then imagine my further surprise when I asked Dr. Sinclair about the reports . . . and he told me he gave them to *you*, Francis— that you personally asked for all the victims' reports yourself. Even the one for the Librarian of Congress."

"Ma'am, this is *my* investigation. I have every right to see those reports."

"Then see them *after* he files them. You can read them online like the rest of us."

"I appreciate that, ma'am. So I hope you also appreciate that the way things have been going here lately, I'd rather read from the original sources than trust what gets put online."

"What's that supposed to mean?"

"It means, I am absolutely tired of talking in euphemisms. Ma'am. We both know what you're asking. When Nola Brown's body first arrived from Alaska, that body wasn't Ms. Brown. And Clifford Eddy, Rose Mackenberg, and Amedeo Vacca . . . that's not who they were either, were they? You knew that from the moment those fallen were packed in ice and sent here."

Now Colonel Hsu was the one gripping her hands together, strangling her cell phone.

"Also, ma'am, when it comes to an ongoing investigation, you know I can't talk about any of my findings."

Hsu went to say something, stopped herself, then started again. "Francis, when people hear that this is my command, they assume I'm a serious person—that there's no humor in death. But if I've learned anything at Dover, it's that this place is filled with the absurd. Dead bodies fart. When you embalm someone, their penis engorges. Some things must be laughed at. But that accusing tone in your voice? There's nothing funny about it, Francis. You hearing me on this? If you've altered a word in those reports, you're breaking the law."

"So you don't have a problem with our medical examiner filing false reports? Was that your idea, or were those just orders from someone higher up the chain of command?"

"I told you, be careful with that tone, soldier."

"Not a soldier. A Marine."

Hsu rolled her eyes. "Francis, spare me the bluster. You should've never taken those reports before they were sent to my office!"

"*Me? You're* the one now interfering with an active investiga—!"

There was a loud ring—Master Guns's phone. He looked down at Caller ID. He knew the number. So did Colonel Hsu, who was glancing at it as well.

202-406 prefix. United States Secret Service.

"Why are they calling you?" Hsu asked.

Master Guns didn't answer.

Riiiiiing.

"Pick it up," Hsu said.

He still didn't touch it.

Riiiiiing.

"Francis, pick that phone up *now*. That's an order."

Riiiii—

Hsu's arm shot out like a cobra as she pounded the button for the speakerphone. "This is Colonel Agatha Hsu. Who's this?"

"Terry O'Hara, Secret Service," a strong, determined voice said through the speaker. "I'm looking for Sergeant Steranko."

"The sergeant can hear you just fine. I'm his supervisor. How can we help you, Agent O'Hara?"

O'Hara paused, but not for long. "Ma'am, I'm not sure if you're aware of the subject we've been tracking. We now believe that subject has breached security."

"Breached it *where*?" Hsu asked.

"On base," O'Hara replied. "We've got a full mobilization headed your way. After you activate surveillance and heightened security, we recommend you lock it down until we locate the target."

"What're you—? What target?"

"Horatio, ma'am. We believe Horatio's now inside Dover."

From opposite sides of the desk, Colonel Hsu and Master Guns looked up at each other, both of them confused.

Simultaneously, they asked, "Who's *Horatio*?"

77

FBI Headquarters
Washington, DC

Amy Waggs was having one of those days. One of those years, actually, ever since she tweaked her back hurling down a zip line on that stupid singles cruise her sister Kim talked her into.

At thirty-eight years old, she should've known better than to listen to her sister. Or ride a zip line. All she had to show for it was a herniated disc, $4,500 in chiropractor bills, and a tall, adjustable-height desk that took the pressure off her spine but meant she was on her feet all day.

It was barely 6 a.m.—her favorite time of day, when the office was quiet, when the sky was dark—the best time to think. So here Waggs was, elbows on her adjustable-height desk, clicking through folder after folder, reading Dover report after Dover report, searching for the name Zig had told her this morning.

Horatio.

Three days ago, when Zig first called her to trace Nola's fingerprints, Waggs was doing a simple favor. But somewhere along the way, this became more than just a courtesy for a friend. From the start, this case reeked. She knew it. Covert missions happened all the time. To protect national security, the CIA would regularly mask the names of Dover victims so that agents and sources weren't revealed. But those cases had their own rhythm, their own pattern of governmental checks and clearances. Reports were written. Files were created.

None of that could be found here. And neither could any trace of Horatio, Waggs realized, running yet another search on Dover's intranet.

Still nothing.

For a few moments, Waggs stood there, staring blankly at the only totem she kept on her desk: a Grateful Dead dancing bears soy candle from their reunion tour in Chicago a few years back. A present from her older sister. Growing up in rural Iowa, Waggs's sister loved to color. Her brother used to love mazes. Waggs, though? She loved Connect the Dots. Such a simple treat. From one, to two, to three, to four—follow along and the bigger picture will emerge.

It was no different today.

To move a body in and out of Dover...was that hard to pull off? Not really. Leaning back and doing that stupid stretch the chiropractor gave her, Waggs could think of a dozen different ways. But. The one pattern that kept repeating? In every move across the chessboard, wherever Zig went, someone was always there first. When Zig went to check on Nola's body in Departures, someone had already arranged to take it. When Zig went to Nola's office, someone was already lying in wait. Wherever he moved, they always knew Zig was coming. Like someone tipped them off in advance.

For the next hour, Waggs ran the list of every Dover mortuary employee, checking it against the entrance records of every person who had gone in and out of Dover during the last few weeks. She checked flight manifests to see who landed there, then rechecked those same manifests to see who flew out. She even put in a request for phone records, specifically those of Colonel Hsu and Master Guns, just to be safe. Then she ran all those names, crosschecking to see who had ties to Zig, to Alaska, to Nola's office at Fort Belvoir, to the Secret Service, even to the White House itself. And of course to that name. *Horatio.*

Despite all the dots, no pattern emerged. That is, until Waggs reached for the thick padded envelope that'd been sitting on the edge of her desk. There was no stamp in the corner. Hand-delivered, just like Waggs asked.

The bubble wrap popped as she tore open the envelope. Inside was a small black device made with mil-spec hardware. The Fang—the machine Zig used when he first scanned "Nola's" finger-prints.

"You mind grabbing it for me?" Waggs had asked yesterday when she heard that an FBI colleague was headed to Dover for an errand.

"Something wrong with its scanners?" he'd asked.

"Just needs a tune-up," she'd lied.

It was a Hail Mary for sure, but every day, Waggs pulled bio-metrics from terrorists' weapons and explosive devices. That was her specialty—what people leave behind.

Standing at her desk, Waggs spread cyanoacrylate—liquid superglue—across the smoothest part of the scanner. It attached quickly to whatever moisture residue was there. A UV penlight did the rest, revealing the one thing she was hoping for, and making her feel like Sherlock Holmes with her very own magnifying glass.

A fingerprint. Two of them, actually.

Ten minutes later, Waggs was staring at her screen, waiting on the FBI's database. Somewhere, servers whirred.

Two pictures popped on-screen. The first, as expected, was Zig. But the second...

Waggs swallowed hard.

No. That's— Can't be.

But it was.

Waggs whispered his name, barely hearing her own words. *"Ho-ratio's... Oh, shit."*

78

Dover Air Force Base, Delaware

D ino always started with the plain M&M's.
Those were his favorites. He was a purist, preferring the plain ones to peanut—and of course to those abominations with peanut butter or dark chocolate, or that bluewrapped disaster, the pretzel M&M.

No, plain were the best. Which explained why Dino always restocked them first in the candy machine—in the moneymaker slot, third row from the top, eye level, center position.

From there, he added his full murderers row of candy: Snickers, Reese's, Crunch bars, Twix, 100 Grand bars, Heath bars, Original Skittles, Sour Skittles, the ultra-underrated Take 5 bar, and in the very last slot on the right, white chocolate Kit Kats. Because why have the same candy machine as everyone else?

Dropping the last pack of plain M&M's into place, Dino glanced around the breakroom. This early in the morning, Dover's mortuary was quiet. It wouldn't be for long.

One by one, he restocked each row, tilting each chocolate bar backward, just right. If the candy leaned forward, it'd get caught in the coil, stuck in the machine. On a military base, with the tempers here? That was never good for anyone.

Kneeling down to work the bottom row, he added extra granola and protein bars—the colonel's favorites—humming a song to himself, Cher's "If I Could Turn Back Time." How the hell'd that get stuck in his head?

With a slam and the twist of a key, Dino shut the front of the machine and, as always, gave it a test. C5. Plain M&M's.

Rrrrrrrr.

The coil began to spin, the plastic kicker at the end of it giving the bag of M&M's its final shove...

Tuuunk.

Reaching into the vending machine, Dino pulled out the M&M's. It was still early, but... C'mon. This was the best perk of being the Candyman. Actually, second-best.

Dino tossed back a few M&M's, shoved the rest in his pocket, then quickly restocked the boxes onto his hand truck. That was the job. Every day, putting back what others took.

Heading out into the hallway, Dino opted for the long way around, toward the executive offices of the mortuary—home of carpet walkers like Accounting and Human Resources, who never saw bodies—but also where both Zig's and Master Guns's offices were.

Zig had already snuck onto the plane. Dino was sure of that. As for Master Guns, the light was on in his office, though based on the open door, Master Guns wasn't there.

In the corner, Colonel Hsu's light was on as well. Her door was shut.

This early in the day? She and Master Guns were both inside. Dino made a mental note.

By now, back at the bowling alley—at the Kingpin Café—the first pot of coffee should finally be done brewing.

Throwing back a few more M&M's and still humming "If I Could Turn Back Time," Dino wheeled the hand truck through the office, toward the front door. The few secretaries he passed didn't even bother looking up.

That's how it was, every day.

No one looked twice at the Candyman.

79

First, Waggs called Zig.

No answer.

She called him again.

Same. Straight to voicemail. Didn't even ring. Like his phone was off.

Then Waggs called Master Guns.

Same. No answer.

She called again.

Still no answer, but it rang three times. He wasn't picking up.

She sent Master Guns a text. "You there?"

No response. And then...those three gray dots appeared, the ellipsis that told her Master Guns was writing back.

"In a meeting. All ok?" Master Guns texted.

"No. Emergency. Call me," she texted back.

"Can't. With Colonel and Sec Service. Base going on lockdown. You safe?"

Waggs stood there at her adjustable-height desk, debating whether to text the words. She had no choice.

"I know who Horatio is." She hit *Send*.

The three gray dots came up immediately, then disappeared as... Her phone rang, vibrating in her hand.

"You're on speaker," Master Guns announced as she picked up. "I have Colonel Hsu and Agent Terry O'Hara from the US Secret Service. You were saying about Horatio..."

"I know who he is!" Waggs insisted. "I found his...I found fingerprints on the Fang."

"That doesn't mean—"

"I looked through Dover's entrance records, checking to see when he swiped into the building. He's there every time Zig is, leaves every time Zig leaves! He's been watching all along!" she added, pulling up an image on her phone and hitting *Send*.

There was a pause and a buzz as the image popped up on Master Guns's phone screen.

"That's him. *That's Horatio!*" Waggs said, still staring at the employee photo of the one man who had access to every building at Dover, the one man who knew everything Zig was up to.

Dino.

80

At Dover, most buildings had names. The military is tidy; it prefers names.

So officially, the mortuary was known as the *Charles C. Carson Center for Mortuary Affairs*. The military museum where Dover stored dozens of old classic airplanes was called the *Air Mobility Command Museum*.

But the building Dino was currently headed to as he carried a large cardboard box with a Snickers logo on it? Building 1303. That's what it was called on Dover's official maps. But to those who worked on base, it had another name. *The Graveyard*.

A bit melodramatic, to be sure. But as Dino readjusted the Snickers box and eyed the security forces' black SUV in the distance, even Dino had to admit, it was an apt name.

Back in 1978, during the Jonestown massacre, preacher Jim Jones asked his followers to drink cyanide-laced grape punch, killing over 900 people, including over 200 children. Since Dover specializes in mass fatalities, 913 corpses were sent here. But with a number that large, the only way to store the bodies was to convert an old 1960s-era metallic warehouse into a massive morgue. Building 1303.

"Anybody home?" Dino called out toward the warehouse's broken windows, which were boarded up. He didn't like coming here—no one liked coming here—not since those nine hundred Jonestown corpses were covered in white sheets and spread out across the warehouse's concrete floor. When it happened, the then-colonel at Dover said to give it time, that people would eventually forget and the building could be put back into regular use.

It almost worked, until a decade ago, when a C-5 Galaxy, the military's largest plane at the time (over six stories high), took off from a runway at Dover and mysteriously crashed right after it flew over this exact spot. No one on the plane was killed. Voodoo, everyone called it, blaming it once again on Building 1303—one of the few places at Dover that people actively avoided.

"*Hello...? Anyone...?*" Dino called out again, crossing around to the side of the warehouse and checking one last time over his shoulder.

The military SUV was long gone. This far south on the base, there were only long, barren cornfields on one side of the building and a scattering of parked airplanes on the other.

Using his chest to pin the cardboard box to the wall, Dino reached for the rusted old doorknob and gave it a tug. He knew it'd be open. He unlocked it days ago.

"*Delivery!*" Dino called out, stepping inside and ignoring the metallic whiff of wet coins and rusted old pipes. It was dark inside—they shut off the electricity years ago—the only light coming from a boarded-up skylight that wasn't boarded up as well as it should be.

"Back here," a man's voice called out.

Dino glanced to his left, where stack after stack of 1950s-era gurneys—at least two thousand of them—were piled one on top of another, each stack ten feet high, forming makeshift walls and an instant maze that Dino followed deeper into the wide warehouse.

After 9/11, when the Iraq invasion began, the government was keenly aware that every new war brings a massive increase in dead young soldiers. To handle the demand, Dover got $30 million for a new mortuary, filled with $10 million in state-of-the-art equipment. But as all the new items arrived, everything from the old mortuary—which dated back to Vietnam and Korea—had to be thrown away. Or at least stored somewhere no one would notice.

"You're late," the man's voice called out.

"I'm doing my best," Dino replied. He meant it. His entire life, Dino worked hard, but somehow, it was never good enough. In high school, he barely passed. In community college, he scraped by. As a valet, an ice cream store manager, a Piercing Pagoda employee, even a health club trainer, he struggled, struggled, and struggled. Even now, as he tried to pick up his pace, it led to more stumbling. Dino was a big guy, with a big gut, who lumbered when he walked.

"Wait...that's not— Where'd you go?" Dino called out, hitting a dead end down an aisle of thirty-foot-high metallic racks that flanked him on both sides. Back during Vietnam, these casket racks held all the new caskets—six thousand at a time—when the war was at its peak. Now they were filled with old desk chairs, lamps, and leftover office furniture.

"Did I tell you this place was something?" Dino shouted, doublebacking down a different aisle, still trying to navigate the stacks of old metal desks, battered embalming tables, vintage casket carriages, fifty-gallon drums of formaldehyde, as well as metal storage racks filled with scalpels, forceps, draining tubes, separators—every mortician's tool you can think of, all smelling like mildew and decay, all covered in rot and rust—like an entire 1960s funeral home was dumped into a warehouse and forgotten.

"By the way, you were right about Zig," Dino called out, his arms holding tight to his cardboard box. "According to the entry records, he came in first thing this morning. Driving a hearse. That means Nola was probably in back, huh?"

No answer.

"You hear what I said?" Dino added, cutting around a huge wooden crate marked *Warning: Carcinogens* in bright red letters.

The crate was filled with glass bottles of embalming fluid. "That means Nola—"

"What's in the box?" a deep voice interrupted.

Dino spun toward a man with buzzed gray hair, a pitted face, and a faded scar that split his bottom lip in a pale zigzag, from where it was torn open years ago. Dressed in tan-and-green camouflage—an army combat uniform—the man stood there, arms behind his back, his greedy eyes taking Dino apart.

"Jesus on a pogo stick—don't *do* that!" Dino blurted. "I hate scary movies!"

"The box. What's in it?" the man asked.

Dino hesitated, but not for long. "It's for my payment. You said you'd—"

"I know what I said." From behind his back, the man pulled out a manila envelope, thick with cash. "If it makes you feel better, you did the right thing."

Dino grabbed the money, then turned away, studying the envelope and avoiding eye contact. He took no joy in what he'd done. But at this point, he didn't have a choice, not with all the debt he was buried under.

It started six months ago, when his old manager from Piercing Pagoda told him about an opportunity to get in on the ground floor: a brand-new PVC piping company—with the filament it used, you could make it yourself on a 3-D printer. "Miraculous!" everyone called it. "A game-changer!" Dino looked it up; it all checked out. Together, they could buy the distributorship for the entire East Coast.

This was Dino's chance—his chance to get away from the candy machines, to get out of the bowling alley...his chance to step out of Zig's shadow and finally build something for himself, something that Zig didn't help him with. All he had to do was pull together the cash: his savings, second mortgage, plus the $20,000 he borrowed from his bookie. Sure, it was a risk, but what great reward came without risk? This was Dino's *chance*.

Unfortunately, it was also a scam—one that took Dino for nearly $250,000. For months, he thought he could dig out. Then Dino's car got repossessed. He told Zig it was in the shop. Then the bookie sent a guy who wore a gold razor blade around his neck. A few times, Dino was tempted to ask Zig for help, but God Almighty, he'd spent his whole life asking Zig for help.

Eventually, the banks stopped calling and instead started knocking on his door. They threatened to take his house, his wages. They even started going after the joint account his grandmother asked him to cosign so Dino could help pay her rent and bills. She was ninety-three! If they took that account, Grandma Ruth would be out on the street!

So when a man approached Dino, offering to pay Dino's debts, Dino knew there had to be a catch. And there was. All Dino had to do was tell the man where Zig was going and what he was up to.

"Are you out of your mind?" Dino replied. No way. He'd never screw over his friend.

That is, until the man explained that he didn't want to hurt Zig either. He just wanted information: where Zig was on base...who he was talking to. If anything, considering the people Zig was investigating, it would save Zig's life. More important, the man explained, if Dino wouldn't help, he'd find someone else who would.

It was that last point that Dino couldn't argue with. At least this way, Dino could keep an eye on everything, managing the situation and keeping Zig safe. Did Dino feel bad that day when he knocked Zig in the head? Of course. He felt awful. But at that point, to grab Kamille's items from the room and to make sure Zig didn't spot him, Dino had no choice. Keeping Zig in the dark meant keeping Zig safe. Plus, with the influx of cash, Dino could pay off his debts, keep his car and house, and pay for Grandma Ruth. All of his financial problems would disappear. Like magic.

"You hear what I said about Zig and the hearse?" Dino asked, staring down as he clutched the envelope of money, tempted to open it. Somehow, though, it felt rude. "I'm telling you, Nola's on that plane to Alaska."

"No," the man said quietly. "She isn't."

There was something in the man's voice, something that made Dino want to turn around. He didn't, though. "How d'you know?"

Those would be the final words Dino ever uttered.

Behind him, Dino didn't see the man pull out his gun. Didn't hear as the man cocked a bullet into the chamber. Dino was too busy dropping the envelope into his cardboard Snickers box, congratulating himself for picking such a good hiding place.

"Dino . . ." the man said.

Following the sound, Dino glanced over his shoulder. The gun was already at Dino's temple, the angle just right so when they later found the gun, along with a pile of collection notices, even the best investigators would be convinced it was a suicide.

Ftttt.

A jagged black hole appeared in Dino's temple, burn marks scorching his skin. His head whipped sideways, chasing the bullet, followed by his torso, then his body, all his weight dragged to the side like a toppling tree.

Thuuud.

As Dino hit the concrete floor, a single spurt of blood gushed like a tiny waterfall down his temple, across the side of his nose. Then another. That was it.

For a moment, the man with the pale zigzag scar stood there. He wasn't looking at Dino. He was staring straight ahead, out into the warehouse.

"I know you're here," he called.

No one replied.

"You think I'm a fool?" the man added. "You followed Dino here, didn't you, Nola?"

There was a noise on his left. A click. Like a gun being cocked. From behind a tall stack of 1950s metal desks, Nola just stood there, her gun pointed at the man.

"Horatio, huh?" Nola asked. "That's what you're calling yourself now?"

The man laughed—a soulful, hearty laugh that came from deep in his belly. The man who knew IDs better than anyone. "Don't be so formal, Nola. I know it's been a while," Royall said, flashing his wolfish grin, "but you can still call me *Dad*."

81

Homestead, Florida
Ten years ago

This was Nola when she was sixteen. On the day she almost didn't make seventeen.

Royall was screaming about mayonnaise.

"Did you taste it!? It turned! Went bad!" he shouted, gripping his sandwich in a fist, shoving it toward Nola's face.

She was trying to clean up lunch, hoping to get out of there. At the smell of the sandwich, she recoiled.

"You smell that, right!? Shit smell like that and you still served it to me?"

Avoiding eye contact, Nola stayed focused on wiping crumbs from the counter.

"Why would you serve it if it smelled like that?"

Nola stayed silent.

"Answer me!"

Nola paused. He asked again. Finally, she whispered, "It smelled fine before."

That was it. Fuse lit.

"Fine? You think *this* is *fine?* Or better yet—" Royall opened the fridge, pulled out the old tub of mayo—a massive price-club size that'd been sitting in the fridge for the better part of a year—and quickly unscrewed it, ramming the open tub toward Nola's face.

Again, she recoiled at the smell.

"You think I'm a fucking moron? You did it on purpose, didn't you!?" Royall asked, hitting his own next level. "*You knew it was spoiled, and you served it!*"

Nola shook her head, but it was true. She thought the mayo might've turned. It was a small victory, but she'd take it. Like when she'd spit in his pancake batter every Sunday.

"Okay, smart-ass—if it's good enough for me, then it's good enough for you!" Royall insisted. From the counter, he grabbed at a ceramic utensil holder, knocking it over and sending two whisks and a metal cheese grater flying across the counter.

From the utensil holder, he pulled out a wooden spoon, scraped it inside the tub, and pulled out a big dollop of mayo, like a runny scoop of ice cream. He rammed it at Nola's face.

"C'mon, you think it's so good, take a bite!"

Nola kept her head down, trying to sidestep him.

"*Take a bite!*"

Nola shoved his hand aside. "Get *off*!" she blurted, already regretting it.

In a blur, Royall slapped her across the face so hard, blood flew from her mouth. She knew that taste. The coppery tang of blood wasn't new to her.

She was still getting her bearings.

He grabbed her by the throat.

"I said. *Take. A. Bite*," he growled, tightening his grip around her neck and slowly moving the spoon of mayonnaise to her lips, like he was feeding a baby.

The cloud of mayo smelled foul, looking thicker and yellower than it should. Nola shook her head back and forth, her lips pressed together.

Royall held tight to her throat, and with a violent shove backward, half a dozen wooden spoons and the cheese grater fell to the floor. Royall lifted her up on her tiptoes. Nola couldn't breathe. Her face was tomato red.

"Eat it," he rumbled, his breath matching the smell of the lumpy glob of mayo that was now touching her lips.

Nola had no choice. She opened her mouth to gasp for breath. The sour mayonnaise passed her lips, and she felt it coat the front of her teeth, then the roof of her mouth. She swallowed hard, using her tongue to force it down. It was like eating a pudding of bad eggs.

"*All of it,*" Royall said, still gripping her throat.

She gagged on the first bite, then gagged again, her body violently jerking.

"Don't you dare throw up."

Too late.

A thick spray of Nola's salami lunch spewed through the air. Royall stepped out of the way just in time. It landed in a thick Jackson Pollock splatter across the linoleum.

At the sight of it, Royall tightened his fists.

"*You think you're done?*" he screamed.

She tried to run.

He grabbed her by the hair, then the back of her neck, her body bending backward, like a childhood game of limbo. She was off-balance and falling. Royall held tight, twisting her around, forcing her to her knees. He pushed her face toward the floor until her nose was inches from the vomit. "I said *all of it.*"

Nola pushed back, trying to raise her head.

Royall held her in place. Nola was shaking, the bile smell bringing tears to her eyes, mucus running from her nose.

"*All of it. Lick it up!*" Royall insisted.

And then Nola whispered the one thing that she'd never said in ten years.

"*No.*"

She muttered the word to herself. But Royall could feel it, could sense it, even if he couldn't hear it.

"What'd you just s—?"

Royall never finished the question. Down on the ground, mucus dangling from her nose into the vomit, Nola reached for the nearby cheese grater. Gripping it in her fist, she swung backward with all her might. The metal grater caught Royall in the face. It tore open his bottom lip, taking with it a hunk of skin that ran down his jaw. He'd have this zigzag scar forever.

"*Naaaaaah!*" Royall screamed, Nola already all over him.

"*You don't get to touch me! You never get to touch me!*" she howled, clawing at his face, at his throat, at his eyes, snot still raining from her nose. A flurry of punches spread the blood from Royall's cheek, now covering her fists. She even kicked at his left knee, remembering when he twisted it a few years back. In a matter of seconds, a decade of rage erupted and overflowed. For a moment, she thought she'd won. But Nola had never been trained to fight—and as she wound up with another punch—

Royall planted his meaty fist directly into her left eye. The singular blow turned Nola's world black, then bright with stars. She flew backward, crashing into the sink and tumbling to the floor. The cheese grater went flying. She couldn't hear a thing. Royall had hit her before, but never with a ferocity like this.

"*You're dead! Y'hear me!?*" he screamed, letting out a roar as spit flew from his lips. In a blur, he gripped her by the hair and dragged her to her feet. His eyes were dark, like she wasn't even there.

Nola thought she'd seen all his levels. She'd never seen this one. He wasn't cursing, wasn't screaming, wasn't even calling her his nigger. No. He was simply silent.

Gripping the back of her neck, Royall thrust her toward the back screen door, using her forehead to shove it open, tossing her outside. Her toes dragged through the grass as they headed for—

Of course.

A vicious kick sent the kiddie pool flying across the yard, but instead of shouting a time at Nola—*fifteen minutes . . . twenty minutes . . . half an hour*—Royall tossed her into the hole.

She landed on her side, her shoulder on fire, dislocated.

"Lay down."

"Royall—"

"*LAY DOWN!*" he snarled, his voice booming through the backyard.

She did, well aware of what would happen if she didn't. The blood was still pouring from his face.

"*R-Royall, please, don't do this!*"

He already was, leaping in after her and grabbing the shovel.

"You move, and I'll put this in your heart," he said coldly, standing over her and pressing the point of the shovel into her chest. "You understand?"

She nodded, lying there on her back, her shoulder burning.

Climbing out of the hole, Royall slid the blade under a mound of fresh dirt that was at the foot of the shallow pit.

She wanted to scream, wanted to cry. *No!* Even he wouldn't do this.

He lifted the shovelful of dirt into the air and didn't pause. He dumped it on Nola.

As the dirt rained down, she was coughing, gasping, trying to shield her face. She could feel it sticking to the slurry of snot under her nose. The musky smell of dirt. It wouldn't take much to cover her.

Royall loaded up again with another round of fresh dirt.

Nola looked up at him, pleading. He stared down, straight into her eyes, unblinking, like there was no one inside his head.

With a twist of his wrists, he dumped the dirt on her again. And again. And again.

Nola shut her eyes, spitting between each shovelful. Her legs were covered first, then her waist, the heavy blanket of dirt feeling like a thousand pounds.

She should run. *Run now!*

"*Don't you move,*" he warned as she started to squirm.

He won't go through with it. Even he wasn't that nuts, Nola told herself. *He was just making a point.* But then she thought back all those years ago, to that first night of digging, in South Carolina. He said it from the start. She was digging her own grave.

A clump of dirt hit her chest as she covered her eyes. She cupped her hands together, trying to make a little air pocket for her face.

Another clump hit.

She was spitting, her breathing heavy now. Her lungs were ready to burst. *No... don't hyperventilate...*

A clump hit her in the waist. Then another in the neck.

Since they moved here, it took most of the year for her to dig this hole. It took Royall less than five minutes to fill it.

Nola was covered now, up to her neck.

Royall stomped the blade into the dirt, scooping out his final mounds.

Nola's hands were still cupped over her face. She thought about praying, but learned long ago there'd be no answer. Instead, she went to a different place, tried to imagine a better place than this. It wasn't hard. She could see it in her mind's eye, saying the words for the first time. *Mongol... Faber... Staedtler... Ticonderoga... Swan.*

Another clump hit, right at her wrists.

Mongol... Faber... Staedtler... Ticonderoga... Swan.

And then...

The next clump of dirt never came.

Royall stood there.

"Had enough?" he asked.

Nola's hands were shaking. She lifted them up, letting the light in. Spit again. Blinked away the dirt.

She could barely see Royall. He was standing there, at the foot of the hole. She lifted her head for a better look. Blood ran from his chin, his lower lip looking like it wasn't attached.

Down in the hole, Nola was covered up to her neck, her head the only thing still free. Dirt was in her ears, in her nose, in her teeth, in her hair. Another good shovelful and she'd be completely under.

"You better learn your place," Royall warned, his voice low and steady, sounding slurred from his cut lip. "You understand?"

Nola's own lips were pursed. She was breathing heavily, short quick bursts to keep the dirt from her throat.

"*You understand?*" he repeated.

She nodded over and over and over. "I-I'm sorry...so sorry," she gasped, meaning it.

With a flick of his wrists, Royall tossed a final shovelful of dirt onto her face. Not enough to cover her. Just to remind her of the consequences.

She spit out most of the dirt, her face still covered in mucus and saliva. By the time she looked up, Royall was headed back to the house.

"*Let's go!*" he called out.

The dirt wasn't packed tight. With a little effort, she sat up straight. Her eye was already swelled shut from where he punched her. The shovel was at her feet. She spit out more dirt, her head still ringing.

"How you feeling?" Royall asked.

She kept her head down, not answering as she used the shovel like a crutch, crawling up from the hole.

"You look like a zombie," Royall teased, seeing all the mud and filth still stuck to her. "Don't get that shit in the house," he added, heading for the back door.

As Royall stepped inside, even from here, Nola could smell the acidic stench of salami vomit that was still sprayed across the kitchen floor. "What a hot damn mess," he called out, nearly tripping over the tub of mayonnaise turned on its side, which spun like a top into the mayo-covered spoon he'd used to force-feed her.

Behind him, through the screen door, Nola was outside, taking off her clothes. She made sure he wasn't peeking. For those few moments, he did the right thing, giving her some privacy.

Then, for no reason, he turned just slightly, glancing over his shoulder. Just a little peek. Just as Nola was winding up. "Nola, you better get in here and clean this shit u—"

Klang.

The side of the shovel hit Royall with a wallop as it smashed him in the temple.

Wielding the shovel like a baseball bat, Nola had swung with all her might. At the impact, Royall's head twisted so hard, it looked like it was about to unscrew from his neck.

For Nola, the sound alone—a sickening bonecrack of metal against skin—was worth it.

Royall's body corkscrewed, bouncing off the kitchen counter and crumpling to the floor. Nola wound up for another hit, but Royall was already slumped across the ground, unconscious.

That day, Nola ran nine miles, not stopping until she reached Ms. Sable's house.

By the time the police arrived at Nola's place, Royall was long gone.

It would be the last time Nola and Royall saw each other—until that frozen afternoon, out by the runway in Alaska.

82

M.K. Air Base—Constanta, Romania
Four months ago

O kay to sit?" asked the man with the long eyelashes and
pale zigzag scar across his lip.

"Free country," the man named Rowan replied. "At
least I think it's still free." His fox-shaped face contorted as he took
a bite of his steak sandwich.

The two of them sat in the PX food court, both of them eating
over red plastic trays from Charley's Steak Sandwiches—a little
piece of home on this air force base in Romania.

"How's the steak?"

"Crappy. And amazing," Rowan said, barely looking up.

"So like all PX food?" the man with the scar joked, his voice like
a woodchipper.

Rowan didn't answer. He was eating faster now, trying to get out
of here.

"That one of ours?" the man added, motioning with his chin toward the small computer case that sat next to Rowan's red tray.

"Yeah. Why?"

The man took a bite of his own steak sandwich, grease
and oil raining from the bottom. A few determined chews.
Swallowed it quick. Licked his lips. "You're the one they call
Houdini—the paying agent, yeah? Usually they ship you around
place to place, but they said you got assigned to Colonel Price's

unit. I hear you do amazing work. Can make all sorts of things disappear."

Houdini sat up straight, his glare tightening on the man with the zigzag scar. No uniform. Green stripe across his ID. "You're a contractor?"

"For Colonel Price's unit. Welcome to Bluebook."

"You been with them long?" Rowan asked.

The man nodded. "I get our people the right paperwork. It's more important than you think. But I also make sure that no one tries to rip us off. And that's what caught my eye here— you said that computer there is one of ours, but if it is, you should've filled out a hand receipt. But when I looked, I didn't see a hand receipt from you. Which makes me wonder: Why is the new guy suddenly carrying a computer bag without a computer?"

"I use it for storage. I like the bag."

"It's a good bag. Probably holds . . . what? . . . about eleven pounds? That's heavy. Equal to a big bag of sugar, a medium bowling ball . . . or if you use those bricks of cash we pay people in . . . eleven pounds is about five hundred thousand dollars. Give or take." The man gripped his steak sandwich, squeezing the grease and oil from it.

"I should run," Houdini said, starting to stand. "I got a flight to catch."

"I noticed. I also noticed that everyone else in Bluebook is flying out of here first thing tomorrow morning. The colonel included. But for some reason, according to the manifest, you're flying out in the next few hours. Why you rushing away from us?"

Houdini froze there a moment, midway between standing up and sitting. Then he sat down.

"I should probably get running myself," the man added. "If a computer goes missing—or even a computer bag—it's good to file a report. That way they can check everyone's belongings before they fly out. You wouldn't believe what people take from here." He looked straight at Houdini, who looked straight back.

"What'd you say your name was again?" Houdini asked.

"I didn't," Royall replied as he went to get up. "Again, I should run."

"Wait, wait, wait—before you go..." Houdini said. "Maybe we should have ourselves a talk."

83

Deutsch Air Base
Copper Center, Alaska
Five days ago

Nola was staring at a hole in the ceiling when she made the decision. She didn't remember what caused her to look up—a stray bird that swooped through the airplane hangar?—but there it was: a pinprick of light shining through the roof.

She couldn't help but wonder what caused it. A squirrel? Hail? No. A gun. In every army base on the planet—including this tiny outpost near the national park in Alaska—there was a roof with a stray bullet hole.

"Passengers, head to the aircraft. Prepare to board!" a young airman with droopy eyes called out. "And please don't leave any trash in my terminal!"

A small group of passengers collected their belongings by the bench area, readying their boarding passes. At the front of the group was an older man in a wool winter coat. He was the VIP—Librarian of Congress Nelson Rookstool. Leading the pack, he headed quickly toward the tarmac and the Air Force tech sergeant gripping a clipboard.

Holding her own boarding card, Nola was about to join them—but right there, as she stared up at the hole in the roof, she turned the other way.

"*Wait . . . you're leaving?*" a female voice called out.

Nola didn't hear her. She was already at the exit, pushing her way through the clear plastic strips that covered the doorframe and kept the warmth from leaking out.

"*Sergeant Brown! Sergeant Brown!*" the woman added, barreling through the flaps, her breath making tiny clouds. "It's me! It's—"

Nola turned, eyeing the young woman with the flat nose and silver cuff earrings. Nola knew exactly who she was. Intimately. Nola painted her portrait yesterday, even let her keep the canvas when she started crying over how beautiful it made her look, a moment that Nola still couldn't shake. Kamille.

"Sorry to bother you, Sergeant Brown, I just— On the flight . . . Are you *going?*"

Nola studied her, Kamille once again leading with her squinty eyes. At her neck hung a pair of aviator sunglasses.

"Why?" Nola asked.

"They gave me leave because of— *Y'know* . . ."

Nola just stood there.

"Anyway, I tried getting on this flight and they told me there were no more seats. But if you're not gonna—" Kamille stopped, getting her first good look at Nola. "*You okay, Sergeant Brown?*"

Nola was looking to her left, toward the runway. Nearly a football field away, a snow-camouflaged Hummer was backed up toward the plane. A man in his mid-fifties loaded supplies. It was him. Most definitely him. Nola first spotted him yesterday. She was getting in a car; it was just for a split second. But she'd never forget his face. Royall was here. On base.

"You look like you've seen a ghost," Kamille added.

She had. Nola was up all night, debating what to do. For sure, she'd seen him—but had he seen her? No, not yet. That was her advantage . . . and the only way to keep it was to stick to her schedule. Get on the plane. Avoid attention. Now that she knew where he was, she could track him easily, even come back for him. Prepared.

It was a fine plan, especially considering what she almost did last night with the shovel she found in a supply room. Yet now, as the Librarian of Congress climbed aboard the plane, and the pilot walked around it, doing his final preflight checks...just the thought of Royall leaving...of losing him again... No. After all these years, no way could she risk that.

"I need to go," Nola said, still staring at Royall, who was out on the runway and loading a final box, a small suitcase, onto the plane.

"Because of *him*?" Kamille asked, following Nola's gaze.

Nola turned. The girl was sharp, had a nose for details. Nola realized it yesterday while she was doing her portrait. It's why Nola had spent the past few years painting those who tried to take their own lives. People saw them as victims. And they were. But they were also much stronger than everyone thought.

"How do you know him?" Kamille asked.

Nola didn't answer.

"Bad history, huh?" Kamille said.

"Something like that."

Kamille nodded, more to herself, as Royall climbed into his snow-camouflaged Hummer. "He looks old," Kamille said. "Doesn't even look that tough."

"You have no idea," Nola blurted, hating herself for even saying something so stupid.

Kamille watched the way Nola stepped sideways, out of his line of sight. "You're really scared of him, huh?" Kamille asked.

Nola didn't even hear the question. In her pocket, she was fidgeting with the colored pencils she carried everywhere. It was in that moment that Nola realized just how many of her old fears had settled back onto her chest. She didn't like it. "I need to go," Nola said, sidestepping Kamille.

"Wait, wait, wait. Before you— What about your seat?"

"*What?*"

"Your seat. On the plane. You know how the Air Force guys are. They said they already filed the manifest—that the plane was full. But if you let me take your spot..."

"I don't think so," Nola said.

Right there, Royall glanced their way. For barely a second. Nola turned her head, making sure he didn't get a good look.

Kamille stood there, watching. Finally, she whispered, *"What'd he do to you?"*

Nola shook her head like it was nothing.

Kamille didn't believe her. Soldiers were masters at hiding it, but just from her body language, Nola wasn't just *looking* at Royall. She was *running* from him.

"Is he on the flight?"

Nola shook her head *no*, her back still to Royall.

"Then c'mon—switch with me. The next flight isn't for three days. I'll be back before you leave."

"Passengers, last call!" the young airman shouted from inside. Unlike on commercial flights, once you check in, the military rarely rechecked IDs. They just looked to see if your name was on the manifest.

"Please, Sergeant Brown? After everything that happ— Let me say it like this: I need a good weekend. *Desperately.* I've got a fiancé I haven't seen in weeks. He doesn't even know what I—" She stopped herself again. "I know it's stupid, but I'm trying to surprise him. It's his birthday."

Nola was about to say no. Then she noticed Kamille's backpack. Sticking out of the top of it was a rolled poster. Not a poster, a canvas—the painting Nola did. Kamille was taking it with her, to show her fiancé.

Twelve days ago, Kamille Williams did a Whip-It full of bug spray in the hopes of taking her own life. Today, she was bouncing anxiously on her heels, a pleading smile on her face.

"Here," Nola said, handing over the boarding pass.

For the next ten seconds, Kamille squeezed Nola in an exuberant hug—the happiest Nola had seen her. Kamille didn't even realize Nola was just standing there, arms at her side, not hugging back.

"You won't regret it!" Kamille said, darting toward the airplane hangar. As she plowed through the clear plastic strips, she took a final glance at Nola, who was still standing in the cold, her back to Royall.

"*Last call!*" the airman with the clipboard shouted. "*I'm looking for Nola Brown!*"

"That's me! Sorry! Here I am," Kamille added, running for the plane and waving her boarding pass like she'd just won the lottery. "I'm Nola Brown!"

84

Y ou're never leaving this building. I'm gonna write your
death in fire."

"*Death in fire?* That's how you start our reunion?" Royall
asked, a thin grin still on his lips. "After all these years... Surely, in
your head, you practiced something better than that?"

Nola kept her gun pointed at him. Just seeing her father
again... getting a clear and close look at him... Royall was never a
handsome man, but now, with his hair gray, the color of smoke—
the way his face was thicker and puffier from age— Life worked
hard to wear him down. But as always, Royall fought against it. His
knuckles were worn and red from those fights. He had the survival
instincts of a rat, hustling and clawing his way out of whatever trap
he was in.

She saw it in his posture. Shoulders back, chest out. Someone
taught him how to stand at attention. It gave him an air of authority, respectability. But Nola quickly tightened her glance. His feet
weren't together; he carried all his weight on his left leg. Plus the
way he cocked his camouflage cap, like John Wayne rather than
the proper placement... No, whoever he stole that uniform from,
Royall wasn't proper military. Most likely a contractor.

"You look tired, Nola. And angry as ever," Royall said, trying to
make it sound like a compliment. Age brought a calmness to his

tone. He no longer clenched his fists when he spoke. But there are only so many things you can unlearn. As he turned her way, a glint of light hit his eyes. He always had such greedy eyes.

"You really should let go of that anger," Royall added, taking a step toward her. "It'll eat you up f—"

"Don't. Don't move. Not another damn inch," she said, aiming her gun.

He didn't put his hands up. He just stood there, a few feet from Dino's lifeless body. "How many years has it been, Nola? A dozen? If it makes you feel better, I'm not the man I used to be."

"You tried to kill me."

"No. You brought this on yourself."

"Royall, this isn't— In Alaska— You did something to the plane, didn't you? You murdered those people. You killed Kamille, and the Librarian of Congress. You took seven people's lives when you put that airplane down. And for what? Because you thought I was on it?"

"Did you hear what I said? This is on *you*, Nola. *You're* the one who came sniffing for trouble. I made something of myself. Do you have any idea how much we'd invested in Bluebook?"

She did. She learned two days ago, during her interrogation of Markus on the boat. Blue Book was an old Harry Houdini trick— the way he'd reveal fake fortune-tellers and also communicate with other magicians. Zig knew that. But what he didn't know, and what Nola didn't tell him, was that Bluebook's real moment came when one of Houdini's friends, a guy named John Elbert Wilkie, was put in charge of the US Secret Service. Wilkie was a magician himself—and he admired the way Houdini used his own Blue Book to separate truth from lies when it came to the great beyond. Of course, the real secret of Houdini's Blue Book had nothing to do with speaking to the dead or returning from it. Its real power came from Houdini's people, who covertly found it and exposed it—the people who worked with Houdini and hid so perfectly in his audience during the show. It was a private corps made up of friends like Rose Mackenberg, Clifford Eddy, and Amedeo Vacca. The ultimate insiders.

Over time, Wilkie turned Bluebook into a full-fledged government program, sneaking undercover agents and troops into key locations. It started during the Spanish-American War. When Teddy Roosevelt rode into battle, three US sharpshooters were right there, secretly dressed as Cuban rebels, protecting Roosevelt and catching the Spanish army by surprise. A perfect trick. And a sure way to avoid death.

By World War II, Bluebook had grown to three dozen Marines, all of them embedded in German physics labs, secretly reporting on the development of German weaponry. And by the 1980s, at the height of the Cold War, Bluebook had put thirty Navy SEALs into Russian language programs at universities around the country, since that's where the KGB did most of their recruiting.

Today, Bluebook was still kept purposefully small—and had a permanent home on that university path, secretly enrolling our best soldiers in the nation's top university computer programs, from MIT to Caltech. Filled with students (and easily influenced social misfits), those programs were top targets for hacking and cyberterrorism recruiting.

When Nola first learned of Bluebook, she was doubtful that the government would put that much energy into infiltrating civilian life. Then she started checking class rosters in the computer science labs at Stanford, Berkeley, and the University of Michigan. Among the skinny brainiacs and future Mark Zuckerbergs, she kept finding a beefy thirty-year-old who'd spend every day getting great technical training while trying to hide his muscles in a cheap button-down shirt. Some blended in better than others. But one thing was clear: Even in the military, not all fighting happens with guns.

In the end, to keep an eye on potential terrorists and to infiltrate anyone who would recruit them, the Bluebook soldiers were the ultimate observers, hiding in plain sight, just like Harry Houdini's hidden assistants. And to keep the program a secret, they'd run the entire operation out of the Library of Congress.

Zig was right about that. That's why the President appointed a friend to manage the program. Just like Houdini, he needed someone he could trust. Also, with Rookstool on the plane, it provided the perfect cover story that the rest of the "students" could hide behind. With the Librarian of Congress on board, the last thing anyone suspected was an undercover operation. The big move covered the small one. But like any good magic trick, it only worked if everyone in the military kept their mouths shut.

"How'd you pull it off, Royall? Bluebook was classified at the topmost levels. So who was so dumb that they'd tell you about it?"

"You're making assumptions, Nola. Like I said, I'm not the man I used to be."

Nola wanted to rush at him right there, wanted to stuff her thumbs into his venous return and starve his heart as she told him he was full of shit. Not yet, though. Not until she got her answers.

The day after she ran away, Royall changed his name. She knew that for sure. That's how he'd disappeared. "New name, new driver's license—you must've loved using your skills on yourself. The thing is, you're still—"

"You don't know anything about me," Royall said. "You have no idea who I became—or what I gave up when I left you. My home, my contacts, my relationships...everything I built... Your damn art teacher sent the cops to Mr. Wesley! *You took my life!*" he shouted, his voice ricocheting through the metal warehouse.

"All those years creating new identities, I helped give people a second chance. But to start my own life from scratch... You think you know what it's like, but you don't. I took you in; I gave you food. But to truly be out there alone? To leave my car behind because I couldn't fill it up? It was death," Royall said, swallowing hard, finding his calm.

"After a year, I eventually reached out to Mr. Wesley. My timing was perfect. He had a new job for me—a big one—three hundred

IDs plus backup documents. The group was coming in on a boat. It was my chance to rebuild. But neither of us knew that the Feds were listening in. They never went away. They nabbed us both. It's a federal crime, so I—"

"You snitched," Nola said.

"I made a deal."

"You gave up Wesley and testified against him. Then the government *what*? They liked your work?"

"They *loved* my work. When the Feds saw what I could do... They realized I didn't just forge documents—I forged *lives*. Do you have any idea how many uses the military has for that? They tested me at first. I was better than anyone they'd ever seen. Over time, they assigned me to Bluebook. I made new lives for our 'students,' hiding Marines at universities around the country, providing them with a paperwork trail that was so untraceable, you'd never guess we planted them there.

"This was my calling. I became a new man. I was resurrected, Nola. But do you know what my real trick was for coming back? Even now, when I look at the shitty life we had together, and compare it with the new one I built—do you know what the difference was between the two?

"*You*, Nola. Once you were gone from my life, that's where I found success. And you want to know why? Because you're a fungus—you infect everything you touch. On my darkest days, I would spend hours focused on shedding my old life and making it disappear. But the truth was, all I needed to shed was *you*. And that's the great irony, Nola. Everything that's happened here... everything I've built... even everything I found with Bluebook and the death of that girl Kamille... it's all thanks to you."

Nola shook her head. He was still the same manipulative ass. "Y'know, for a few seconds, Royall, I almost believed you. I thought maybe you actually *did* make something of yourself with Bluebook. But no matter how high you rise, you're still just that lowlife hustler, aren't you?" she asked, her finger still tight on the trigger.

"Watch your mouth."

"Or what? You won't tell me how you blew it all up in your own face? It's not hard, Royall. Maybe at Bluebook, you were doing good work for a while. But you were forever keeping your eye out, looking for an opening that you could jump all over. That's how you always operated, always working an angle. So lemme guess: One day, you found out the name of their paying agent—a guy they nicknamed Houdini."

The warehouse was quiet now, Royall just standing there. He was no longer smiling.

"I'm right, aren't I?" Nola added. "Usually, Houdini moved money to make the government's disasters disappear. But in this case, he became the disaster. Houdini was supposed to reach out to the undercover 'students,' doling out little bits of money so no one could trace their funding back to Uncle Sam. But you realized he was dirty. And then you saw it, Royall. An opportunity."

"You have no idea what you're talking about," Royall said coldly.

"And you have no idea how predictable you are. Every few months, there's a greedy paying agent who gets arrested for skimming cash from all the money he's carrying around. That's who Houdini was, wasn't he? It's hard to make thirty grand a year—especially while he's trying to ignore the few million that he's dragging everywhere. For Houdini, who made things vanish, no one would notice if some extra cash flowed into his wallet as well—especially when a brand-new pile of money was set to arrive."

Nola knew that like any other military endeavor, Bluebook had its own operational requirements. At least twice a year, they'd bring their undercover agents together—to debrief and compare notes—usually in some isolated location, like an abandoned military base or—in the case where specialists from Russia were brought in to talk about Putin's latest infiltration attempts—one that was tucked away in Alaska's nearby national park. That was where Houdini had planned to make his move.

"You found out about him, though, didn't you? You figured out that Houdini was skimming money from the cash that he was carrying around. Maybe you confronted him and asked for a piece of the action—though knowing you, you went in like a hammer, threatening to tattle on him unless he slid some of it your way. Maybe Houdini started cutting you in—or maybe that's when he panicked and told you about the brand-new pile of money they were about to send him for this special event in Alaska. Now you saw the chance for your favorite thing of all—the big payday— life-changing money, Royall. That's what you used to call it, right? And with all that cash suddenly coming, you couldn't resist. You're far too greedy.

"From there, you started using the nickname *Horatio*, and you and Houdini joined forces to take—*some?*—*all?*—whatever it was, you were eyeing the massive pile of cash that was about to arrive in Alaska. Maybe you even called in a few of your old scumbag friends, Lord knows you always had plenty of those. The irony is, your Bluebook bosses were so busy bringing the Bluebook 'students' in, they didn't even realize that Houdini and you—their paying agent and some greedy parasite who specialized in fake IDs—were about to rob them blind."

"That's enough."

"Was it your idea to go for the big haul? Or did you have enough dirt on Houdini that you talked him into it?"

"*I said, that's enough,*" Royall growled, his head cocked just enough that Nola realized he was no longer making eye contact. Something was wrong, though her brain still hadn't registered it. Royall was looking past her. Like he was talking to someone else. Someone behind her.

Oh, shit.

Nola was in mid-turn, cursing herself. He'd never come here by himsel—

There was a snap, like a chicken wing being ripped apart. Nola heard the noise before she felt the pain—a red-hot fire in her leg— as a sharp blade sliced the cord of her hamstring behind her knee.

She fell backward instantly, like her body was a bike and her kickstand had been knocked over.

Her head slammed into the concrete with a muted thud. The world went black, filled with stars. *Don't pass out!* She'd lived through plenty of pain, but not like this. *Don't pass out!* Her body twisted uncontrollably. She grabbed at her knee, writhing, rolling on her side. She blinked hard, trying to clear away the stars, but they were still twinkling.

She started to scream. *No! Don't scream! Don't give them that!*

A black shadow appeared over her—her attacker—moving like a blur, hovering over Nola as she continued to twist along the floor. Nola grabbed the back of her own knee. It was wet. Blood. She was bleeding.

Nola stared up at her attacker, who was backlit by the skylight, a muddy and hazy blur. But from the outline—from the weapon, the four blades coming out of her attacker's fist, like a tiger's claw— Nola knew who it was. The tall Native American woman with the ice blue eyes.

"Nola, I believe you've met The Curtain," Royall said. "Teresa, this is my daughter. Nola."

Raising the tiger's claw into the air, The Curtain slashed down, aiming straight at Nola's throat.

85

Nola still didn't scream.

She should've, especially as The Curtain sliced at the stitches in Nola's neck, reopening her collarbone wound. The pain was unbearable, a lightning shower of anguish that ran from her collarbone to her knee. But even then, Nola still didn't make a sound.

Rolling on her side, she pinched the web of skin between her thumb and pointer finger. It was a trick she'd learned from her time with Royall. Squeeze that skin as hard as you want. It can swallow all pain.

"Y-You should've killed me," Nola warned The Curtain, still on her side, a long spiderweb of drool dangling from her lips.

"You think she didn't ask?" Royall said from across the room, slowly walking toward them. "*I'm* the one who deals with you. That's *my* privilege."

Nola tried to get up, tried looking for her gun. The world was still blurred, but— On the floor— Something gray. Was that her gun? She reached out . . .

The Curtain raised her foot, stomping down on Nola's wrist and digging her heel into the wound that Nola got last night.

Nola wanted to howl. Her eyes flooded with tears. Her mouth was open wide, like she was in mid-yell, though nothing came out but a high-pitched hiss of air. Twisting from the knifelike agony, Nola pinched the web of skin so hard, she thought it'd tear in half.

"Nola, y'know what the saddest part of all this is?" Royall asked, his voice louder now. He was close. She could feel his fury from here. "This could've all been avoided."

"Y-You never change— Y-You're a monster—! A murderer!"

"That's always been your problem. You can't just let a good thing be, can you?" Royall asked, reaching down and picking something up. Nola's gun. He gave it a look, noting its weight. "You always have to spoil it. Everything you touch turns to ash, to shit."

Nola thought she told him to go screw himself, but she was just imagining it. Her nose was running. Her heartbeat was thumping in her forehead—and she couldn't feel the fingers on her hand. Her body was in shock, and suddenly she was thinking of that folded-up greeting card she used to carry around with her in junior high. *This will make you stronger.* That card was a damn lie.

"What really amazes me, though," Royall added, kneeling down next to her, "is just how fanatical you've become. How many years were you searching, Nola? How much of the Army's resources did you waste looking for me? And for what? So you could track me down in some craphole army base in Alaska?"

Nola was on her back now, squirming in pain as Royall kneeled next to her. He was in that same pose, at that same angle from when she was little and he'd sit down on the edge of her bed— when he thought Nola was asleep.

"Who told you where I was, Nola?"

She looked away, refusing to face him. "Y-You're what you've always been . . . a vampire."

Lifting the gun, Royall pressed it into Nola's cheek, her skin bunching toward her nose. Royall leaned so close, she could see, coming down from his lip, in the fleshy white scar she gave him all those years ago, a few stray black hairs that no razor would ever reach. He smelled of Brut aftershave and wet wood. Same as all those years ago.

"Who was it?" he asked, his finger now around the trigger. "It's a very simple question, Nola. Did they tell you my new name, or just that I was in Alaska? Someone needs to pay for that."

Nola took a deep breath, staring up at Royall. It didn't matter how long they were out of each other's lives. Even the most estranged father and daughter could have a whole conversation—an opera of emotion—with just the exchange of a single dark glance.

You're a dead man.

Your skin is lighter. But you still look like a nigger.

"Three seconds, Nola. Who told you?" Royall pressed the gun harder into her face. "I need a name. Who told you I was in Alaska!?" His finger tightened around the trigger. "Two seconds. One..."

Nola's eyes slid sideways. She looked away.

"Wait," he asked. "Are you saying—? *Noooo...*" Royall started to laugh. "*Jesus H!* All this time, I thought— I figured someone ratted me out, but—" He laughed again, that rat-a-tat-tat laugh that told her trouble was coming. "When you showed up in Alaska, you weren't even looking for me, were you? You were just painting, just doing your crappy job. But when you spotted me there..." His laugh was louder than ever. "*Jesus H!* And here I thought you'd been hunting me for years. What a narcissist I am, right?"

"Y-You're not leaving here alive," Nola insisted. She believed it, even as the heartbeat in her forehead reached a deafening level. *Don't pass out...!* Her eyes flicked back and forth. She tried staying locked on Royall, but the world was now a circle that was shrinking at the edges. *Don't pass out...!*

"Did I miss something? What the hell is going on?" The Curtain asked, standing just behind Nola's head. "I thought you said she tracked you to Alaska."

"I was wrong," Royall said, never taking his eyes off Nola, still holding the gun to her face. "Oh, Nola, our little reunion... It wasn't because you're some great detective, was it? You finding me in Alaska...that was just your gift from the universe. A bolt of what you thought was dumb luck. But as always with you, it was just *bad* luck."

Nola whispered a curse word, her eyes half closed. Her shirt was soaked. She'd lost too much blood. *M-Mongol...Faber... Staedtler...*

"It's enough. Pull the trigger," The Curtain said. "Let's get out of here."

Royall moved the gun to Nola's head, directly at her temple, nudging her with the barrel to make sure she was awake. "I want you to know something, Nola," he said as his finger tightened around the trigger. "Even when you were little, I always knew you were a—"

Pop.

A splatter of blood hit Royall's face. The blood wasn't Nola's. It sprayed him from above. In the forehead. From where The Curtain was standing.

Still kneeling, Royall looked up, following the sound.

The Curtain was already stumbling backward, fighting for air and gripping the bullet hole that was now in her chest.

Pop. Pop.

One shot ricocheted off a metal rack with a spark. A miss. The other hit The Curtain above the collarbone. A burst of blood exploded at her neck. Her arms went flat as her body twirled awkwardly at the impact. The metal tiger's claw fell to the floor.

"*Hhhhhh,*" The Curtain gasped, her blue eyes wide with shock as small flaps of her neck skin waved like a flag.

Nola was down on the ground, unconscious. She had no idea what was going on.

Pop.

Royall grabbed at his own shoulder, like he was swatting a mosquito. "*What in the f—!*" he roared. It wasn't until he put his finger into the bullet hole in his shoulder that he realized he'd been shot. He looked up to see who was responsible.

Stepping out from behind a tower of rusted metal desks, Zig held out his gun, still aiming it at Royall.

"*Drop your gun! Drop it, or I swear I'll shoot you again!*" Zig shouted, wishing he'd spent even more time with the base's infantry guys when they taught everyone to shoot.

Royall dropped his gun, which skittered on the concrete.

As the two men locked eyes, a chill crawled up Zig's ribcage. Zig knew that face, knew exactly who he was. They hadn't seen each other in nearly two decades, not since that night in the ER. But even back then, these two men had nothing but hate for each other. Zig knew it all those years ago. *No heart.*

"You got old," Royall said.

Zig didn't take the bait. He was too focused on...

"*Nola! You okay!?*" he called out.

She didn't move. Didn't answer. Zig saw the blood, saw the way her leg was twisted so awkwardly.

"*Step away! Get away from her!*" Zig shouted, racing toward Nola, his gun still on Royall.

At Nola's knee, her blood was dark, a deep maroon, and wasn't pulsating. It oozed slowly from her wound. That was good. No active bleeding, Zig realized. Whatever The Curtain sliced open, it wasn't an arterial injury. More likely, Nola was unconscious from the pain, not loss of blood.

"You better pray she's okay," Zig said, turning his attention back to— There was a noise. Footsteps. Someone running.

Mothertrucker.

Zig looked to his right, toward the back of the warehouse.

The Curtain was dead. Nola was exactly where he'd left her.

But Royall—along with his gun—were gone.

He wouldn't get far.

86

Zig moved slowly, taking small side steps down the dark aisle. His breathing was heavy the entire way.

Passing a row of stacked metal bedframes, Zig had his gun out in front of him, following the blood.

There were drops along the ground. Royall had run this way, deeper into the warehouse. There was no back door. No back exit. *No way out,* Zig thought, picking up the pace.

He was careful about his speed. Move too fast and he wouldn't see what was coming; move too slow and Royall would get away.

"I didn't come here alone!" Zig shouted. "Security's on their way right now!"

It was a lie. Zig came here straight from the plane. He tried calling Master Guns. Hsu as well. But with the base on lockdown, it would take hours before anyone made their way back here. Still, by saying people were coming, maybe it would get Royall to run.

The warehouse was silent. No reaction.

Rounding the corner past stalagmites of stacked rusted trash cans, Zig searched the floor for the trail of blood. There wasn't any. Maybe Royall didn't come this way. Or maybe he put pressure on the wound, and the bleeding finally stopped.

Sticking to the edges of the aisle and gripping the gun tighter than ever, Zig closed his eyes, trying to listen. No heating system.

No hum from fluorescent lights. No water running through pipes. For a moment, he held his breath, searching for footsteps, for movement, for anything. The only sound was the high-pitched flow of blood through his own ears, reminding Zig of the familiar quiet that greeted him every day in the...

Morgue. That's why this place seemed so familiar. That's what this warehouse was. The whole building—filled with stacks of out-dated gurneys, rusted casket carriages, 1960s coffin racks, even all the ancient file cabinets, furniture, and old red buzz saws—everything here came from the morgue where Zig used to work.

The embalming tables on his left—the porcelain tops of them standing up and leaning one against the other like surfboards—were the exact tables Zig worked on when he first came to Dover.

As his shoulder slowly brushed against them, he saw chips in the old porcelain, stained pale green from decades of chemicals and use—and now Zig was thinking of the very first fallen soldier he ever worked on years ago: a thirty-two-year-old pilot whose legs were crushed in a helicopter crash, and whose wife asked that a roll of quarters be put into his casket since he loved to play the slots. Darren Lee Abramson. Fallen #1.

Reaching the next aisle, Zig peered around the corner, his finger tight on the trigger. Like every other aisle, this one was dark. He couldn't see far, but he could see it was narrow. On both sides were fifty-gallon drums, set like massive bowling pins, all of them marked:

DANGER

FORMALDEHYDE

AVOID INHALATION AND SKIN CONTACT

Beyond that, the aisle was empty. No one there.

C'mon, Royall. You gotta be somewhere.

Moving to the next aisle and turning the corner, Zig noticed half a dozen ashtray stands, all without their tops. Tucked into one of them were umbrellas, in another were tall wooden rulers, and in a third were long metal rods.

Huh.

Zig grabbed one of the rods, pulling it out like the sword from the stone. It was an old trocar—a mortician's tool to aspirate fluid from the body. After embalming was finished, Zig would take its sharp steel tip, insert it under the ribcage, and use the trocar to remove all the blood from the abdomen, chest cavity, heart, and everywhere else. Zig wasn't sure why he grabbed it. Maybe as a weapon—maybe to make sure Royall didn't grab it instead.

Today's trocars were light and nimble. This one was heavy, substantial—like a hollow baseball bat with a pointy metal tip. It felt familiar in Zig's hands, another totem from years past. But as he slowly continued down the aisle, craning his neck and searching every nearby shadow, what brought back even more memories was a strangely familiar smell.

Rubbing alcohol, mixed with chemicals and...formaldehyde.

Zig smelled it before he saw it—and then, there it was—a puddle growing along the floor. Moving like a leak. It seeped out from below a black particleboard bookshelf filled with faded file boxes.

That smell. Zig knew that smell from his first days as a mortician. And every day since. Only one thing in the world reeked like that.

Embalming fluid.

The metal drums a few aisles back. Royall must've opened one of them.

Further up the aisle, another puddle appeared, engulfing the floor. These days, embalming fluid was a gel. Easier to work with; less splash. The wet puddles here... This was the old kind, liquid, from back in the day, when embalming fluid was more corrosive and— Flammable.

Oh, crap.

"*Nola, get up! GetupGetupGetup!*" Zig shouted, sprinting back the way he came. "*He wants to— He's gonna blow it up!*"

Tearing around the corner, Zig was moving full speed, gun in one hand, trocar in the other. *"Nola, you hear what I sai—?"*

The fist pummeled Zig's face, crashing into his jaw and cutting him off mid-syllable.

Zig stumbled sideways, off-balance. He tried standing up, tried lifting his gun, but momentum had him as he turned to face—

Royall towered over him, a human freight train barreling at top speed.

The next thing Zig saw was Royall's fist hammering down with another brutal punch.

87

Zig went to squeeze the trigger. The gun was no longer there.

There was a clatter along the concrete. Then a metal clang. The gun and the metal trocar, both knocked from his hands.

Stupid old man, Zig cursed himself, seeing the gun slide up the aisle, through the puddle of embalming fluid. The trocar was closer. If he could get to that—

"*What'd she promise you!?*" Royall growled, unleashing another violent punch. Then another, deep into Zig's face. Royall's opposite shoulder was soaked with blood from where he was shot. If he was in pain, he wasn't showing it. "*What lie did she tell to get you to come here!?*"

Zig crashed back on his ass, smashing into a forest of tall, outdated halogen lamps. *Make a plan. Find a distraction.*

Zig kicked at the lamps, sending them flying toward Royall. It didn't slow Royall down. Swatting them away, Royall plowed toward him, his face red with rage, angrier than ever.

"You trust that little nigger over one of us?" Royall asked.

From what Zig could tell, Royall wasn't military trained. He was a brawler, nothing more. Fought with no plan, no art. All Zig had to do was take a few hits. *Take the pain*, Zig told himself. *Lure him in.*

Zig crabwalked backward, halogen lights tumbling in all directions.

Royall stormed toward him without hesitation, fist raised.

That's it, meathead, come closer, Zig muttered, still on the floor. He eyed Royall's ankles and knees. Joints. Easiest way to do maximum damage.

Zig unleashed a sharp kick at Royall's left knee. To Zig's surprise, he missed. Royall spun in a side step. He was fast, like he knew it was coming.

"Cheap shots!? You think that'll save you!?" Royall roared.

Zig was still in mid-kick as Royall grabbed him by the ankle.

Zig thrashed wildly, fighting to pull his leg free. Royall wouldn't let go. He was flushed with adrenaline.

Yanking Zig closer with one hand, Royall pounded Zig with the other, landing a blow to Zig's thigh, then his stomach, then— *whap*—a low blow right between Zig's legs, hitting him square in the testicles.

"Ruuuuh!" Zig screamed. The pain was a flash fire, short-circuiting his insides. Squirming in pain, Zig lashed out, kicking even more wildly, over and over.

"Enough!" Royall shouted, still holding tight to Zig's ankle. Tugging hard on Zig's leg, he dragged Zig out of the pile of lamps, tossing him back into the aisle. Back toward— There. Behind Royall.

The trocar!

There it was. Across the aisle—just shy of the still-growing pool of embalming fluid. It was tucked under the bottom lip of one of the bookcases.

Royall couldn't have seen it yet.

As Royall whipped him around, Zig knew this was his chance. Using his momentum, Zig rolled to the side, reaching out. In one fluid movement, he grabbed the trocar, twisted around, and swung it like a bat toward—

Fap.

Royall caught the trocar in midair, tearing it out of Zig's grip. "You think a weapon will help you?" Royall asked.

He raised the trocar like a police baton. Zig tried to spin out of the way.

Royall swung down with full fury. Zig rolled, taking most of the punch out of it, but the metal club still clipped Zig in the side of the head.

Zig's world went pitch black. No stars. No nothing.

Royall arched his arm back, swinging harder this time. Zig again tried to move, but even as he blocked the full weight of it with his forearm, the baton collided with his throat, near his windpipe.

A burst of liquid flooded Zig's throat. In his mouth...that coppery taste. Blood. Zig was bleeding and gasping for air. *No, if he crushed my larynx...*

Royall wound up again. Zig curled in a ball, fighting to cover his own head. If the trocar were a baseball bat, Zig would be dead. It was hollow, but still enough to do damage.

"You know what you cost me!?" Royall roared, unleashing another hit, then another—spit flying from his mouth as he swung the trocar like a club, pummeling Zig in the arm, in the ribs, then a ruthless shot in the jaw, which sent Zig's head spinning.

Blood flew from Zig's lips. He was coughing now, choking on...*ppttt*...a dislodged tooth. He spit it to the ground in a phlegmy wad of blood.

Royall still didn't let up, winding up yet again.

With each swing—each impact—it was harder for Zig to breathe. His ribs...the sharp pain...his lung was punctured, no question about that.

Krkk.

The metal baton hit him in the forearm. Ulna broken.

Zig was breathing in shallow gasps. Blood filled his mouth. And then—time itself began to churn, Zig knowing all too well the limits of what the human body could take.

Zig was curled in a ball. From the corner of his eye, he saw Royall standing over him, the wintry glow from the skylight framing Royall from above, making him look...angelic. That was the only word for it, even with the bloodlust in Royall's eyes.

When Zig was younger, like most kids, he thought he'd have a spectacular death, an ending where he went out in style, wrestling a giant squid or leaping a rocket cycle over the Grand Canyon. As he got older, Zig realized that the very last thing you want in life is a spectacular death. Indeed, the more mundane your closing chapter is, the luckier you'll likely be.

Still, even as a child, deep down, Zig knew his ending would come too soon. In the life he chose—he was always attracted to Death, and Death was attracted to him. For years, he could feel Death there, standing two steps behind him and watching. And of course, there was that day when Death followed him home. In recent years, as more and more souls came through Dover, he felt Death take another step closer, perched there on his shoulder, his ever-present raven, just sitting there, anxious to be fed.

Zig's eyes rolled skyward. Above him, Royall was still in slow motion, adjusting his grip on the metal trocar. Royall held it up like a spear, aiming its metal tip toward Zig's chest. Though Zig's mouth wasn't moving, he found himself saying the prayer he always said, the prayer for his daughter.

Usually, Zig prayed that one day, he'd see his Magpie. Today, lying there across the cold concrete, his face a purple pulp, he knew that part was assured. He'd see her for sure. What he prayed for now was that he'd see her quickly, so they could—

Pop. Pop, pop.

Gunshots. Zig tried turning his head, tried following the sound as slow motion sped back to reality. The noise...it came from the end of the aisle.

There. Down on the ground.

Nola was on her stomach, propped on her elbows. Her leg was

bleeding, a long smear of blood curving behind her. She had army-crawled around the corner, holding a gun in her shaking hands. Pointed right at Royall.

"I told you, I'm gonna write your death in fire," she warned, a wisp of smoke twirling from her gun.

88

Nola had pulled the trigger.

Royall froze. He looked down at himself, patting his chest. There was the old blood from the wound in his shoulder...but other than that— He started to laugh.

"You dumb shittard. *You missed!*" he hissed. He looked up, like he was about to take off.

"*Don't! Not a step!*" Nola warned, her voice not nearly as strong as usual. The color was wiped from her face. To crawl all the way here, she lost so much blood. She was down on her stomach, her hands quaking. But no way was she letting him go free.

Fifty feet away, halfway down the aisle, Royall stood there, catching his breath and eyeing her like prey. The only thing between them was the shallow puddle of embalming fluid, the skylight reflecting off it, adding an odd serenity to the dark warehouse.

"Nola, if you think you have the balls to pull the trigger—"

Pop.

Nola fired again. There was a ping and a spark. The bullet ricocheted off something in the distance.

"Another miss?" Royall asked, a thin grin lifting his cheeks. "That's gonna cost you your life." If he wanted, he could've darted to his right, back toward the halogen lamps, and cut over to the aisle that ran parallel to this one. Escape. Instead, he stood his ground, readjusting the metal trocar in his hand.

Behind him, Zig was slumped across the concrete, unmoving.

Nola wanted to pull the trigger again, but the way her vision was darkening, the way the world was tilting—she'd lost so much blood. She wanted to get up, wanted to put her hands around his throat, but right now, she couldn't feel anything below her waist. And no matter how hard she tried, she still couldn't stop her hands from shaking.

"Always such a stubborn bitch, aren't you, Nola? I can see the pain in your face. You can't even see straight, can you?"

Nola stayed silent, refusing to tell him there were three Royalls staring back at her. *Aim for the one in the middle.* But every time she lifted her head, she felt woozy, like she was on a life raft and the room was bobbing. Her heart raced, fighting to compensate for the blood loss. If she fired again—he was too far—wouldn't be a direct hit. Still, Nola held tight to the trigger, her eyes struggling to stay on the man who buried her all those years ago.

"C'mon, Nola, take your shot. I'll give you a free one," Royall said, sticking his chest out, spreading his arms wide, like he was up on the crucifix.

A thin line of mucus ran from Nola's nose. She fought to keep her head up. The gun felt like an anvil in her hands.

"*No?* That's it? You give up?" Royall asked, lowering his arms, still holding the metal trocar. He gave a quick glance behind himself to make sure Zig was still out. Unconscious.

"That's the part I want you to remember, Nola. In the end, despite all your pushy interference, when you finally got to the finish line, *you're* the one who surrendered. Like always, you gave up. Never able to finish the job. The same lazy nigger you've always been."

"G-G-Go fu—" Nola began, though the words wouldn't come. Her head bobbed low again, but she could still see Royall, could see that satisfied smile on his face. He was having fun now, especially as he took his first step toward Nola.

He choked up on the trocar. Then his foot made a small splash as his heel hit the puddle of embalming fluid.

Now Nola was the one grinning.

Royall could've avoided the puddle, could've walked the long way around to make sure he didn't come into contact with the flammable fluid. But that was Royall's flaw. It'd always been his flaw. Ever since he took her home as a child, Nola knew, *she* was the one who was Royall's greatest weakness.

Nola tipped her gun forward, aiming it diagonally toward the ground, straight at the puddle of fluid. Even now, with her head bobbing, it was the one shot even she couldn't miss.

Royall froze. His eyes became saucers. "Nola...*DON'T!*"

Too late.

Nola's finger curved around the trigger. Royall tried running. He looked terrified, then enraged, then terrified again, all in the span of half a second as the two of them shared a long final glance. The angle they were at—him looking down on her, like he was standing at the door of her bedroom—it was as if Nola was seven years old, and he was her dad, and he'd just brought her home on that first night, tucked her into bed, and all might be well in the world, even though young Nola, even back then, knew it wouldn't be.

She wanted to say something vengeful, wanted to tell him how long she'd waited for this moment, wanted to tell him how much pain he was about to be in, and of course how much he deserved every bit of it. Instead, she pierced him with a dark glare, staring unflinchingly into Royall's now-wide eyes.

"*Nola...!*" he pleaded, his voice cracking.

She squeezed the trigger.

Pop.

There was a spark as the bullet hit the embalming fluid. Then a deafening *boosh*, like a gas main being lit. Royall was still in mid-run, frozen with one foot in midair, as a thick column of fire rose from the puddle, swallowing him whole.

"*Nahhhhhh!*" Royall screamed, his clothes, his hair, his face, all of it engulfed in bright blue flame.

Nola knew what was coming next.

Down on the ground, she tucked herself into a ball, covered her head, and turned away from the puddle.

Within seconds, the fire spread across the top of the puddle, snaking its way back to the original metal drum of embalming fluid. Nola counted to herself. *Three . . . two . . .*

There was an earsplitting roar—a thunderclap two aisles away—as a massive explosion sent a black-and-orange fireball mushrooming to the roof. The warehouse rattled and shook. It felt like a mortar hit, the metal drum taking off like a bottle rocket, zigzagging toward the front of the warehouse.

The onslaught of heat came so fast, even two aisles away, Nola thought her back was burned. By the time the heat receded and she finally looked up, Royall was on the ground, thrashing frantically, rolling back and forth as he tried to put the flames out. "*Please . . . someone . . . my eyes! It's in my eyes! Nola . . . please!*"

Nola didn't move.

Royall kept rolling, twisting along the concrete. Behind him, the puddle was still burning at knee height. Then he was just lying there, a black charcoaled brick, flat on his back and barely moving as steam rose off him.

Twelve seconds. That's all it took. The skin on Royall's face bubbled and boiled. Parts of his hands were bright white, other parts were black and charred. His chin took it worst, a mess of bloodied, melted blisters. Plus, there was that smell, of burnt hair and skin. Still on his back, Royall was moaning, making a noise like a kicked dog. He was alive, though. No longer a threat, but alive.

Nola's reaction was instantaneous.

"Ghh," she grunted, army-crawling on her elbows, straight toward Royall, her hand still shaking as she pointed her gun at his head. Time to finish the job.

On her left, all the bookcases were on fire. Some furniture too.

Small campfires burned all around her from the rusted drum's explosion, but since the warehouse was filled with mostly porcelain and metal, she wasn't worried the place would go up in flames. Even if it did, she wasn't sure she cared.

A few feet away, Royall's chest rose and fell. He was still breathing. Not for long.

"Nola, don't do it," a familiar voice called out.

She looked to her right. On the opposite side of the burning puddle, Zig was awake, curled on his side, his face a purple mess from Royall's beating with the trocar.

Stop talking, she thought to herself, crawling forward on her belly, her arm outstretched, the barrel of her gun getting closer to Royall's head.

"Nola, don't let him turn you into a killer!" Zig added. "It's over. He's done. He'll pay for his crimes."

No. He won't, Nola thought, throwing her elbow forward with a grunt. *He'd escape again, take on another new name, disappear into yet another new life. It was his specialty.* The room was still swaying and bobbing. Her breathing was heavier than ever. She was a fool to keep moving. But as she stared at the rise and fall of Royall's chest—for this piece of shit?—she didn't mind being a fool.

"Nola, listen to me," Zig begged. "Those people on that plane—that woman Kamille—she wouldn't want you to do this!"

This isn't for them, Nola thought. *It's for me.* She was less than two feet away. Almost there.

Her outstretched arm was quivering so much, she put the butt of the gun on the ground, pressing it down into the floor, just to keep it steady.

"It'll haunt you forever, Nola! Whatever pain he caused you," Zig added, "when you take someone's life—you can't take that back!"

Nola pressed the gun against Royall's head. Wisps of his burnt, smoke-colored hair curled around the barrel. It reminded her of a painting...she wanted to do a painting of this moment, of the shiny barrel against his charred skin. She was memorizing details, saving them for later as her finger slowly slid around the trigger. She gripped it tight. *Pull*, she told herself. *Just pull.*

But she didn't.

There was a crackle and a loud pop a few aisles away. The fire consumed yet another lost piece of military history. In the distance, outside, she could hear the faint sound of an approaching siren. Fire alarm must've gone off. Help would be here soon.

Nola let go of the gun, which clattered to the floor.

"Nola, you made the right choice," Zig said, still lying there on the opposite side of the low-burning puddle.

In front of her, Royall's body twitched, like he was lost in a dream—or when she used to sneak past his room, praying he wouldn't wake up when he was drunk on Tuesday and Saturday nights. At that, she remembered their old car and how it smelled of cigarettes and Armor All on those nights when she'd sleep in the backseat. She remembered the burnt steaks. The screaming. The shoveling and all the dirt. Dooch the skunk. And of course, that first night, being dragged from the LaPointes. Most of all, she remembered the promise she made to herself all those years ago. If she ever saw him again. The promise that brought her here today.

In one quick movement, Nola grabbed the gun, pointed it at Royall's head, and pressed it to his temple—

"*Nola, no!*"

Pop.

A burst of blood sprayed across the concrete, hunks of Royall's skull scattering in every direction.

Finally.

Promise kept.

Zig was yelling something, louder than ever. Nola didn't hear it. The room was bobbing up and down uncontrollably now, the world again shrinking around the edges. Her heartbeat was deafening, pounding and thumping in her temples, in her fingertips, in her tongue, blood still pouring from behind her twisted knee.

I just need to put my head down, Nola said, though her lips never moved. *Just a little rest, a little nap, right here*, she added. Then she did just that. As half a dozen fractured fires continued to burn around her, Nola put her head down on an overstuffed, fluffy pillow, not even realizing it was the cold hard concrete.

89

Nola woke up after the surgery.

It was a full day later—the following morning—though the way a wave of nausea pulled from the inside of her throat, it seemed like it'd been a week.

All at once, she heard the beeps and boops—the chorus of droids—from the half a dozen electronic monitors she was hooked up to. A TV on the opposite wall was already on, with an old episode of *Family Feud*.

"—elcome back, sleepyhead," said a black nurse with a wide oval face and crooked teeth. She was standing at the far side of the bed, checking the dorsalis pedis pulse in Nola's foot. The nurse asked a question. Nola barely heard it.

On Nola's right, a beige recliner was pulled close to the bed. Like someone had been visiting. On her left was a dry-erase board with the logo for Kent General Hospital. Delaware. She was still in Delaware.

The board also had Nola's name, blood type, birth date, and an emergency contact, with a number Nola didn't recognize. 202 area code. Washington, DC. She read the number three times, unable to place it. Her brain wasn't working right. That tug in her throat. She was dizzy again, nauseous.

"Here, if you need to throw up..." the nurse said, placing a plastic yellow bedpan on Nola's chest. "Our barf bags don't hold squat."

Nola nodded, like it all made sense. Her right leg was immobilized, numb, wrapped in gauze. Surgery. She'd been through surgery. That explained the nausea, the drugs.

Yet what Nola noticed more than anything else... Outside. In the hallway. There was a man. Tall forehead, thick neck, military build. Skin the color of bronze. He was in full military dress, standing guard. Single silver bar on his shoulder board. First lieutenant.

Not a soldier. An officer.

He looked over at Nola, not saying a word.

It made no sense, Nola thought, but the world was again being squeezed at the edges, the room tilting and starting to spin. W-Why... Why would they send an officer?

90

W here's his body?"

"Still at Dover," Master Guns said.

"They're not transferring him to Torbert's?" Zig asked, referring to the local funeral home where Dover sends most civilians.

Master Guns made a noise, like a grunt. "You want the bad news or the bad news?"

"Like I have a choice?" Climbing out of his hospital bed, Zig headed for the bathroom in the corner, lifted his medical gown, and took a long, frightfully satisfying piss. As he washed his hands, he caught his own reflection in the mirror.

"Don't look in the mirror," Master Guns called out.

"I'm not," Zig said, staring straight at himself.

Busted lip, two black eyes, a severe orbital rim fracture, fourteen stitches between his forehead and chin, plus a ruthless dark bruise that turned his cheekbone into a purple pillow.

Zig had seen worse. This would heal. Or at the very least, could be covered up.

"Gimme the bad news first."

"I spoke to Dino's sister," Master Guns said. "She's devastated, of course. Making flight arrangements now. She should be here by tomorrow."

Heading back to the hospital bed, Zig picked at the cast on his broken arm and took a long look at his friend. Standing at the center of the room, posture forever perfect, Master Guns was silent.

"Tell me what you're not saying," Zig added.

"Listen—"

"When you say *Listen*, I'm already listening. What else did she say?"

"Nothing. She just— For Dino's funeral—" He cleared his throat. "She requested that *you* be the one to work on his body. Asked for you by name."

Zig nodded. He expected as much. When Zig was little, Dino's sister used to drive them to high school. Bought beer and wine coolers for him and Dino too.

"Ziggy, you don't have t—"

"Tell her I'll do it."

"I can make an excuse. Let her know you're in the hospita—"

"Stop. I'm doing it," Zig said, reaching for the red-and-white duffel that Master Guns brought from Zig's home. Zig pulled out a pair of old jeans, quickly climbing into them.

"Ziggy, what're you—?"

"You said his sister will be here tomorrow. If I don't start now—"

"Are you a moron? Your doctors— They said they want you under observation for at least another day. Your concussion—"

"I'm fine."

"You're not fine—and if you think I'm letting you back in the mortuary—"

"You said Dino took a bullet to the head. That's where Royall shot him, right? You think you got enough pieces of his skull to put him back together?"

Master Guns didn't respond.

"Dino's family is Catholic. I helped bury their mom. Their dad too. His sister Denise, she'll want an open casket. Do you even have an intact face, or is that gonna need major sculpting and a rebuild too?"

"Ziggy..."

"You think we're having a discussion. We're not," Zig shot back. "When Denise gets here tomorrow, she's expecting an open casket. I'm giving her an open casket. Okay? I'm doing it. Fallen #2,358. I need to do it," Zig said, buttoning his jeans. As he pulled a fresh shirt over his head, a Rorschach blot of blood seeped from his forehead into the chest of his T-shirt.

"You're one stubborn pain in my ass, you know that?" Master Guns said.

"You really thought I'd sit here in a hospital and let you give this case to Wil?"

Master Guns nodded at the mention of Zig's fellow mortician. "He's definitely a bigger a-hole than you are, Ziggy. Plus, I hate the way he spells his name with one L. Douchebaggery."

Zig went to smile, but the tug on his skin from the stitches hurt too much. Still, if Master Guns was making jokes, he was prepping Zig for another bomb.

"If it makes you feel better," Master Guns added, "we've been tearing through Dino's records—phone, email, all of it. His financials were—" Master Guns paused, taking a big breath through his nose. "Ziggy, he had some pretty bad debts."

"How bad?"

"Really bad. As in, taking money from his own grandmother bad. Whatever his goal was, he was flailing. His debt was well into six figures, and from what we can tell, if he didn't pay soon, someone would've dropped by his house and offered him the claw side of a hammer."

"That doesn't excuse it."

"Not saying it does. But whatever Dino did—whatever money he was taking from Royall to pay back his debt—I don't think for one second Dino was purposely trying to hurt you."

Zig stayed silent, pulling out a pair of socks and taking a seat on the side of the hospital bed. "What about his sister? What're you telling her?"

"You think I have any say there? This is coming from the top. The real top. 456 number," Master Guns said, referring to the prefix for the White House. "Did I tell you the President called me?"

"You told me. Tell me about Dino."

"If I was a wagering man—and I'm always a wagering man—I'm guessing they'll be using words like *innocent bystander*. They'll tell her that Dino was doing his job—stocking Reese's Pieces in the candy machine when suddenly he was shot by Royall—poor Dino being just another victim in the wrong place at the wrong time."

Zig acted surprised, but he wasn't. At Dover, he saw it every day, the government choosing to tell a half-truth to ensure that a military secret stayed secret. In this case, what Royall did—finding out about a paying agent who was skimming money, and then the two of them using that info to plan their own super heist—it'd put Operation Bluebook on the front page of every newspaper. Even worse, it would risk exposing the identities of every current and previous soldier who worked undercover for it.

"The President loves the program. Apparently, he's a Harry Houdini fan too. He was hoping to protect Bluebook at all costs. That's why, when the plane crash first happened, they rushed everyone so quickly through Dover. Keep it hush-hush and keep the program intact. The body that they thought was Nola's just got swept up in that. No one would've raised an eyebrow—until, of course, you realized it wasn't her. And that's also why he put one of his oldest friends—the Librarian of Congress—in charge of Bluebook to begin with. Unlike our generals, when the Librarian is flying somewhere, no one looks twice at who's sitting there next to him."

"So Rookstool was doing real work in Alaska?"

"Real work. He was the point man all the so-called 'students' reported to. It's been like that for decades. He was flying back with three of them, since they never like putting them all on the same plane. Apparently, Harry Houdini donated his books to the Library of Congress for a reason. Who knew librarians could be so dangerous?"

Zig was still silent, sliding each foot into a sock, then into his shoes. Today, the government was hiding soldiers on college campuses, in computer science training programs, so we can track potential hackers and terrorists. Tomorrow, we'd have different problems; we'd hide them somewhere else. But there would always be a need for Harry Houdini's Blue Book and the covert corps that went with it.

"Y'know, for a while," Zig said, "when we were looking for who was behind it all—I was worried it might be you."

"Yeah, well, I forgive you," Master Guns said, forcing a laugh. "President Wallace thought the same."

"Then I thought for sure it was Hsu. She was the last person I saw on that day the President came to see the bodies—right before I got smashed in the head and knocked unconscious."

Master Guns went silent, both of them replaying that morning in the mortuary, populating it with Dino instead of Colonel Hsu. She was investigating just like they were—and was the only one smart enough to be suspicious of Dino; she even questioned him in her office.

"So Hsu has *heart*, huh?" Zig asked.

"I have to say, I thought she was *No heart*. But after this? *Heart*."

Zig thought about that. "I hate being wrong."

"Frickin' A."

Crumpling up his hospital gown into a small, compact ball, Zig gripped it tight, like he was trying to keep it from expanding.

"Y'know, Ziggy, there's just one little detail that still makes no sense to me," Master Guns said, glancing over at the TV on the wall and pretending to watch, even though it wasn't on. "When you snuck back into Dover and got on that plane to Alaska, I talked to the pilots. They said that the plane had pretty much taken off, but you threw a holy fit, convincing them to stop right there on the runway."

"I told you—"

"—you realized Nola pulled another fast one and wasn't in the coffin. I remember. I've heard you tell the story three times now. You're lucky the pilots listened to you. Nola might've been dead if they didn't."

Master Guns was still eyeing the blank TV, admiring it.

"But what I still can't figure out, Ziggy, is...well... When you got off that plane, you went running straight to the Graveyard," he said, referring to the old warehouse. "Straight to where Nola and Royall were as they tried to kill each other." He was still studying the TV. "So answer me this, Ziggy. How'd you know to go there?"

"I'm not sure I understand the question."

"You scrambled off the plane. All of Dover was on lockdown. With all the hell that was breaking loose, even if you had called for help, I get it. There was no time. You had to make a spilt-second decision. But even so, don't bullshit me, Ziggy. How'd you know Nola and Royall were in that old warehouse?"

Zig looked up from the hospital gown he was still clutching like a miniature world. But he didn't say a word.

"She told you, didn't she," Master Guns said. It wasn't a question. "Nola texted you for help. She reached out and told you she was in that warehouse."

Zig studied his friend, knowing that tone in his voice. He seemed pretty confident in his assessment. "You went through that burner phone I was carrying, didn't you?" Zig asked.

Now Master Guns was the silent one. "This is my job, Ziggy. And truthfully, I'm not even that surprised she texted you to come running. But what I still can't figure out is *why*? Even on her best day, Nola never asks for help, not from anyone. So when I look at a situation like this, I just need to know: Was she simply panicking in a moment of desperation—or did you actually manage to ingratiate yourself enough that she somehow, by some miracle, put a tiny bit of genuine faith in you?"

Zig went to say something, then decided against it. "I can live with either."

Master Guns nodded, finally turning away from the TV.

Tossing his hospital gown aside, Zig hopped off the bed and headed for the door. Back to the mortuary, back to work.

"Ziggy, can I say one final thing?"

"I thought that final thing was the final thing?"

"About Dino's body...for the embalming... I understand why you want to work on him. It's a little weird and Addams Family–ish, but I get it. Closure's good." Master Guns took another breath, his voice softer than before. "After that, though, maybe it's time for a break."

"What kind of break?"

"A break. A *real* break. Enough with so much death. Every day, you're around it, surrounded by it. Maybe you...I don't know..."

"Are you firing me?"

"I'm not your boss, Ziggy. I'm your *friend*."

"Then say what you're saying."

Master Guns stood there a moment, shoulders straight, chest out. Unreadable. "Two days ago, when we were trying to figure out this Bluebook stuff, we started wading through all the real details about Harry Houdini's life."

"Is this another magic story?"

"It's a *death* story, your favorite topic. Anyway, during the research, I found out that before Houdini died—and this is true— he gave secret passwords to those closest to him—to his wife, to his brothers, even to those in his little corps: Clifford Eddy, Rose Mackenberg, and Amedeo Vacca. Each got an individual code—a word known only to them. That way, if the person died and there was a séance, Houdini would know if the so-called ghost that the medium said had 'appeared' was the real deal or not."

"So the ghost would say the magic word to the medium, and then Houdini would know he wasn't being scammed?"

"I know. The guy was more obsessed with corpses than you are—but as we kept digging, we also found that Houdini gave one of these passwords to his mom. *She* was the ghost he wanted to speak to most of all. Apparently, he never got over her death. When she passed... It was such a devastating loss, it tore him apart for the rest of his life," Master Guns said, glancing over at Zig.

Now Zig was the one looking up at the blank TV.

"Here's what caught my eye, though, Ziggy. Y'know what his mom's secret password was? After all the death in Houdini's life, after spending so much time obsessing over it and chasing fake mediums, and going after spiritualists, and spending part of every show proving that every fortune-teller was a sham... y'know what code word he gave to the one woman he wished he could have back more than anyone else? It was a single word. *Forgive.*"

Zig turned from the blank TV. *"Forgive?"*

"Listen to the man. It's good advice."

"I thought we were chatting about my job. About me taking a break."

"We are."

"Then make your point," Zig insisted.

"You're not dead."

Zig laughed. "Thanks for the sagacious advice."

"I'm serious, Ziggy. You're not underground; there's no dirt on your face. You've spent so many years around these lifeless corpses, thinking they're the ones you're helping, but... It's time for you to come back to life."

"I *am* alive."

"Not just alive, Ziggy. It's time to *live* again. It's the one trick Houdini could never pull off. But you can."

Zig thought about that.

"My point is..." Master Guns took another breath through his nose. "Maybe when this is over and you've finished working on Dino's body, maybe you step away from Dover for a bit. Maybe go to a plain old, regular funeral home and just... work on some civilians. Old ladies. Ninety-year-old men whose hearts finally gave way. People who are missed, but who don't have you up to your eyebrows every day in a full-fledged tragedy."

"You know that's not my—"

"Or better yet, hit the road. Forget Delaware. Go be a pirate again—travel around—see the country. For the average funeral home, when there's a hard case, they usually recommend a closed casket. But with your sculpting skills…what you can do for people, for their families…that's a dying art. Go be a pirate again, and share it. Forgive. Live. It'll do you good."

"My life's here," Zig said, though what he was really thinking was a far simpler truth, a truth he wasn't about to share: *What other life do I have?*

Master Guns stared at his friend, then took off his glasses, polished them on his shirt, and slid them back on his face. His eyes never left Zig.

"Don't look at me like that. You know I can't just leave this place," Zig said.

"Ziggy, everyone has an arrow in their life. For all these years, you followed that arrow. But maybe it's time to follow a new one."

"You practiced that arrow metaphor, didn't you? No way did you just make that up on the spot."

"Your jokes don't work on me, Ziggy. Maybe it's time for a new challenge."

"I like working with the troops, with our fallen. I like helping them. I'm not leaving."

"You do what you want, Ziggy. But just think about it, okay? That's all I ask."

Zig nodded, like he appreciated the advice. But as he headed for the door, he already knew his answer.

"I'm not leaving," Zig called out, turning the corner and stepping into the hospital hallway.

He meant it.

91

Three days later

I assume someone's coming to pick you up?" Nurse Angela asked.

"They're on their way," Nola said.

It was a lie. Hospital rules said that, for liability purposes, Nurse Angela had to roll Nola's wheelchair down to Discharge and stay by her side until her ride arrived. "I just spoke to them," Nola explained.

Nurse Angela nodded, pushing and not really caring.

Ten minutes later, they were waiting in the hospital lobby, Nola still in the wheelchair, her leg extended in the Frankenstein brace they gave her to keep it immobile after surgery. Behind her, Nurse Angela stood there, staring outside at the few double-parked cars, baby clouds rising from their tailpipes as they waited for their loved ones.

"Miss Nola, you sure they're on their way?" Nurse Angela asked.

"Absolutely. Any minute."

Nola liked Nurse Angela, liked the way she called her *Miss Nola* and always had a chewed pen in her breast pocket. *Anxious. Real worry for her patients.* But also impatient.

By Nola's calculation, it wouldn't be long before Nurse Angela got antsy and excused herself. Forget hospital rules. Angela still had another eight patients to deal with. Once she was gone, Nola could call a cab and get the hell out of here. Truth was, she could call one right now, but she didn't want anyone in the hospital knowing her personal details.

"Miss Nola, if it's okay with y—"

"*There she is!*" a man's voice announced.

Nola turned just as the sliding doors parted ways. Zig walked in, big smile on his face as he headed toward her.

"Sorry I'm late. Someone's pinball machine bounced out of a pickup truck and onto Route 1, so traffic on the highway was biblical," Zig said, shaking the nurse's hand, holding it extra long to turn on the charm.

Nurse Angela stared at Zig's face, at the stitches and his black eyes and bruises. His left hand was in a cast. "You were here a few days ago."

"Zig. Some call me Ziggy."

Nurse Angela didn't answer. "You know this person?"

"Of course I know her. I'm her ride," Zig said.

"I'm talking to *her*," Nurse Angela shot back, turning to Nola and pulling her own hand from Zig's grip.

"Yeah," Nola said from the wheelchair. "I know him."

"You want me t—"

"He's harmless," Nola said. "Plus, I can hit him with these," she added, raising the metal crutches that were wedged alongside her in the wheelchair.

Nurse Angela stood there a moment, trying to decide if she believed her. She didn't, but she didn't have much choice. "On behalf of Kent General and all the liability insurance that goes with it, you're officially discharged. Miss Nola, you have a nice afternoon. I've got patients to see, like Mr. Robbins, who keeps complaining of the smell, even though he's the one farting up his room."

Zig and Nola watched the nurse disappear up the hallway, neither of them saying a word until she stepped inside an elevator and the doors slammed shut.

"Why are you here?" Nola asked.

"You need a ride, right?" Zig dangled his keys. "I own a car."

Nola looked up from her wheelchair and saw the grin in Zig's eyes, the way he was biting the inside of his cheek. *Excited. Hopeful.*

"I'll take a cab," she said.

"To Washington, DC? You're going home, right? You know what a cab will cost from here? At least three hundred, maybe four hundred bucks. You think you can afford that right now? I'm a free ride. Don't be such a mule."

She shot him a look, her pointy features hitting him like a spear.

"Fine. Be a mule. But don't be so stubborn that you make a decision you'll regret in two minutes. C'mon. You don't even have to talk to me."

Nola didn't like Zig. She understood him more, but she still didn't like him. "My bag's behind the—"

"I see it. I got it," Zig said, grabbing the shopping bag that hung off the push bar of the wheelchair. It was filled with clothes, meds, and post-surgery instructions.

"Watch your feet," Zig added, steering the wheelchair out the front door, to an old 2011 Honda Odyssey.

"A minivan?"

"Borrowed it from work. Figured it'd have more legroom for you."

"Dover has minivans?"

"Most mortuaries do. When you're moving caskets, the seats go down in back and—"

"I got it," Nola said. Outside, in the cold, she noticed an Asian woman with a weak chin—a doctor—on her cell phone, pacing back and forth. The doctor had cracked, dried lips, which she kept licking. No lip balm. *Unprepared. Or lazy. Or maybe just strong.*

As they reached the passenger side of the van, Zig went to help Nola out of the wheelchair.

She waved him off, maneuvering the crutches into place and hopping up on one foot. She opened the door herself, sliding into the front passenger seat.

Inside, the minivan smelled lemony fresh, no dust, the dashboard all shine. Better than most in the military, but that's how everything was at Dover. Still, Nola noticed that one of the knobs was missing from the radio, the front windshield had a small chip from where a rock hit it, and down by her left hip, there was a stray thread in the stitching of her leather seat.

"You buckled in?"

She nodded.

Neither of them said another word as they headed past the mom-and-pop shops that dotted Main Street, half the redbrick storefronts looking new and refurbished, the other half dwindling and marked with *For Lease* signs, as if the town itself still hadn't decided if it was living or dying.

Nola stayed silent as Zig turned left onto 301 South, the landscape widening out and looking like every other four-lane commercial byway in America, all the mom-and-pops replaced by Walgreens and Pizza Huts.

Within a few miles, the landscape expanded yet again, the storefronts now gone. On either side of the highway was nothing but acres upon acres of farmland, for as far as the eye could see, all of it dusted with patches of snow.

"Those are wheat and barley fields," Zig said, pointing to a wide swath of land on their right. "You'd think the frost would be bad, but it's actually warm under the snow. Helps the smaller grains thrive."

Nola lowered her visor to block the orange sun that teetered in the late afternoon sky as it waited to set in the distance. As the shadow hit her face, her leg was in pain. She shifted in her seat, but didn't say a word.

"I'm sorry you got fired," Zig said after a moment.

Nola turned toward him, trying to decide if she was surprised the news traveled so fast. So far, the White House had been able to keep it out of the papers—and apparently was still working with local law enforcement to avoid prosecution—but after all that Nola had done: sneaking back onto her old base, attacking Markus and dragging him onto that boat, plus pulling the trigger on both Houdini and Royall...

Self-defense. That's what Nola's military-appointed lawyer called it. The White House didn't argue. They'd never admit it, but the President's team was probably thankful Royall and Houdini were gone. With them dead, cleanup would be that much easier. Operation Bluebook would get a new name, everyone who worked there would stay protected, and their good work could continue. Life moves on. Nola knew the truth, though; she knew it days ago. Even if the White House was happy, this was still the military. Doesn't matter if you save the day—once you kick the chain of command, there had to be consequences.

"I saw they named a new Artist-in-Residence," Zig added. "That must've been a tough job to say goodbye to."

Nola didn't answer.

"After all you did, though... I'm surprised they only gave you a general discharge."

"Under honorable conditions," she clarified.

He nodded. "You can apply for a recharacterization in six months. I bet they'll change it. They'll bust balls, but you'll get your honorable discharge."

Nola stared straight ahead, the shadow from the car's visor making it look like she was wearing a blindfold.

"Nola, if it makes you feel better, I told them how helpful y—"

"Why are you here, Mr. Zigarowski? Are you looking for a thank-you? Is that why you made the trip?"

Zig didn't even turn at the question. He knew it was coming.

Tapping his thumbs on the steering wheel, Zig let out a sigh. His voice was soft, softer than she'd ever heard it. "Master Guns told me you were healing just fine, but I guess... I wanted to see for myself. Wanted to make sure you were okay, see what you were doing next."

"And that's it?"

"That's it."

The car hit a small bump, a divot in the road, sending a flash-bulb of sunlight into Nola's eyes and another shockwave of pain through her leg.

She glanced over at Zig. The orange sun lit him up, revealing all the lines in his face. Smile lines. Frown lines. And so many worry lines.

"Painting," she blurted.

"Pardon?"

"They fired me... You asked what I was doing next. Painting. I'll keep painting."

"Like for a gallery?"

She hit him with the kind of look that twenty-six-year-olds give to fifty-year-olds. *Don't be a shmuck.* "The Army made me their Artist-in-Residence for a reason. I like seeing the world. I figure I'll take my pastels, travel around, see what I can find."

"So kick up some trouble?"

Nola shot him another look, rolling her eyes. She then reached for the glove compartment. Inside, she found a pad and an old Cracker Barrel pen. She rested the pad on her good leg and began sketching. "I was thinking of starting in New Orleans. Never been there."

"You'll love it," Zig said, watching her pen scratch at the page.

"What about you, Mr. Zigarowski? You staying at Dover?"

He nodded. "This is where my life is. Plus, all the fallen soldiers... I like the job. Lets me help people."

Ahead of them, the road veered to the right, past the longest wheat and barley field they'd seen thus far, Zig thinking that when the winter was done, this whole field would be replanted with soy-beans. Same dirt—just depends what you put in it.

"Nola, in your art, in all the canvases I saw at your office—why were you always painting attempted suicides?"

"Why do you spend so much time around the dead, Mr. Zigarowski?"

"I told you. I like helping people. So. Why suicides?"

Nola was still sketching, working the outer edges of whatever she was drawing. Looked like a snake. Or a lake. Something long. "I don't know. There are lots of kinds of deaths. Suicides just interest me."

"It does more than interest you. It's in every painting."

"What are you getting at, Mr. Zigarowski?"

"I want to know if suicide—" He thought about when they were back at the motel, about the scars on her wrist. "Is it something you've thought about *yourself*?"

Nola said nothing. Her body went still and her hand stopped moving. She didn't look up from her sketch. "Not for a while."

For the next mile or so, the road continued to veer right, at one point intersecting with a narrow street called Strawberry Lane that held only an enormous steel-lattice transmission tower.

"Nola, during your time in the military, you ever meet a man named Dr. Robert Sadoff?" Zig finally asked.

Nola sensed a lecture.

"Sadoff works in my field, spends a lotta time around death," Zig added. "I saw him speak at a conference years ago—they call him the father of modern forensic psychiatry. When there's a murder in the military—or anywhere, really—they would bring in Dr. Sadoff to testify. He'd use forensic science and medical details about the human mind, then tell the court whether the suspect had the mental competence to commit such a crime."

"So he says whether people are crazy or not?"

"That's his job. The real point is, Dr. Sadoff is a man of science. His decisions hinged on medical facts. But when I saw him speak, he insisted he was also a man of deep religious faith. Loved God. Said his prayers. And when someone asked about his faith, Sadoff traced it back to when he was five years old in his hometown of Minneapolis. One morning, a fire engine was flying toward an emergency when its driver missed a turn, sending the truck straight at the local drugstore that was owned by Sadoff's father. The fire truck slammed headfirst into the prescription counter where Sadoff's dad worked every day. But on that day," Zig explained, "Sadoff's dad had stepped out of work for a few hours to say religious prayers for a relative who had just passed away. For the rest of Dr. Sadoff's life, this man of science pointed to *this* moment as absolute *proof* that the universe has a divine plan.'"

Nola stared down at her sketch pad, thinking about it for nearly thirty seconds. "Not for me," she finally offered.

"Me either," Zig agreed, both of them smiling, then, to their own surprise, laughing. Actually laughing.

On Nola's notepad, with another few lines, the picture slowly bloomed into view. It was a drawing of her extended leg, wrapped in its elastic Ace bandage and protected by the bionic-looking knee brace with its hinges and adhesive straps. From Nola's point of view. Her wound.

"Y'know I knew her," Nola blurted.

Zig glanced over, confused.

"Maggie," she said, the words hitting like a bomb. "Your daughter."

Zig's head tilted almost imperceptibly. "I-I thought— Back at the funeral home . . . you said—"

"We weren't friends. Never even sat near each other. But it was seventh grade. I knew who she was. Everyone knew who she was. I saw her every day."

Zig sat there, staring straight ahead, trying so hard to listen. But Nola could see the way he was clutching the steering wheel like it was a life preserver.

"I can't say she was ever really nice to me," Nola added. "I don't think we ever said two words to each other. But one day, at the end of gym class, everyone was playing Do It and You're Cool—"

"*Do It and You're—?*"

"It's a game. Seventh grade. Someone dares you to do something, then everyone chants, '*Do it and you're cool! Do it and you're cool!*' until you—"

"I get it."

"Think *Truth or Dare*. But with less truth. And more assholey-ness. Regardless, on this day, a girl named Sabrina Samuelson—"

"I remember Sabrina! She was in Girl Scouts."

"I remember her too. Nasty little shit goblin who always wore a French braid and rhinestone Keds. On that day, Sabrina was leading the charge, demanding that I show everyone the tampon that she somehow spotted in my backpack. It was a trap, of course. If I took the tampon out, the entire seventh grade would know about my menstrual cycle; if I denied having one, they'd crucify me for being behind the curve," Nola explained. "But there was Goblin Sabrina, riling up the crowd.

"*Do it and you're cool! Do it and you're cool!*" Nola chanted. "*Omigod, she's about to cry!*" Nola recounted the tease with perfect clarity. Her voice returned to normal. "That wasn't true. The only thing I was about to do was take the combination lock I was holding and smash it into Sabrina's face."

"I'm sorry they did that to you."

"Stop apologizing. Just listen. The crowd was in a lather now—*Do it and you're cool! Do it and you're cool!*—and before I realized what was happening, your daughter Maggie appeared from nowhere. She was on her own mission, racing up to Sabrina, grabbing her by the arm, and telling her, 'Lucas just asked out Charlotte M.!'

"In a fit of teenage giggling, Maggie and Goblin Sabrina went running, the crowd of prepubescent sheep now following them to a brand-new childhood nightmare."

"Why're you telling me this?" Zig asked.

"When they were leaving—Sabrina and Maggie—the two of them were leading the pack, running down the hallway from the central locker area, cackling like seventh-grade bitches. But just as they turned the corner and disappeared, Maggie glanced back over her shoulder. I saw it right there, Mr. Zigarowski—on her face—in her anxious green eyes. Even back then, I knew real concern when I saw it. When she pulled Sabrina away, Maggie knew what she was doing."

"So you became friends?"

"Maggie never said another word to me. Not once. Not even after my ear got burned at the campfire. And I'm not saying she was some saint—she was too well aware of her own popularity for that. But on that particular day, when the crowd and the pitchforks were pointing my way, your daughter—" Nola paused, searching for the right phrase. She couldn't find it. "You raised your daughter right."

Zig was worried his voice would give him away. So he just nodded. He smiled. He clutched the steering wheel, amazed he was actually holding it together. That lasted a full three seconds.

Zig's chin quivered first, then his lips, then the full emotional earthquake hit, sending shockwaves through his body, rippling upward as they climbed his face and squeezed the tears out from behind his eyes.

Nola wasn't surprised. He's a father. He missed his daughter.

And he did. He missed Maggie every day.

But for Zig, these weren't tears that came from a loss. They were tears that accompanied a *return*. For fourteen years, Zig had grown accustomed to Maggie being gone, grown accustomed to having her birthday marked by quiet, or having the day she died be equally ignored. It was the most profound pain that death delivered: the utter numbness that comes from when you can't get over it but somehow get used to it.

For fourteen years, Zig knew the contours of Maggie's death. The rules of it. The limits. And then, with a single two-minute story about vengeful seventh graders, Zig had what he never thought he'd have again—new details of her life. And just like that, his daughter, his Little Star, was alive again. He had a new memory of her, something he never thought he'd ever get.

He was smiling now—and crying—doing both of them together

as tears of joy pushed out from behind his eyes. "Nola," he said, turning to her...

"You're welcome," she said, her eyes down, focused on her sketch pad. "And I'll consider us even if you don't hug me when we get to DC."

Zig laughed, knowing she meant it. "Can I just—? What you said about Maggie—"

"Just enjoy the ride, Mr. Zigarowski. Can we do just that?"

"But what you said— I just need to know...that night at the campfire—"

"Enjoy the ride," she insisted, pointing the tip of her pen toward the front windshield. Outside, the road stretched out in front of them, the orange sun so low, it turned the entire sky tangerine.

Breathtaking, Zig and Nola thought simultaneously.

Nola memorized the color for a future painting.

Next to her, in the driver's seat, Zig hit the gas, still replaying Nola's words in his head. *Enjoy the ride.*

And for the first time in a long time—in maybe fourteen years—he did.

92

Two weeks later

Balancing a six-pack of beer on his hip, Zig fumbled with his keys, fighting to turn the lock on his front door.

With a click, the door opened. He wiped his feet, the mat perfectly in place.

Heading for the kitchen, he pulled two receipts from his left pocket—one from lunch, one from Donnie's Liquors—plus a folded-up business card from the peppy new woman who was just hired in Veteran Affairs. Every month brought new faces to Dover; few people could handle it for too long.

He threw it all in the trash.

Next to the toaster, his daughter's red hair band was gone. These days, he was wearing it around his wrist.

"You have no messages," the robotic answering machine announced as Zig hit the button in the kitchen. Just like the night before. And the night before that.

Two minutes later, Zig was in his backyard, ritual beer in hand.

"How's everyone tonight, ladies?"

"Mmmmmmmmmmmmmm," the bees sang as Zig opened the roof of the hive and added some food—a homemade sugar-and-water mixture he called bee cupcakes.

As he slid into his favorite rusty lawn chair, Zig threw his coat aside. The weather had turned over the last few nights—it was still fifty-five degrees, but after the recent cold spell, Zig was determined to make the most of the respite.

"By the way, I met the new candy guy today," Zig told the hive, which was buzzing with life, swarming the landing board. Bee cupcakes always kicked off a dance party. "Twix are out. New M&M's with caramel are in. Can you imagine? No Twix? *Blasphemy!*" Zig said. "I mean, how do you even explain poor decision-making like that?"

"*Mmmmmmmmmmmmmm,*" the bees hummed.

"I agree. Cultural bias. Like the SAT," Zig said, taking a swig of beer, then licking a bit of excess from his lips.

For the next twenty minutes, Zig sat there in his lawn chair, nursing his drink and enjoying the private concert of the bees' low-pitched *mmmmmmmm*. A crescent moon lit the sky; the cool air felt nice. It was a near-perfect night.

On his far left, past the barbeque, a single stray honeybee swirled in the air, making wobbly loop-de-loops and bouncing a few times off the wooden fence. Guard bee? No. This bee was bigger, longer. A forager. The ones who get to leave the hive, since they always come back.

Zig watched the bee do another shaky loop-de-loop, ramming itself yet again into the fence, like it was drunk or trying to escape. In reality, it was just old. Foragers were the elders, dying in huge numbers every season. But that didn't slow them down.

In the next few months, with the arrival of the first blooms, full foraging would begin, thousands of bees flying up to four miles to get nectar and pollen to nourish their hive.

Foragers were stubborn too, Zig thinking about how many times he'd come home and find a bee so weighed down with pollen and nectar, they'd be twisting in the grass, struggling to get back to the hive. Wonderful creatures, committed to their mission.

Still, after decades of intense study, there was one question about foragers that scientists couldn't answer: Where do they die? Every single day, foragers go out and come back home. Out and home. Out and home. But for some reason, 99 percent of deaths happened *away* from the hive. That's not just luck. That's a trait. An instinct. A natural law.

For years, like most scientists, Zig assumed it was a way to protect the hive, keeping it free from sickness and disease. Or maybe it was Darwinism—the weaker foragers would go out, but didn't have enough strength to make their return. Yet tonight, as Zig sat there in his lawn chair, watching this stubborn, lonely bee make yet another fruitless loop-de-loop, he couldn't help but think that maybe, deep in the bee's psyche, it knew what was coming. It knew the end was near. So when it left for that final flight, instead of yet another mission for the hive, maybe, just maybe, it would go off on one final adventure.

Or who knows? Maybe more than one.

With a final swig of beer, Zig pulled out his phone. His thumb hovered past Facebook, tapped on a browser, and quickly navigated to one of those online travel sites with a purposely weird name that you could never remember.

Flights.

One way.

Destination?

Zig sat there a moment, wondering if he was being impulsive. Then a new thought hit his brain—the words of The Amazing Caesar, who told him there were only four different magic tricks: You make something appear. You make something disappear. You make two things change place. Or, the one Zig liked most: *You change one thing into something else.*

Zig stared down at the red hair tie on his wrist. It'd be fun to pirate again. Go around, see the world. And of course, do some good. So where to start?

New Orleans, he typed into the search box. He'd heard it was nice this time of year.

There are many kinds of death, Zig thought to himself. But there are also many ways to live. It's one of the few things they never teach you at mortician school. Sometimes you need to bury your old life—and make a new one.

ABOUT THE AUTHOR

Brad Meltzer is the #1 *New York Times* bestselling author of *The Inner Circle* and ten other bestselling thrillers. He is also the author of the Ordinary People Change the World series of picture book biographies—which includes *I am Neil Armstrong*—and is the host of the History Channel television shows *Decoded* and *Lost History*, in which he helped find the missing 9/11 flag. He lives in Florida. You can find out much more about him at BradMeltzer.com. You can also see what he's doing right now at Facebook.com/BradMeltzer and on Twitter @bradmeltzer.

SANTA BARBARA PUBLIC LIBRARY

3 __447 01654 9640

YOU'RE READING THE
WRONG WAY!

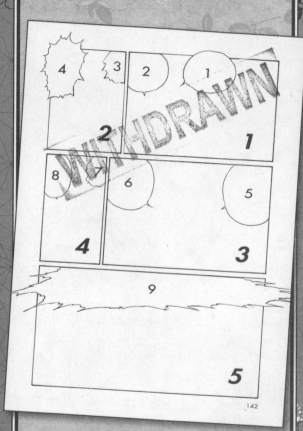

DEMON SLAYER: KIMETSU NO YAIBA
reads from right to left, starting in the
upper-right corner. Japanese is read from
right to left, meaning that action, sound
effects and word-balloon order are completely reversed from English order.

IN A SAVAGE WORLD RULED BY THE PURSUIT OF THE MOST DELICIOUS FOODS, IT'S EITHER EAT OR BE EATEN!

"The most bizarrely entertaining manga out there on comic shelves. *Toriko* is a great series. If you're looking for an weirdly fun book or a fighting manga with a bizarre take, this is the story for you to read."

—*ComicAttack.com*

TORIKO

Story and Art by Mitsutoshi Shimabukuro

In an era where the world's gone crazy for increasingly bizarre gourmet foods, only Gourmet Hunter Toriko can hunt down the ferocious ingredients that supply the world's best restaurants. Join Toriko as he tracks and defeats the tastiest and most dangerous animals with his bare hands.

TORIKO © 2008 by Mitsutoshi Shimabukuro/SHUEISHA Inc.

ratings.viz.com
www.shonenjump.com
www.viz.com

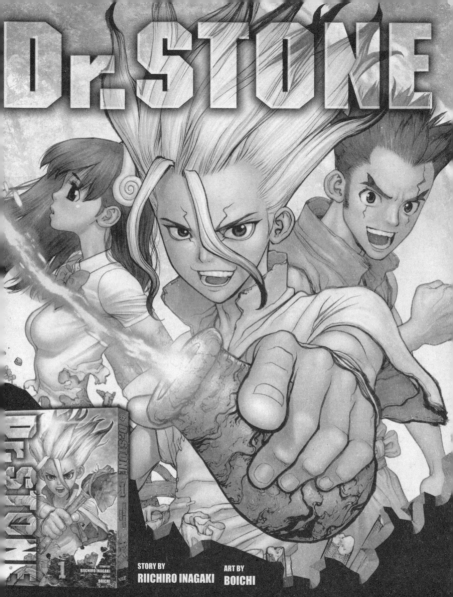

Dr. STONE

STORY BY
RIICHIRO INAGAKI

ART BY
BOICHI

One fateful day, all of humanity turned to stone. Many millennia later, Taiju frees himself from petrification and finds himself surrounded by statues. The situation looks grim—until he runs into his science-loving friend Senku! Together they plan to restart civilization with the power of science!

DR. STONE © 2017 by Riichiro Inagaki, Boichi/SHUEISHA Inc.

OOOF!

WHUMP

HASHIBIRA, DO YOUR FRONT BUTTONS!

BOMP

OH! IT'S NEZUKO THE BAKER'S DAUGHTER! SHE'S BITING BREAD AGAIN TODAY. HOW CUTE!

GYAAAH!

BONK

HEE HEE

NO PLAYING WITH MARI BALLS!

GOOD MORNING, NEZUKO!

AGAT-SUMA...

THIS JOB SUCKS.

UNGH

TOMIOKA SENSEI...

HOMF!

MMF!

FURF!

GAR!

HOMF!

GNAW!

BUT THIS IS MY NATURAL COLOR!

SWAK

...I TOLD YOU, NO DYEING YOUR HAIR!

SO CUTE...

SHE'S JUST LIKE THE HEROINE IN A SHOJO MANGA!

THE MOST WELL-MANNERED BOY AT KIMETSU ACADEMY

I KNOW EARRINGS ARE AGAINST SCHOOL REGULATIONS, SO I APOLOGIZE.

...AT KIMETSU ACADEMY'S JUNIOR HIGH AND HIGH SCHOOL.

THERE ARE MANY PROBLEM STUDENTS ...

IF YOU KNOW THE RULES, DON'T BREAK THEM... EVEN POLITELY!

I'M ON THE SCHOOL'S DISCIPLINARY COMMITTEE, EVEN THOUGH I DON'T WANT TO BE.

MY NAME IS ZENITSU AGATSUMA.

THEY'RE THE LAST MEMENTO OF MY FATHER.

NO EAR-RINGS!

HEY, YOU!

SNIFF OKAY. I'LL LOOK THE OTHER WAY. BEAT IT!

HUH ?!

BOW

VOLUME 6 – TRIAL BY HASHIRA (THE END)

DO *YOU* HAVE ANY LAST WORDS?

SIGH

YES.

THIS ONE'S GONNA DIE TOO.

I'M DYING.

GULP

IT ALL GOES AS LORD KIBUTSUJI WISHES.

...I WILL DIE BY YOUR OWN HAND.

GLEAM

I AM IN A DREAM! BECAUSE...

SILENCE.

I AM NEVER WRONG. I CANNOT MAKE MISTAKES.

YOU'RE WRONG! I...

I...

NO...

YOU HAVE NO RIGHT TO OBJECT.

WHAT I SAY IS RIGHT *IS* RIGHT.

ALL AUTHORITY IS MINE. AND WHAT I SAY IS ABSOLUTE.

...WARRANTS DEATH.

YOU CONTRADICTED ME, AND THAT...

...I WOULDN'T FAIL TO MAKE GOOD USE OF IT!

BLOOD!

IF YOU COULD GIVE ME A LITTLE MORE BLOOD...

I'D BE A STRONGER DEMON AND FIGHT!

THUNK

ROLL

ROLL

TOSS

HOW VERY IMPUDENT. KNOW YOUR PLACE.

WHY SHOULD I REWARD YOUR FAILURE WITH MY PRECIOUS BLOOD?

NO, I DIDN'T HEAR ANY MUSIC!

I FAILED?! WAS IT THAT BIWA PLAYER'S POWER?

UGH... WHY CAN'T I REGENERATE?

?!

DO YOU HAVE ANY FINAL WORDS?

WHAT CAN YOU DO AT YOUR CURRENT STRENGTH?

EXACTLY *HOW MUCH* GRACE? AND HOW WILL YOU BE OF USE?

...I'M SURE I COULD!

I CAN STILL BE OF USE! IF I COULD HAVE JUST A LITTLE MORE GRACE...

MY ONLY CHANCE IS TO RUN!

THE FOOL.

SOME-
HOW...

I HAVE TO GET AWAY SOME-HOW...

EVERY TIME YOU ENCOUNTER ONE OF THE DEMON SLAYER HASHIRA, YOU WANT TO FLEE.

NO!

...

NO I DON'T! I RISK MY LIFE FOR YOU!

ARE YOU *CONTRADICTING* WHAT I SAY?

...THE MOMENT THAT NEZUKO ARRIVED, KIBUTSUJI KNEW WHERE UBUYASHIKI'S HEADQUARTERS WAS.

BECAUSE...

TAMAYO'S AND NEZUKO'S EFFORTS...

TO THIS POINT, HOWEVER, KIBUTSUJI HAS NOT GRASPED THAT.

...AND KIBUTSUJI STILL DOESN'T KNOW IT.

...HAVE REMOVED KIBUTSUJI'S CURSE...

MUZAN KIBUTSUJI CAN READ THE THOUGHTS OF THOSE TO WHOM HE HAS GIVEN HIS BLOOD.

IF HE CAN SEE THEM, HE CAN READ THEIR MINDS. THE FARTHER AWAY THEY ARE...

...THE LESS CLEARLY HE CAN READ THEM, BUT HE CAN ALWAYS DISCERN THEIR LOCATION.

...WHEN NEZUKO WAS TAKEN TO UBUYASHIKI MANSION, IT WAS A TERRIBLE THING FOR THE DEMON SLAYER CORPS.

HE KNOWS WHERE THEY ARE.

WHICH MEANS...

UPPER

IN ORDER:

UPPER RANK:
ONE, TWO, THREE,
FOUR, FIVE, SIX

LOWER RANK:
ONE, TWO, THREE,
FOUR, FIVE, SIX

THE STRONGEST
IS UPPER-1.

THE WEAKEST IS
LOWER-6.

THE TWELVE
KIZUKI ARE
DIVIDED
INTO
UPPER
RANKS
AND LOWER
RANKS.

ONE	TWO	THREE	FOUR	FIVE	SIX

LOWER

ONE	TWO	THREE	FOUR	FIVE	
					SIX

THE
DEMONS IN
THE UPPER
RANKS
DISDAIN
THEM.

DEMONS IN
THE LOWER
RANKS ONLY
HAVE A
NUMBER
ENGRAVED
ON ONE EYE.

CHAPTER 52: CRUEL AND HEARTLESS

THE ONES WHO PUT THE DEMON-SLAYING HASHIRA IN THEIR GRAVES ARE ALWAYS IN THE UPPER RANKS. BUT WHAT ABOUT THE *LOWER* RANKS? HOW MANY TIMES HAVE THOSE MEMBERS CHANGED?

FOR MORE THAN A CENTURY, THE MEMBERS OF THE UPPER RANKS OF THE TWELVE KIZUKI HAVE NOT CHANGED.

YOU CAN ANSWER MY QUESTION.

"WHAT ARE WE SUPPOSED TO SAY TO THAT?"

WHAT ARE WE SUPPOSED TO SAY TO THAT?

WHAT HAS YOU SO WORRIED?

TELL ME.

CRINGE

?!

HE CAN READ OUR THOUGHTS?

UH-OH!

RUI WAS KILLED. HE WAS LOWER-5.

WHY ARE YOU MEMBERS OF THE LOWER RANKS SO WEAK?

I WANT TO ASK ONLY ONE THING.

YOU MUST EAT MORE PEOPLE, GET STRONGER, AND BECOME MORE USEFUL TO ME.

JOINING THE TWELVE KIZUKI IS NOT THE END... MERELY THE BEGINNING.

IT'S LORD MUZAN! THAT'S LORD MUZAN'S VOICE.

I DIDN'T KNOW. HIS APPEARANCE AND AURA ARE DIFFERENT THAN BEFORE. IT'S AN INCREDIBLE DISGUISE.

YOUR APPEARANCE AND AURA ARE DIFFERENT, SO—

M'LORD...

MY APOLOGIES!

WORMS! YOU MAY NOT SPEAK ON YOUR OWN.

ONLY ANSWER MY QUESTIONS.

QUIVER

SHAKE

QUIVER

WHO SAID YOU COULD SPEAK?!

WHAT IS SHE?

...AND BOW!

LOWER YOUR HEADS...

BOW

BOW

WHO IS THIS WOMAN?

THE BLOOD DEMON ART, AGAIN!

WE'VE MOVED!

LOWER-3

LOWER-1

LOWER-2

LOWER-4

ONLY THE LOWER RANKS OF THE TWELVE KIZUKI HAVE GATHERED.

THIS IS THE FIRST TIME.

LOWER-5 STILL HASN'T COME.

KABOOM

I'M GONNA KILL YOU, YOU THANK- LESS BRAT!

HE'S SORRY! REALLY, HE'S SORRY!

...INOSUKE MOVED LIKE AN OCTOPUS UNDERWATER, SO I ACCIDEN- TALLY LET OUT MY AIR!

AND RUNNING WAS SO EXHAUSTING! AND DURING OUR BREATH- HOLDING TRAINING...

TANJIRO ENCOUR- AGED ME THE WHOLE TIME.

HE'S A GOOD BROTHER, NEZUKO.

BUT I LIKE BEING ABLE TO DO MORE THAN I COULD BEFORE.

AHH, THEY'RE SO PRETTY. THE BLUE-GRAY HAS A FAINT SHINE.

AN ELEGANT COLOR THAT BEFITS A KATANA.

SHWNN

...

IF THEY SERVE YOU WELL IN BATTLE, I'LL BE HAPPY.

I FORGED NEW SWORDS FOR YOU, LORD INOSUKE.

NOD

NOD

IT'S MY FIRST TIME MAKING KATANAS FOR A TWO-HANDED FIGHTER.

MOO

HOW DO THEY FEEL IN YOUR HANDS?

MOO

POF POW BIF

OW OW OW.

GOOD. INOSUKE'S BLADES WERE TERRIBLY CHIPPED.

SWIP

LORD INOSUKE ?

?

TMP TMP

CLOMP

CLOMP

THE KATANA BROKE BECAUSE YOU WERE WEAK!

I DON'T CARE! THAT DOESN'T MATTER! IT'S YOUR FAULT! IT'S ALL YOUR FAULT!

OTHER-WISE, WOULD *MY* KATANA BREAK?!

POKE

I'M SO SORRY!

...WAS SUPER STRONG!

BUT REALLY... I WAS ABOUT TO DIE! MY OPPONENT...

HE CHASED ME AROUND FOR AN HOUR.

37 YEARS OLD

I'M GOING TO KILL YOU!

...IS TWICE AS STRONG AS ANYONE ELSE'S.

WELL, HAGANEZUKA IS A PASSIONATE ARTISAN. HIS LOVE FOR KATANAS...

...I'M KANAMORI.

OH...

W-WHY...?

FWSH

GYAAAH!

I CAN'T BELIEVE IT!

I CAN'T BELIEVE YOU BROKE MY SWORD!

YAHOO!

HURRY! HURRY!

YEAH! A CROW JUST TOLD ME!

REALLY?!

HEEEY!

CWHSH

MR. HAGANEZUKA!

...   ...

MR. HAGANEZUKA!

HEY! HEY!

...WELL?

TMP

HAVE YOU BEEN...

TMP

TMP

TP

TP

TP

IT'S BEEN SO LONG!

NINE DAYS LATER, ZENITSU AND INOSUKE HAD MASTERED TOTAL CONCENTRATION: CONSTANT.

SHE CHEERED FOR *ME* MOST OF ALL!

I DID IT! GRAAH!!

Good for you!

AND TANJIRO WAS TRULY *AWFUL* AT TEACHING PEOPLE.

WOOHOO

WOOHOO

Yahoo!

SHINOBU WAS SKILLED AT TEACHING.

SHINOBU!

I HEAR THAT MY REFORGED NICHIRIN SWORD ARRIVES TODAY!

INOSUKE! ZENITSU!

THE TECHNIQUE TANJIRO MASTERED IS CALLED *TOTAL CONCENTRATION: CONSTANT.*

BY DOING TOTAL CONCENTRATION BREATHING EVERY MINUTE OF THE DAY...

...PHYSICAL FITNESS DRASTICALLY IMPROVES.

IT'S A BASIC MOVE... A BEGINNER'S TECHNIQUE, SO OF COURSE...

...HE COULD *DO* IT...

...BUT MASTERING IT REQUIRES INCREDIBLE EFFORT!

CHAPTER 51: THE NICHIRIN SWORD RETURNS

AND INOSUKE CAN'T BEAR TO DO ANYTHING SLOWLY.

I'M NO GOOD AT WORKING HARD.

WE REALIZED WE WERE TOTAL LOSERS.

...EVEN WHEN HE TAUGHT US CAREFULLY, WE DIDN'T GET BETTER.

GO LIKE THIS... AND LIKE THIS...

THEN LIKE THIS...

MAYBE BECAUSE TANJIRO WAS SO FAR BEYOND US NOW...

Inosuke playing on the mountain.

Deer
↓

Zenitsu hiding and stealing food.

Manju is delicious!

TONK

I DID IT!

...

BUT *DID* HE?

HE WON!

SETTING IT ON HER COUNTS!

UH-OH!

YAY
TEE HEE HEE!
AH HA HA!
YA HOO
YIPEE
YAY
YAY
YAY

I GOT PAST HER!

I'D FEEL BAD IF I DUMPED IT ON HER.

THIS MEDICINAL TEA STINKS.

TAN

FEELZ

DO IT!!

PLEASE, KEEP DEFENDING NEZUKO.

KEEP UP YOUR FIGHT, TANJIRO.

WITHOUT REASON...

...JUST ON INSTINCT, THEY KILL PEOPLE.

DEMONS ALWAYS LIE TO SAVE THEM-SELVES.

...AND I FEEL BETTER INSIDE.

FWOOO

WHEN I THINK THAT YOU'RE SUCCEEDING AT MY SISTER'S DREAM, IT SOOTHES MY ANGER...

I'LL DO MY BEST.

HWSH

EVEN AS SHE DIED, SHE PITIED THE DEMONS.

SHE FELT SYMPATHY FOR DEMONS.

IF THERE'S A WAY TO AVOID KILLING PITIFUL DEMONS, I MUST TRY TO FIND IT...

BUT IF THAT WAS MY SISTER'S WISH, THEN I MUST TRY TO CARRY IT OUT.

I COULDN'T THINK LIKE HER. PITY SOMEONE WHO KILLS PEOPLE?

...WITHOUT LOSING MY SUNNY DISPOSITION, WHICH MY SISTER ALWAYS LIKED.

THAT'S RIDICU-LOUS.

...IT REALLY TIRES ME OUT.

BUT...

...THE ANGER IN ME GROWS DEEPER AND STRONGER.

EVER SINCE A DEMON MURDERED MY BELOVED ELDER SISTER...

...WHENEVER I SEE A DEMON, OR PEOPLE WHOSE LOVED ONES HAVE BEEN STOLEN BY DEMONS...

...ANY OF THEM WILL HARM HER. ALSO, BECAUSE IT'S THE MASTER'S WILL.

NOW THAT THEY'VE SEEN NEZUKO, WHO HASN'T EATEN ANY PEOPLE, AND SENSED HER TRUE NATURE, I DON'T THINK...

DEEP INSIDE MY BODY, THERE'S HATRED THAT I CAN'T QUIET.

ANYWAY, MY SISTER WAS A KIND PERSON LIKE YOU.

IT'S THE SAME FOR THE OTHER HASHIRA.

ARE YOU ANGRY?

...YOU ALWAYS SMELL SORT OF ANGRY.

EVEN THOUGH YOU'RE ALWAYS SMILING...

...YOU COULD SAY I'M ANGRY.

WELL...

I GUESS...

...

...

YOU HAVE A PURE HEART.

...AND YOUR INJURIES WERE HORRIBLE.

BECAUSE WE LEARNED THE TRUTH ABOUT NEZUKO...

WHY DID YOU BRING US HERE?

...

...

UMM...

DREAM?

YES.

I'M SURE YOU CAN ACHIEVE THAT.

MY DREAM OF GETTING ALONG WITH DEMONS.

ALSO...

...I THOUGHT I COULD ENTRUST YOU WITH MY DREAM.

YOU'RE REALLY DEDICATED.

YOUR TWO FRIENDS RAN OFF SOMEWHERE.

ONCE I CAN DO IT, I'LL TEACH THEM HOW!

NOPE!

PWIP

AREN'T YOU LONELY BY YOURSELF?

...YOU BROKE MY SWORD.

I CAN'T BELIEVE...

URO...

UROKO...

I'M REALLY SORRY.

UROKODAKI MUST BE REALLY ANGRY. RIGHT NOW I'M HAVING IT REFORGED, BUT...

SORRY...

CONCENTRATE ON YOUR BREATHING!!

CONCENTRATE! CONCENTRATE!

HELLO...

HELLO...

HELLO THERE!

HUH?!

EVEN THAT CAT LOOKS AT ME DISAPPROVINGLY.

I FOUGHT ONE OF THE TWELVE KIZUKI BUT DIDN'T GET ANY OF ITS BLOOD.

...

FIF- TEEN DAYS LATER ...

I CAN RUN MORE THAN BEFORE, AND MY LUNGS HAVE GOTTEN STRONGER, SO THIS IS GOOD.

NO NEED TO RUSH.

GOOD.

MY STRENGTH IS COMING BACK.

...BREATHE SLOWLY AND DEEPLY—CIRCULATE AIR ALL THE WAY TO MY FINGERTIPS.

FWO

OOO

DURING THE DAY, I RUN AROUND, WORKING OUT MY LUNGS WITH FAST MOVEMENTS. NOW IT'S TIME FOR ME TO...

UROKODAKI SAID THAT. UROKODAKI...

MEDITATION IMPROVES CONCENTRA- TION.

THAT SKINNY GIRL BURST ONE OF THESE?!

AND THESE ARE SPECIAL GOURDS, EVEN HARDER THAN NORMAL ONES.

UH-HUH!

HUH? ME? BURST THIS?!

A DRIED GOURD?!

TA-DAH

...THIS GOURD.

RIGHT NOW, KANAO IS WORKING ON...

AND AS THE TRAINING WENT ON THE GOURDS GOT BIGGER.

I GOTTA TRY!

...BIG!!

THAT'S...

BLOW INTO THE GOURDS?

TUNK

THAT'S INTERESTING TRAINING! DOES IT MAKE A SOUND?

OH!

YES. WHEN SHINOBU WAS TRAINING KANAO, SHE OFTEN MADE HER BLOW INTO GOURDS.

...

MUNCH

OH!

BURST ....?!

NO. YOU'RE SUPPOSED TO BURST THE GOURD.

HOOOO

BREATHING BEGINS WITH THE LUNGS. IF MY LUNGS ARE BAD, I CAN'T DO ANYTHING.

I'LL GET UP EARLIER AND RUN. AND I'LL PRACTICE HOLDING MY BREATH.

WHEN YOU'RE IN TROUBLE, GO BACK TO THE BEGINNING!

I CAN'T DO ANYTHING IN THIS CONDITION.

I SUCK!

HARD WORK BUILDS DAY BY DAY. LITTLE BY LITTLE IS FINE. JUST KEEP MOVING FORWARD!

I'LL GIVE IT MY ALL! THAT'S ALL I'VE EVER BEEN ABLE TO DO—TRY MY BEST!

LET'S BRING HIM SOME RICE BALLS.

YEP.

TP TP

TANJIRO WORKS HARD EVERY DAY.

YEAH.

AND GOURDS.

HRAAAH!

WHEN I TRY TO DO TOTAL CONCENTRATION BREATHING FOR A LONG TIME, I FEEL LIKE I'M GONNA DIE.

IT'S TOO HARD. MY LUNGS HURT. MY HEAD HURTS. MY EARDRUMS POUND...

KOFF

HFF HFF HFF HFF

THERE'S NO WAY I CAN DO IT!

I JUST CAN'T!

AGH!

HFF HFF HFF

SWIP

SWIP

FOR A SECOND, I THOUGHT MY HEART WAS GONNA COME OUT MY EARS!

THAT WAS TERRIFYING!

EVEN WHILE SLEEPING?

IS THAT EVEN POSSIBLE?!

...

NO, I DON'T.

ALL THE HASHIRA... AND KANAO.

SOME PEOPLE ARE ABLE TO DO IT.

YOU SHOULD TRY!

IT'S PRETTY HARD USING TOTAL CONCENTRATION BREATHING EVEN JUST A LITTLE.

SO ALL DAY WOULD BE...

BEING ABLE TO DO THAT MAKES A WORLD OF DIFFERENCE.

YES.

I'M GOING TO GIVE IT A TRY! THANK YOU!

GREAT IDEA!

OH!

THANK YOU!

HOW KIND!

HERE'S A TOWEL.

SHWF

?

UM...

...TANJIRO, DO YOU DO TOTAL CONCENTRATION BREATHING 24 HOURS A DAY?

DO YOU DO TOTAL CON-CENTRATION BREATHING WHEN YOU SLEEP?

MORNING, NOON, AND NIGHT?

HMM?

...

I THINK HER EYES ARE DIFFERENT.

UM...

TANJIRO...

SHE EVEN SMELLS DIFFERENT. HER SCENT IS CLOSER TO THAT OF THE HASHIRA.

TANJIRO...

AND HER EYES...

FIRST OF ALL, THE SPEED OF OUR REFLEXES IS COMPLETELY DIFFERENT.

ON MY BEST DAY I'D PROBABLY STILL LOSE.

HMM

...

UHH

UMM

...

UHH

WHAT IS IT?

WHOA! YOU SURPRISED ME!

SORRY.

GLOOM GLOOM

...

IF YOU DON'T WANT TO COME, THEN YOU DON'T HAVE TO EITHER!

NO! THERE'S NO NEED TO BOTHER WITH THEM ANY LONGER!

SKF SKF

GOOD WORK TODAY...

I LOST FOR TEN MORE DAYS.

I WON'T GIVE UP!

I'LL WORK HARD FOR ALL OF US! THEN I'LL TEACH THEM HOW TO WIN!

WHAT ARE THE DIFFER-ENCES BETWEEN US?

WHY CAN'T I BEAT HER?

SKDDD

INOSUKE
...

WE LOST TO KANAO FOR FIVE DAYS STRAIGHT.

...NEVER TOUCHED A SINGLE HAIR ON KANAO'S HEAD.

SPLASH

AND ZENITSU
...

I DID GOOD... FOR ME!

UH-HUH!

ZENITSU JUST ACCEPTED HIS FATE.

CAN I GO NOW?

...SO HE TOOK IT REALLY HARD.

INOSUKE
...

INOSUKE ABSOLUTELY HATED LOSING...

MAYBE THEY'LL COME TOMORROW
...

JUST YOU?! I CAN'T BELIEVE THOSE TWO!

BOW

BOW

SORRY.

THEY BOTH STOPPED COMING TO THE TRAINING ROOM.

MAYBE.

NO ONE COULD HOLD DOWN HER CUP OR DRENCH HER.

KANAO WAS UNBEATABLE.

MAYBE I SHOULD JUST CHANGE MY NAME TO MONITSU ...

EVEN WITH MONITSU HERE, WE FINISH EACH DAY SOAKED.

...

IF YOU THINK I KNOW, YOU'RE DUMBER THAN ME.

WE JOINED THE CORPS THE SAME TIME AS HER, SO WHY IS SHE SO MUCH BETTER?

I WON THE GAME...

...BUT LOST THE FIGHT!

THROB

...HE DIDN'T GET TO ENJOY IT.

WAHOOO!

GLOM

HE ALSO WON DURING THE FULL-BODY TAG TRAINING, BUT...

OW!

HRAAAH!

SPLASH

GRAAAH!

MEAN-WHILE, INOSUKE HATED TO LOSE.

...THAT WAS ALL THAT WENT SMOOTHLY FOR ZENITSU AND INOSUKE.

PLEASE, WATCH YOUR HANDS!

WHOOP

WHOOP

BUT...

Kyah! Put me down!

I'M SO EMBAR-RASSED.

I'M THE ONLY ONE WHO KEEPS LOSING.

DRIP DRIP

....

AND IN THE REFLEX TRAINING GAME, HE BEAT AOI EVERY SINGLE TIME.

SWFF

TCK

AND HE TRIED TO LOOK COOL, BUT...

DON'T WORRY. I'D NEVER THROW A DRINK IN A GIRL'S FACE.

THE GIRLS HAD A FLINTY LOOK IN THEIR EYES.

...HE SPOKE TOO LOUDLY, SO EVERYONE OVERHEARD.

GWOO

THEY BOTH GOT EXTREMELY FOCUSED.

BUT NOT ME.

FOR BETTER OR WORSE, ZENITSU'S PARTICIPATION RAISED THE STAKES.

YANK TUG

GRIP

YA HA HA HA HA

DURING RUBDOWNS, ZENITSU LAUGHED CONTINUALLY DESPITE INTENSE PAIN.

THAT WASN'T NORMAL.

I THINK IT'S BAD TO TRAIN WITH SUCH IMPURE MOTIVATIONS.

...HE MEANT EVERY WORD. THAT HURT SO BAD I CRIED, BUT HE'S LAUGHING.

WELL, I'LL SAY THIS...

HMMM

WAAAH, JOOOY!

FLOP

FLOP

JOY!

BOING

Whoa!

I BET YOU HAVEN'T SPENT ANY TIME WITH GIRLS BEFORE! SO YOU NEVER LEARNED!

AW, HOW SAD!

OH, CRY ME A RIVER! YOU GREW UP IN THE MOUNTAINS ANYWAY!

LOSING TO THOSE TINY GIRLS IS EMBARRASSING!

STOP TALKING NONSENSE!

I'VE *STEPPED* ON PLENTY OF GIRLS!

THAT'S AWFUL!

WHAAAAT?!

SNORT

WHY DID YOU COME BACK EVERY DAY ACTING LIKE YOU'D BEEN THROUGH HELL WHEN YOU WERE ACTUALLY IN HEAVEN?!

YOU SAY YOU'RE SORRY!

YOU GUYS SHOULD APOLOGIZE!

BOW DOWN DEEPLY AND APOLOGIZE! OFFER TO COMMIT SEPPUKU!

YOU WERE HAVING A JOLLY TIME PLAYING GAMES WITH GIRLS, BUT EVERY DAY YOU CAME BACK LOOKING WRECKED!

FWUP

FWIP

HOP

HI-SE

IF YOUR OPPONENT HOLDS DOWN YOUR CUP BEFORE YOU CAN RAISE IT, THEN YOU HAVE TO "DRINK."

EACH OF THESE CUPS CONTAINS MEDICINAL TEA THAT CAN BE APPLIED TOPICALLY.

YOU WILL COMPETE TO SEE WHO HAS TO TAKE THE MEDICINE.

FINALLY, FULL-BODY TRAINING.

SIMPLY PUT, WE PLAY TAG.

YOUR OP-PONENTS ARE ME AND KANAO OVER THERE.

HMPH

EXCUSE ME, MAY WE HAVE A MOMENT?

SLUMP

GLOOM

...

THE TRAINING ROOM.

THE NEXT DAY.

I'm scared...

I'm scared...

...SO I'LL EXPLAIN IT ALL AGAIN!

HMPH

TODAY ZENITSU STARTS HIS TRAINING...

TADAAH

THEN REFLEX TRAINING.

...YOU WILL LIE DOWN AND THOSE GIRLS WILL LOOSEN UP YOUR STIFF MUSCLES.

FIRST, OVER THERE...

HMPH

HMPH

HMPH

I'VE NEVER HEARD ANYTHING LIKE THEM BEFORE.

THE SOUNDS THAT SHINOBU MAKES ARE UNIQUE.

BUT THEY'RE WEIRD, SO THEY'RE KINDA SCARY.

GLOW

BEAM

*MIRROR

THEY ALL CAME TO HER IN TEARS.

BUT SHE WAS LIKE A GODDESS WHEN SHE HEALED THE PEOPLE WHO BECAME SPIDERS.

HER FACE IS SO BEAUTIFUL.

AND SHE'S REALLY ATTRACTIVE.

CHAPTER 49: REHABILITATION TRAINING, PART 1

HELLO!

WHEN SHINOBU ARRIVED, MURATA LEFT IMMEDIATELY.

GOTTA GO! SEE YA!

FWOOSH

ALL HE DID WAS COMPLAIN.

GRUMP GRUMP GRUMP GRUMP GRUMP GRUMP

I'M FEELING A LOT BETTER.

gotta pee.

THANK YOU FOR ASKING.

BOW

SMILE

HOW ARE YOU ALL FEELING?

"REHABILITA-TION..."?

SOMETHING WAS ABOUT TO START.

THEN IT'S ABOUT TIME TO START *REHABILITATION TRAINING!*

BEAM

GRIN

BRIGHT

HI!

MURATA!

ZUUUUN

← Jammed finger.

THOSE HASHIRA ARE SCARY!

IT WAS HELLISH!

GLOOOM

Who's that?

MURATA WAS INVITED TO THE HASHIRA MEETING TO GIVE A DETAILED REPORT ON THE EVENTS AT MOUNT NATAGUMO.

UGH

IT SEEMS SOME OF THOSE SENT TO MOUNT NATAGUMO DIDN'T OBEY ORDERS. SO THEY ASKED ME WHO THEIR TRAINERS WERE.

NGH

NGH

UGH

THEY WERE ALL ANGRY. THEY SAID CORPS FIGHTERS THESE DAYS ARE DROPPING IN QUALITY.

NG

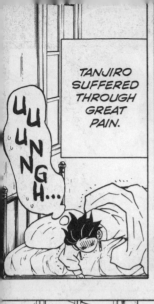

TANJIRO SUFFERED THROUGH GREAT PAIN.

UUNNGH...

NEZUKO SLEPT A LOT.

ZZZ

THE FOUR WERE ABLE TO REST AND RECOVER IN BUTTERFLY MANSION.

SEE YA!

...SO WEAK.

SORRY FOR BEING...

INOSUKE WAS EXTREMELY DEPRESSED.

HAVE I HAD MY LUNCHTIME MEDICINE?!

DID ANYONE SEE ME TAKE IT?!

ZENITSU FUSSED MORE THAN EVERYONE ELSE COMBINED.

OH!

UNTIL A VISITOR CAME.

EACH DAY, THE SAME THING.

YOU WERE AWESOME!

HANG IN THERE, INOSUKE!

BUT THE OTHER TWO ENCOURAGED HIM.

YOU'RE GREAT!

MULTIPLE CUTS AND ABRASIONS ON FACE, ARMS AND LEGS.

SPRAINS ALL OVER HIS BODY, PLUS PULLED MUSCLES AND CONTUSIONS ON HIS LOWER JAW.

TANJIRO

NUMBNESS IN RIGHT ARM AND LEG.

TREMBLING IN LEFT ARM.

ZENITSU

POISONED BY DEMONSPIDER VENOM.

CRUSHING TRAUMA TO LARYNX AND VOCAL CORDS.

INOSUKE

LACK OF SLEEP!

NEZUKO

DON'T WORRY ABOUT IT.

THAT'S OKAY.

IS THAT INO- SUKE?!

HIS VOICE ....!

AT THE END HE LET OUT A LOUD CRY, SO HIS THROAT IS IN REALLY BAD SHAPE.

I DON'T KNOW THE DETAILS, BUT HIS NECK WAS SEVERELY INJURED.

Tissues!

Tissues!

HE HURT *HIMSELF* ?!

WHAAAT?!

APPARENTLY, HIS THROAT GOT CRUSHED.

BWONG

WHY ARE YOU LAUGHING LIKE A WEIRDO? WHAT HAPPENED?

WEE HEE HEE!

I THINK HE'S DEPRESSED. HE'S TOTALLY MELLOW, WHICH IS REALLY FUNNY.

HEY.

DROOP

I DON'T KNOW WHO MURATA IS, BUT INOSUKE IS RIGHT HERE.

HE'S BEEN HERE ALL ALONG!

I DIDN'T NOTICE!

WHMP

HEY! YOU'RE RIGHT!

...

I'M GLAD YOU'RE ALL RIGHT!

SORRY I COULDN'T HELP YOU!

INOSUKE!

ZENITSU!

WILL YOU PLEASE PIPE DOWN!

MOAN

SOB

TRMBL

TRMBL

HMPH! GRRR!

TP TP TP

IF YOU DON'T BEHAVE, WE'LL TIE YOU DOWN!

GRR GRAR

WE'VE EXPLAINED IT OVER AND OVER!

I HAVE TO DRINK THIS FIVE TIMES A DAY?!

IT'S SUPER BITTER! AND THICK!

NOOOOO!

AND KEEP THAT UP FOR THREE MONTHS?!

JUST TAKING MEDICINE WILL HEAL MY ARMS AND LEGS? REALLY?!

I'LL BE TOO FULL TO EAT!

STOP

IS THAT GUY *STILL* FUSSING ?!

WHAT HAPPENS IF I MISS A DOSE?!

I WANT ANSWERS!

WAAAH

WAAAH

PLEASE, BE QUIET.

TELL ME!

WHO THE HELL ARE YOU?!

HE'S INJURED, EH?

ARE YOU KAKUSHI?

COME THIS WAY.

LADY KOCHO SAID...!

UMM

UUH

OH! WE, UM...!

WAVE

FLOP

She's fast!

She's fast!

HUP HUP

TMP TMP TMP

...

A TSUGUKO IS A CORPS FIGHTER WHO'S BEING TRAINED BY A HASHIRA.

AND SHE'S A GIRL. IMPRESSIVE, HUH?

ONLY THE MOST TALENTED AND HIGHLY SKILLED FIGHTERS GET SELECTED.

MAY WE ENTER THE MANSION?

BOW

WE COME ON ORDERS FROM LADY KOCHO.

I SAW HER AT FINAL SELECTION.

WHOA

HE DIDN'T NOTICE THAT SHE STEPPED ON HIM LAST NIGHT.

UH...

SMILE SMILE

IS IT ALL RIGHT ...?

UMMM ...

...WE?

MAY...

BEAM

SMILE

GRIN

SMILE

KANAO
TSUYURI.

MAYBE WE CAN GO AROUND TO THE GARDEN?

BUT I DON'T THINK WE SHOULD JUST GO IN.

SORRY FOR...

NO ONE IS COMING TO GREET US.

PARDON THE INTRUSION!

THAT'S, UM... OH, RIGHT!

OH, *THERE'S* SOMEONE!

IT'S A TSUGUKO!

SORRY. I'M IN PAIN. MY WHOLE BODY HURTS.

CAN'T YOU WALK BY YOURSELF?

WHATEVER, GRANDPA!

HER NAME IS...

SHE'S A TSUGUKO.

WHAT'S A TSUGUKO?

...QUITE RUDE.

INTERRUPTING THE MASTER IS CONSIDERED...

...PAYING ATTENTION AFTER ALL!

SEEMS LIKE MUICHIRO IS...

HOW COOL!

LORD TOKITO!

BLINK

S-SORRY, MASTER SIR!

TANJIRO...

SHUFFLE

PANIC

Quickly!

Hurry!

FLUSTER

Y-YES, SIR!

HURRY NOW. GO.

KAMADO CAN WAIT FOR US IN MY MANSION.

HUH?

GRIN

So sweet!

SIGH

WHOOSH

EXCUSE ME!

OKAY, TAKE HIM AWAY!

CLA

CLA

Hasn't shown up yet. →

Taisho Whispers & Rumors

Ubuyashiki is said to have five children. The one with black hair is a boy and his heir. The boy in House Ubuyashiki is sickly, so he was raised as a girl until age 13.

IN MODERN TERMS THIS IS CALLED 1/F FLUCTUATION.

HEAD OF THE DEMON SLAYER CORPS:

KAGAYA UBUYASHIKI

IT'S AN ABILITY POSSESSED BY MANY PEOPLE WHO ARE CHARISMATIC AND HAVE THE STRENGTH OF PRESENCE TO MOVE MASS AUDIENCES.

THE RHYTHM OF HIS VOICE AND MOVEMENTS SOOTHES THOSE HE ADDRESSES.

IT IS TIME FOR THE HASHIRA COUNCIL TO BEGIN.

THAT IS ENOUGH TALK ON THIS SUBJECT. TANJIRO...

...YOU MAY LEAVE.

OKAY.

UH...

...DO NOT BE MEAN TO YOUNGER CHILDREN.

SANEMI AND...

OBANAI...

AS YOU WISH.

UNDER-STOOD.

...

HFF

PFF

NAD

NAD

THROUGH LABORIOUS TRAINING, THEY HAVE IMPROVED THEMSELVES, DEFIED DEATH...

YUP, THAT'S RIGHT!

IT GOES WITHOUT SAYING THAT THE HASHIRA IN THE DEMON SLAYER CORPS ARE EXTREMELY TALENTED.

...AND DEFEATED MEMBERS OF THE TWELVE KIZUKI.

...

?

TANJIRO, YOU MUST BE CAREFUL HOW YOU SPEAK.

THAT IS WHY PEOPLE RESPECT AND WARMLY WELCOME THE HASHIRA.

I SWEAR...

WE WILL NOT FAIL!!

NEZUKO AND I WILL DEFEAT MUZAN KIBUTSUJI!

I'LL USE MY BLADE TO BREAK THE CHAIN OF SADNESS!

OKAY.

YOU'RE NOT READY FOR THAT YET. FOR NOW, DEFEAT ONE OF THE TWELVE KIZUKI.

NO, NO, NO!

I MUSTN'T LAUGH.

...FROM NOW ON, TANJIRO AND NEZUKO WILL FIGHT FOR THE DEMON SLAYER CORPS TOGETHER.

SO...

PROOF WAS NEEDED, AND NOW WE HAVE IT.

IT'S DIZZYING...

HFF

HFF

HFF

WHAT IS THIS FEELING?

IF YOU DO, THEY WILL ACCEPT YOUR WORDS AND RECOGNIZE THE VALUE OF YOUR PRESENCE.

DEFEAT ONE OF THE TWELVE KIZUKI.

IT'S A STRANGE, GIDDY FEELING!

...HIS VOICE MAKING MY HEAD FEEL SO LIGHT?

IS IT...

WHAT ARE YOU DOING, TOMIOKA?

...

NEVERTHELESS, SOME WILL STILL VIEW NEZUKO UNFAVORABLY.

TANJIRO ...

GASP

...AND DIDN'T BITE IT.

HFF HFF

...HIS BLOODY ARM FOR HER TO FEED, BUT SHE CONTROLLED HERSELF...

SHINAZUGAWA STABBED HER THREE TIMES THEN OFFERED...

...NEZUKO HAS PROVEN SHE WON'T ATTACK PEOPLE.

IN THAT CASE...

!!

!!

THE DEMON GIRL TURNED AWAY.

WHAT HAPPENED?

!

...ARE...

PEOPLE
...

...TO BE
HELPED
AND
PROTECT-
ED.

I MUST
NEVER
HURT
THEM.

I CANNOT
HURT
THEM.

KCH

NEZUKO!

PLEASE, EASE UP A LITTLE.

IGURO, YOU'RE PUSHING HIM DOWN TOO HARD.

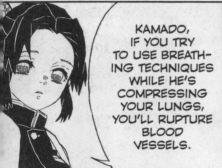

KAMADO, IF YOU TRY TO USE BREATHING TECHNIQUES WHILE HE'S COMPRESSING YOUR LUNGS, YOU'LL RUPTURE BLOOD VESSELS.

BUT HE KEEPS TRYING TO BREAK FREE, Y'KNOW?

SMSH

NGH

KRCH

URRR...

HNGH...

HNGH...

UGH!!

THAT SOUNDS COOL! GOOD! DO IT! RUPTURE 'EM!

YAY

RUPTURE BLOOD VESSELS ?!

NAMU AMIDA BUTSU...

POOR, WEAK, PITIFUL CHILD...

NEZUKO!

SWIK

STOP
IT!

IF YOU DON'T GO INTO THE SHADE, THE DEMON WON'T COME OUT.

...IT WON'T WORK IN THE LIGHT.

SHINAZ-UGAWA...

I SERVE YOU.

MY APOLO-GIES...

... MASTER.

...MAY HAVE SEEN SOMETHING UNEXPECTED IN NEZUKO AS WELL.

...

AND IT'S POSSIBLE KIBUTSUJI...

...

...

DO YOU UNDER-STAND?

LETTING A HUMAN LIVE IS ONE THING, BUT NOT A DEMON. I CANNOT AGREE. THERE IS NOTHING NORMAL ABOUT IT.

NO, MASTER, I DO NOT UNDER-STAND!

GNG
GNGH
GRGAH
GRG

START WITH KIBUTSUJI'S ABILITIES, AND THEN...

SHHH

FWP

HE MAY MERELY WISH TO SILENCE HIM, BUT FOR THE FIRST TIME...

...KIBUTSUJI HAS SHOWN HIS TAIL AND WE HAVE GRABBED IT. I DON'T WANT TO LET GO.

KIBUTSUJI HAS SENT HIS FORCES AFTER TANJIRO.

ARE YOU SAYING THAT THOUGH NO MEMBER OF THE HASHIRA HAS EVER FACED HIM...

NO WAY!

?!

...*THIS KID HAS?!*

WHAT WAS KIBUTSUJI DOING?

DID YOU FIGHT?

WHAT DID HE LOOK LIKE?! WHAT ABILITIES DID HE HAVE?! WHERE IS HE?!

DID YOU FIND HIS LAIR?!

SHUT UP! I ASKED FIRST!

HEY! ANSWER ME!

...

...THEN YOU MUST OFFER SOMETHING *GREATER* THAN URUKODAKI'S PROMISE.

IF YOU WOULD REJECT THIS...

ARGH!

...

!

FURTHER-MORE, TANJIRO HAS CROSSED PATHS WITH KIBUTSUJI.

I CANNOT GUARANTEE OR CONFIRM THAT SHE WILL NOT ATTACK PEOPLE.

THAT IS CORRECT.

HOW— EVER...

...YOU CANNOT PROVE THAT SHE *WILL* ATTACK PEOPLE.

...AND THREE PEOPLE HAVE STAKED THEIR LIVES ON HER.

IT IS A FACT THAT NEZUKO HAS NOT BITTEN ANY- ONE FOR OVER TWO YEARS...

IF HE WANTS TO DIE, HE CAN ROT!

IT DOESN'T PROVE A THING!

SO *WHAT* IF HE'LL COMMIT *SEPPUKU*?!

IF SHE KILLS AND EATS SOMEONE, IT'S IRRE-VERSIBLE!

THE DEAD WON'T COME BACK!

SHINA-ZUGAWA IS RIGHT!

THIS LETTER ARRIVED FROM FORMER HASHIRA SAKONJI UROKODAKI.

I WILL READ A PORTION OF IT.

"...PLEASE, FORGIVE TANJIRO FOR BEING WITH HIS SISTER WHO IS A DEMON."

"THROUGH STRONG SPIRITUAL STRENGTH, NEZUKO MAINTAINS HER HUMAN REASON.

EVEN WHEN STARVING, SHE REFUSES TO EAT PEOPLE."

"SHE HAS PERSISTED IN THIS WAY FOR MORE THAN TWO YEARS."

"IT IS DIFFICULT TO UNDER-STAND, BUT IT IS UNDENIABLY THE TRUTH."

"SHOULD NEZUKO EVER ATTACK SOMEONE...

...TO-GETHER WITH TANJIRO KAMADO..."

MASTER, I RESPECT YOU FROM THE BOTTOM OF MY HEART, BUT I DO NOT UNDERSTAND THIS. I AM AGAINST IT...

...WITH ALL MY STRENGTH!

HSS HSS

I CAN'T BELIEVE IT. MORE THAN ANYTHING...

...I HATE DEMONS.

PLEASE, PUNISH BOTH KAMADO AND TOMIOKA.

THE DEMON SLAYER CORPS *KILLS* DEMONS.

YES.

WELL THEN...

...THE LETTER.

I, TOO, MUST STYLISHLY OPPOSE.

I CAN'T ACCEPT A CORPS MEMBER CONSORTING WITH A DEMON.

AHH...EVEN THOUGH MY MASTER REQUESTS IT...

...I CANNOT CONSENT.

KLIK

FWIP

KIT

...

NO MATTER WHAT HAPPENS...

...I'LL FORGET RIGHT AWAY.

I WILL DO ANYTHING YOU SAY, MASTER!

YES. MY APOLOGIES FOR SURPRISING YOU.

HE DIDN'T SEEM TO HAVE ANY MANNERS BEFORE, BUT NOW HE'S BEING INCREDIBLY POLITE!

AND I WANT EVERYONE ELSE TO DO THE SAME.

I HAVE ACCEPTED TANJIRO AND NEZUKO.

!

IT IS GOOD TO SEE YOU SO HEALTHY.

MASTER, I SINCERELY PRAY FOR YOUR INCREASED HAPPINESS.

I'D LIKE TO GREET THE MASTER.

I WISH I'D SAID THAT!

THANK YOU, SANEMI.

...ABOUT THIS CORPS MEMBER WHO TRAVELS WITH A DEMON, TANJIRO KAMADO?

...BEFORE THE HASHIRA MEETING, WOULD YOU BE SO KIND AS TO TELL US...

I'M SORRY, BUT...

THE SKY IS A PERFECT BLUE, ISN'T IT?

GOOD MORNING, EVERYONE.

IT FEELS LIKE A BEAUTIFUL DAY.

...WITHOUT ANY MEMBERS HAVING CHANGED.

IT MAKES ME VERY HAPPY THAT WE CAN HAVE OUR TWICE-YEARLY *HASHIRA MEETING*...

Taisho Whispers & Rumors

Sakura colored

Please, don't tell anyone!

Turns green about here.

I hear Mitsuri loves sakura mochi and that she ate so much that her hair changed color.

Sakura Mochi

THE MASTER OF THE MANSION HAS ARRIVED.

WELCOME...

...MY DEAR DEMON SLAYERS.

?!

IF YOU CAN'T TELL THE DIFFERENCE BETWEEN A GOOD DEMON AND A BAD DEMON...

...THEN YOU DON'T DESERVE TO BE A HASHIRA!

YOU'RE *DEAD!*

WHY YOU...

SORRY.

BWA HA

TOMIOKA'S DISTRACTION HELPED, BUT IT'S STILL AMAZING HE LANDED A BLOW ON SHINAZUGAWA.

KRIK

AAAH!

I WON'T LET *ANYONE* HURT MY SISTER!

I DON'T CARE IF YOU'RE A HASHIRA OR WHATEVER!

PLIP

PLIP

... COMPLETELY IMPOSSIBLE, YOU FOOL!

LADY KOCHO, WE APOLO-GIZE!

HE HAS EVEN MORE SCARS THAN BEFORE! HOW RUGGED!

SHINOBU SOUNDS ANGRY. THAT'S RARE. HOW COOL!

SHINAZUGAWA, DON'T DO ANYTHING RASH.

THAT'S INCRED-IBLE! AMAZING! WHY, THAT'S...

YOU SAY SHE CAN PROTECT PEOPLE AND FIGHT FOR THE CORPS?

WHAT ABOUT THIS DEMON, BOY?

IS THAT THE IDIOTIC CORPS MEMBER WHO TRAVELS WITH A DEMON?

TMP

TMP
TMP

JUST WHAT IS GOING ON HERE ANYWAY?

WIND HASHIRA: SANEMI SHINAZUGAWA

MY SISTER HAS FOUGHT ALONGSIDE ME!

SHE CAN FIGHT *FOR* THE DEMON SLAYER CORPS AND PROTECT PEOPLE!

SO...

NO, LORD SHINAZUGAWA!

SAAAY... THIS IS GETTING SORTA INTERESTING.

PLEASE, PUT DOWN THE BOX!

WHAT BIRD IS THAT?

HMM...

SHE HASN'T BITTEN ANYONE? AND SHE ISN'T GOING TO?

JUST WORDS! *SHOW* ME! IMPRESS ME!

THIS CONVER- SATION IS JUST SPINNING IN CIRCLES.

THE *MASTER OF THE MANSION* MUST BE AWARE OF THIS...

UH...

I'M NOT SURE ABOUT THIS.

...

...

...

SHOULDN'T WE WAIT UNTIL HE GETS BACK?

THROB

...

...SO SHOULD WE REALLY HANDLE IT ON OUR OWN?

AWW... HE'S POS- SESSED BY A DEMON.

HURRY UP AND KILL THIS CHILD TO SET HIM FREE.

I DON'T TRUST ANYTHING ANYONE SAYS, AND I ESPECIALLY DON'T TRUST YOU.

STOP SPEWING SUCH NONSENSE.

SHE'S YOUR SISTER! OF COURSE YOU'LL PROTECT HER!

IT'S BEEN MORE THAN TWO YEARS SINCE SHE BECAME A DEMON!

IN ALL THAT TIME, SHE HASN'T BITTEN ANYONE!

PLEASE, HEAR ME OUT!

I BECAME A SWORDS- MAN SO I COULD PROTECT NEZUKO!

WE CAN CONSIDER A SUITABLE PUNISHMENT LATER.

WE NEEDN'T WORRY ABOUT HIM. HE CAME ALONG WITHOUT A FIGHT.

I'M MORE INTERESTED IN QUESTIONING THE BOY.

INSECT HASHIRA: SHINOBU KOCHO

TOMIOKA IS ALL ALONE—KEEPING HIS DISTANCE.

ADORABLE!

BOMP

...!

NNGH

BECAUSE OF ME, TOMIOKA IS...

KOFF KOFF KOFF

SHWF

YOUR JAW IS HURT, SO DRINK SLOWLY...

...THEN YOU CAN TALK.

HERE. DRINK SOME WATER.

POK

YOUR WOUND HASN'T HEALED, SO DON'T OVERDO IT.

IT CONTAINS A PAIN-KILLER, SO YOU'LL FEEL BETTER.

GLUG
GLG

SHE HASN'T...

...AND SHE WON'T!

NEZUKO WILL NEVER HURT ANYONE!

MY SIS-TER WAS TURNED INTO A DEMON...

...BUT SHE HASN'T EATEN ANY HUMAN FLESH!

WHAT SHALL WE DO ABOUT THIS? HOW SHALL HE TAKE RESPONSIBILITY? WHAT PRICE SHALL HE PAY?

KOCHO SAYS TOMIOKA BROKE CORPS RULES TOO.

RIGHT NOW HE'S JUST WANDERING AROUND FREELY, AND THAT GIVES ME A HEADACHE.

SERPENT HASHIRA: IGURO OBANAI

HE'S RELIABLE, WHICH IS NICE.

AS USUAL, IGURO IS AS COOLY MENACING AS A SNAKE.

WATER HASHIRA: GIYU TOMIOKA

NEZUKO!

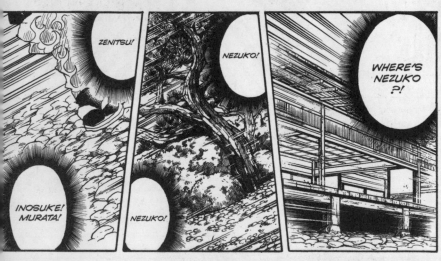

ZENITSU!

NEZUKO!

WHERE'S NEZUKO?!

INOSUKE! MURATA!

NEZUKO!

?!

FORGET ABOUT HIM. WHAT ARE WE GOING TO DO ABOUT TOMIOKA?

LET'S JUST LOP OFF HIS HEAD ALONG WITH THE DEMON'S!

PROTECT-ING A DEMON IS CLEARLY AGAINST CORPS RULES!

THERE'S NO NEED FOR A TRIAL!

FLAME HASHIRA: KYOJURO RENGOKU

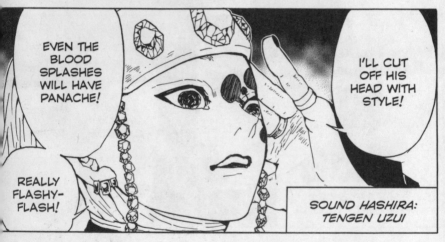

EVEN THE BLOOD SPLASHES WILL HAVE PANACHE!

I'LL CUT OFF HIS HEAD WITH STYLE!

REALLY FLASHY-FLASH!

SOUND HASHIRA: TENGEN UZUI

...PAINS ME. IT'S TOO MUCH.

EEEH!? KILLING SUCH A CUTE KID...

LOVE HASHIRA: MITSURI KANROJI

LOWER-RANKED CORPS MEMBERS DIE INCREDIBLY QUICKLY, BUT THE HASHIRA ARE DIFFERENT.

THEY PROVIDE STABILITY TO THE DEMON SLAYER CORPS.

...ARE THE NINE DEMON SLAYER CORPS MEMBERS WITH THE HIGHEST LEVEL OF SWORDSMAN-SHIP.

THE HASHIRA ...

CHAPTER 45: TRIAL BY HASHIRA

HASHIRA?!

WHAT IS THE "HASHIRA"? WHAT DOES THAT MEAN?

WHERE AM I?

CHAPTER 45: TRIAL BY HASHIRA

WHO *ARE* THESE PEOPLE?

...PUT...

...ON *TRIAL.*

THIS IS THE DEMON SLAYER CORPS HEAD-QUARTERS. AND YOU, TANJIRO KAMADO, ARE ABOUT TO BE...

GOOD. SECURE HIM.

HE HAS A SCAR ON HIS FOREHEAD.

THESE AGENTS ARE CALLED...

...THE KAKUSHI.

AW, I HATE TO TIE HIM UP.

LOOK... IS HIS JAW BROKEN?

MOST MEMBERS OF THIS GROUP LACK ANY SWORD SKILLS.

THEY CLEAN UP AFTER THE DEMON SLAYER CORPS BATTLES DEMONS.

!!

CAPTURE THEM AND RETURN TO HEADQUARTERS!!

CAPTURE TANJIRO AND THE DEMON NEZUKO!

ARE YOU NEZUKO?

THE DEMON NEZUKO HAS A BAMBOO GAG!

TANJIRO HAS A SCAR ON HIS FOREHEAD!

KAWW!

MESSAGE! MESSAGE!

MESSAGE!

?!

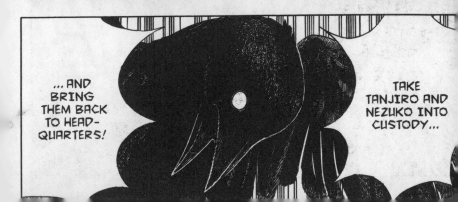

...AND BRING THEM BACK TO HEAD-QUARTERS!

TAKE TANJIRO AND NEZUKO INTO CUSTODY...

HOW ABOUT JUST SAYING *SOMETHING*?

...OR ARE YOU JUST GETTING BACK AT ME BECAUSE I SAID PEOPLE HATE YOU?

OH NO. IS THIS GOING TO BE ONE OF YOUR LONG, RAMBLING STORIES? ARE YOU *TRYING* TO BORE ME...

I THINK IT WAS TWO YEARS AGO...

GRIP

GRIP

GRIP

SQUEEZE

...BUT WHAT *YOU'RE* DOING *IS* AGAINST THE RULES.

...

EXPLAIN YOUR-SELF!

YOU'RE INTERFERING WITH THE SLAYING OF A DEMON.

JUST KILL DEMONS, LIKE I WAS TAUGHT!

DON'T THINK ABOUT IT...

SHE'S JUST RUNNING. NOT ATTACKING AT ALL.

WHY?

...THERE'S NOTHING WRONG WITH THAT.

I'M CHASING DOWN A DEMON TO KILL IT...

WILL I HAVE TO LEAVE THE DEMON SLAYER CORPS?

THEY WON'T ACCEPT A SWORDSMAN WHO TRAVELS WITH A DEMON... AND MY SISTER IS A DEMON!

BUT I MUST KEEP GOING! THE PAIN! I WANT TO SCREAM!

ARGH! MY WHOLE BODY HURTS!

KEEP GOING, KEEP GOING...

KEEP GOING, KEEP GOING...

TOMIOKA...

!

THANK YOU!

I'M SORRY!

WHSH

...

THIS IS AGAINST CORPS RULES.

YOU KNOW ...

...I'LL USE A GENTLE POISON TO KILL HER SO SHE WON'T SUFFER.

!

CAN YOU MOVE?

...

TAKE YOUR SISTER AND FLEE.

EVEN IF YOU'RE HURT, GATHER YOURSELF UP AND GET GOING.

...

BOY!

YES?!

THAT'S DANGEROUS. SO GET OUT OF THE WAY AND...

PSSt

PSSt

YOU'RE LYING ON TOP OF A DEMON.

OH! IS THAT SO? HOW SAD.

IN THAT CASE...

SHE'S MY LITTLE SISTER!

AND...

NO!

YOU'VE GOT IT ALL WRONG! WELL... NOT WRONG, BUT...UMM...

NOW MOVE, TOMIOKA.

WHY DID YOU SAY THAT EVERYONE HATES ME?

I SHOULDN'T HAVE SAID ANYTHING. MY APOLOGIES.

I GUESS YOU NEVER REALIZED THAT PEOPLE HATED YOU. SORRY.

OH DEAR ...

THEY'RE REALLY CLEANING UP QUICKLY.

???

YES. TAKE THE WOUNDED TO MY PLACE.

DO THEY GO TO BUTTERFLY MANSION TOO?

SHE HAS THE SAME HAIRPIN AS THE GIRL WHO WRAPPED US UP.

AND WASN'T THAT GIRL AT MY FINAL SELEC-TION?

DROOP

DUNNO.

WHAT'S THIS?

I'LL TAKE CARE OF ANY DEMONS NEARBY, SO YOU CAN WORK WITHOUT FEAR.

WHO ARE THESE PEOPLE?

CHAPTER 44: AGAINST CORPS RULES

CHIRP

I'M ALL WRAPPED UP.

*LABELS: TREATMENT COMPLETE

CONTENTS

**TRIAL
BY
HASHIRA**

INOSUKE HASHIBIRA

He also went through Final Selection at the same time as Tanjiro. He wears the pelt of a wild boar and is very belligerent.

ZENITSU AGATSUMA

He went through Final Selection at the same time as Tanjiro. He's usually cowardly, but when he falls asleep, his true power comes out.

SAKONJI UROKODAKI

A trainer in the Demon Slayer Corps and Tanjiro's master.

SPIDER DEMON

Obsessed with the idea of having a family, he uses fear to bind his minions to him and calls them his family.

MUZAN KIBUTSUJI

The one who turned Nezuko into a demon. He is Tanjiro's enemy and hides his nature in order to live among human beings.

SHINOBU KOCHO

Another Hashira in the Demon Slayer Corps. Familiar with pharmacology, she is a swordswoman who has created a poison that kills demons.

GIYU TOMIOKA

The Hashira who invited Tanjiro to join the Demon Slayer Corps.

TANJIRO KAMADO

A kind boy who saved his younger sister and now aims to avenge his family. He can smell the scent of demons and an opponent's weakness.

Tanjiro's younger sister. A demon attacked her and turned her into a demon. But unlike other demons, she fights her urges and tries to protect Tanjiro.

NEZUKO KAMADO

STORY

In Taisho-era Japan, young Tanjiro makes a living selling charcoal. One day, demons kill his family and turn his younger sister Nezuko into a demon. Tanjiro and Nezuko set out to find a way to return Nezuko to human form and defeat Kibutsuji, the demon who killed their family!

After joining the Demon Slayer Corps, Tanjiro meets Tamayo and Yushiro—demons who oppose Kibutsuji—who provide a clue to how Nezuko may regain her humanity. On a new mission, Tanjiro goes to Mount Natagumo with Zenitsu Agatsuma and Inosuke Hashibira. There, they encounter a group of demons pretending to be a family as they wipe out out Demon Slayer Corps members. Tanjiro finds himself in a tight spot until Giyu Tomioka rushes in to save him. Then another senior member of the corps joins the battle…

6

THE DEMON SLAYER
CORPS GATHERS

DEMON SLAYER

KIMETSU NO YAIBA

**KOYOHARU
GOTOUGE**

DEMON SLAYER: KIMETSU NO YAIBA VOLUME 6

Shonen Jump Edition

Story and Art by
KOYOHARU GOTOUGE

KIMETSU NO YAIBA
© 2016 by Koyoharu Gotouge
All rights reserved. First published in Japan
in 2016 by SHUEISHA Inc., Tokyo. English
translation rights arranged by SHUEISHA Inc.

TRANSLATION John Werry
ENGLISH ADAPTATION Stan!
TOUCH-UP ART & LETTERING John Hunt
DESIGN Adam Grano
EDITOR Mike Montesa

The stories, characters and incidents mentioned
in this publication are entirely fictional.

No portion of this book may be reproduced or
transmitted in any form or by any means without
written permission from the copyright holders.

Printed in Canada

Published by VIZ Media, LLC
P.O. Box 77010
San Francisco, CA 94107

10 9 8 7 6 5
First printing, May 2019
Fifth printing, December 2020

PARENTAL ADVISORY
DEMON SLAYER: KIMETSU NO YAIBA is rated T for
Teen and recommended for ages 13 and up. This
volume contains realistic and fantasy violence.

ratings.viz.com

viz.com

KOYOHARU GOTOUGE

I did it! I'm Gotouge. I get to bring out volume 6, and thanks to everyone's support I get to work enthusiastically on manga again today. Thank you for the letters of support, snacks, Valentine's Day chocolate, drinks and clay Tanjiros. With support from everyone, an author can lean into their work, be a fighter and work hard. Sorry for taking so long to say thank you. [*crying*]